MICHELLE REID

BRIDAL BARGAINS

MILLS & BOON

All the characters in this book have no existence outside the imagination of the author, and have no relation whatsoever to anyone bearing the same name or names. They are not even distantly inspired by any individual known or unknown to the author, and all the incidents are pure invention.

All Rights Reserved including the right of reproduction in whole or in part in any form. This edition is published by arrangement with Harlequin Enterprises II B.V./S.à.r.l. The text of this publication or any part thereof may not be reproduced or transmitted in any form or by any means, electronic or mechanical, including photocopying, recording, storage in an information retrieval system, or otherwise, without the written permission of the publisher.

This book is sold subject to the condition that it shall not, by way of trade or otherwise, be lent, resold, hired out or otherwise circulated without the prior consent of the publisher in any form of binding or cover other than that in which it is published and without a similar condition including this condition being imposed on the subsequent purchaser.

® and ™ are trademarks owned and used by the trademark owner and/ or its licensee. Trademarks marked with ® are registered with the United Kingdom Patent Office and/or the Office for Harmonisation in the Internal Market and in other countries.

Published in Great Britain 2013
Mills & Boon, an imprint of Harlequin (UK) Limited,
Eton House, 18-24 Paradise Road, Richmond, Surrey TW9 1SR

BRIDAL BARGAINS © Harlequin Enterprises II B.V./S.à.r.l. 2013

The Tycoon's Bride © Michelle Reid 2000
The Purchased Wife © Michelle Reid 2005
The Price of a Bride © Michelle Reid 1998

ISBN: 978 0 263 90583 0

026-0313

Harlequin (UK) policy is to use papers that are natural, renewable and recyclable products and made from wood grown in sustainable forests. The logging and manufacturing processes conform to the legal environmental regulations of the country of origin.

Printed and bound
by CPI Group (UK) Ltd, Croydon, CR0 4YY

Michelle Reid grew up on the southern edges of Manchester, the youngest in a family of five lively children. Now she lives in the beautiful county of Cheshire, with her busy executive husband and two grown-up daughters. She loves reading, the ballet and playing tennis when she gets the chance. She hates cooking, cleaning and despises ironing! Sleep she can do without and produces some of her best written work during the early hours of the morning.

THE
MICHELLE REID

COLLECTION

February 2013

March 2013

April 2013

May 2013

June 2013

July 2013

THE TYCOON'S BRIDE

MICHELLE REID

CHAPTER ONE

'ADOPTION?' Claire repeated in dismay. 'You want me to give Melanie away to strangers?'

Standing there, white-faced and shaking in the shabby sitting room of her equally shabby little flat, Claire stared at her aunt as if she had just turned into a real live she-devil. In truth, she was having trouble believing that any of this was really happening. In the last few tragic weeks it felt as if her whole life had been wrenched out from under her.

Now this, she thought wretchedly. 'I am going to pretend you never said that, Aunt Laura,' she said, cuddling the sleeping baby just that little bit closer as if trying to shield her from what was being proposed here.

'No, you're not,' her aunt countered sternly. 'You're going to listen to me. Do you honestly think I would be suggesting this if I believed you were coping?'

'I *am* coping!' Claire angrily insisted.

Wearing a pin-neat chic little two-piece grey suit and with her perfectly made up face and elegantly groomed blonde hair, Laura Cavell only needed to send her coldly fastidious eyes on a brief scan of their surroundings to completely denounce that declaration.

The place was in a mess, every available space cluttered with all the usual baby paraphernalia—the floor, the chairs, the unit tops in the attached tiny kitchen. It was only October but the notoriously unpredictable British weather was already wintry. Yet what small amount of heat there was coming from the electric fire was being blocked off behind a clothes-horse laden with wet baby clothes. The washing had to be dried somehow and Claire had no other way of doing it now she could no longer afford to use the laundrette in the high street. So the windows were steamed up, the air inside the chilly little room damp with hanging condensation.

Claire herself looked no better, her once outstandingly pretty face ravaged by too much grief, by too much worry, and by too many disturbed nights caused by a baby who only seemed to sleep when she was holding her.

'I only asked you for help with my rent, for goodness' sake,' she mumbled defensively, feeling like a stray cat that had dared to beg at a queen's front door.

'And sometimes people have to be cruel to be kind,' her aunt replied with a cold little shrug of her elegant shoulders. 'If that means I have to use ruthless methods to make you see the error in what you're trying to do here, then so be it.'

Which, Claire presumed, was her way of saying that she wasn't going to part with a single penny. But then, Aunt Laura had never been known for her charity.

'Melanie isn't even your child, Claire!'

'But she is my sister!' Claire angrily flashed back. 'How can you want to have her taken away from me?' It was a cry from the heart—a copiously bleeding heart that had known too much pain and grief over the last half year.

Her aunt winced—but her stance didn't alter. 'Your *half*-sister,' she corrected her. 'You don't even know who her father is,' she added, her red-painted mouth pursing with real distaste as she glanced down at the dark-haired, olive-skinned baby cradled in Claire's arms.

'What difference is that supposed to make?' Claire demanded, her blue eyes widening in affront at the rude remark. So, her mother had a fling with a Spanish waiter—so what? she wanted to shout. At least she'd still been able to attract a man—which was something after what she had been through with Claire's father! 'Melanie is still my flesh and blood, and I am still hers!' she declared, only just managing to bite back the angry reminder that her aunt was supposed to be their flesh and blood also!

Not that it had ever shown. Claire's mother had always

said that Aunt Laura had no heart to speak of. She was hard, she was tough, and the fact that she held down a very important job playing PA to the top dog at one of Europe's biggest merchant banks meant that she was also totally dedicated to her career.

The moment that Claire had dared to ask for help, she must have been racking her brains looking for a solution that would put an end to what she must be seeing as the beginning of years of hassle. So, to a woman who had found it very easy to sacrifice love, marriage and the prospect of her own children for the sake of that career, telling her own niece to give her sister away came easy to Aunt Laura.

Claire felt sick to her stomach.

'You're only twenty-one years old, damn it!' Aunt Laura sighed out impatiently when she caught a glimpse of Claire's expression. 'Until a month ago you were still a student. Now you've dropped out of university but you have no job,' she listed. 'No means whatsoever to support yourself, never mind a small baby! And now you tell me you can't even afford to pay the rent on this awful place!'

'I will find a job soon enough, I'm certain of it,' Claire stated proudly.

'A job doing what?' she was instantly challenged. 'Waiting at tables like that—child's father did? Cleaning floors? Skivvying for others when you could be doing what your mother wanted you to do, and getting your degree? And who is going to look after Melanie while you do scrub floors?' her aunt pushed on remorselessly. 'It takes a lot of money to employ a good baby-minder, Claire,' she warned. 'Your mother's estate barely left enough to bury her.'

The derision in that final remark cut Claire right to the quick. 'I have rights! I must have rights!' she cried. 'Surely the State will help me!'

'Of course,' her aunt agreed. 'But only as much as it absolutely has to do. The days are long gone when the State was prepared to pay up without much of a murmur. They encourage self-help these days—which is just another way of telling you to go away and get on with it,' she derided. 'And Melanie has rights too, you know; you seem to have overlooked that. Do you think *she* is going to thank you for bringing her up in poverty when she could be living with the kind of people who could give her everything?'

With the sheer brutality of her aunt's words scoring deep grooves into her already lacerated soul, Claire reeled away in an agony of mind-numbing confusion.

Would it be better for Melanie if she gave her up? she actually found herself wondering. Suddenly she was starting to see the future through the baby's eyes. And her aunt could well be telling the truth; Melanie would have no grounds to thank her for condemning her to the kind of life she could provide for her.

Silently she moved across the room to go and place the sleeping baby in her crib in the corner. She was so thin now that the pair of jeans and stretch-cotton blouse she was wearing were hanging on her body. Only a couple of months ago they would have been as tightly fitting as you would have expected any healthy young woman's clothes to be.

But a couple of months ago Melanie had not been born. And Claire's mother had still been here, happily looking forward to giving birth to a new life, which she'd seen as the path to a whole new beginning, after what the previous few years had put them through.

Just three years ago Claire had been the only child of two utterly doting parents. Then her father had died at his own hand when he couldn't face the fact that his business had failed, taking just about everything they owned along with it. They'd lost their home, their furniture—even most of their clothes had to be sold to pay back their debtors. By then they had moved from the Holland Park area of London into rented accommodation here in the East End.

Victoria Stenson had never really recovered from the way her husband of more than twenty years had bailed out of life, leaving her to pick up the pieces. On top of all that, she'd had to watch so-called friends melt clean away as her circumstances altered. Claire had had to leave her private school to finish her final year of education at the local state school. She too had had to watch her friends disappear in much the same way her mother had done.

It had been a tough, painful time that left Victoria Stenson feeling very disillusioned and bitter. She'd had to find a job, which, having spent the last twenty years of her life being taken care of, wasn't at all easy. Oddly enough, it was Aunt Laura who'd helped then. She'd found her sister a job working in an up-market fashion boutique where her natural flare for style and what suited people had come in useful.

But then, Victoria Stenson had been a very classy lady. As a tall and slender natural toffee-blonde, at forty-two years old she had still been a very attractive woman who proved to be very good at her new job. So when the lady who owned the boutique had suddenly taken ill and could not go on a planned trip to Madrid to check out one of her fashion suppliers, she'd felt no qualms in sending Victoria in her place.

The rest was history. By the time she'd come home again, Claire could not believe the change in her mother. She'd looked almost happy; more relaxed, more—at peace with herself. A couple of weeks later she'd found out why.

'I'm pregnant,' her mother had announced. And eight months later little Melanie was born. Small, sweet, olive-skinned and with a crop of black hair that they'd both found so comical when compared with their own fair colouring. It was love at first sight for all three of them.

They'd brought Melanie home here to this small flat with its two small bedrooms and tiny kitchen and bathroom. A couple of weeks later Victoria had gone back to work. It was August, and Claire was on her long summer break from university, so it had worked well that she could care for Melanie while her mother was out. They would have to find a baby-minder later—they had been aware of that—but for now they were both happy to share the caring between them and all in all things were beginning to look up for them, they'd thought.

Then tragedy had struck yet again. Victoria Stenson had suffered a massive haemorrhage that she'd never recovered from, leaving Claire shell-shocked and utterly grief-stricken, with a baby to care for and nothing much else to help her to do it.

Outside a car horn sounded. Behind Claire, her aunt Laura took a glance at her wristwatch and frowned. 'I've got to go,' she murmured impatiently. 'Oh—for goodness' sake,' she then snapped out. 'Will you leave the child alone for a moment and listen to me?'

As if she could actually feel her aunt's animosity towards her, the baby let out a soft yelp. It was purely instinctive for Claire to reach down and brush a soothing caress across the baby's petal-soft cheek, and as she did so a well of love came surging up inside her.

It wasn't fair, she thought tragically. It just wasn't fair what life was throwing at her! She wanted to keep Melanie with her! She wanted her mother back. She wanted her father back. She wanted her life back how it used to be before all of these horrible things began to happen.

'What are our options?' she questioned thickly, tears clearly not far away.

Behind her, her aunt sensed success coming closer and smothered a smile of satisfaction. 'There are waiting lists longer than you can imagine of childless couples who would be very grateful to you for—'

'I don't want gratitude,' Claire cut in, straightening to slice the older woman to ribbons with a razor of a look.

'No.' Wrong move, Aunt Laura realised. 'People who would give her a loving home, then,' she quickly back-tracked. 'And a loving family life with all the security that comes along with that.'

But I would not have a place in her life, Claire thought bleakly. And tried to imagine strange arms cradling her sister, strange hands caring for her, feeding her, clothing her—loving her...

A cold sense of despair went chasing through her system, her eyes blurring as the tears tried to follow.

'There are discreet ways of going about it,' her aunt was saying. 'Private agencies that only accept the very best of society onto their books. The kind of people who would make sure Melanie wanted for nothing for the rest of her life. Surely it is at least worth considering the idea—if only for Melanie's sake...'

For Melanie's sake. Having found the right button to push, the super-sharp PA to one of Europe's top bankers was now using it ruthlessly.

'You could go back to university and finish your degree,' Aunt Laura continued. 'I would be prepared to help you to do that, because I think it's the right thing for you to do. But not this, Claire,' she murmured, with another contemptuous scan of their surroundings. 'I will not help you to wreck two lives when both you and Melanie deserve better than this...'

Melanie.

'I'll—think about it,' Claire heard herself whisper. But even as she said the dreadful words it felt as if someone was reaching down inside her and ripping her bleeding heart from her breast.

'Good,' her aunt murmured approvingly. 'While you do that, I will approach some of the agencies for you,' she offered. 'See what is required and how m—'

The car horn sounded again, cutting her off mid-word. And, on a small sigh of irritation, Laura Cavell glanced at her niece, saw the dreadful misery now apparent on her pale face—and relented a little. Opening her small clutch purse, she withdrew a slender leather wallet.

'Look, take this...' she said, sliding a folded wad of paper money out of the wallet which she placed on the arm of the sofa. 'It should see you through until I can get back to you in a couple of days. By then I will expect you to have made a decision.'

Staring at the money, Claire nodded. 'Thank you,' she breathed, but they both knew she didn't really feel grateful.

'Please try to think with your head, not your heart, Claire,' was her aunt's final volley as she walked to the door.

Then she was gone, leaving Claire standing there staring at the money she had left behind her.

Her thirty pieces of silver, she likened tragically, and had to wrap her slender arms around her body in an effort to still the icy chill that suddenly ran through her blood.

Because that's what this money is, she acknowledged as she made herself walk forward and sit down beside the wad of notes. The price of betrayal of those we love most.

With her heart throbbing dully in her breast, she reached out with a hand and picked up the folded wad with the grim intention of finding out how much that betrayal was worth these days.

But she didn't even get as far as counting the notes when something dropped out from in between them that had her launching herself off the sofa and running to yank open the door.

Her flat was on the first floor. She made a dive for the stairwell just as the main front door downstairs slammed shut. Muttering a couple of choice curses that would have drawn her mother's wrath if she had been alive to hear them, Claire began racing down the stairs in pursuit of Aunt Laura with the wad of bills still clutched in her hand—and with them a gold plastic credit card.

An ice-cold north-easterly wind hit her full in the face as she dragged open the heavy front door. She paused and shivered, her thin blouse no protection as she stood there at the top of the steps urgently searching the street in front of her for a glimpse of her aunt Laura's distinctive figure.

It was a narrow street but a busy one, used as a cut-through between two main highways. It was lined on both sides by high Victorian-style terraced houses that would once have been quite elegant until time and decay, and greedy property developers, had turned them into cheap tenement dwellings.

The two rows of cheap and old cars parked up against the kerb reflected the quality of the tenants. So the long, sleek limousine Claire could see her aunt climbing into stood out like a rich dark hybrid rose amongst a tangle of briar. It was parked on the other side of the street and facing towards her with its engine already running.

'Aunt Laura!' she called out, trying to catch her attention before she disappeared into its spacious rear compartment. But the wind whipped her voice away, the rear door closed her aunt inside and almost instantly the limousine inched into movement.

Without thinking what she was doing, Claire darted forwards, the thin-soled ballet slippers she wore around the flat no protection from the cold, hard pavement as she ran across it then out into the street with the intention of stopping the car before it had gained momentum.

What came next happened so very quickly that the whole became lost in a blur of confusing sounds and images. She had a feeling, for instance, that she would remember to her dying day the sound of a horn shrilling furiously at her. Just as she would always have a rather curious image of her own golden hair fanning out in a shimmering arc around her face and shoulders as her head spun to register the delivery van bearing inexorably down on her.

Then there was the ear-piercing sound of screeching brakes, the acrid smell of burning rubber, and the warning cries from helpless onlookers who were seeing as clearly as she was seeing what was about to happen.

And even as the adrenaline did the exact opposite of what she needed it to do for her and froze her utterly to the spot instead of jolting her into taking avoiding action—she still managed to note the terrible look on the delivery driver's face when he too realised that he was not going to be able to stop without hitting her.

Yet—interestingly—the impact itself she barely registered. She felt a thump to her right-hand side, but not the pain that should have come with it.

The next thing she knew, she was lying in the road and a dark-eyed stranger was leaning over her while someone in the background was talking wildly in a choked, shocked, shaking voice. 'She just ran out in front of me!' he was saying over and over. 'I didn't stand a chance! She just ran out in front of me—she just ran out in front of me…'

Was he referring to her? Claire wondered dizzily, and on a frown of confusion attempted to sit up.

'Don't move,' a quiet voice commanded. Vaguely she registered the hint of a foreign accent, liked the deep velvet sound of it and smiled accordingly.

'OK,' she complied. Crazily, it really did seem that simple. She still felt nothing, and, in those first few conscious moments, she remembered nothing, which didn't seem to matter either. A strange state of mind, she decided—all fluffy and floaty.

'Am I dying or something?' she wondered curiously.

'Not while I am here to stop you,' replied the stranger.

She found herself smiling at that too. Arrogant devil, she thought. And became aware of a hand resting on one of her shoulders while another hand was dispassionately travelling all over her body as if it had every right to do something like that. Yet—oddly—she let him. Her worry-bruised deep blue eyes solemnly studied him as he carried out his examination. He wasn't young, she noted, but he wasn't exactly old either. And his skin—like his voice—was definitely foreign, bronzed and sleek, and he had a nicely defined mouth that, for some reason, she wanted to reach up and trace with her fingertips.

But really it was his eyes that held her attention. They were dark—so dark it was like looking into nothing.

Catching her studying him, he sent her a brief grim smile that made something alien stir inside her. She didn't understand it—didn't recognise the feeling, but it was disturbing enough to make her close her eyes and shut him out again as a wave of dizziness rolled over her.

She began to shiver suddenly—though she wasn't sure why unless the cold was beginning to get her—yet she didn't feel cold—not at all, actually—which was strange in itself considering the icy weather.

Something warm and silky landed on top of her, and she realised that he had taken off his jacket and covered her with it.

It was only then that it occurred to her that she shouldn't be lying here; that she had been in a hurry to get somewhere—though for the life of her she couldn't remember where she was supposed to be going.

'I said—don't move!' the deep voice insisted.

'Did I?' she asked, frowning confusedly because she certainly wasn't aware of moving.

In fact she didn't feel able to do anything very much—even breathing in air was strangely difficult. Her chest felt tight, her limbs heavy.

And for all she knew she could be very seriously injured. It was well documented, wasn't it—that the worse you were, the less you felt? 'My chest hurts,' she confided, meaning to reassure herself with that bit of information.

He didn't seem to understand that, though, because she heard his harsh expletive muttered beneath his breath. 'Has someone called the emergency services?' he demanded of—whoever. Claire wasn't sure who, nor cared that much really. But she did become aware of hurried footsteps coming towards her.

'I've seen to it,' another voice announced breathlessly. Then, 'I can't believe she just ran out in the street like that!' the voice added angrily.

Her aunt. Claire winced on a rush of total recall.

'Did that hurt?' the stranger enquired concernedly. He was touching her right wrist, and, yes, it did hurt, she realised belatedly. But that wasn't why she had winced.

A pair of handmade Italian court shoes appeared beside her. 'What made you do such a stupid thing?' her aunt demanded furiously.

Lifting up her injured wrist, she opened her fingers with effort. Lying there, half hidden amongst the crumpled wad of notes, was her aunt's plastic gold card. 'You left this behind,' she explained. 'I thought you might be needing it...'

For the space of thirty long, taut seconds, no one else made a single solitary sound as they stared at the gold card in Claire's palm.

Then the stranger spoke. 'You know this girl?' he demanded sharply of her aunt Laura. 'She is the niece you came here to see this morning?'

'Yes,' Laura Cavell confirmed with enough reluctance to make Claire wince all over again.

How can anyone be so uncomfortable with the fact that they possess family? Claire wondered bleakly. And at last managed to pull herself into a sitting position while everyone's attention was elsewhere.

'Look, Mr Markopoulou...' Aunt Laura was saying, sounding unusually anxious for her. 'If you want to leave this situation to me now, you could still just manage to catch your flight to Madrid.'

That was the moment when Claire realised that the tall, dark stranger was none other than Aunt Laura's hot-shot tycoon employer! No wonder she is sounding so anxious, she mused ruefully.

'I thought I told you not to move,' the dark voice censured.

'I'm fine now—really,' she lied. 'No one needs to miss their flight. In fact, I think I would like to get up now.'

'I think not,' the stranger drawled, his black eyes autocratic. 'You will remain exactly where you are until the emergency services arrive to check you over.'

No way, Claire thought. If they took her to hospital then Aunt Laura would have her certified as unfit to take care of Melanie before she could even turn around!

Then, 'Oh, no!' she gasped, scrambling shakily to her feet. She'd left the baby in the flat on her own!

Her head felt groggy, her shoulders stiff, and her insides were shaking so badly that they were making her feel sick.

'Where do you think you are going?' the stranger demanded, vaulting to his feet like a well-honed athlete.

'I have to go now,' she murmured hazily.

Barely registering the small crowd clustered around them, she took a few staggering steps forward—then remembered the gold card still clutched in her hand—the cause of all of this trouble in the first place, she acknowledged mockingly as she spun back towards Aunt Laura.

'Here...' she said, plucking the card out from amongst the crumpled bank notes and handing it over.

Her aunt took it in grim silence, her red-painted mouth tight with angry embarrassment.

Turning back to find the stranger had moved to stand directly in her path, Claire mumbled an awkward, 'Thanks for your trouble,' went to divert around him only to come to yet another confused halt when she noticed the pristine whiteness of his shirt.

No jacket...

Glancing behind her, she was appalled to see his jacket lying on the road where it had slid away from her unnoticed when she'd got up. 'Oh—I'm so sorry!' she gasped, making a move to go and collect it.

He got there before her, though. Tall, dark, whipcord lean, he bent to retrieve it in one smooth movement.

'I'm so very sorry.' Claire apologised a second time.

His idle shrug dismissed the oversight. 'Here...' Instead the jacket landed back around her shoulders. 'You seem to need it more than I do at this moment,' he explained. Then he bent his head towards her to add gently, 'You are shivering.'

'But...' The rest of what she had been going to say got lost in a sudden wave of dizziness. Her wrist was hurting, her chest felt very tight, and her head was beginning to thump. She became aware of a cluster of blurred faces all staring at them in rapt curiosity.

An arm came gently about her shoulders. 'Come on,' her aunt Laura's boss said coolly. 'Show me where you live and I will see that you get there...'

'It really isn't necessary,' she protested.

'It is, I assure you,' he insisted rather grimly. 'For I am not leaving until I am sure you have been checked out professionally.'

And it was amazing—but he meant it! He even sounded as though he cared! Hot tears suddenly filled her eyes, though she had no idea why they did. 'It isn't even as though it was your car that hit me!' she choked out in something between a sob and a protest.

'No, my van did that,' another male voice intruded. 'Are you sure you're all right?' the newcomer then enquired worriedly.

'Yes—really.' Seeing the shock still whitening the driver's face, she sent him a reassuring smile. 'A bit winded,' she confessed. 'But otherwise I'm OK. I'm sorry I was so stupid.'

'No problem—no problem,' the other man said, and he walked off looking relieved to be getting away from it all without getting into more trouble.

Claire felt another wave of dizziness wash over her. The arm resting across her shoulders suddenly became supportive. 'Lead the way, Miss Cavell,' his grim voice commanded.

Silent as a grave and stiff-backed as a corpse, Laura Cavell stalked into the house while they followed behind her. Her aunt was going to despise her for showing her up like this in front of her boss, Claire thought wearily as they trod the stairs. 'You don't have to go to this much trouble, you know,' she muttered uncomfortably. 'I really am all right.'

'No, you are not,' the man beside her replied. 'Your right wrist is injured. You have a cut on your head that needs attention. And when you breathe you gasp—which suggests you may have cracked a rib or two.'

An injured wrist. A cracked rib or two. Claire closed her eyes and wondered bleakly when something good was going to happen.

There didn't seem to be much use in hoping for it, she decided heavily. Things around her seemed to be going from bad to worse with every passing minute.

When they reached her flat she broke free from him so she could precede him through the door. Laura was standing by the clothes-horse—valiantly trying to hide it, Claire suspected, with the first hint of humour she'd felt in weeks.

Then, from behind her, she could sense her aunt's boss running his gaze over his shabby surroundings and all hint of humour completely left her. Outside in the street stood a limousine belonging to a man who was rich enough to travel everywhere in absolute luxury. His clothes shrieked of bespoke tailoring. No doubt his many homes were large and palatial, and here he was, Claire concluded, standing in what was probably the shabbiest abode it had ever been his misfortune to experience.

Shame washed through her. Why she didn't know, because the feelings of a complete stranger really shouldn't matter to her. But something made her turn around to confirm the look of distaste she just knew would be written all over his lean, dark, super-elegant features.

It was there.

She felt hurt, so very hurt.

Then, as if to completely demolish her, a soft snuffling sound came from the corner of the room, and the way his expression altered to a look of shocked horror as he accurately registered just what that sound belonged to finally wrecked what was left of her fragile composure. In an act of teeth-gritting defiance, she whipped off his jacket and threw it at him.

Startled, his black eyes widened on her. 'You don't have to come in,' she clipped, suddenly alight with a bristling hostility. 'And actually I would prefer it if you didn't.'

'Claire!' her aunt objected furiously.

'I don't care!' she flashed. 'I just want you both to get out of here!'

Angrily she spun away to hurry over to the small baby crib where Melanie was still sleeping peacefully, she was relieved to discover.

But the tears weren't far away. She could feel them coming as she stood there leaning over the crib with an aching wrist hanging limply by her side and her ribcage beginning to pain her badly.

Behind her the silence went on and on. They hadn't gone and she wished that they would because she was beginning to feel rather hot and shaky.

'Please go,' she pleaded. Then, without warning, she fainted.

Maybe he saw it coming. Maybe he was already walking over to where she stood without her being aware that he'd moved. Whatever, as Claire felt herself going, as the blood slowly drained away from her head and her legs began to go limp, a pair of arms came securely around her, and the last thing she recalled was hearing the distinctive wail of an ambulance siren as she slumped heavily against him.

After that everything became a bit hazy, and she didn't really start making sense of what was happening to her until she was travelling in the ambulance—accompanied by none other than Aunt Laura's boss who was cradling Melanie.

But no Aunt Laura.

'She will be joining us later,' the stranger replied when Claire queried her aunt's absence. 'She needed to attend to some urgent business.'

Frowning at him through huge, pain-bruised blue eyes, she wondered why he wasn't taking care of his own urgent business. But their arrival at the local hospital forestalled any more conversation between them when she was taken away to be examined and x-rayed.

Her ribs, she discovered, were only bruised, but her wrist was a different matter. A broken scaphoid, the doctor called it, and they would have to put her out briefly to reset it.

'What about Melanie?' she fretted as the pre-med they had given her began to send her brain fuzzy. 'How am I going to cope with my wrist in plaster? Where's Aunt Laura?'

'If you want your aunt here, then I will get her here,' a deep voice that was starting to sound very familiar quietly promised. She had expected Aunt Laura's boss to melt away once they reached the hospital, but to her surprise he had stayed with her the whole time.

'No,' she sighed in shaky refusal, shifting restlessly where she lay because he didn't understand. It wasn't that she wanted her aunt—she just needed to know where she was and what she was doing because she didn't trust her not to take matters into her own hands where Melanie was concerned, while she was in no fit state to stop her.

'Don't let her take her away from me,' she mumbled slurredly.

'I won't,' the voice promised.

That was the last thing she remembered for the next hour or so, so she had no idea that he continued to stand there beside her bed grimly watching over her until they came to wheel her away.

When she did eventually resurface, it was to find herself lying in a small side room with her wrist encased in its new plaster cast and secured by a sling. They had left her fingers and thumb free at least, she noticed—not that she felt overwhelmed with gratitude for that because she knew she still wasn't going to be able to handle a baby.

What did concern her was that it was going to take up to eight weeks to mend.

Eight weeks…

Sighing heavily, she closed her weary eyes and tried pretending that this was all just a bad dream.

'Worrying already?' a deep voice dryly intruded.

CHAPTER TWO

CLAIRE'S eyes flicked open, something disturbingly close to pleasure feathering across her skin as a tall, dark figure loomed up in front of her in the very disturbing form of Aunt Laura's hot-shot tycoon banker.

'How are you feeling?' he enquired politely.

'Dopey,' she replied, with a shy little grimace.

His dark head nodded in understanding. 'Give yourself time to recover a little from the anaesthetic,' he advised. 'Then—if you feel up to it—they say you can go home.'

Home... That sounded good. So good in fact that she made herself sit up and slide her feet to the ground. It was only then that she realised what a poor state her clothes were in. Her jeans were scored with dust and tar from the road, and her blouse had managed to lose half of its buttons.

No wonder he threw his jacket over me, she thought wryly, making a half-hearted attempt to tidy herself. But it was difficult to look pin-neat after the kind of day that she'd had, she decided heavily. While this man, whose eyes she could sense were watching her so intently, still looked elegant and sleek and clean even though he had spent most of the day rescuing fallen maidens, abandoned babies, and—

'Where's Melanie?' she asked sharply, unable to believe she had been so irresponsible as to not give the poor baby a single thought until now!

For the first time today, he suddenly looked cross. 'I would have expected by now that you would trust me to ensure your child is perfectly safe and well taken care of,' he clipped out impatiently.

'Why?' Claire immediately challenged that. 'Because my aunt Laura works for you?'

Something made his broad shoulders flex in sudden tension, though what made them do it Claire had no idea, but she felt her own tension rise in response to it.

'Just because you were gracious enough to pick me up and dust me off, then condescended to accompany me here instead of going off to Milan, that does not automatically win trust, you know,' she pointed out, coming upright on decidedly shaky legs.

'Madrid,' he corrected her absently—as if it really mattered!

'I don't know you from Adam,' Claire continued as if he hadn't spoken. 'For all I know you may be one of those weirdos that prey on innocent young females in vulnerable situations!'

A wild thing to say—a terrible thing to say considering what he *had* done for her today. Watching the way his elegant frame stiffened in affront, Claire was instantly contrite.

But as she opened her mouth to apologise he beat her to it—by retaliating in kind.

'Young you may be,' he grimly conceded. 'What are you, after all—not much more than eighteen? And vulnerable you certainly are at the moment—one only has to look at your face to know that a relatively minor road accident was not enough to cause quite that amount of fatigue in one so young. But innocent?' he questioned with cutting cynicism. 'One cannot be innocent *and* give birth to a child, Miss Stenson. It is, believe me, a physical impossibility.'

Two things hit her simultaneously as she stood there absorbing all of that. One was the obvious fact that he had got her age wrong. And the other was his mistaken belief that Melanie was her daughter!

Had Aunt Laura not bothered to explain anything to him? she wondered. And who the hell did he think he was, standing in judgement over her, anyway?

'I am not eighteen—I am twenty-one!' she corrected him angrily. 'And Melanie is not my daughter—she's my sister!

Our mother died, you see, just two weeks after giving birth. And if you hadn't been so quick to send my aunt off to do whatever business you felt was more important to her than we are,' she railed on, regardless of the clear fact that she had already managed to turn him to stone, 'then maybe she would have had the chance to explain all of this to you, so you didn't have to stand here insulting me! And my innocence or lack of it is none of your damned business,' she tagged on for good measure.

At that point, and giving neither of them a chance to recover, the door swung open and a nurse walked in carrying Melanie.

'Ah, you're awake.' She smiled at Claire, seemingly unaware of the sizzling atmosphere she had walked into. Stepping over to the bed, she gently laid the sleeping baby down on it. 'She has been fed, changed and generally spoiled,' she informed them as she straightened. 'So you need not concern yourself about her welfare for the next few hours.'

'Thank you,' Claire murmured politely. 'You've all been very kind.'

'No problem,' the nurse dismissed. 'If you feel up to it, you can leave whenever you want,' she concluded, and with a brisk squeak of rubber on linoleum was gone again—leaving a tension behind her that stuck like glue to Claire's teeth and her throat, making it impossible for her to speak or swallow.

So instead she moved to check on the baby. As the nurse had assured her, Melanie looked perfectly contented. Her left hand went out to gently touch a petal-soft cheek while he looked on in grim silence.

'I apologise,' he murmured suddenly. 'For the—altercation earlier. I had no right to remark upon either your life or your morals. And I certainly had no right to make certain assumptions about either you or your situation. I am, in fact, ashamed of myself for doing so.'

Quite a climb-down, Claire made note, nodding in acceptance of his apology. 'Who are you?' she then asked curiously. 'I mean—what is your name? It seems crazy that we have spent almost half the day together and I don't even know your name.'

'Your aunt never mentioned me?' he questioned.

Claire shook her head. 'Only that she worked with the head of a merchant bank,' she told him.

He seemed to need a few moments to take this information in, which Claire thought was rather odd of him. 'My name is Andreas Markopoulou,' he then supplied. 'I am Greek,' he added, as though he felt it needed saying.

Feeling suddenly quite painfully at a loss as to what she was supposed to do with his name now that she had it, all Claire could come up with was another small nod of acknowledgement.

Consequently, the silence came back, but it was a different kind of silence now as they stood there eyeing each other as if neither quite knew what to do next. It was all very strange, very—hypnotic, Claire thought hazily.

Then he seemed to give himself a mental shake and stepped up to the other side of the bed. 'Maybe we should leave now,' he huskily suggested.

'Oh, yes,' she said, and bent with the intention of scooping Melanie up with her good arm.

But he stopped her. 'I will carry her,' he insisted, adding almost diffidently now that they seemed to be trying very hard not to tread on each other's feelings, 'Perhaps you would accept the use of my jacket again? The day is drawing in and it must be quite cold outside...'

A hesitant nod of agreement had him rounding the bed as he removed his jacket so he could place it across her slender shoulders, then he was turning to get Melanie. And without another word passing between them they made their way to the hospital exit.

Just as he had predicted, it was cold outside, but within

seconds of them appearing his car came sweeping into the kerb just in front of them. As soon as the car stopped, the driver's door shot open and a steely-haired short, stocky man in a grey chauffeur's uniform stepped out.

Rounding the car's shiny dark red bonnet, he touched his peaked hat in greeting and deftly opened the rear door, politely inviting Claire to get into the car.

Wincing a little because her bruised ribs didn't like the pressure placed on them to make the manoeuvre, it was a minute or two before she felt able to take in the sheer luxury of her surroundings—the soft kid leather upholstery and impressive amount of in-car communications hardware.

It all felt very plush, very decadent. Very—Andreas Markopoulou, Claire mused wryly as the door on the other side of the car opened and the man himself coiled his impressive lean length into the seat next to her—without Melanie.

'Be at ease,' he said before Claire could even voice the alarmed question forming on her lips. 'She is perfectly safe. See, I will show you...'

Reaching out towards his door panel, he pressed a button that sent the dark glass partition between them and the driver sliding smoothly downwards. Having to move carefully so it didn't hurt too much, Claire sat forward a little so she could peer over the front passenger seat—where she found Melanie snugly strapped into a baby car seat fixed to the seat next to the beaming driver.

A car seat just for Melanie? 'You really shouldn't have gone to so much trouble for us,' Claire mumbled awkwardly. 'You've done more than enough as it is.'

'It is nothing,' he dismissed, sitting back and pressing the button that brought the partition window sliding up again.

Claire was edging herself carefully back into her seat when a sudden thought hit her. 'That seat isn't new, is it?' she asked. 'You have borrowed it from someone?' Oh—please let him say it's borrowed! she prayed fervently.

But the arrogant look he levelled at her spoke absolute volumes, and had Claire stiffening in dismay. 'But the expense!' she cried. 'I won't be able to pay you back!'

'I was not expecting you to,' drawled a man to whom money had obviously never been a luxury he couldn't afford to toss away! And with a shrug that dismissed the whole subject as boring he turned his head to glance outside as the car slid into smooth motion.

But Claire couldn't let him just dismiss it like that. It wasn't right that he should fork out for anything for them! 'I will have to ask my aunt if she will reimburse you,' she decided stubbornly.

'Forget it,' he said.

'But I don't want to forget it!' she cried. 'I hate being beholden to anybody!'

Arrogantly, he ignored all of that. 'Please fasten your seat belt,' he instructed instead. Then, 'Leave it,' he advised when she opened her mouth to continue the argument, the sheer softness of his tone enough to still her tongue. 'It is done. The seat is bought. Further argument is futile…'

Lowering her face, Claire began attempting to fasten her seat belt around her with fingers that were suddenly shaking badly. In all her life she had never been spoken to quite like that, even by Aunt Laura, who could be intimidating enough.

'I can't do this!' she sighed after a few taut moments of hopeless fumbling that made her frustratingly aware of how incapacitated she was going to be with one hand rendered completely useless, and felt the tears that were too ready to appear just lately begin to fill her eyes again.

With a smooth grace, he leaned across the space separating them, took the belt from her trembling fingers and, carefully making sure that the belt sat low down on her body so that it missed both her ribs and her plaster-cast, he locked it into place.

He glanced up, saw the tears, and released a soft sigh. 'Don't get upset, because I have a tendency to cut into people,' he murmured apologetically. 'It is a—design fault in my make-up,' he explained sardonically. 'I dislike having my actions questioned, so I react badly. My fault—not yours...'

'You should not have spent money on us without my say so,' Claire couldn't resist saying despite the fact that she seemed to know instinctively that—half apology or not—he wasn't going to like her resurrecting the argument.

Still, if he was angry, he managed to keep his voice level. 'Well, it is done now.' And although the remark was dismissive again at least he cloaked it in a gentler tone. 'How is your wrist?' he enquired, wisely changing the subject.

Glancing down to where the sling held the heavy plastercast against her slender body, she noticed an ugly swelling around the base of her thumb. 'It's OK,' she lied.

In fact it was throbbing quite badly now. But then, so was her head—and her ribcage. Closing her eyes, she let herself relax back into the seat, feeling so tired, so utterly used up now that she had an idea that if she was left to do it she could easily sleep for a whole year.

But she wasn't going to be able to sleep, was she? Instead she was going to have to come up with a way to take care of Melanie while her wrist was like this.

Out from behind the dull throb of her physical pain and her mental exhaustion her aunt Laura's rotten suggestion reared its ugly head. It was enough to make her open her eyes, make her sit up straight as aching muscles knotted up with stress. Unaware of the pair of black eyes that were observing her narrowly, her anxious gaze went dancing around as if on a restless search for deliverance.

'What's wrong?' he enquired levelly.

'Nothing.' She shook her head. For how could she tell him that his highly respected PA could be crass enough to want to give away one of her own nieces rather than help share responsibility for her? It was wicked, simply wicked.

Yet you said you were prepared to consider the option, Claire grimly reminded herself.

Her eyes grew stark, the tired bruising around the sockets becoming more pronounced as the weight of all her many problems began pressing on her once again.

Then other things began intruding on her consciousness. The fact, for instance, that the car was driving them through a part of London that was very familiar to her since she'd used to live around here until three years ago.

But that was a long way away from the East End district where she lived now. Frowning in puzzlement, she glanced around to find Andreas Markopoulou's fathomless black eyes fixed on her watchfully.

'This isn't the way to my flat.' She stated the obvious.

Those dark eyes didn't so much as flicker. 'No,' he confirmed, adding smoothly, 'This is the way to *my* home.'

His home... Claire repeated to herself, and tried to work out why he had used the words with the kind of emphasis that had set instincts firing out all kinds of warnings at her.

'Your driver is going to drop you off first,' she nodded, deciding that was what he had been implying.

But beside her the dark head shook. 'We are all going there,' he said, waited a few moments for his words to sink in—then added gently, 'I am taking you both home with me.'

'But—what for?' she demanded frowningly. 'Will my aunt Laura be there?'

There was a long pause when his eyes continued to hold hers but he didn't answer. He has a beautiful face, she found herself thinking. Good bones and skin and nicely balanced features. It was a shame the whole was spoiled by the cold mask he wore over it...

Then she blinked, realising that he still hadn't answered her but was just sitting there, watching her studying him, and by the sardonic gleam she could see lurking in his eyes he knew exactly what she was thinking but didn't give a damn.

Not just cold, she thought suddenly, but proud of it. And she shuddered as if something unholy had just reached out to brush its icy fingertips along her body.

The car came to a stop. 'We have arrived,' he announced, and leaned over to flick free her safety belt.

Instantly her skin began to prickle, her heartbeat picking up pace as a burst of alarm forced her into taking avoiding action by pressing her body back into the seat.

'Be calm,' he murmured dryly as he carefully guided the belt back into its housing so it didn't whip across her body. 'You truly have nothing to fear from me.'

No? Claire wished she could believe that—an hour ago she *would* have believed that! But since then something about this man had altered subtly and what really frightened her was that she just didn't understand what that something was!

Nikos, the chauffeur, was opening her door then, and offering to help her to alight. Feeling stubborn in the face of her own confusion, she ignored his outstretched hand and climbed out of the car under her own steam. But the effort took its toll, and she had to steady herself with her good hand on the bonnet of the car while her many aches and pains made their presence felt.

She knew this street, she realised, suddenly becoming aware of her surroundings. It was several streets up from the one where she used to live when her father was alive, though this part of Holland Park was a hundred times more exclusive.

But at least she knew where to run to if she needed to get away from here, she told herself. And with that consoling thought, she turned to watch the chauffeur release Melanie from her safety seat, while Andreas Markopoulou stood to one side of him, waiting to receive the baby into his arms.

The baby arrived, all cute and cosy wrapped in a shawl her mother had so painstakingly crocheted throughout her confinement. And, for some crazy, unexplainable reason, remembering that brought on a violent surge of possessive jealousy that made her want to reach out and snatch the baby from him!

Maybe he sensed her resentment, because he turned then, to glance at her sharply. 'OK?' he asked.

No, Claire thought. I am not OK. I want you to give me my baby sister then I want to go home, because every single instinct I possess is telling me I should not be going anywhere with you!

Aunt Laura—Aunt Laura… Like a chant devised to soothe the troubled spirit, she found herself using Aunt Laura's connection to them both as an excuse as to why she was allowing herself to be taken over like this.

'Let's go…' Her new guardian led the way towards one of the elegant town houses that stood in the middle of an elegant white-painted row.

The door fell open even as they arrived at it, a short plump lady with hair a similar colour to the chauffeur's appearing in the opening with a warmly expectant smile on her face. The moment she saw Melanie she let out a soft cry of delight, clapped her hands together then opened them up in greedy readiness to receive the baby.

'This is my housekeeper, Lefka,' Andreas Markopoulou informed Claire as he dutifully placed the baby in the other woman's arms. 'As you can see from her expression, she is ecstatic to be given this opportunity to take care of the child while you are here.'

'Oh, but—' Claire began to protest, but even as the words began to form on her lips the housekeeper began speaking over the top of her, in what Claire had to assume was Greek. Then, without a by-your-leave to anyone, she turned and proceeded to disappear with Melanie into the bowels of the house!

'Usually her manners are much better than that,' Andreas Markopoulou dryly remarked as they watched the woman go. 'No doubt she will recover them once her bout of ecstasy has subsided.' Then, more formally, he invited Claire to enter his home.

The interior was more or less what she had expected—

large and warm and beautifully furnished in a tasteful mix of modern and antique.

Light hands smoothly removed the jacket. Glancing up and around, she mumbled a wary, 'Thanks,' but felt uncomfortably lost without the jacket to hide in.

Leading the way across the square hallway, he opened a door and invited her to precede him through it. In silence she went, still telling herself that she was going to find her aunt Laura waiting there—*needing* to find her aunt Laura waiting there.

But, except for the obvious fact that this was a man's very comfortable study—with its roaring log fire, light-oak-panelled walls and heavy oak furniture—the room revealed no sign of Aunt Laura.

Behind her, the door closed. She turned to confront him.

'Where's my aunt?' she demanded.

Sleek black eyebrows shot up. 'I do not recall saying that your aunt would be here,' he replied, moving gracefully across the room to where a big solid desk stood with its top clear of papers.

Had he said it? Claire's brow puckered up as she tried to remember just what he had said about her aunt, and found she couldn't say for sure.

But the impression had been drawn, she was sure of it. 'Then why have you brought us here?' she asked, puzzled. 'If it wasn't to meet up with Aunt Laura?'

He had switched on a small laptop computer and was studying whatever had appeared on the screen while casually tapping at one of the keys—though his head lifted at the question, his dark eyes drifting up the full length of her then back down again in a way that raised every fine hair on her body. 'I would have thought that was obvious,' he replied, his attention already back on the computer screen again. 'You are a mess, quite frankly,' he stated bluntly. 'And in no fit state to take care of yourself, never mind a helpless young baby. So, for the time being at least, you will stay here with me.'

'But I don't want to stay here!' Claire cried, too horrified by the prospect to dress up her protest.

That brief grim smile of his that he liked to use so much registered her horror. 'I wasn't aware,' he drawled, 'that I was giving you a choice.'

No choice? Who did he think he was, for goodness' sake? 'It isn't your problem.' She flatly refused the offer. 'We will manage somehow,' she insisted with more confidence than she really felt. 'My aunt—'

'Your aunt,' he interrupted, 'is already out of the country. And since we both know that she would rather—break *both* wrists,' he said, with a telling glance at Claire's plaster-cast, 'than be forced to play housemaid to anyone, then I think we can take her out of the equation, don't you?'

Out of the country—out of the equation? 'But it's you who says where Aunt Laura goes!' she pointed out confusedly.

He didn't even deign to answer that. Instead he lost interest in whatever was written on the computer screen and snapped it shut then straightened to give Claire his full attention.

She was still standing where he had left her, looking pale, drawn, and totally bewildered. A short sigh whispered from him. 'Look—why don't you sit down?' he suggested. 'And at least allow me to call the kitchen and order you something to eat and drink. I have been with you for most of the afternoon but as far as I have seen you have only taken a couple of sips of water in all that time...'

As it was, she had already determined that she wasn't accepting anything else from this man until she knew just what it was that was going on here, so the desire to tell him where to put his offer was strong.

But she was thirsty and cold, and at this moment she was ready to kill for something hot inside her stomach. 'A cup of tea would be nice,' she nodded. 'Please,' she added belatedly.

Then—seemingly because she had given in to one craving—she found herself giving in to another. While he began talking into the telephone, she turned to walk over to where two dark red velvet recliners sat flanking the blazing log fire.

Sitting down hurt. But then, just about every muscle she possessed was beginning to ache now, and the other thing she really wished for was a long soak in a piping-hot bath.

No chance of that, though, she thought, glancing dully at her plastered wrist. 'Don't get it wet,' they'd said. 'Tape a plastic bag around it when you bathe.'

But who taped the plastic bag? she asked herself dully, closing her weary eyes as her body sank into the softest velvet. And how did she undress herself, wash and dry herself? How did she manage all of those other little necessities that she'd taken so much for granted until today?

'Claire...' a deep voice prompted softly.

Her eyes flicked open. Had she been asleep again? She wasn't sure. All she did know was that she felt warm and comfortable at last. As she turned her head against the back of the chair, her sleepy eyes met with fathomless dark ones.

'I'm sorry to disturb you,' he said. 'But Lefka needs to know how Melanie likes her formula milk prepared?'

Melanie's formula milk? she repeated sluggishly to herself. Oh, good grief! How could she—how could she have forgotten all about the poor baby—again?

Without thinking what she was doing, she jolted to her feet. 'Aggh!' she cried out, as pain went screaming round her system.

She had jarred her bruised ribs and she could hardly bear it!

Then he was right there beside her. His long-fingered hands slid around her narrow waist to offer support while her slender body shook with violent spasms as she stood there, half bent over, trying desperately to ride the storm.

'You little fool!' he muttered angrily.

'Sh-shut up,' she gasped, needing his reproof like a hole in the head right then.

Grimly, he was silenced. And for the next few minutes the only sound in the room was her fight with her own body. When it was eventually over, she wilted like a dying flower against his chest—then stayed there, feeling so utterly used up that it was a long while before she began to notice little things about him. Like the padded firmness of his breastplate acting as a cushion for her cheek. And the lean tightness of his waist where her good hand had decided to come to rest. He felt big and warm and very tough, and there was a faint spicy smell floating all around her. It was pleasantly intoxicating.

'There is nothing of you,' he grunted.

And broke the spell.

'I'm all right now,' she said, pulling carefully away from him.

He let her go, his hands dropping slowly to his sides while he continued to stand there at the ready—in case she did anything else just as stupid.

'Melanie's formula,' she prompted flatly. 'I didn't bring any out with me.' No formula, no bottles, no nappies, nothing. 'I'll have to go home.'

'We have everything you will need right here,' he assured her.

Now what was that supposed to mean? she wondered wearily, sensing another battle in the offing. 'Don't tell me you've been out and bought the whole lot along with the car seat!' she sighed out heavily.

He didn't even deign to answer that. 'I will take you to the kitchen so you can show Lefka what she has to do.'

It was like dealing with an armoured tank driver, she thought grimly. What he didn't want to bother with, he rolled right over!

'Lead the way,' she said heavily, letting him have that small victory—for Melanie's sake, she told herself as she followed him out of the study and down the hallway towards the rear of the house.

The kitchen was a housewife's dream, all lovingly waxed wood and red quarry-tiled flooring. There was a huge Aga sitting in what Claire presumed had once been the fireplace, the kind of smells coming from the pots busy simmering away on its top enticing enough to make her stomach cry out in appeal.

A young dark-haired woman of around her own age was standing near to the Aga, close to a baby's travel cot. As Claire made eagerly for the cot, the young woman melted silently away.

Melanie was lying there, wide awake for once, and looking curiously around her. She had been changed, she noticed, and was wearing what looked like a brand-new sleep suit in the softest shade of pink that showed off her olive skin and jet-black cap of fine straight hair.

There was nothing about her that resembled her dead mama, Claire observed sadly—and felt the tears begin to threaten as they always did when she let herself think of her mother.

'Please...' she murmured a little thickly to the man who was standing silently by. 'I need to hold her—can you get her for me?'

Common sense told her not to attempt to bend down there and scoop Melanie up for herself.

'Of course,' he said, and with an economy of movement he bent to lift the baby, straightened and turned towards Claire—only to pause indecisively.

'How will you do this?' he asked, frowning over the problem. 'You don't want to put any stress on your bruised rib-cage.'

Looking around her, Claire decided it was probably best to ease herself into one of the kitchen chairs; at least then she could use the tabletop as an aid to take some of the baby's weight.

A moment after she had settled herself, Melanie arrived in the crook of her arm, and, resting it on the table, Claire released a long, soft, breathy sigh, then lowered her face to the baby's sweet-smelling cheek.

If anyone, having witnessed this moment, could still wonder if she really loved this baby, then they would have had to be blind.

Andreas Markopoulou wasn't blind. But he was moved in a way that would have shocked Claire if she'd happened to glance at him.

Angry was the word. Harshly, coldly—frighteningly angry.

'Ah, you come at last.' Lefka suddenly appeared from another room just off the kitchen, the sound of her heavily accented voice bringing Claire's head up. Looking at Claire with Melanie, the housekeeper smiled warmly. 'You love this baby,' she said, not asking the question but simply stating a fact. 'Good,' she nodded. 'For this baby is an angel. She has stolen my heart.'

Claire had a feeling that she meant it, too; her dark eyes definitely had a love-struck look about them.

'But she will not be happy with me if I do not feed her the bottle soon. So you will show me, please—what to do? My daughter Althea will hold the child.'

By the time Claire had escaped from the kitchen, as reassured as ever anyone could be that Melanie was in safe and loving hands, she had come to a decision.

Going in search of her host, she found him sitting behind his desk, his fingers flying across the laptop keyboard while he talked on the telephone at the same time.

By now, it had gone truly dark outside, and the dark red velvet curtains hanging behind him had been closed, the room softly lit by several intelligently placed table lamps that didn't try to fight against the inviting glow of the fire.

As he glanced up and saw Claire standing there, she saw that the whole effect had softened and enriched his

Mediterranean skin tone, helping to smooth out the harsher angles to his lean-boned face so he looked younger somehow—much less intimidating than he had started to appear to her.

'I'll stay here,' she announced.

CHAPTER THREE

'FOR Melanie's sake,' she added, knowing she sounded surly, but then, she was resenting her own climb-down so her voice was projecting that.

But the last hour spent with Melanie had turned out to be a tough lesson in how little she was able to do for the baby in her present state. And, although witnessing the way Lefka and her daughter Althea had been efficient and gentle and unendingly caring as they saw to her sister had been the main factor that had brought about her decision, her stubborn soul found it a bitter pill to take.

So Claire stood in stiff silence, watching those thoughtful eyes study her, and waited with gritted teeth for him to ask her why she had changed her mind.

Yet he didn't do that. All he did was nod his dark head in mute acceptance of her decision.

A diplomat, she thought, mocking his restraint.

'I will show you to your room, then,' he said, coming gracefully to his feet.

'No need.' She shook her head. 'Althea is going to do that. But I do need some things from my flat,' she then added. 'Fresh clothes and—things,' she explained, feeling a faint flush working its way into her cheeks when she saw the way his gaze dropped automatically to the disreputable state of the 'things' she was presently wearing.

In truth, she felt a bit like a bag lady that had been brought in off the street and allowed to experience how the other half lived.

'If you give Althea a list of your requirements, I will send her with her father to collect them.'

Definitely the diplomat, she reiterated silently as she picked up on his carefully neutralised tone.

'Thank you,' she murmured politely. Then, 'Her father?' she questioned, realising what he had just said.

'Nikos, my chauffeur,' he nodded, coming around his desk. 'They have the top floor to this house as a self-contained apartment.'

As he talked he had been walking smoothly towards her, and the closer he came, the more her nerve-ends began to flutter. Why, she wasn't sure. Then he came to a stop in front of her and reached out to gently cup her chin, arrogantly lifting it so she had to look at him—and she knew exactly why her nerve-ends became agitated whenever he came too close.

Her flesh liked to feel his flesh against it, and that implied a sexual attraction that she just did not want to acknowledge.

'Stop being afraid of me,' he commanded, obviously seeing something flash in her guarded blue eyes.

'I'm not.' She denied the charge, but pulled away from his touch anyway.

Sighing slightly, he turned away from her, but not before she had glimpsed a hint of irritation with her. 'I have the keys to your home,' he announced, as cool and flat as calm waters. And, at her soft gasp of surprise because she hadn't given a single thought as to where her keys were, he turned back again, to flick her with one of his unfathomable looks. 'As you were being transferred into the ambulance, I instructed Nikos to make your flat safe and lock up,' he explained.

'Then if you have my keys,' she shot at him sarcastically, 'I'm surprised you didn't have the whole place transferred here while I couldn't stop you!'

She was referring to the very unpalatable fact that her sister seemed to have acquired a complete new wardrobe of clothes—plus just about every gadget ever invented to make a mother's life an easier one!

To her amazement he stiffened up as if she had just hit him! 'I would not be so ill-mannered as to remove anything from your home without your permission!' he informed her haughtily. 'It would be tantamount to stealing!'

'Yet you felt no qualms about stealing me!' Claire shot back.

Irritation really showed on his hard face now. 'I—stole *both* of you.' He made that fine but seemingly important distinction. 'For your own good, since we both know you cannot manage without my help. Now, can we drop this—conversation?' he went on impatiently. 'It is serving no useful purpose—and I have more important work to do!'

Stung by his tone and being made to feel like an awkward child who had just been severely reprimanded by an adult, Claire turned without another word and reached for the door.

'Don't...' The gruff voice sounded too close to her ear.

'Don't what?' she mumbled, the too ready tears not far away.

He didn't reply; instead he reached around her with his arm, his hand appearing in front of her misted vision as it closed over her own hand and gently prised it free of the door handle. Just as gently, he turned her round to face him and Claire found herself looking at the blurred bulk of his white-shirted chest once again.

She heard him sigh, and wished she could stop being so pathetic! It was humiliating to keep wanting to cry like this! 'This isn't going to work,' she choked.

'Just because we fight,' he replied, his deep voice completely wiped clean of all hint of anger, 'it does not mean that we cannot get along with each other. It simply shows that we are two very strong-willed people who both like to win in an argument.'

It seemed to Claire that he had been winning every single battle they'd fought today—which didn't say much for her own strength of will.

'Well, try not to be so arrogant,' she advised, firmly pushing herself away from him. 'And maybe we will get through this without killing each other.'

With that she turned back to the door, opened it and walked away, rather pleased for grabbing the last word for a change—and surprised that he'd let her have it without cutting the legs out from under her.

Althea showed her to a rather elegant bedroom suite decorated and furnished in a tasteful range of soft blues through to watery greens. There was a large white *en-suite* bathroom that seemed to have been stocked with just about every requirement anyone could possibly look for, plus a cavernous walk-in dressing room lined with custom-designed shelves and hanging space.

Her pathetically few items of clothing were going to look really great in here, Claire thought ruefully, turning her attention back to the main bedroom and looking around her to decide where she was going to place Melanie's crib when it arrived.

Then she stopped, realising suddenly that she wasn't going to be able to have Melanie in here with her! Not unless Althea or her mother came along with the baby—for how was she supposed to deal with nights feeds when she couldn't even manage to fix a teat into a bottle, never mind everything else?

'Where is Melanie going to sleep?' she asked Althea, who was waiting for her to compose the list of things she needed from her flat.

And even the writing of a simple list was going to be completely beyond her, she realised next. She was going to have to dictate it to Althea.

Softly spoken, gentle, introverted and shy, Althea answered carefully, 'Mamma suggests, if you agree to it, that perhaps the little one would be best sleeping next to my bed?'

Which placed not just a room between her and Melanie— but a whole wretched floor. It hit her hard, that. It had her standing there gazing helplessly around her, feeling a bit like a boat that had lost its rudder.

The list didn't take very long to dictate. After all, what did Claire need here but a few changes of clothes and the odd personal item? But it was only as Althea left to go and find her father that another thought suddenly struck her, bringing with it a rather ugly clutch of shame at the knowledge that Althea, who was used to living like—this, was going to walk into her shabby little flat and see what Claire and Melanie were more used to.

And pride, Claire Stenson, is a very poor companion! She immediately scolded herself for allowing it to encroach. Hadn't she already learned that salutary little lesson years ago when she and her mother had lost everything—even so-called lifelong friends *and* most of the clothes off their backs?

With that stern reminder, her chin came up, and she turned her attention to something much more important. Namely, needing to use the bathroom quite urgently. Whereby she spent the next ten minutes encountering a whole new set of obstacles that took some trouble to overcome.

She would have liked to fill the bath with hot, fragrant water and lie down in it for ever, but that was so much out of the question that she didn't even bother to do much more than *think* how wonderful it would be. But a shower was a different proposition, she mused, with a thoughtful look at the clear glass cubicle over in the corner...

Spying a long white terry-towelling robe hanging behind the bathroom door made her mind up for her. And with a sudden determination that eventually turned into a panting frustration she struggled out of her dirty clothes.

She only hoped that Althea wasn't long, because there was no way she was putting those clothes back on her body, she decided as she stood there, naked, giving the small pile in the corner of the bathroom a distasteful glare before turning away from it.

Which was when she caught a glimpse of herself in the full-length mirror that was fixed to one of the tiled walls, and all normal thought processes stalled for the moment as dismay completely froze her.

She looked as if someone had given her a good beating. The cut at her temple was pretty minor but the lump that had formed beneath it was distorting the shape of her face! And the bruising on the left-hand side of her lower ribcage had already begun to turn an ugly back and blue.

But that wasn't all of it, she noted woefully. Not nearly all of it. Though the rest was purely personal. A painfully personal view of herself as the man downstairs must have been seeing her each time those dark eyes had settled on her, she realised with a small shudder.

How much weight had she actually lost? she asked herself as she stood there feeling the shock of self-awareness ricochet through her for the first time since her mother had died.

Two months ago she'd had a nice figure—even if she did say so herself! Slender and sleek, not thin and bony! Even her breasts…these small, pointed breasts had absolutely no fullness left in them!

And her hair… Her good hand went up to touch her lank, lifeless hair where it hung around her pale and sadly hollowed-out face.

What had she been doing to herself? Where had she gone? She used to be happy, bright, always smiling, with hair and skin that glowed with health, and a well cared for, athletic body. Not this thin, lank, dull-eyed person who looked as if she'd been kicked black and blue.

She was suddenly filled with an almost overwhelming urge to toss herself in the corner of the bathroom where her ruined clothes lay discarded!

Yet, surprisingly, seeing a vivid picture of herself, sitting there slumped in the corner along with her torn shirt and dirty jeans, was so comical that she laughed.

By the time she had managed to have a shower *and* shampoo her hair whilst keeping her plaster-cast dry by winding her arm around the outside of the cubical wall whilst the other hand did all the work, she emerged from the steamy confines refreshed, smelling sweet, and feeling generally a whole lot better all round. Mainly, she suspected, because she'd managed to do it all for herself without having to ask for any help.

Encouraged by her own success and thinking on her feet now, she decided to let the terry bathrobe do the job of soaking up the excess moisture from her skin so she didn't have to jar her bruises by attempting to dry herself with a towel. In fact, the only task that defeated her was knotting the robe belt around her middle. And that was such a minor thing after all the other obstacles she had so successfully negotiated that she thought nothing more about it as she walked back into the bedroom, dabbing a towel at her damp hair—only to stop dead in her tracks.

'Oh!' The stifled exclamation of surprise left her throat like a sigh, yet he heard it, and it brought him twisting on his heel to face her. Then, for a few short, thickening moments, neither of them moved again.

It's like having time stand still, Claire thought as she stared at his lean, dark face and felt the strangest sensation wash over her—like a sharp implement being drawn down her backbone, setting off a sensory chain reaction that had her whole system tingling.

Then he spoke. 'For goodness' sake,' he bit out. 'Do you have to look so disturbed that you find me here? I have not come to ravish you—though it may be prudent for you to— do something about the robe,' he suggested, with a grim flick of the hand that sent her wide eyes jerking downwards.

In an agony of dismay she dropped the towel so she could whip the two sides of the robe together across her naked front, then clamped them there with her plastered wrist.

'Have you never heard of knocking?' she choked, almost suffocating in her own embarrassment.

'I did knock,' he replied. 'But when I received no answer I let myself in, believing you may well be sleeping.'

'Which makes it all right, does it?' She flashed him a hot, resentful glance. 'You see nothing wrong in coming into a guest's bedroom while she sleeps in blissful ignorance of your presence?'

If she said all of that to hit back at him for embarrassing her, it didn't work. All he did was throw up his arrogant head and glare at her as if he was waiting for *her* to apologise for *his* intrusion!

Then he let out an impatient sigh. 'This is all so unnecessarily foolish,' he muttered, and began striding towards her with the kind of purpose that had Claire backing warily.

'Stop it!' he hissed, reaching down to grab hold of the two ends of the robe belt that were hanging at either side of her. With a firm yank he brought her to a standstill, then proceeded to tower over her like some avenging dark angel.

He was angry, she could see that. But there was something else going on behind that hard, tight expression that seriously disturbed her—though at that moment she wasn't sure why.

Then he bent towards her. He's going to kiss me! she thought wildly, and gasped out some kind of shaky little protest as her heart gave a painful thump against her ribs then began palpitating madly when panic erupted in a roaring mad rush that set her brain spinning.

What he actually did do was knot her robe belt around her middle. It was like being on a helter-skelter ride of out-of-control emotion. Instead of feeling high as a kite on panic, she suddenly felt dizzy with the effects of a sinking relief.

Then he kissed her.

And after everything else that had gone before it she had nothing—nothing left to fight him with. The sense of relief had relaxed all the tension out of her, so he caught her undefended, his mouth crushing hers with a ruthless precision that literally shocked her breathless.

Warm, smooth, very knowledgeable lips fused warmly

with hers. Blue eyes wide open with shock and staring, she found herself looking straight down into the black abyss of his. The rest of her followed, free-falling into that terrible darkness without the means to stop herself.

Then he was gone. As abruptly as he had made the contact, he withdrew it.

'Now be afraid,' he grimly invited, and while she stood there just staring at him with huge blank blue eyes he turned on his heel and strode off to the other side of the room.

In the sizzling taut silence which followed she could have heard a pin drop on the thick carpet beneath her bare feet. She was too stunned to speak and he was obviously still too angry.

For anger it had been that had made him kiss her like that; she wasn't so punch-drunk as not to have recognised that. It had been a kiss to punish, not a kiss to frighten. He had already warned her several times today that he reacted badly to challenge.

Well, she had just received personal experience of that bad reaction, Claire acknowledged. 'If you ever do that again, I will scratch your eyes out,' she informed him shakily.

'Before or after you expose your body to me?'

He was such a merciless devil! If her legs hadn't felt so shaky she would have gone over there and scratched his eyes out anyway!

Then she remembered what it had felt like to fall into them, and shivered, the will to fight shrivelling out of her because she never wanted to risk looking into those eyes like that again.

So instead she began looking around her in a rather dazed effort to remember what she had been doing when she'd discovered him here.

She saw the white towel lying on the deep blue carpet and remembered she had been using it to dry the excess water off her wet hair. Knowing that bending to pick it up again was completely beyond her physical abilities at the moment, she ignored the towel and went over to the dressing table where, earlier, she had spied a hairbrush.

He was standing with his back to her, in front of a polished wood tallboy inside which, Althea had shown her, were housed a television set and a very expensive-looking music system.

The room with everything, she thought sarcastically, and grimaced as she picked up the hairbrush and began drawing it through her damp hair.

'What are you here for anyway?' she asked, needing to break through the silence. 'I presume you did have a reason to come in here?'

He turned, stiff, tense, and supremely remote—like a man sitting alone on the top of a mountain, she thought, and felt a return of her earlier sense of humour at the absurd image.

No apology forthcoming this time, she noted, and the smile actually reached her eyes.

He saw it, didn't like it and frowned, something interestingly like the pompous male equivalent to a blush streaking a hint of colour across his dark cheekbones. Fascinated by that, Claire turned more fully to face him so she could see how he was going to deal with this momentary loss of his precious composure.

Recognising exactly what she was doing and why, he released a heavy sigh. 'How are the ribs?'

Ah, a diversion, she noted. 'Sore,' she replied, telling the blunt truth of it.

'And the wrist?'

'Agony,' she grimaced.

'Then maybe I did the right thing coming in here to bring you—these...' He was holding up a small bottle of what had to be tablets. 'Pain-killers,' he explained. 'Issued by the hospital. I forgot I had them.'

Half turning, he placed the bottle on the top of the tallboy. Then he turned back to Claire. 'Where is your sling?'

Glancing down to where her plastered wrist was hanging

heavily at her side, 'I must have left it in the bathroom,' she replied, putting down the hairbrush so she could use her hand to lift the cast into a more comfortable position resting against her middle.

Without another word he strode off, his composure intact now, and his arrogance along with it, she observed as she watched him disappear into the bathroom then come out again carrying the modern version of a sling in his hand.

About to approach her, he paused, thought twice about it, then—sardonically—requested, 'May I?'

Her wry half nod gave her permission and he came forward. By then she had moved to ease herself into a sitting position on the edge of the dressing table, so he really towered over her this time as he coolly looped the sling-belt over her head then gently took hold of her plastered wrist.

'You didn't even get it wet,' he remarked.

'I'm a very clever girl,' she answered lightly.

'And sometimes,' he drawled, 'you are very reckless and naïve.'

'How you can make such a sweeping remark about me when you've barely known me for a day is beyond me,' she threw right back. Then she broke the banter to issue a wince and a groan as he gently eased the weighty plaster-cast into its support.

Instantly his eyes flicked upwards to her face, wondrously lustrous curling black lashes coiling away from those dangerous black holes to reveal—not anger, but genuine concern.

'How much pain are you actually in?' he demanded huskily.

A lot, she wanted to say, but tempered the reply to a rueful, 'Some,' that was supposed to have sounded careless but ended up quivering as it left her.

The anger came back then. 'How much and where?' He grimly insisted on a truthful answer.

'All over,' she confessed as all hint of flippancy drained

right out of her and her throat began to thicken with pathetic, weak tears.

On a soft curse, he moved away from her again, going back into the bathroom to return carrying a glass of water. Not even glancing her way, he strode across the room to pick up the pill bottle. Coming back, he handed her the glass of water then shook two small pills into his palm. In grim silence he offered them to her. And in tearful silence she took them and washed them down with the water.

A tear trickled down her cheek. She went to wipe it away with the glass—but he got there before her, his long fingers gently splaying across her damp hair while he smoothed his thumb pad across her cheek.

And the worst of it was, she wanted to lean right into those splayed fingers. She wanted to bury her face in his big hard chest and sob her wretched heart out!

'I can't even stand up!' she confessed despairingly 'My hip's gone all stiff—and my thigh and my ribs!'

A moment later she was being lifted into his arms and it hurt like blazes but she didn't care.

'I am such a pathetic baby!' she sobbed as he carried her across the room towards the bed.

'You are hurt. You are shocked. You are exhausted,' he responded sternly. 'Which means you are allowed to be pathetic.'

A joke! She laughed, and the tears stopped.

Laying her carefully on the bed, he reached across her and flipped the other side of the king-size duvet over her. His face was still stern, but she found she liked looking at it now.

'How old are you?' she asked curiously.

He paused as he was about to straighten. Looked into pool-deep blue eyes—and offered her a cold little grimace. 'As old as the hills,' he drawled—and stood back. 'Now rest,' he ordered. 'And let the pain-killers do their job. We eat in...' he took a quick glance at the paper-thin gold watch he had wrapped around his hair-peppered wrist '...two hours. By then Althea should be back with your things. So you may get up and join me for dinner downstairs, or you can eat up here. The choice is yours.'

With that he turned and was gone. It was like having the fire go out suddenly, Claire decided with a shiver, then frowned, wondering why she was comparing him to a fire when he was more like a freezer most of the time...

She went downstairs for dinner. Mainly because she didn't want to be a bigger nuisance to these people than she was already being—and because she was desperate to see Melanie, who was being bathed and fed by Lefka while Althea unpacked Claire's clothes then helped her to dress in a fresh pair of jeans and a simple black tee shirt that was loose enough and baggy enough to pull on and off without causing her too much trouble.

Althea showed her into a large drawing room that was nicely decorated in champagne golds and soft greens. Another fire was burning in the grate and the soft sounds of classical music floated soothingly in the air.

Andreas was there, dressed in a fresh pale blue shirt and a pair of steel-grey trousers that sat neatly on his lean waist. But what really surprised her was to find him holding Melanie comfortably at his shoulder.

'You look better,' he remarked, bringing her eyes up from the baby to find him running his gaze over her now shiny gold hair. It had dried on its own while she'd rested and really needed styling, but its own slight kink had saved it from looking a complete fly-away mess.

'I feel it,' she nodded, with a smile that brought his eyes into focus on hers. Whatever it was that was written in those dark depths, Claire suddenly found herself remembering that kiss earlier, and had to break the contact quickly before she embarrassed herself by blushing.

'How has she been?' she then asked anxiously, looking

back at Melanie who looked so tiny against the broad expanse of his chest.

'Like an angel,' he drawled. 'So Lefka informs me. She is smitten,' he confided—then said more softly, 'And I cannot blame her.'

He really meant it, too, Claire realised as she briefly flicked her eyes back to his face to find it softening as he glanced at the baby.

'She is awake. Would you like to hold her?'

'Oh, yes, please...' No one—unless they'd experienced it—could know what it felt like to be separated from the baby she had taken care of single-handedly since their mother had died.

'Perhaps if you sit down on one of the comfortable chairs then you can cradle her in your lap,' he suggested.

Claire didn't need telling twice; walking over to one of the champagne-coloured easy chairs, she sank carefully into its comfort-soft cushions then eagerly accepted the baby.

The moment that Melanie saw Claire's face smiling down on her, her tiny mouth broke into a welcoming smile.

'She knows you,' he said, sounding surprised.

'Of course,' Claire answered. 'I'm her surrogate mother—aren't I, my darling?'

After that she completely forgot about Andreas Markopoulou, who, after a moment or two, lowered himself into the chair opposite them then sat looking on as Claire immersed herself in the sheer pleasure of her mother's baby, talking softly to her while Melanie looked and listened with rapt attention.

Dinner was pleasant. Nothing fancy, just simple but tasty vegetable soup followed by boiled rice and thin slivers of pan-fried chicken that she could easily manage to eat by only using her fork.

Refusing the deep red full-blooded wine he was drinking with his meal, she asked for water instead. And they talked quietly. Well, she talked—Claire made the wry distinction—

while he encouraged her with strategically placed questions that resulted in her whole life to date getting aired at that dinner table.

When she eventually sat back, talked-out and replete, having refused any dessert to finish her meal, she made herself ask the question that had been troubling her on and off throughout the whole day.

Only one day? She paused to consider this with a small start of surprise. It was beginning to feel as if she'd spent a whole lifetime here with this strangely attentive, very intriguing and enigmatic man.

'Why did you send my aunt away?' she asked him.

He sat back in his own chair to idly finger his wineglass while he studied her face through faintly narrowed eyes.

'She was never very close to you or your mother, was she?' he said, frustratingly blocking the question with a question.

Still, Claire answered it. 'They never got on,' she admitted with a shrug. 'My mother was...' She stopped, her soft mouth twisting slightly because what she was going to say sounded as if she was being critical of a mother she'd adored—when in actual fact it wasn't a criticism but a flat statement of fact. 'A bit frivolous.' She made herself say it. 'Aunt Laura was the older sister. Much tougher and...less pretty,' she added with wry honesty.

'People liked to spoil my mother.' Even I did, she thought, glancing at those slightly narrowed, intent black eyes then away again quickly. 'Aunt Laura would have bitten their heads off for trying the same thing with her,' she went on. 'She's a staunch feminist with a good business brain and she likes to use it.'

He nodded in agreement and once again Claire felt herself being subtly encouraged to continue. 'She has no time for—sentimentality.' Claire thought that described her aunt best. 'Her philosophy is that if something goes wrong you either fix it or throw it away and start from scratch again,' she explained sadly.

'And which category do you and Melanie come under?'

'She wants me to have Melanie adopted,' she replied, her expression turning cynical. 'So you tell me because I still haven't decided whether that particular solution is supposed to be fixing us or throwing us out.'

'Which means,' he concluded, 'that you also have not decided whether to take her advice or not.'

Shrewd devil, Claire thought bitterly, and rose tensely to her feet as the rotten truth in that statement hit sharply home. 'Why don't you try answering my question for a change?' she flashed back in sheer bloody reaction. 'And tell me why you sent her away when it has to be obvious that we needed her here right now!'

'I don't need to answer the question,' he replied, super-calm in the face of her sudden hostility. 'For you have just answered it for yourself.'

'What's that supposed to mean?' she demanded frowningly, not understanding what he was getting at.

He didn't seem inclined to explain it either, she observed as he sat there, eyes hooded, face grim while he stared fixedly at his wineglass as if he was weighing up his options.

But—what options? Claire wondered in despairing confusion. She didn't even know why she knew what he was doing! Yet the suggestion stuck while she stood there simmering with frustration and anger, waiting for him to make up his mind.

Then he announced, 'I have a proposition to put to you,' and got to his feet, obviously having made that decision! 'But we will go through to my study before I say any more. For we require privacy and it cannot be guaranteed here when Lefka or Althea could walk in at any moment.'

With that he turned and strode off, obviously expecting Claire to follow him. She did so, frowning and tense again—

very tense as every suspicious thought she'd had about this man and his motives came rushing back.

By the time Claire arrived at the study door he was already standing across the room where a tray of bottles stood on an antique oak sideboard.

'Please shut the door behind you,' he instructed without turning.

Doing as he said, she watched in silence as he selected, uncapped and poured a rather large measure of a dark golden spirit into a squat crystal tumbler.

Clearly, he needed something more fortifying than wine before he put his proposition to her! she noted, and felt her wary tension move up another couple of notches as she waited for him to speak.

'I sent your aunt out of the country on business today,' he began quite suddenly, 'because I decided to get her about as far away from you as I could possibly manage.'

Claire gave a surprised start. 'But—why?' she gasped. 'Why would you want to do that?'

He didn't answer immediately; instead the glass went to his mouth so he could sip at the spirit, gathering tension all around them as it did so.

It was odd—that tension—full of a tingling sense of dark foreboding that even he seemed affected by. As Claire stood there by the door with her wary eyes fixed on his hard, lean face, she gained the strong impression that, despite the decision he seemed to have come to in the dining room, he was still heavily involved in a rather uncharacteristic struggle with himself.

'I have a—personal problem that is threatening to cause me a certain amount of—embarrassment,' he said suddenly. 'I do have a workable solution, however,' he added, glancing back at his glass and tipping it slightly so the golden liquid clung to the sides. 'But it requires a wife and a child to succeed. Meeting you today,' he went on levelly, 'seeing where you live and, more importantly, how you live—it occurred to me that you may well be the ideal candidate for the position...'

'What position?' Claire asked, utterly lost as to what he was getting at.

He grimaced into his glass—she presumed because she was forcing him into being more explicit about what he was talking about.

'As my wife,' he enlightened her. Then, when she still continued to stand there blank-faced and frowning in bewilderment, he lifted his eyes until they fixed sardonically on hers and said, 'I am asking you to marry me, Claire...'

CHAPTER FOUR

CLAIRE released a gasp in stunned disbelief. 'You want to *marry me*?' she repeated.

Then, almost instantly, she decided, No, I've heard him wrong, and laughed—or rather emitted a nervous little giggle that she regretted as soon as it left her lips because the effect it had on him made her feel cruel, as his lean face closed up as tight as a drum.

He's actually serious! she realised. She felt her legs threaten to collapse beneath her and had to move over to one of the dark red recliners and lower herself carefully into it.

'Please do not misunderstand me,' he said, suddenly standing high on his mountain of dignity again. 'I am not suggesting an intimate relationship. Just a—marriage of convenience if you like. Where we will maintain an appearance of intimacy. But that is all...'

No intimacy, she repeated to herself, and as quickly as that her eyes went blank as her imagination shot off to a place where she'd stared into this man's eyes while his mouth had been fused very *intimately* with her own.

'I will, of course, ensure that the—arrangement is a beneficial one for you,' he coldly continued. 'The advantages in being the wife of a very wealthy man do, I think, speak for themselves. And it need not be a lifetime thing—although I will have to insist that I become Melanie's legal father or it will not work.'

'What won't work?' she questioned helplessly.

But he gave a shake of his dark head. 'I can only reveal that if I gain your agreement,' he said. 'But in her becoming my legal daughter,' he went on as if she hadn't made the interruption, 'I will be assuring Melanie's future—which can

58

only be a good thing for her, since she will also become my sole heir. And if and when you decide that it is time for you to leave me so you can get on with your own life you will not go empty-handed.'

Claire's mind was starting to scramble. She was sure that what he was actually saying here, in a carefully veiled way, was that he wanted Melanie, but if Claire had to come along with her, then he was prepared to agree to that.

'I think you're crazy,' she told him.

He grimaced, but didn't argue the point.

'You don't even know me!'

This time it was a shrug. 'I am a man who has always relied on my first impression of people—and I like you, Claire,' he said, as if that should mean something special to her. 'I even admire you for the way you have been coping on your own with a child and little to no help from anyone.'

'I do have help!' she cried, her hackles rising at his too accurate reading of her.

'Do you mean—this kind of help?' he asked, and from his trouser pocket he withdrew a wad of bank notes.

As she stared at them as if she had never so much as laid eyes on paper money before, it took a few moments for it to sink in what he was actually showing her.

Her eyes shot to his. 'Is that the money Aunt Laura left for me today?'

'You dropped it on the floor in your flat when you fainted,' he explained. 'I picked it up and placed it in my pocket for safekeeping. I counted it earlier; there is exactly one hundred pounds here,' he informed her grimly. 'Knowing the dire straits of your circumstances, that you owe at least four times that amount on your rent *and* being fully aware that you also have to exist somehow, your aunt condescended to leave you a paltry one hundred pounds.'

To Claire, who had nothing, one hundred pounds was an absolute fortune! But it obviously wasn't to this man. For the way he tossed the money aside made his disgust more than clear.

'In effect, what she was doing,' he went on, remorseless in his determination to get his own point across, 'was wearing you down so that you would begin to look on her proposal more favourably. I got that much out of her while you were half comatose,' he inserted tightly. 'And she was trying her best to explain to me why her only relatives were living in that kind of squalor.'

Claire closed her eyes, the word 'squalor' cutting right to the heart of her.

'You already knew about her suggestion before I told you,' she breathed, feeling the sharp sting of one that had been well and truly tricked by his quiet interest in her during dinner.

Maybe he saw it. 'I am sorry if that offends you,' he said. 'But it is important here that you keep your mind focused on what is best for you and Melanie. And if it has come down to a choice between having the child adopted and my offer, then I think mine is your better option.'

'But then you would, wouldn't you?' Claire pointed out, and came stiffly to her feet. 'Now I want my baby and I want to go home,' she informed him with enough ice-cold intent to match any he could dish out.

It made his face snap with irritation. 'Don't be foolish!' he rasped. 'That is no solution and only promises you more misery!'

I'm miserable now, Claire thought unhappily. 'I thought you were kind!' she burst out, blue eyes bright with a pained disillusionment. 'I thought you genuinely cared about what had happened to me! When all the time while you've been shadowing me around today you've been plotting this!'

Her voice rose on a clutch of hurt. He winced at the sound of it. 'I *am* kind!' he growled, looking faintly uncomfortable with his own role here.

Claire's thick huff of scorn made his eyes flash warningly,

then, with a grimace, he seemed to be allowing her the right to be scornful.

'I can be kind,' he amended huskily, scraped an impatient set of long fingers through his hair, then even amended the amendment. 'I will be kind,' he declared in a voice that made it a promise.

Still, it held no sway with Claire. 'Thank you for the offer but no, thank you,' she refused, moving stiffly towards the door.

'Before you walk through that door, Miss Stenson, don't you think you should take a moment to consider what your decision is going to mean to your sister...?'

Smooth as silk, his voice barely revealing an inflection, his words still had her steps faltering and growing still, the fine quiver touching her soft mouth sign enough that, just like her aunt, he had managed to find the right button to press without having to look very hard for it.

'But—why?' she cried, lifting perplexed blue eyes to his deadly ruthless face. 'If you feel such a strong need to will your possessions to someone, then why not get a family of your own?'

It didn't make sense—none of it did. Neither did the way he suddenly stiffened up as if he'd been shot. 'I will never marry again,' he said. 'Not in the way you are suggesting anyway.'

'You've been married before?'

'Yes. Sofia—died six years ago.' The confirmation was coldly blunt.

'Oh...I'm so sorry,' Claire murmured, her expression immediately softening into sympathy.

His did the opposite. 'I have no wish to discuss it,' he clipped, and the way he said it was enough to stop Claire from daring to ask any more questions.

But she was curious. Suddenly very curious about the woman he had lost whom he must have loved very deeply if he never wanted to marry again. Not for real, anyway, she dryly tagged onto that.

'There are other ways these days to get children without having to commit yourself to marriage, you know,' she pointed out gently. 'Medical science has become quite clever in that respect.'

'I am Greek,' he replied as if that explained everything. And he didn't elaborate. Instead he pulled everything back to the main issue. 'I want you to consider very carefully what you will be gaining if you agree to marry me. For you will get to bring up your mother's child in the kind of luxury most people only dream of.'

Humility is not one of his strongest points, Claire made wry note.

'Think of it,' he urged. 'No more living from hand to mouth. No more having to go without so you can ensure that the child is clothed and fed. No worrying where the next week's rent is coming from. Instead,' he concluded, listing the advantages of his so-called proposal in much the same way her aunt had done when talking about Melanie's adoption, 'you will receive a generous monthly allowance to do with what you will. And since all our homes will have more than enough paid staff to relieve you of the less enjoyable chores involved in caring for a baby you will have the time and the leisure to enjoy life rather than sacrificing it to your baby sister.'

'I don't see it as a sacrifice.' Her chin came up, blue eyes glittering with indignation. 'And I resent the implication that I may do.'

'My apologies,' he retracted instantly. 'It was not my intention to offend.'

No, Claire could see it wasn't. This was just too important to him to want to risk offending her—which immediately brought about her next question. 'Why does it mean so much to you to get me? To get Melanie?' she asked. 'You could walk out of here right now and simply pick up a dozen women with children who could fill this role just as well as we can!'

'But I want you both,' he stated simply. 'Why don't you ask yourself why it is that you are so afraid of what I am offering you?'

'Because it feels wrong,' she replied, then added honestly, 'And I'm too young for this role.'

'Or is it me who is too old?'

He's the type who will never be old. 'How old is that exactly? And don't give me the flippant answer I got the last time I asked you that question,' she warned. 'Because I'm serious. If you want me to consider your proposition I need to know.'

'Thirty-six,' he replied, and grimaced at her astonished expression.

She gave a small sigh, then turned to lean back against the closed door. 'This is crazy,' she muttered, thinking out loud. But what was even crazier was the knowledge that she was beginning to waver.

No more worries, she told herself. No more living from day to day in a place she hated with no prospect of ever getting something better—if you didn't count what was being offered here. Then there was Melanie to consider. Melanie, who would want for nothing for the rest of her life, if his sincerity was to be believed.

It was all very seductive, she mused, lifting her hand to gently rub at the bump on her temple as her head began to ache.

He saw the gesture and was instantly all concern. 'It is clear that you have had enough for one day,' he murmured huskily. 'Let us leave this for now, and come back to it tomorrow when you are feeling more rested.'

He was right—and she had taken enough, Claire acknowledged wearily. But she said, 'No.' She shook her head. 'I won't sleep for worrying about all of this unless we resolve it now.'

She lifted tired, bruised, anxious eyes to his. 'Will you please tell me *why* you need a ready-made wife and baby?' she begged.

There was a pause, then he asked smoothly, 'Are you telling me you are going to accept my proposition?'

He isn't going to give a single inch to me, she noted. 'I'm thinking about it,' she replied.

'Then while you think I will think about telling you why I want you to marry me.'

Cat and mouse. Cut and thrust. 'Then goodnight,' she said, and turned back to the door.

'I like the hair, by the way...'

Her hair? Her hand went up, self-conscious fingertips lightly touching the ends of a fine silk tendril.

'It is such a wonderful colour...'

'Thank you,' she murmured, blushing slightly at the unexpected compliment.

'Neither blonde nor red,' he softly observed. 'But a rather fascinating mixture of the two... I wonder what colour it will go with a Greek sunset pouring all over it?'

'I've never been to Greece,' Claire sighed, heard the wistful note in her voice and knew that he must be able to hear it too.

'You'll love it,' he promised as he walked towards her. 'Sizzling hot days and delightfully warm nights. Though you will have to protect your fine white skin from the sun,' he warned. 'But Melanie's skin will love it. Whatever nationality her father was, he gifted her with the rich olive skin of a true Mediterranean.'

'Spanish,' Claire inserted. 'Her father was Spanish.' Then a sudden thought had her glancing sharply at him. 'Is that why you want her?' she asked. 'Because she has the right skin tone to be passed off as your daughter?'

But he shook his dark head. He was standing so close to her now that she could actually see the wry humour hovering in his dark eyes. 'With a golden-haired, pale-skinned English wife, my child could have been blessed with her colouring,' he pointed out.

Looking away again, Claire frowned, the conundrum behind his reason for wanting them beginning to irritate her like an itch she couldn't quite reach. 'Well...' She gave a small shrug of one narrow shoulder as if the itch were situated there, and turned away from him yet again. 'I'll...'

'My family is trying to make me marry again, and produce an heir to my fortune.'

He caved in so suddenly and produced the information that for a moment Claire couldn't believe that he'd actually done it! It went so against what she'd believed she'd already learned about his calculating nature!

'They have my proposed bride already picked out for me,' he went on. 'And the pressure is mounting because my grandmother is ill. She wants to hold her great-grandchild before she dies. And since I am the only grandson she has it is up to me to grant her that wish.'

'How ill?' Claire asked gently.

'Very.' The shadowy outline of his mouth flicked out that grim brief smile again. 'She is ninety-two years old and has just suffered her second stroke. She does not have long left on this earth.'

And he loves her and is going to miss her dreadfully, Claire realised as she saw a darkness come down over those unfathomable eyes, and felt her heart give a pinch of well understood sympathy.

'I don't have time to play around with alternatives,' he admitted. 'So your arrival in my life was a piece of good fortune I could not afford to dismiss. As I have told you before, I respond to my instincts. And my instincts tell me that we three could make a good team.' His eyes flicked up, clashed with her eyes and Claire suddenly felt as if she were falling again. 'When my grandmother is no longer here to see it happen, you can leave whenever you are ready to...'

No hearts compromised, no feelings touched. 'More like a temporary job, in fact.'

'For you, yes,' he agreed, with a small shrug. 'But not for Melanie...' he made firmly clear. 'Melanie will be my daughter in every way I can make it so. I want her, Claire,' he added huskily. 'I *need* her.'

'But will you *love* her?' she challenged.

'As my own and all my life,' he vowed. And he meant it; Claire could see that in the fierce glow of a powerful intent that suddenly lit his eyes.

I wish somebody wanted me like that, she found herself thinking wistfully. 'And when I decide to go—what happens to Melanie?'

'She goes with you,' he said—but only after a hesitation that hit a warning button inside her head. 'So long as you will promise to respect my rights as her legal father, we will agree on an affable arrangement which will suit both of our needs where she is concerned. For Melanie's sake alone, it has to be her best chance in life, don't you think?'

For Melanie's sake, Claire repeated silently, knowing exactly where she had heard those words before, and not liking the sensation that trickled down her spine at the connection.

But, despite that nasty sensation, one important thing she did know for sure was that, having once lived in privileged comfort herself—though not anywhere near the style he was offering Melanie here—and having gained tough experience at the poorer end of the scale, Claire knew which end of that scale she preferred to be.

'I'll do it,' she heard herself say. 'For Melanie's sake.'

And only wondered as she did so whether this hadn't been a case of him caving in first, but simply a very astute man knowing exactly when to play his final card.

'Thank you,' he murmured. 'I will promise you, Claire, that you will never have cause to regret this decision.'

But she was already regretting it as early as the next morning when she came down the stairs ready to tell him that she had changed her mind.

At which point she discovered that Andreas Markopoulou had pulled yet another tactical move on her, by going abroad on business for the next frustratingly long week.

Melanie, in the meantime, was beginning to bloom with all the tender loving care both Lefka and Althea were ladling upon her. Claire didn't hear her cry once!

Secretly she found it hurtful. For, under Claire's exclusive care, the little girl had hardly ever *stopped* crying since their mother had died.

Then, most hurtful of all, was the way her aunt hadn't once bothered to get in touch with her. Whether that was her aunt's own indifference or Andreas Markopoulou's doing she didn't know. But, knowing Aunt Laura as well as she did, if she'd wanted to contact Claire then she would have done, no matter what her big tycoon boss might say.

But, as the week slid by, at least her body began to heal; the bump on her temple disappeared altogether and her bruises began to fade. Even her hurt feelings had given way to a dull acceptance—along with her acceptance that she could no more take Melanie away from what she was receiving here than sprout wings and fly.

So it was that she was sitting in the solarium at the back of the house, gently pushing Melanie's pram to and fro to rock the baby to sleep, when a voice murmured to one side of her, 'You look a lot better...'

She didn't turn to look at him, but her hand stopped rocking the baby carriage. And her heart gave an excited leap that left her feeling tense and shaky.

Still, at least her voice was steady when she answered coolly, 'A week is a long time.'

'Ah...' He came forward, his footsteps sounding on the quarry-tiled floor beneath his feet. 'I thought it best to leave you alone to—come to terms with your decision.'

So he was admitting to a retreat, she noted, and was oddly

pacified by that—then even more so when he paused at the pram to bend down and inspect Melanie.

'She's asleep,' he whispered. But it was the way he stroked a gentle finger over the baby's cheek in much the same way that Claire did that touched a warm spot inside her.

Then, pulling up one of the other cane chairs, he sat down beside her. 'How is the wrist?' he enquired.

'Better,' she told him.

'And the ribs?'

'They don't hurt when I laugh any more,' she replied with a grin she turned to offer directly to him.

Then wished she hadn't when her heart gave that funny leap again, making the tiny muscles deep in her stomach coil up in reaction. He looked lean and dark and sun-kissed, as if he'd just stepped off a plane from a place where the weather had been a lot pleasanter than it had been here in England.

She felt a tingling urge to reach out and touch his face just to feel if it was as warm as it appeared to be. 'Where have you been?' she asked instead, leaving the less tactile medium of words to assuage her curiosity.

'You sound like a wife,' he mocked, his dark eyes flickering slightly as he scanned her face where even Claire had noticed the stray-waif look was beginning to fade.

'Not yet,' she drawled in answer. 'And for all you know I may have changed my mind.'

'Have you?'

The urge to prolong his agony and lie almost got the better of her, but in the end she said, 'No,' and they were both silent for several minutes. The baby made a snuffling sound and she began rocking the pram again. It was all very— ordinary.

'I've been in Greece,' he announced, answering her earlier question. 'With my grandmother,' he added, and though his tone was level Claire knew instinctively that something was wrong.

'She's worse, isn't she?' she said.

'Fading fast,' he grimaced—then added briskly, 'So I have set her a task to do to keep her mind occupied. She is planning our wedding as we speak.'

Startled, Claire straightened in the chair. 'Our wedding?' she repeated. 'But I thought you wanted to present her with a *fait accompli*!'

'No.' He shook his head. 'That would not have worked quite so successfully as the story I have now fed her.'

'Which is—what?' she demanded, only managing to keep her angry voice down in respect of the sleeping Melanie.

'That you are young and very beautiful...'

Beautiful? Claire stared directly ahead and wondered how he could lie so glibly, because the one thing she wasn't was beautiful! Passably attractive when at her best, she conceded. But nothing more than that.

'I told her that we had shared a—liaison some time last year,' he went on. 'But because of your youth I broke it off, not knowing I was leaving you carrying my child...'

Lie number two, she counted, and began to see for the first time what mire of deceit she was about to fall into.

'But I could not get you out of my mind—which was why I found it so impossible to agree to marry another woman while I still wanted you. So I went to see you,' he explained. 'And as for the rest—' he shrugged '—it tells itself.'

It certainly did, Claire agreed, seeing herself as this tragic young woman who'd fallen for the big handsome Greek tycoon who was, by the sound of it, not far off his dotage.

'Actually,' he said, 'the new slant I have put on our—story—' he used the word dryly '—was done to serve a second purpose...'

Now what? Claire wondered, feeling the fine hairs on the back of her neck begin to prickle warningly.

'For this way you don't have to *like* the fact that you are marrying me,' he explained. 'Being the arrogant dictator that everyone seems to think I am—including you—no one is going to question the idea that you have been—coerced into becoming my wife for the sake of our child. Which also means you get your own bedroom without tongues wagging,' he pointed out. 'While I must—earn your affections again.'

'And thereby ends the tale when I eventually turn my back on you and walk away,' Claire finished for him. 'Not quite the stuff of a romantic novel, is it?' she mocked.

'Life rarely is,' he drawled, sounding suddenly so cold that Claire couldn't believe her ears! With one lightly mocking comment she seemed to have turned him to stone!

Stiffly, he came to his feet. 'We leave for Greece in the morning,' he announced. 'Now I have some work to do. So if you will excuse me...' And, with a curt little bow, he was gone!

What was all that about? Claire found herself wondering in blank bewilderment. And spent the next half an hour trawling over every single word they'd said to each other without coming up with a single thing which could have caused that kind of reaction!

His grandmother: she finally decided to blame it on her. It had to be because he was worried about her.

But deep down inside she somehow knew that wasn't true.

CHAPTER FIVE

THEY flew out to Athens by private charter then transferred
to a helicopter for the final leg of the journey. It was all very
comfortable, a very trouble-free way to travel in fact.

Claire was impressed—despite not wanting to be, for she
still hadn't forgiven Andreas for his sudden coldness the day
before.

Melanie was with them, which had surprised her rather.
She had expected him to insist that the baby travel with Lefka
and her family, who were to close up the London house before catching a later flight. But what really astonished her
was the way Andreas took personal responsibility for the
baby by seeing to her needs throughout the whole journey.

He was more relaxed than she had ever seen him before.
A bit quiet, maybe, but very attentive. So much so that it
was a shame that she was still feeling so annoyed with him,
because she suspected that he was doing all of this as a way
to make up for his bewildering attitude.

Yet he hadn't apologised for it, or explained it. He blew
hot and cold on her so swiftly that it seemed to be easier to
withdraw and keep herself aloof from him rather than risk
having it happen all over again.

'Here, let me help you...' Cradling the baby in one big
arm, he offered Claire the steadying strength of the other to
help her negotiate the long step down from the helicopter.

With one hand out of action and because she was wearing
her only good suit today—a summer-blue silk-linen mix with
a fitted jacket and skirt that would not allow her much flex-
ibility in her steps—she needed his help, so she couldn't
refuse. But feeling that rock-solid forearm flex beneath her

palm had such a disturbing effect on her that she removed her hand just as soon as she could do it.

But, worse, she knew that he had sensed her reluctance to touch him when she saw his mouth tighten as he turned away to carry Melanie away from the noise of the rotor blades.

Smothering a heavy sigh, Claire followed more slowly, feeling decidedly at odds with herself and most definitely at odds with him. She hadn't slept last night for worrying and fretting about this whole crazy situation. Now she felt tired and fed up and...

'Oh,' she gasped, coming to a surprised standstill at his side as she focused at last on her new surroundings.

Set in vast formal gardens, the house stood like a statement to all that was right in grace and architectural posture. No one feature had been allowed to dominate. The walls were painted in the softest cream, the woodwork glossy white, and the roof was constructed in flat grey slate rather than the terracotta she would have expected. A first-floor veranda ran right across the front of the house, casting gentle shade onto the terrace below, where the palest blue-cushioned wooden garden furniture waited invitingly.

Over to one side of the house, she could see a large swimming pool shimmering in the afternoon sunshine, and even spied a second pool under a high domed glass roof attached to the house itself. If there was a road nearby, she could neither see nor hear any evidence of it, but a long straight driveway led off into the distance, lined on either side by tall cypress trees.

'But this is lovely,' she murmured.

'Praise indeed,' he drawled with cutting sarcasm. 'I was beginning to think that nothing was going to please you.'

With that he turned his back on her again to walk off towards the house. With a small grimace, Claire followed, half allowing him his right to have lost his grasp on all of that quiet patience he had been doling out to her all day.

He had stepped beneath the shaded end of the terrace before pausing to allow her to catch up with him, his long, lean body making a half turn so he could watch her approach through slightly hooded eyes.

Glancing up and noticing his scrutiny, Claire felt a self conscious flush of heat wash through her system and quickly looked away again. What was he seeing when he looked at her like that? she wondered. A very big mistake walking towards him?

While she saw a tall, dark, very handsome man with cold black eyes, an unsmiling mouth, and a proud tilt to his chiselled chin that seemed to be trying to tell her something.

Though what that something was, she couldn't have said. The man was a complete enigma.

Hot-cold. Soothe-cut. Approach and retreat. She listed these characteristics of his behaviour with a rueful tilt to her unhappy mouth that seemed to further annoy him. He shifted slightly, looking stiffly tense. The baby woke up with a start and gave a small cry. Claire covered the final few yards in a couple of light dancing steps, her mothering instincts alerted without her even being aware of it.

In the end she wasn't needed. When he glanced down at the baby to find her eyes were open, all the hardness simply melted clean out of him as he lifted a finger to gently touch the baby's small, pointed chin.

But what really took Claire's breath away was the way Melanie's sweet little smile appeared. She knows him already! she realised with a shock.

'Hey,' she complained, peering over his arm so she could look at her sister. 'Those smiles are supposed to belong to me!' she scolded.

As she heard her voice, Melanie's eyes found her face and stuck firmly to it. 'That's better,' Claire grinned, so engrossed in the baby that, far from being disturbed by his closeness, she didn't even notice the way she was leaning against Andreas so she could monopolise the baby's attention.

If she had, she would have realised how still he had gone.

How his hooded eyes had become even more hooded as he settled them on the top of her golden head.

'What a seductive picture,' a beautifully cultured but coldly sarcastic voice intruded. 'I wish I had my camera,' it drawled. 'Then I could capture the image for posterity and you could hang it on the wall as an example of perfect family harmony...'

Two heads came up, one dark, one fair, both faces revealing different expressions. Claire's was startled by this totally unexpected attack; Andreas's was—resigned.

'Desmona...' he greeted smoothly. 'How—nice to see you.'

But it wasn't nice. Desmona wasn't nice and Andreas wasn't being nice. The warm Greek air had suddenly turned chilly and Claire shivered accordingly as she watched the other woman begin walking towards them along the shaded terrace.

She was outstandingly beautiful. A tall and willowy silver-blonde in her early thirties, at a guess, whose silver-blue-silk-encased body glided gracefully as she moved. Money, class and a lifetime of believing herself to be special were reflected in that walk, Claire noted.

Though it was Desmona's eyes that held her thoroughly captivated. If Andreas's eyes could remind her of black ice sometimes, then the silver-grey ones looking at her now could have been set in permafrost, and they intimidated enough to have Claire inching backwards in wary retreat.

The back of her head hit a firmly cushioned shoulder at the same time as an arm curved around her, angling across her rigid back so long, lean brown fingers could rest on her narrow waist. Claire never even considered the idea of moving away from him—not while those silvery eyes were fixed on her anyway.

Was she family? Did she live here? she wondered curiously.

I hope not, she prayed, with a small shudder.

'This, Claire,' Andreas informed her levelly, 'is my sister-in-law Desmona Markopoulou...'

Sister-in-law? With a small start, she flashed him a frowning glance. She was sure he had told her that he was the only grandson.

'*Widowed* sister-in-law.' It was Desmona herself who unwittingly cleared the puzzle as she came to a smooth stop just in front of them. But Claire didn't even like the way she said that.

'May I be the first to welcome you to your new home?' Desmona murmured graciously.

'Thank you,' Claire politely replied.

She was offered a long-fingered, very slender white hand. Claire's own palm began to tingle in anticipation of having to brush against the other woman's satin-smooth skin.

Then the need to touch each other at all was suddenly saved when Claire remembered belatedly that her right hand was in a sling—at about the same moment that Desmona noticed it.

'Oh, you are injured,' she remarked. Her English was superb, spoken with an accent that was barely noticeable.

Claire smiled nervously. 'An accident.' She didn't bother to elaborate. 'So I am afraid I can't...' She gave a jerky gesture towards Desmona's outstretched hand; the hand fluttered a little then dropped.

Clearly picking up on the tension suddenly surrounding them all, Melanie let out another protesting cry. Desmona's eyes flicked from Claire to the baby, and in the sudden taut silence which followed something in her expression subtly altered.

'She is like you, Andreas,' she remarked casually enough, though.

'She is my daughter,' he answered just as casually. 'What else would you expect?'

No reply was forthcoming, but the silence lashed to and

fro with the kind of bitter words Claire could sense but not follow.

Then the silver eyes were shifting back to Claire, and the cold mask, which had slipped slightly, was suddenly back in place as Desmona politely excused herself before walking gracefully away along a formally set pathway that took her around the side of the house.

'Good grief,' Claire breathed as the air left her body in a single relieved whoosh. 'What was all that about?'

For a moment Andreas didn't answer, his attention thoughtfully fixed on Desmona's steadily receding figure. Then he surprised Claire with a short, sardonic laugh. 'You have just met the family choice for my bride,' he said dryly.

'Your late brother's *wife*?' she gasped, tipping her head back to stare at him in shocked disbelief.

He was already looking down at her, so their eyes clashed. The surface of her skin began to tingle, her insides along with it. She could feel herself beginning to fall into those devilish black eyes again and couldn't seem to do a single thing to stop it.

'Timo was a lot older than me,' Andreas was explaining, seemingly unaware of the strange sensations Claire was beginning to experience every single time she looked into those eyes now. 'They think I owe his widow something for inheriting on his death.'

'But that's archaic,' she denounced, having to struggle to keep her mind locked on the conversation and not on the man she was having the conversation with. 'When did your brother die?'

The bleak, pained look that came into his eyes occasionally was beginning to make more sense now, she realised as she watched it appear again. 'Just over a year ago,' he replied.

So, he had lost a wife he loved six years before, and a brother only recently. 'I'm sorry,' Claire murmured.

'So am I.' He smiled that brief grim smile. 'I miss him.'

'I know.' She nodded in understanding. 'You catch yourself looking round to speak to them only to feel that dreadful clutch of emptiness when you find they're not there and you remember...'

His dark lashes gave a flicker. Claire's breath caught on a softly inhaled little gasp when she saw the usual knock-back on its way. So she was totally unprepared for it when instead he bent his head and kissed her fully on her mouth.

If this was another punishing kiss for encroaching where he didn't want her to, then it didn't quite work out like that. Caught so off guard with her lips parted and her body relaxed, she was powerless to stop what happened next as she fell headlong into that kiss.

I don't need to be looking into those eyes to feel like this, she realised as her whole mouth softened and drew him deeper, touching tongues—tongues that caused a sharp, hot electric charge to go racing through her blood. It was devastating, the most passionate encounter she had ever experienced. And if he wasn't feeling it with her, then he was certainly feeling something that made a muffled groan break in his throat and his chest heave against her resting head before he completely caved in and threw himself passionately into that kiss.

If he hadn't been holding Melanie, Claire had a horrible feeling he would have fallen on her like a ravenous wolf. As it was his stance shifted slightly and the hand resting at her waist became a clamp to wedge her back hard up against the full length of his side with a need to increase and compound upon what was suddenly running rife between them.

It was crazy—totally crazy, she kept on telling herself over and over. This wasn't supposed to happen. This was a business arrangement. No intimacy.

No intimacy. But if this wasn't being intimate then she didn't know what was. And she could smell the clean spicy smell of him—was being enveloped by it—stormed by it! Even her bruised ribs weren't bothering to put up any protest at being clamped so tightly against him—they were too busy being under attack from the other side where her heart was pounding wildly in response to the whole mad, hot onslaught.

Then he groaned again, and in the next moment she was abruptly set free. In a dizzy haze of complete and utter disorientation, she reeled away. Legs like lead, eyes in a fog, she stumbled from beneath the terrace overhang and out into the sunshine.

'Where are you going?' His voice sounded hoarse and husky. But it brought her to a stop.

'I—don't know,' she answered honestly, too confused to care how stupid she must sound.

Or stupefied, she then thought numbly, and wished the grass beneath her feet would open up and swallow her whole so she didn't have to make herself turn around and face him.

Not that she needed to look to know exactly what she would see—a dark devil who had the kiss of hell in his repertoire, she thought fancifully.

A dark devil no less, who was cradling a sweet little baby on his arm, she added, and let out a strangled laugh that seemed to echo plaintively in the somnolent warmth of the afternoon quietness.

Yet he didn't sound like a devil when he said, 'Come back, Claire,' very gently. 'You're quite safe here; please believe me…'

Safe, she repeated to herself. Tears sprang. Wretchedly she blinked them away. Then, on a small, tight, thickened suck of air, she attempted to pull herself together before turning round again.

She didn't look at him—refused to do so as she made her shaking limbs carry her back into the shade. Coming to her side, he paused for a moment, and her senses began to sting in an agony of need for him to say not another word!

He must have sensed it and held his silence, which was something else she was realising about him—he picked up her feelings very easily.

Which made her what? Claire wondered dizzily as they

both began walking in silence along the terrace towards the door. Pathetically transparent? 'I...' Desperately she searched her foggy brain for something casual to say so she could pretend the kiss just hadn't happened. And found it when the sound of a car engine powering into life reminded her of Desmona. 'Does Desmona live here in this house?'

'She has her own apartment in Athens,' he replied. 'But she comes to visit my grandmother quite regularly. Claire, listen to me,' he then urged huskily.

'Oh, good,' she cut in, agitatedly aware he was going to say something about that wretched kiss, and equally sure she did not want to hear it. 'Then I won't have to watch my back for flying knives,' she joked, and managed to gain some reassurance from the fact that she *could* joke while she was feeling like this.

They turned together into a vast hallway with a white ceramic floor, cream walls and a white-painted staircase that swept gracefully upwards to a galleried landing above. It was all very grand. Very—

At which point her brain ground to a stop when she found herself confronted by a long line of shyly smiling and expectant faces.

Oh, what now? she groaned inwardly, eyeing the long row of what could only be the staff needed to run this big house, looking at the uniform neat pale pink dresses and white aprons the females were wearing, while it was white shirts and dark trousers for the men.

Then, on a sudden flashback to a few minutes ago, her face suffused with mortified colour. 'Do you think they saw us outside?' she breathed for his ears alone, while having a sudden horrendous vision of them all crowding at the windows to watch Andreas kissing her.

'If they did,' he drawled, 'then we will have no need to labour the game-plan.'

It hit her then just what had been going on outside. That kiss had been part of this deception! No impulse, she realised.

But merely part of his precious game-plan to make their liaison appear genuine.

She felt oddly cheated. No, worse than that. She felt used.

'Shall we get this over with?' he suggested, while she was still struggling with the appalling proof of just how ruthless this man could be!

With a light touch to the rigid line of her spine he prompted her into motion. For the next five minutes, face after face went by in a blur of smiles and curiously craning necks as his staff tried to get a peep at the sleeping baby lying in the crook of their employer's arm.

In fact the only face that registered was that of a young girl on the end of the row who reminded her of Althea. She stepped forward and shyly offered to take Melanie from Andreas. While Claire stood by, intensely conscious of everyone's eyes on her, Andreas exchanged a few words in Greek with the young girl before he handed over Melanie.

'I don't believe you put me through that,' she hissed when eventually he began leading the way up the staircase to the landing above, giving the staff the chance to crowd around the young girl holding Melanie.

'It was not set up for your benefit but for theirs,' he came back crushingly. 'They need to know who it is they are going to be dealing with since you will in effect be the lady of the house.'

Lady of the house? Claire almost tripped over the next stair in trembling dismay! His hand came out to steady her—she didn't even notice! 'But I can't order those people around, Andreas!' she protested, not noticing either that she had used his name for the first time in her urgency to get her point across. 'I just wouldn't know how!'

'You will get used to it,' he murmured indifferently.

'But I don't *want* to get used to it!' she snapped, and at last realised he was touching her again and angrily tugged her arm free.

'Fine,' he concurred, letting her go—but only, she suspected, because they had reached the top of the stairs anyway, so she wasn't likely to trip over again. 'Then let Lefka do it when she arrives,' he suggested carelessly.

She had forgotten all about Lefka, who, she had learned in London presided over whichever household Andreas was staying in. So—yes, she thought in relief, let Lefka do it. And felt her pounding heart settle down to a steadier pace. She was used to dealing with Lefka...

She followed Andreas along a galleried upper landing to a glossy white-painted door that led, she discovered, to a suite of rooms very similar to the suite she had been allocated in his London home, only this suite was decorated in neutral shades of the palest gardenia and grey.

While Claire walked over to the window to check out the view, Andreas walked across the thick carpet to another door and pushed it open.

'My rooms,' he announced, bringing her swinging abruptly to face him. 'But no key,' he dryly pointed out. 'So you will just have to trust me to behave myself.'

Was he really insensitive enough to joke about it after *that* kiss? Claire wondered furiously, and turned her back on him to walk over to the other side of the room where she opened another door, hoping to find a bedroom where Melanie would sleep. But a bathroom done in colours to match the bedroom gleamed cleanly back at her.

'Where is Melanie going to sleep?' she turned to ask.

'In the nursery on the other side of the house,' he said. 'I will show you later...'

He was already striding towards the only other door left in the room to open. Claire watched him, wondering what could be left to uncover. She remembered the huge dressing room in the London house and once again was ruefully envisaging her sad wardrobe inside it.

The door came open at his touch, and he turned to Claire. 'Come and look,' he invited.

Not a dressing room, then, she assumed, walking curiously

forward—only to go still in a state of breathless surprise when she realised that she was not only right and that this was indeed a dressing room, but also that her wardrobe of clothes certainly would be lost inside it—amongst the racks and rails and shelves already filled to bursting with the most exquisite things she had ever seen.

Expensive clothes. Designer clothes. Some of them very formal evening clothes. Yet still the kind of modern clothes any fashion-conscious twenty-one-year-old would die to possess.

'For me?' she asked breathlessly.

'Yes,' he replied, and watched grimly the way her fingers trembled as she lifted them to cover equally tremulous lips.

'I don't know what to say,' she whispered.

'Your response says it for you,' he responded quietly.

'I will never be able to wear this much!' she cried, her eyes beginning to shine with unshed tears of excitement as those same trembling fingers reached out to touch a fine georgette top in smoky mauve with a matching shantung silk skirt to go with it.

'Try,' he invited.

Then she suddenly thought just what she was doing. 'You must think me very mercenary,' she groaned, turning to find him leaning lazily against the open door, his dark eyes fixed on her expressive face.

'I think you are exquisite,' he answered deeply, reaching out to touch his cool fingertips to the satin-smooth heat in one of her cheeks, his expression so unimaginably sombre that it trapped the air inside her chest.

Then he was turning away from her in that now familiarly abrupt way of his. 'Enjoy,' he invited with a careless wave of his hand. 'Enjoy.'

And he was gone, disappearing through the connecting door to his own room, leaving Claire standing there with her own palm now pressed where his fingertips had been. Her thoughts locked on that terrible—terrible expression she had glimpsed on his face before he'd walked away from her.

It hurt so much to see it that she had a sudden urge to run after him, throw her arms around his neck and tell him not to be so sad, for she loved him; surely that had to count for something—?

Is that what I'm doing? Claire asked herself starkly. Am I falling in love with him?

He picks you up off the road, dusts you off, takes you home and feeds you. He then sweeps all your troubles away by replacing them with a whole new set of troubles—and you decide he's the man to fall in love with?

Sold, she grimly mocked herself. For the price of a big house and a load of designer clothes, to the ruthlessly calculating man in the corner with the attitude problem worth falling in love with!

Well… Her chin came up, the light of a battle entering her eyes, though she knew the battle was now with herself. Marching forward, she firmly knocked on his door then swung it open.

'I want to talk to my aunt Laura,' she announced forcefully.

And thereby learned just how *he* must have felt when she'd walked out of the bathroom in his London home, with her robe hanging open down her naked front!

OK, she allowed as her senses roared into an overdrive she had never, ever before had to contend with. So he wasn't quite naked. But there was only one piece of clothing left on his big, sleek, muscle-rippling dark golden body for him to take off—and those black silk briefs were not hiding very much!

Certainly not the powerful build of his legs or the kind of muscular torso Atlas himself would envy! Wonderful wide shoulders, she listed bemusedly. Lean, powerful hips, and the dynamic evidence of a—

'Get the hell out of here!' he snarled.

Claire almost left her skin behind as she jumped in response. Her eyes flickered then focused too late—much too late—to save her own dignity, never mind his. For it was only then that she realised just where she had been staring!

She whipped out of that room as fast as her shaking legs could take her. Pulling the door shut behind her, she wilted weakly against the wall beside it, squeezing her eyes tight shut so she could beg whoever it was who could make these things happen that they take back the last thirty dreadful seconds!

No chance. She wasn't even allowed a few minutes to recover her composure before that damn door was shooting open again.

Pausing to scan the room for her, Andreas found her standing there cringing like an idiot against the wall with her eyes squeezed tightly shut. Swinging himself around, he slapped his hands on the wall at either side of her head so he could push his face up close to hers like the dark avenger in search of a victim.

'What the hell did you think you were doing barging into my room like that?' he raked at her furiously.

'I'm sorry,' she choked, feeling his angry breath warm on her face, but keeping her eyes shut because she still wasn't ready to take on board how she had been so crass as to stare at his body like that. 'I didn't think. I just—'

'Didn't think?' he interrupted. 'Have you any idea how close you came to completely embarrassing both of us?'

Oh, yes, she thought, with a telling little shudder, she had a very vivid idea how close she had come. 'I'm sorry,' she repeated. 'I'm sorry—I'm sorry!'

Small white teeth appeared, biting hard into her bottom lip, her only good hand clenching into a fierce fist while she tried very hard to dismiss the image that was still cruelly filling her head.

Another sigh rasped her face. 'You idiot,' he murmured, and the anger seemed to be easing out of him. 'Next time knock and wait until you are invited before opening that door, and save both our blushes.'

'Ditto,' she found the presence of mind to counter.

It took him a moment, then he huffed out a laugh. 'I suppose you do have a point,' he conceded. 'Are you all right?' he asked then. 'You have gone a really strange shade of puce. Never actually seen a man naked before, hmm?'

He was taunting her! she realised. 'Don't you dare laugh at me!' she flashed, her eyes shooting open in sheer reaction.

Oh, good grief. He was very close. She hadn't realised just how close until she found herself staring into those devilish black eyes bare inches away. But at least he'd stopped long enough to pull on a robe, she noted with relief.

'And of course I've seen men naked before,' she lied, lifting her chin to throw the words at him like a challenge. 'Loads of them as a matter of fact,' she added for good measure. 'And you weren't naked.'

'Oh, I don't know,' he drawled. 'I certainly felt it.'

His mocking tone sent her eyes tight shut again. This isn't really happening, she told herself firmly. It's all just a very bad dream.

This time it was a soft huff of laughter that brushed across her heated face. Then—thankfully—he straightened away from her. 'Now, what did you want?'

Claire shook her head. 'It doesn't matter.' In truth, she couldn't remember now what had sent her into his room like that.

'You mentioned your aunt, I seem to remember.' The rotten swine knew she had forgotten.

'Where is she?' she demanded. 'Why hasn't she been in touch with me?'

'Probably because it is more than her job is worth to try,' he answered laconically.

Claire frowned, beginning to relax a little now he had put a bit more distance between them. 'If you dislike her so much—' and it was obvious that he did '—then why do you employ her?'

His lips compressed, his dark eyes hooding over in a way that told Claire he wasn't going to answer that question even before he confirmed it. 'If you never take anything else from me, Claire, then take this small piece of advice,' he suggested very seriously. 'Forget your aunt. Or even that she works for me. She is not worthy of a single one of your thoughts. Now,' he added, giving her no chance to challenge all of that before he was turning back to his room, 'I am going for my shower. You have approximately half an hour to prepare yourself for an audience with my grandmother, by the way,' he told her blithely before shutting himself away.

His grandmother...? Couldn't he have told her that before?

'Oh, heck!' she gasped, and dropped everything else right out of her mind to make room for this much more nerve-racking prospect.

CHAPTER SIX

BOTH nervous and anxious about the coming ordeal, Claire rummaged quickly through the rails of her brand-new wardrobe of clothes, and eventually decided on a misty grey silk-lined linen dress that she felt she could easily slip into. Taking it through to the bedroom, she laid it on the bed.

But it was only while she was tackling the difficult task of pulling on a pair of fine silk hold-up stockings with only one hand to do it with that she suddenly realised there was no way she was going to be able to pull up the zip running the full length of the back of her chosen dress!

Puffing and panting from her excursions, she was standing there in her bra and panties feeling very hot and very flustered, and about to go and select something less difficult to put on, when a light knock sounded on the outer door.

Peering warily around a thin crack in the door, she was so relieved that it wasn't Andreas catching her in a state of undress yet again that she almost dragged the young maid into her room in her eagerness.

'Oh, thank goodness,' she sighed, smiling with relief. 'Do you speak English?' she asked hopefully, and at the girl's nod said, 'Then will you please help me to do up the zip on the back of this dress?'

Scurrying over to the bed, she snatched up the dress, feeling the seconds ticking ever further onwards towards her next ordeal when what she really wanted to do was lie down and rest because her neck was aching after having to take the weight of her wrist in its sling all day.

Never mind all the stress and tension, she tagged on hectically as she shimmied into the dress. 'What's your name?' she enquired curiously as the zip rasped up her backbone.

'My name is Lissa,' the maid replied shyly, probably wondering if Claire had any brains at all, when it had only been an hour ago that she had been introduced to her downstairs.

Which, Claire decided, was probably true because her brains seemed to have gone begging from the moment Andreas had dared to kiss her outside in the garden.

And remembering that right now was stupid! she scolded herself as her insides went haywire at the memory. Then she remembered the most recent scene that thoroughly outranked the one with the kiss. And the two together played merry havoc with just about every sensitive nerve she had in her system.

Oh, stop it! You don't have time to fall apart at the seams right now! she told herself crossly. She was just slipping her feet into a new pair of grey low-heeled shoes whilst carefully feeding her plastered wrist back into its support when another knock sounded.

At the connecting door.

Both Claire and the maid turned to stare at it, and, as quick as that, the tension was back, singing across the room to ricochet off that closed door and back at her—and that was without so much as setting eyes on the perpetrator of it all!

At least he's practising what he preaches, she noted wryly when the door remained resolutely shut. She moved to answer it—the little maid scurried in the opposite direction with a mumbled excuse.

Deserting the sinking ship, Claire thought. Then she was gritting her teeth and setting her chin before reaching for the door handle.

It was like opening the door on a hot oven. The power of this man's newly recognised sexuality flooded over her in burning waves. Stifled by it, she could neither breathe nor think. So she just stood there staring at him while his dark eyes hooded over as they began a slow scan of her from shining head to neatly shod feet.

Then she began to notice that he was wearing the most

casual clothes she had seen him in to date. The lightweight
chinos hung loosely from his narrow waistline; the white soft
cotton knit polo shirt moulded his well remembered torso like
a second skin.

No, don't think of that! she told herself sternly. 'Will I
do?' she asked, anxiously searching those unrevealing eyes
as they made the same journey back up her again.

To her consternation, he emitted a rather odd laugh. And
his head gave a small shake as if he couldn't believe what
he was actually seeing. Then those wretched dark eyes
flicked downwards again, prompting Claire's gaze to follow
them to discover what it was that was bothering him.

And at last she became aware of the incredible amount of
leg the short dress had left on show! Her mind shot off,
seeing through this man's eyes what his ninety-two-year-old
grandmother was going to see: a tall, leggy female who must
be a brazen hussy to wear a skirt this short! 'I'll get changed,'
she announced, turning jerkily away from him.

'You will not.' His hand capturing her good one stopped
her in her tracks. 'You will *do* fine,' he added softly at her
frowning expression.

'That wasn't what you were thinking when you first saw
me,' she pointed out candidly.

To her surprise, yet again he uttered one of those odd
laughs. 'You don't want to know what I was thinking,' he
mocked her dryly. Then, before she could respond to that, he
said, 'Come on, let's go.'

His hand tightened on her hand to keep her firmly beside
him when she would have pulled slightly away. And like that
they walked across her room and out onto the galleried landing. In silence she let him lead her, his hand warm around
hers and faintly comforting, which confused her rather because she knew she should be shying right away from his
touch.

At the head of the stairs he walked them beneath a deep
archway that led into another wing of the house. With no

natural light flooding in from the gallery, in here it was darker, and there was a different atmosphere—a hushed silence that felt slightly suffocating as they travelled along a carpeted corridor towards a pair of double doors at the other end.

'Where's Melanie?' Claire asked in a hushed whisper—it was most definitely a whispering kind of place.

'The nursery quarters are in the other wing,' Andreas informed her. 'She will not be meeting my grandmother today.'

'But I thought that she was the sole reason why we are both here at all.' She frowned in confusion.

'My grandmother is ninety-two.' He seemed to feel he needed to remind her. 'She lives by a different set of social morals than you or I do. She will not acknowledge Melanie until we are married.'

Oh, great, Claire thought heavily. I am about to meet a ninety-two-year-old puritan with the kind of moral codes that will file me under the heading marked 'loose woman' for being so free and irresponsible with my sexual favours!

The short dress was as big a mistake as she'd suspected it would be, she realised as she stood there with Andreas beside her, his arm casually resting across her narrow shoulders now while his grandmother inspected Claire.

Ninety-two was certainly old, Claire noted as she, in turn, studied the elderly lady. She looked thin and very frail, sitting there in an old-fashioned wing-backed chair which suited the old-fashioned possessions that surrounded her.

The light in the room was unnaturally dim, made so by a tall folding screen that had been pulled across the window, and the air was so warm it was stifling, yet his grandmother was draped from shoulders to feet in shawls and blankets as if the blood in her veins must be too slow to help keep her warm any more.

But the pair of beady amber eyes in her withered face were certainly very much alert. She snapped something at her grandson in Greek. He replied smoothly.

'You ought to be ashamed of yourself!' the old woman scolded, switching to scathing English.

'Resigned to my lot is the truth of it,' Andreas threw back lazily. 'The too old and the too young.' He dryly marked the distinction. 'Both of them the bane of my wretched life.'

To Claire's surprise the old woman laughed, the sound shrilling the stifling air with a high-pitched cackle. 'I will speak to you later,' she informed her grandson once she had recovered her composure.

Then she flicked her sharp eyes back onto Claire's face. Claire stiffened in response, readying herself for the blast of criticism she sensed was coming her own way next. The hand Andreas had curved around her shoulder gave a gentle squeeze as if in reassurance. He was still very relaxed himself—which had to mean something, Claire told herself as she waited.

As perceptive as her grandson at picking up other people's vibrations, the old lady challenged, 'Scared of me, are you? Wondering what I am going to say to you as you stand there next to my grandson with your short skirt and your long legs enough to tempt a saint out of celibacy. Did your mother never warn you that men are weak of the flesh?'

'My mother is dead,' Claire answered levelly.

'Your father, then.' Death, it seemed, held no excuse to the old woman.

'Dead also.' It was Andreas who answered this time, his tone revealing just the slightest hint of a warning. 'And treading carelessly on other people's feelings is unacceptable, even for a dying old woman.'

Claire's shocked gasp was ignored as the old woman flicked her eyes back to Andreas and glowered at him. 'Oh, come over here,' she then commanded him impatiently. 'I want my kiss now...'

At last he deserted his post beside Claire, walking gracefully across the room to bend over the old lady. They embraced, exchanged a few softly spoken Greek words that somehow made Claire feel rather sad.

'You next!' the sharp voice then snapped out at Claire as Andreas straightened again.

Going over to her, Claire obediently bent to brush a kiss on the old woman's lined cheek. 'What did you do to your hand?' she then asked curiously.

Claire explained. The old woman grimaced then pushed back the blanket to reveal her left arm, which she tried to move but clearly couldn't. 'Snap,' she murmured ruefully.

A joke, Claire realised, even if it was a wretched joke. And impulsively she bent to drop another sympathetic kiss upon a withered cheek. The old lady didn't reject it, and there was something very close to a sad vulnerability in her eyes as Claire straightened again.

But the voice was as surly as ever when she said, 'Now go away, the pair of you; I'm tired. I will see you later, Andreas, before I retire,' she prompted as Claire moved back to his side.

'Of course,' he nodded, making Claire aware that this must be something he always did when he was here.

'But you come back tomorrow to discuss your wedding dress,' Claire was then commanded. 'And we will see if we cannot add ten years to your age to save this family from another scandal.'

Another—? Claire thought sharply. But that was as far as that thought went as Andreas placed his hand on the base of her spine and urged her into movement.

'I like her exactly as she is,' he threw over his shoulder in a firm warning.

'You think we do not already know that?' the old woman snarled scathingly after him.

He just laughed and was still laughing when the door closed behind them. 'It keeps her will alive to spar with me.' He seemed constrained to explain the banter between the two of them.

'Yes, I realise that,' Claire nodded as they began walking back down the corridor.

He nodded too, pacing beside her. 'I know she is surly,' he added after a moment. 'But she feels the weight of her own helplessness. It makes her—

'Surly,' Claire acknowledged. 'At least while she snaps people listen.'

'Yes.' He sounded almost relieved she understood that. 'But she means no harm by it. And, as she will no doubt tell you herself, she does not have the time or the energy to find out what she wants to know by more devious methods. So she jumps straight in there. She meant no offence regarding your mother and father.'

'None was taken.' Claire frowned, wondering, as they walked along, why he felt it necessary to explain all of this to her. 'Actually,' she added, 'I liked her.'

'Good,' he murmured as they reached the arch that would take them back into the other part of the house.

Claire stepped sideways slightly so they could both move through it. Andreas did the same—and the front of their bodies brushed. Claire stopped breathing. She had a horrible feeling that he had done the same. Tension was rife. She attempted to break it by sliding away from him—but, on a thickened sigh that was all the warning she got, Andreas placed the flat of his palm on the centre of her back, drew her harder against him—and took hungry possession of her mouth.

It was no use trying to delude herself that this kiss was anything other than it was because it didn't pretend to be. It was need, pure and simple. Even Claire, with her inexperience of these things, recognised that telling little fact as she was pressed back into a darkened corner of the arch and held there by the kind of need that was not going to take no for an answer.

Not that she was saying no—or considering saying it. Because from the moment his mouth moulded to the shape of her mouth her lips parted to welcome him. With his expertise to show her the way, she delved into the kind of heated passion that was utterly new to her. She felt hot and breathless, the dim quietness of the hallway helping to fill her head with a steamy mist that made him and what he was doing to her the only thing that mattered.

His hand drifted downwards to splay at the base of her spine so he could gently urge her into deeper contact with that part of him that so clearly needed it. He was aroused and pulsing; her gasp of awareness was breathed into his mouth. His other hand was making long stroking movements down her body, stimulating senses she hadn't even known were there but made her subside against him in drowning pleasure.

It went on and on, growing deeper and more intimate with each heated second as his hand made its way down to one of her silk-covered thighs then began a pleasurable stroking upwards again. Long fingers made contact with bare flesh above her lace edged stocking. Claire responded by arching her spine closer to him.

In all her life she had never experienced anything like it. It was hungry, it was intense, and it was deeply, deeply sensual, the whole thing coiling around them in burning tendrils of pleasure that poured fire into her veins.

A door opened somewhere down the quiet corridor. They broke apart like guilty teenagers.

Both dazed and momentarily dysfunctional, he muttered something—a curse, Claire suspected. Then another—and another while he blocked her from sight with his big body as someone walked down the hallway and in through another door.

By then she had wilted weakly into the corner, eyes closed, heart fighting to regain control of itself.

He seems to like pinning me up against walls, she found herself thinking, and choked on a laugh that wasn't really a laugh. She couldn't believe she could be thinking such ridiculously flippant things at a time like this!

'Don't,' he rasped softly, and his fingers threaded themselves into her hair so his thumb pad could stroke gently across the new pulsing fullness he had brought to her mouth.

Don't—what? Claire asked herself half hysterically. Don't laugh? Don't cry? Don't fall apart at the seams in confusion because what just happened was not supposed to happen?

'Don't look to yourself to find the culprit...'

He thought she was blaming herself? Claire glared at the floor between their two pairs of feet and mulishly refused to answer.

After a few taut seconds of this stubborn refusal to offer him a single word, he sighed heavily and his hand fell away, leaving her traitorous mouth pulsing all the hotter. 'It is my fault, not yours. I am—attracted to you,' he confessed, seemingly forced into saying that by her silence. 'But you can trust me not to let this—situation get out of control...'

Could she? At last she found the strength to straighten away from the wall. There had been no control in either of them only a few moments ago. And it was getting worse every time they kissed like that!

'I do not seduce innocent virgins,' was his final stiff offering of what she presumed was supposed to be reassurance.

Where it came from she did not know, because she had never done anything like it before. But, like a cobra rearing up for a sudden attack, she came away from that wall and pushed him violently out of her way, then stalked angrily off, shaking and trembling and wishing the pompous devil in hell!

It was the word 'innocent' that had triggered her reaction; she knew that because the condescending sound of his voice saying it was still buzzing inside her head!

Because the last thing she felt right now was *innocent!* She thought crossly as she paced the pale grey carpet in her room. What she did feel was hot and restless and excited!

If it hadn't been for Lissa, the little maid, coming to offer
to show her where the nursery was, she probably would have
started throwing things just to ease her wretched frustration!

I hate him, she thought as she went off to spend the next
couple of hours helping where she could with Melanie.

I hate him! she repeated after spending ages arming herself
ready to face him across the dinner table, only to find that
the lucky devil had escaped to calmer places. 'A business
dinner,' the staff called it.

Claire begged to differ. She already recognised the tactics.
Playing the advance and retreat game was just another fetish
of his. So, having advanced, he was now in retreat, hiding,
because he was afraid she might decide to call the whole
thing off if he stayed around to let her!

The next morning she came awake to find Althea standing
over her with a breakfast tray carrying her usual tea and toast.
Surprised, she pulled herself up the pillows then blinked the
sleep from her eyes. 'Hello. When did you arrive?' she asked
curiously.

'Late last night.' Althea smiled. 'Andreas wanted to leave
you to sleep this morning,' she then explained apologetically.
'But his grandmother is already asking for you. So…'

Enough said, Claire acknowledged ruefully as she watched
Althea place the tray across her lap and begin pouring her
tea for her, just the way she liked it.

After that, the two of them fell back into a harmonious
routine they had perfected during her stay at the London
house. Half an hour later, showered, dressed in a pair of
tailored pale blue trousers and a simple white top, she was
walking along the gallery to attend the royal summons.

Althea was with her, by order of the grandmother, so
Claire had been told. Knocking lightly on the old lady's door,
they then waited for the terse, 'Enter!' before stepping inside.

The room looked quite different this morning. The tall
screen had been moved from the window to allow the morn-

ing sun to stream in, and was now shielding a corner of the room.

And what had looked like heavy and dark old-fashioned bits and bobs yesterday suddenly looked interestingly aged, making Claire want to walk around the room and study them.

But the old lady was sitting there in her chair by the window looking cross and impatient. 'What time do you call this?' she snapped. 'We get up at dawn in this country, not the end of the day.'

Knowing it was only nine o'clock in the morning, Claire smiled at this gross piece of exaggeration. 'But at least I came here first and without even going to see my baby,' she remarked, taking her lead from the way Andreas had spoken to his grandmother yesterday, and deciding to take her on when she snapped.

'What baby?' the old woman shot back.

'The...' Ah, Claire thought, biting back the sarcastic reply she had been about to make. Taboo subject, she recalled as those beady eyes dared her—just dared her to say anything more about Melanie.

The frail old head nodded when Claire remained wryly silent. Then she was turning her attention on Althea. 'Althea, go into my bedroom and bring the dress that is hanging on my wardrobe,' she commanded.

With an obedient nod, Althea hurried away, and Claire was ordered to come and sit down in the chair set beside the old woman.

'Now,' Andreas's grandmother said once Claire was seated, 'you will explain to me, please, while Althea is away, what you have done to upset my grandson. He was here an hour or two ago,' she informed Claire, 'and he was bad-tempered and restless. Have you two argued?'

No, Claire thought ruefully, we just kissed each other senseless. Then I pushed him away and he went off in a huff! 'I haven't even seen him since I left here with him yesterday.' She avoided the straight answer.

'You mentioned his first wife to him; that is what you did,' the old woman decided.

Claire immediately stiffened. 'I did not,' she denied.

Those amber eyes that had so much life left in them while the body they belonged to was wasting away fixed on her narrowly, looking at her as if they had the ability to see right through the blueness of her eyes to the brain that worked behind them.

'Then take my advice, young woman,' she said eventually. 'If you care anything for Andreas, then never mention her to him, do you hear?'

Yes, I hear, Claire thought, inwardly shocked by the amount of passion the old lady had fed into her words. But I don't understand.

And she was not offered enlightenment—except... 'He needs no more heartache dishing out to him—especially by a nubile young English girl with independent ways and legs that reach up to her armpits! Ah!' she then exclaimed in pleasure as Althea came back into the room. 'This is what I want to show you!'

And the other subject was dropped, leaving Claire sitting there wondering bleakly just how deeply Andreas had loved his first wife for even his grandmother to worry about the fragile state of his emotions.

But—nubile? she then repeated to herself with a grin. Such an old-fashioned word! Yet, coming as it had from this hypercritical old woman, she found it rather a compliment.

'Why the grin?' the sharp tongue demanded. 'You don't like my dress? You think it is funny?'

Dress—what dress? Claire frowned, clicking her eyes into focus on what Althea was carefully holding up so the long skirt didn't touch the ground.

'Oh!' she cried out as she jumped to her feet. 'How absolutely lovely!'

'You like it,' the old woman sighed in satisfaction—then

instantly went back to being stern. 'It was my wedding dress. Now it is yours.'

'Oh, but I can't—'

Even as Claire turned to gasp out her protest, the old lady was talking over her. 'Of course you can!' she snapped. 'It is my wish! So try it on—try it on and let us see how little different my young figure was to yours at your age!'

She sounded so animated—alive and excited—that Claire didn't have the heart to protest a second time. But as she looked back at the long, soft lines of the beautiful dress she felt like a dreadful fraud.

A deceiver of a vulnerable old woman.

But, by the time she emerged from behind the tall screen, having had Althea help her out of her clothes and into the dress, she was already head over heels in love with the dress.

Made of an intricately worked handmade lace worn over the finest silk under-dress, it skimmed her slender body as if it had been made for it. The neckline scooped gently over her breasts. The long fitted sleeves fastened by tiny pearl buttons that ran from wrist to elbow—one of which had to remain unfastened because of her cumbersome plaster-cast. The skirt was a little short, finishing just above her ankle, but even that didn't seem to matter.

It was the nineteen twenties at its most poetic. It was simply exquisite.

And just to see that sheen of tearful joy enter those tired eyes made wearing it a pleasure.

The old lady sighed, then ran on in hushed Greek that didn't need translating for Claire to understand that she was overwhelmed by what she was seeing.

Herself maybe? Claire pondered. Was this old woman who was so very close to the end of her life suddenly seeing herself when she was at the beginning?

'You will do—you will do,' the old lady murmured huskily. Then she said, with a return of her old sharpness, 'Nubile, eh? Was I not nubile also?' she declared triumphantly.

And Claire couldn't help laughing even though she was still feeling like a terrible fraud.

'You will wear it next week when you marry my grandson and he will bless the day he found you because that dress is lucky,' she promised, having no idea that Claire had switched off from the moment she'd mentioned marriage next week, which was news to her. 'I had fifty years of happiness with my husband before the cancer took him. You will have the same luck. You mark my word, child. That dress is lucky…'

'But this whole thing is getting out of control, Andreas!'

Claire was pleading with him across the width of his study desk, having come to search him out the moment she had been dismissed from his grandmother.

'She wants me to wear her own wedding dress!'

'You don't like it?' Sleek eyebrows arched in haughty enquiry.

'Like it?' Claire repeated incredulously. 'It's old, it's handmade, it's utterly unique and it's exquisite!' she sighed. 'But she *loves* that dress, Andreas!' she told him painfully. 'And she loves you! Yet here we are intending to dupe her any which way you want to look at it!'

The only response she got to that was the slow lowering of lazy lashes then the same slow lifting of them again. But then, he was the ice man today, Claire noted impatiently. Yesterday hadn't happened. He had clearly dismissed it from his mind.

'Do something!' she snapped in sheer frustration.

'What would you like me to do?' he asked quietly. 'Go and tell her that this is all nothing but a lie?'

'No,' she sighed, hating him for his smooth simplicity! 'I just feel—' She sighed again, and turned her back on him so she could slump wearily against the desk. 'I hate liars,' she said. 'Yet here I am, lying to everybody I speak to.'

'Is she happy?'

Claire dipped her head to stare at her shoes. 'Yes,' she said.

'Did the dress fit you as it must have fitted her more than seventy years ago?'

'Yes,' she said again, seeing the joy in that old woman's face when she'd seen herself as she would have looked all those years ago.

To her consternation he gave a soft laugh. 'She told me it would.' He explained the reason for the laugh. 'Last night, after having met you, she laid a wager with me that if the dress fitted you then I must buy it from her for you to wear on our wedding day. Oh, don't misunderstand,' he said quickly as Claire turned to stare at him. 'She is a shrewd old thing, and she loves a good wager. The dress is a museum piece and practically priceless. She knows this. She means to fleece me, and will enjoy doing so.'

And thereby keep the weak lifeblood flowing through her veins that little bit longer while they haggle, Claire concluded, beginning to see again what her guilty conscience had blinded her to—the fact that this man was willing to do anything to keep his grandmother alive.

Today it was a wedding dress. Tomorrow it would be something else. Then there was a wedding to plan and a great-grandchild to meet and...

Without really knowing she was doing it, she began planning and plotting herself. 'She wants the wedding to take place next week.' She frowned. 'Perhaps, if I insist that we put it off until my plaster-cast comes off, it will—'

But already Andreas was shaking his dark head, the expression on his suddenly grave face enough to tell her why.

'She hasn't got that long?' Claire questioned thickly.

He didn't answer with a straight yes or no. 'She knows what she is doing,' he murmured. 'Let her set her own timetable, hmm?'

A timetable... She shivered, hating the concept so much

that she sprang abruptly away from the desk. 'I'm going to see Melanie,' she told him as she walked quickly to the door.

For at least Melanie was everything that was bright and optimistic about life, whereas—

'Claire—one more moment of your time before you go, if you please,' that infuriatingly level voice requested.

It reminded her of a softly spoken headmaster she'd once had, who'd used to intimidate everyone with the simple use of the spoken word. Resenting the sensation, she spun around to glare at him. Seeing the glare, he responded with that brief grim smile she despised so much.

'At the risk of infuriating you even more,' he drawled, 'I have to warn you that there will be a party here tomorrow night. My family wish to meet you before the wedding takes place,' he explained, watching the varying changes in expression cross her face. Annoyance, trepidation then eventually dismay. 'It will take the form of a—betrothal celebration.' Smoothly he poured oil on the burning waters.

'No,' she refused, point-blank and unequivocally.

The leather chair he was sitting in creaked slightly as he sat back into it, the morning sunlight pouring in through the window behind him putting his features into shadow so she couldn't see whether he was smiling that smile.

But she knew it was still there! 'I've done everything you've asked me to do to make this lie work for you!' she informed him hotly. 'But I will not be paraded in front of your family to be scoffed at because they think I am a—a fallen woman who trapped you with a baby!'

Despite the sun behind him, she saw his eyes flash. 'Let only one of my family be so crass as to scoff at you and they will never be welcome in my home again.' At last he sounded as if he had some emotions left. 'But if that is your wish—' he stood up, and there was nothing calm or cold in the way that he did it '—then of course I will accede to it. I will go and inform my grandmother right now that she must shelve that particular plan.'

His grandmother. He was agreeing to this party thing because his grandmother wanted it.

She was only agreeing to any of this for Melanie's sake. Grandmother—Melanie. Melanie—grandmother.

What about Claire? she wondered bitterly.

'Oh, have your stupid party,' she snapped. 'But don't blame me if they all think that you've lost your marbles when they see me!'

CHAPTER SEVEN

She was still angry about the emotional blackmail being used on her the next evening as she finished getting ready for the party.

So the dress was a defiance.

Claire knew that even as she stood in front of the mirror frowning in trepidation at the reflection that was coming back at her. Made of pale blue high-stretch gossamer-fine silk tulle, the flimsy bodice was supported by bootlace-slim halter-style straps that held the two triangles of fine fabric over her breasts. From there it followed the contours of her shape with such an unremitting faithfulness that it really was the most daringly thought-provoking garment.

She looked naked beneath it—felt naked! Though she knew that she wasn't if you took into account the tiniest pair of smooth silk briefs and a pair of white hold-up silk stockings. But nervous anxiety was making the hard tips of her nipples protrude to add to the illusion. And because the fabric clung so lovingly to her warm flesh she could even see the way the point high on her stomach between her ribcage was pulsing in tense anticipation of the evening to come.

'I can't wear this,' she muttered on a sudden arrival of common sense that should have hit a lot sooner.

Standing behind her, carefully teasing the final gold-silk strands of a natty fantail knot into which she was dressing her hair, Althea paused to glance over Claire's shoulder.

'I think you are so brave,' Althea confided—which helped not a tiny bit because she didn't feel brave at all!

Not any longer, anyway. This afternoon when she'd picked this dress out off the line of other evening dresses she had been feeling brave—brave, bold and brazen! she mocked her-

self deridingly. Seeing herself *boldly* taking on all those critical looks she just knew she was going to receive for not
being their first choice of bride for their lord and master.

But now, with reality hovering over her like the shadow
of a giant black-winged eagle preparing to swoop, her fickle
emotions had flipped over into cowardice. And she knew now
with absolute certainty that she just was not going to be able
to carry this off!

A knock sounded lightly on the connecting door.

That pulse-point between her ribcage gave a large throb,
and she froze. So did Althea, her gentle brown eyes fixing
on Claire's pale face in the mirror. And silence rained down
on top of both of them in a fine sprinkle of flesh-tingling
static.

How much Althea and her parents actually knew for a fact
about Claire's relationship with their employer Claire didn't
really know. She thought that they at least suspected its lack
of authenticity. After all, did Andreas look like the kind of
man that seduced women like her?

But he does seduce me. She instantly contradicted that
remark. Those increasingly passionate kisses are definitely
seductive. And every time his dark hooded eyes settle on me
now I feel dreadfully seduced even though he is trying his
level best to pretend that it isn't happening.

'What do you want to do?' Althea whispered in a hushed
little voice.

Die a thousand deaths by a thousand knives rather than
open that door! she thought helplessly.

At least you've managed to put on some make-up. She
allowed herself that one small consolation. Discovering today
that she was now able to use the fingers on her right hand
for light tasks meant that she had been able to do a lot more
things for herself—one of them being the application of a
light shadow to her eyelids, some mascara to her lashes without smearing it all over the place, and a rose-pink lipstick

that gave her soft mouth a fullness that had not been there before.

She looked much better for that, even if she did say so herself.

You're not so bad-looking, you know, she informed that reflection. And despite its daring the dress is truly exquisite—the typically fashionable thing any woman slender enough to carry it off would wear today!

The knock sounded again, and she grimly pulled herself together. You've created your own monster here, Claire! she told that frightened face in the mirror. Now live with her!

With that little lecture to bolster her courage, Claire watched her chin come up, soft pink-painted mouth firming a little as the light of defiance sparked back into her eyes.

Seeing it happen, Althea took a step back in silent retreat. And when Claire turned away from the mirror to walk over to the connecting door Althea melted out of the room without another word spoken between them.

The way he was dressed, in a conventional black dinner suit, white dress shirt and black bow-tie, was the first thing Claire noticed as she pulled open the door. And the second thing was that he looked big and dark and dauntingly so-phisticated.

Her pulse quickened; she tried to steady it. He opened his mouth to say something light and ordinary—then stopped when his eyes actually focused on her properly.

Claire gave up trying to control her pulse when it broke free and just went utterly haywire as his gaze rippled over her. There was really no other way to describe it since that was exactly what her skin did as he inspected her slowly from the top of her shining head to rose-pink-painted toenails peeping out from the tips of her strappy silver shoes.

And he wasn't pleased by what he was seeing; she could see that immediately in the way his parted mouth snapped shut then tightened. 'Taking us all on, are you?' he drawled with super-dry sardonicism.

'I don't know what you're talking about,' she answered coldly.

He smiled that smile. 'Then let me put it this way,' he offered. 'I don't think there is going to be any doubt in the minds of anyone here tonight why I find myself having to marry you.'

'Lies can be such uncomfortable things sometimes, don't you think?' She acidly mocked all of that. 'But this one you will have to live with,' she then informed him. 'Because I am not going to cover myself up just to save your embarrassment.'

His sleek black brows shot up. 'Did I say I was embarrassed?'

You didn't have to, Claire thought, and turned away from him as an unexpected wave of disappointment hit. Even with defiance flying as high as a kite from her, she discovered, to her annoyance, that she had still been looking for his reassurance, not his disapproval.

Needing something to do to keep her muddled emotions hidden, she was glad that she had it—in the form of a white stretch-silk sleeve Althea had cleverly fashioned for her to wear over her plaster-cast.

It was waiting for her on her dressing table, and she walked over to get it, stingingly aware of those dark eyes taking in the amount of naked back the wretched dress left exposed.

'Where is your sling?' he enquired levelly after a few moments.

'I don't need it any more,' she said—then, with a half lift of one slender white shoulder, added, 'Well, not all the time anyway.'

'Here—allow me...'

A long-fingered hand appeared from behind her to take the white sleeve from her grasp. 'To cover your cast, I presume?' he said lightly.

The temptation to snatch it back from him and tell him

she could manage very well by herself almost—almost got the better of her. But even in the strange antagonistic mood she was in she knew that would be just too childish.

So she stood silent and still while he came to stand in front of her—her very own giant black-winged eagle, she mused as the feeling of being swooped down on overwhelmed her again. But then, she might be tall at five feet eight inches but he was one hell of a lot taller.

Taller, wider, bigger, darker, she listed as he picked up her injured wrist and began feeding the sleeve over the plaster-cast protecting it.

'Is the age thing a big problem to you, Claire?' he asked her quietly.

Older, tougher, calmer, cooler—the list went on. She gave a shake of her head in reply to his question.

'Perhaps you are still angry with me because I—overstepped the boundaries of our arrangement, then.'

Wiser, she added. Because it hadn't really hit her until he'd said it out loud that this was exactly the reason why she was feeling as emotionally confused as she was.

'You blow hot and cold all the time,' she felt constrained to answer. 'I just don't know how to respond to that.'

'Then I apologise,' he murmured rather grimly.

Gracious, too, she added to the growing list. Because I'd have cut my own throat before I'd have had the grace to apologise as quickly and as sincerely as that.

Giving that small shrug with her shoulder again in acknowledgement of his apology, she then added a small sigh. 'It isn't going to be easy for me, you know, having to deal with all of these people who are coming here tonight, knowing what they will all be thinking when they look at me.'

'I know.'

'Althea said she thought I was brave to dress myself up like this for the party. But I'm not brave, not really. I'm just...' She ran out of words on a discontented sigh.

'Trying to cope the best way you can.' He supplied them for her.

Silly tears tried to fill her eyes because now she was having to add understanding and gentle and sympathetic to her list and it really couldn't get any longer!

Yes, it can. She then had to amend that thought as he put his hand to her cheek and used his thumb to gently draw her chin up so he could look gravely into her swimming blue eyes. Because he was touching her for real rather than touching her through the protection of her plaster-cast, and she now had to add dangerous to that list because his touch made her feel so—!

He bent down to brush his mouth across hers, and the list was halted right then and there as it suddenly raced away from her in a mad, frantic blur of sizzling adjectives.

'Althea should have said beautiful and brave,' he murmured huskily as he drew away again.

So he did like the way she looked! If Claire could have seen her own eyes then, she knew it must have been like watching a dark shadow pass over and the sun coming out.

He smiled; so did she—the first real smile she had offered him in days. And while she continued to stand there feeling starry-eyed and breathless he picked up her other hand and slid something onto one of her fingers.

'A betrothal ring for my betrothed,' he murmured lightly as Claire glanced down then went perfectly still when she found herself staring at the most enchanting little diamond cluster ring she had ever set eyes on. 'It is a necessary part of the game-plan.'

The game-plan. Her heart thumped in her breast. How could she keep forgetting the game-plan?

'And it fits, too,' he added in that same lightly teasing vein. 'Which means Grandmother is going to make me pay for the pleasure of placing it here.'

'It's your grandmother's ring?' Swallowing her silly sense of let-down, Claire glanced up at him questioningly.

'The first of many my grandfather gave her,' he said with a small grimace. 'But this was her favourite. Do you like it?'

'It's a beautiful ring,' she murmured softly; it was not big enough to be ugly, not small enough to be cheap. 'Thank you for allowing me to wear it tonight,' she added, belatedly remembering her manners. 'I promise to take precious care of it for you.'

He had been about to move away from her when she said that. But now he stopped. 'It is yours to keep,' he stated rather curtly. 'I was not expecting to get it back.'

But Claire shook her head. 'No.' This ring did not belong to her and it never would. She could accept the new wardrobe of clothes and the luxury lifestyle she was being treated to here, because they only cost money and, as she had already learned with Andreas, money was a commodity he had more than enough of. But this ring—like the wedding dress—was different. Both had feelings attached to them, memories, for an old lady that belonged to this family, not to Claire, who was only passing through, so to speak.

He knew what she was thinking. She could feel him reading the sombre thoughts as they passed over her face. As she stood there with baited breath, waiting for him to start arguing the point with her, he surprised her by not doing that at all.

'You have integrity, Claire,' he murmured quietly. 'That is a rare commodity; try not to lose it.'

'Integrity?' she repeated, sending him a wry little smile that thoroughly mocked the suggestion. 'Where is the integrity in marrying someone you don't love, even if it benefits the both of us?' she asked him cynically.

He didn't answer, and she didn't blame him because there really was no answer that did not confirm she was telling the truth.

'Come on,' he prompted rather harshly instead. 'It is time for us to go and greet our guests.'

And that small amount of harmony they had managed to

create between them withered and died as they both remembered what this was really all about: a stranger's child that he, for no apparent reason, had decided to adopt as his own. For the first time since he had talked her into this, Claire began to question his reasoning because, knowing him better now than she had when they'd struck this deal, she could no longer accept that he needed to legally adopt Melanie to make this deception work.

After all, no one yet had questioned his claim that Melanie was his child. And if he genuinely needed an heir that badly, then why not find himself an olive-skinned boy-child? Unless choosing a girl was all part of the deception—a clouding of the scent to keep people's minds working on the wrong problem.

Could he be that devious? That tactically calculating? Glancing up at him as they began the long walk down the wide staircase, she saw the ruthlessness and cynicism etched into his dark profile and thought with a shiver, Yes, he can be that calculating.

Which still did not answer the question as to why he was determined to make it all legal. For if this was for his grandmother's sake, and from what he had already prepared Claire to expect his grandmother would not be around for very much longer, Melanie was too young to feel the loss of a father who was not her real father in the first place.

So what was really going on here? She frowned thoughtfully.

'Stop worrying,' he scolded levelly beside her. 'I won't let them eat you.'

But they did—or almost did—with curious looks laced with a disbelief that none of them seemed able to keep hidden, which made her feel uncomfortably like an alien being who was trying to infiltrate their selective society.

Though, to be fair, no one was openly rude or questioning. The older element said teasing things to Andreas in Greek to which he replied with smooth aplomb. The younger ones—

especially the men—ogled Claire in a way that made her
blush and earned them a light but real warning to watch their
manners from Andreas.

All very protective, very—possessive of him, she acknowledged. Like the way he kept her left hand enclosed in his
right hand all the way through the ordeal while cheeks were
brushed against cheeks in typical continental fashion.

'See, it was not so bad in the end, was it?' he drawled
when the introductions were over.

Where were your eyes? she wanted to counter. But, 'No,'
was what she actually said.

One person in particular gave her reason to feel really uncomfortable. Desmona glided in through the door looking
absolutely stunning in the kind of dramatically simple black
sheath gown that made Claire stingingly aware of her own
complete lack of sophistication.

But she had to admire the way the other woman coped
with the small silence that fell on her entrance.

The rejected one, that silence was shouting. Yet not by a
flicker of her silver-grey eyes did she reveal any response to
that.

She kissed Andreas on both cheeks and exchanged softly
spoken words with him in Greek that had him smiling sardonically as he answered. Then she was turning to Claire,
and for the next few minutes really impressed her as she
smiled pleasantly and asked after Melanie.

As Desmona eventually moved away, it suddenly occurred
to Claire that her being here to meet them on their arrival in
Greece could have been pre-planned with this awkward moment in mind.

'A very classy lady, don't you think?' Andreas remarked.

'I feel sorry for her,' she confessed, watching the other
woman join a group of people and begin talking lightly as if
this were just any old social affair.

'Then don't,' was his rather curt rejoinder. 'For she is the sleeping panther in our midst whose teeth are none the less still sharp even though she is not baring them at present.'

As a clear warning to beware—though of what Claire wasn't sure—it certainly sent a cold shiver chasing down her spine.

She found that out later when Desmona decided to sink those teeth into Claire's shaky self-confidence.

Feeling flushed and breathless after having been danced around the large hallway by a rather enthusiastic old gentleman called Grigoris who was apparently to give her away at her wedding, Claire stood on the sidelines, alone for the first time since the whole extravaganza had begun.

She was watching Andreas dance with a rather lovely dark-haired creature whose name she could not recall. He was relaxed, smiling, and looked a completely different man from the one she was used to seeing. More the urbane man of sophistication, enjoying being with his own kind, she thought.

Then a smooth-as-silk voice drawled lightly beside her, 'Have you worked out yet which one is his mistress?'

Mistress? Claire struggled to keep her expression from altering, but the sickening squirm that suddenly hit her stomach sent some of the warmth draining from her cheeks.

Desmona saw it happen. 'You didn't know,' she sighed. 'Oh, how tragic for you—and on your betrothal night, too. I am so sorry...'

No, you're not, you're enjoying yourself, Claire silently contended, aware that she was being baited by a woman who—as Andreas had warned her—was out for her blood.

'He doesn't have a mistress.' She coldly dismissed the suggestion, but in reality she found herself suddenly having to face the fact that he most probably did have one somewhere. A man like Andreas would not put himself in a marriage of convenience without having that side of his needs adequately covered—surely!

'All Greek men of class have mistresses, darling,'

Desmona drawled deridingly. 'You could almost say it is expected of them. So, which one do you think?' she prompted. 'The lovely thing he is dancing with? Or the other one over there who can't take her eyes off him—or maybe the one standing in the corner, who looks too besotted with her husband to even notice Andreas.'

Without wanting them to, Claire's eyes flicked from woman to woman as Desmona pointed them out to her. And all of them—all of them were so beautiful that she wouldn't have blamed him for wanting any of them.

'I would go for the besotted one if I were you,' Desmona advised, not missing a single telling flicker of Claire's blue eyes. 'For the way she is clinging to her husband smacks of desperation to me...'

'I think you're lying,' Claire responded, refusing to let the other woman get to her.

'Then you are a fool,' Desmona replied. 'And maybe you deserve all you are about to receive from Andreas Markopoulou. For he may have good reason to want your child, but I cannot believe that he truly wants you—though he is cold-blooded and ruthless enough to take you if that is the only way he can achieve his aim. There,' she concluded. 'I have said what I needed to say. So now I will leave you to enjoy the rest of your betrothal party. Good luck, Miss Stenson.' She smiled as she turned away. 'I think you may well need it very soon...'

But why had she said it? Claire wondered as she watched Desmona walk smoothly away. To hurt her—Claire—or to hurt Andreas because he had rejected her?

In the end it didn't matter, because now the seed had been planted Claire could feel herself looking at every female face with new suspicious eyes.

Andreas was no longer dancing but talking to the woman Desmona had described as besotted with her husband. Well, she observed, there was no sign of the husband now as she laughed with Andreas, with her big eyes shining up into his.

Was she his mistress?

It's none of your business! she told herself furiously.

But knowing that didn't stop her from studying their body language as Andreas touched a light finger to the woman's shoulder, to her cheek, laughed softly at something she said to him and kissed the hand she used to teasingly cover his mouth when he gave what must have been a wicked reply.

The woman spoke again, only this time her expression turned very serious. With her hand still resting in his, Andreas sobered also, then began glancing furtively around them before giving a grim nod of his head. Then, turning, they moved off into one of the other rooms.

Even with that quick glance around to check that their withdrawal would not be observed, he didn't even notice me, Claire noted painfully. Then she saw Desmona's gaze fixed mockingly on her, and humiliation swept over her in a sickening wave.

It was one thing to deceive but quite another to *be* deceived, she realised, hurt, so very hurt that she didn't quite know what to do with herself as she stood there alone and feeling utterly unable to pretend it hadn't happened.

So when several of the younger guests approached her to say they had set up a disco outside on the pool terrace, then warily asked if she would like to join them, she was so relieved at the diversion from her own hectic thoughts that she accepted eagerly.

Half an hour later she was a different person. A person her mother would have recognised if she'd been there to see the old laughing, teasing, fun-loving Claire who danced disco with enthusiasm rather than stuffy waltzes with reluctance.

If there was something rather desperate about the way she threw herself into the fun, then no one seemed to notice that. They were just pleased to discover that Andreas Markopoulou's newly betrothed was nothing like the hard-crusted English floozy they had all been led to believe she would be.

Someone appeared with a case of champagne they'd pinched from somewhere. And for the next few minutes the small group threw themselves into the fun of making corks explode from bottles then quickly supping at the frothy wine as it spilled over the bottle rim.

After that the wine flowed like water, and as the intoxicating bubbles entered her bloodstream Claire began to let go of what was left of her inhibitions. The music was throbbing—and she danced like a dream. There wasn't one person there who didn't pause to take note of that as her long, slender body swayed and gyrated inside the slinky dress, with the kind of innate sensuality that made the other girls envious and the young men throb to an entirely different beat.

One young man who was bolder than the rest stepped up behind her to slide his hands around her silk-tulle-lined stomach and began gyrating with her. Claire laughed and didn't push him away; instead she began exaggerating her movements to which he had to follow.

'You are wasted on Andreas,' he whispered against her ear. 'He is too cold and stuffy for a wonderful creature like you.'

'I adore him,' Claire lied glibly, when really at that moment she was hating him so badly that she could barely cope with it. 'He's absolute dynamite.'

Not so big a lie, she acknowledged bleakly from some darker place inside her that she refused to go off to. Instead she turned her head against her shoulder and smiled a stunning smile into her new consort's captivated face.

That was how Andreas came upon her. He stopped dead in his tracks. 'Enjoying yourselves?' his deep voice harshly intruded, and effectively silenced the whole group in the blink of an eyelid as heads came up, twisted round, then simply froze to stare at him like guilty thieves caught red-handed.

He was standing in a circle of light being thrown from the open French window that led to the indoor pool just behind him. And even with his dark face cast in shadows there wasn't one of them present who didn't know that he was furiously angry.

Someone had the presence of mind to switch off the throbbing music. Then the silence that followed was truly stunning as he began striding forward.

His hard eyes were on Claire—and specifically fixed on the place where her companion's hands were splayed across her slender body.

Andreas didn't so much as glance at him, but with a sharp click of his fingers he had the young man snatching his hands away from her waist then stepping right back as if he was letting go of some stolen hot property.

Coming to an abrupt halt in front of Claire, Andreas reached out to take the champagne bottle she hadn't even been aware of holding out of her fingers. Then he stood there, impressively daunting, as he held the bottle out to the side in a grimly silent command for someone to take it from him.

Some very brave person did that, for the angry vibrations Andreas was giving off were frighteningly awesome. 'Now you may all return to the party,' he said flatly. And not once—not *once* had he so much as acknowledged a single one of them by eye contact!

Not even Claire, who was standing there rather like a puppet that had had its strings removed while the group responded to his command without a single murmur, disappearing *en masse* through the pool-house doors and effectively leaving her to face the angry wolf alone.

Thanks a bunch, she thought ruefully as she listened to their retreating footsteps fade away.

'Well, that was very sociable of you,' she drawled in an effort to mock her own tingling sense of trepidation at his continuing grim silence.

He didn't even bother to retaliate. All he did do was reach down to snatch up her only good wrist then turned and began pulling her towards the house.

'What do you think you are doing?' Claire demanded, try-ing to tug free of a grip that wouldn't budge.

'You are drunk,' he answered scathingly. 'I have no tol-erance with that, so if you value your life you will be silent.'

'I am not drunk!' She hotly denied the charge—though she had a vague feeling he could well be right. 'Where are we going?' she then queried frowningly when, as they en-tered the indoor pool-room, instead of making for the door which would lead back to the main part of the house, he headed for the private staircase that connected the pool-room to the upper floor.

He didn't answer, but his body language did as he pulled her behind him up the stairs. He was blisteringly, furiously angry.

They emerged onto the upper landing. Below them the party was continuing in full swing. The hallway was crowded with people dancing, others spilling out from adjoining rooms. Peering over the gallery as they walked along it, the first person Claire's eyes picked out was Desmona's choice for Andreas's mistress, dancing cheek to cheek with her hus-band to the slow, smoochy music drifting sensuously in the air.

Two-timer, she thought contemptuously. And flashed the man in front of her a lethal glance.

He opened the door to her bedroom and swung her inside. Only a single small table lamp burned in the corner, casting eerie dark shadows over the rest of the room.

'Now,' he said, shutting the door, 'you are going to pull yourself together and make yourself fit to be seen with me when we return downstairs to our guests.'

'I was *with* our guests,' she threw back. 'And we *were* enjoying ourselves until you came and spoiled it!'

'You mean you enjoyed having that boy paw you?'

A sudden vision of his naked body wrapped around that adulterous woman downstairs had her chin coming up in hot defiance. 'What's it to you if I enjoyed it?' she challenged insolently. 'I don't recall either of us making any vows of celibacy when we decided to deceive everyone!'

His eyes narrowed dangerously. 'Explain that remark.'

Go to hell, she wanted to say, but those narrowed eyes stopped her. 'Let go of me,' she said instead, and tried to pull her wrist away.

He wouldn't let go. 'I said explain,' he repeated.

'What do you think I meant?' she flashed, hugging insolence around her like a protective shield. 'If you think I am going to sit here through this marriage like the ever faithful Penelope while you go off doing your own thing—then you can think again!'

The atmosphere between them was suddenly electric. He wasn't a fool; he knew exactly what she was saying here. If it were possible his eyes narrowed even more. Her blood began to fizz—not with champagne bubbles any more but with a far more volatile substance. Her heart began to pound, the muscles in her stomach coiling tensely as, in sheer self-preservation, she gave a hard yank at her imprisoned wrist and managed at last to break herself free then began edging backwards, attempting to put some much needed distance between them.

But he followed. 'You are not taking a lover while you are married to me,' he warned in the kind of deadly voice that put goose bumps on her flesh.

'You can't dictate to me like that,' Claire protested as she fell back another step—then another, until the backs of her trembling knees hit the edge of the bed. 'I can do whatever I want to do. You promised me that,' she reminded him. 'When I agreed to all of this.'

'And you want to take a lover,' he breathed in taut understanding.

'Why—will you be jealous?' she taunted him, with a sense of horror at her own crazy recklessness.

Something came alive on his lean, dark face that had her

hand shooting up to press against his chest in a purely defensive action meant to keep him back.

'No,' she murmured unsteadily. 'I didn't mean that.'

He said nothing, but his eyes were certainly talking to her. They were gazing down at the hectic heave of her breasts beneath the stretch-silk tulle as if he could actually see this so-called lover's hands on her body. And at last the alarm bells began ringing inside her head, warning her that she had finally managed to awaken the sleeping devil she'd always known must live somewhere inside him.

She should leave, she knew that. She should get the hell out of this bedroom and hide away somewhere until he had got his temper back.

But she didn't move another muscle. Instead she just stood there and trembled and shook.

A little whimper escaped her.

It was enough to bring his eyes flicking up to clash with her eyes—and their darkness was so blisteringly intense that her lungs suddenly stopped working altogether.

He was faring no better, she realised. His heart was pounding; she could feel it hammering against his ribs beneath the place where her hand lay flat against his chest in its puny effort to ward him off. He felt warm and tough, the masculine formation of well developed muscle so intensely exciting to her that she froze on a wave of horrified shock.

'No,' she breathed in shaken rejection—and went to jerk her hand away from him—only he stopped her by covering it with his own hand.

It was then that the heat went racing through her. The heat of fear, the heat of desire, the heat of a terrible temptation.

But what was worse was she could feel the self-same temptation thundering through him! He was still, he was tense, and he was vibrating with a desire so strong that there really was no denying it.

Anxious eyes flicked back to clash with his. 'No,' she repeated in breathless denial of what she saw written there. 'You don't want me,' she whispered shakily.

To her surprise he laughed, the sound so harsh and tight and bitterly deriding that it managed to make her wince. Yet she received the disturbing impression that it was himself he was deriding.

'You fool,' he muttered then, and before she could even feed the words into her brain he had spread one set of long brown fingers across the satin-smooth skin between her shoulder blades, cupped the other to the back of her head. And, with a hard, rough, angrily masculine jerk, he tugged her up against him then took her startled mouth hotly and savagely.

CHAPTER EIGHT

SHE didn't stand a single chance.

Her senses went haywire, every one of them making a mad scrambling surge towards that life-giving mouth like butterflies set free from the bonds of their chrysalis. Her lips fell apart, her tongue going in urgent search of its partner. He shuddered violently at the intimate contact, his hands banding her more closely to him. Like two magnets of opposing poles, they became locked together in a sizzling exchange that left no room for anything but the burning eruption that was taking place between them.

It was wild and it was hot, fuelled by his anger and her refusal to back down no matter what the consequences. It was a lethal combination that flung the whole thing spinning out of control so quickly that neither was able to snatch sanity back.

He took her mouth savagely—and savagely she replied, inciting the whole crazed, potent experience into a frenzy of desire that closed down time and space to this one small zone filled with a vibrant, soaring, passionate energy.

It was devouring—intoxicating. The more he took, the more she gave, arching to the stroke of his hands on her body, literally sighing with pleasure when he touched her breasts. Her injured hand was locked around his neck so her fingers could cling to his hair, her other hand lost inside his jacket, greedily learning every muscle-rippling contour along his back-bone as he jerked and shuddered to her touch.

It was like touching heaven, and if the door to the bedroom had suddenly swung open neither of them would have heard it, they were so lost, so caught up in a conflagration that had been sharply building between them for days.

'Claire...' He groaned her name against her hungry mouth.

Whether in pleasure or in protest she didn't know, but the sudden flare of heat coming from him set her own flesh burning. She gasped when she felt the power of his arousal surge against her. It caused an echoing eruption within herself, locking her thighs in an urgent need to maintain that vital contact as a flare of bright, blinding, blistering desire went shooting through her.

Like seasoned lovers, she thought dazedly. You would be forgiven for thinking that we did this with each other all the time! When in actual fact Claire had never felt like this before—ever!

The halter-style bodice to her dress dropped to her waist-line, his hands feathered over newly exposed flesh, and she gasped on a tremor of nerve-tingling pleasure as her knees gave out and she toppled dizzily back onto the bed.

He followed her downwards so that they landed in a tangle of limbs that only seemed to intensify their excitement. His breathing was fast, his expression intense, his mouth still moist from their long, hot kiss. But it was the look in his eyes that sent Claire completely still beneath him.

In all her life, she had never seen anything like it before. It was hot and it was ravenous but it was also painfully—painfully vulnerable.

'I want you,' he said hoarsely.

'Yes,' she whispered. 'I can tell that you do.' But it was said very gently. For some reason that she didn't understand this big, strong, very arrogant man was hurting enough without her adding to it by taunting him.

Without really having to think about the wiseness of it, she reached up and kissed him—as a lover would kiss a true lover.

Then it was back. The hot, hard, driving passion that had no time or room for gentleness or leisure. He kissed like a man who hadn't done this for centuries, and she responded with a passion that she'd never known she possessed.

Her dress slid away without her even noticing, then his jacket, his shirt and tie. He kissed and licked and caressed and suckled her until she was so lost in the frenzied storm that she had no idea what she was doing any more.

So when she dared to fold her hand around the length of his burgeoning sex it came as a shock to feel him go utterly motionless beside her. Opening heavy, love-glazed eyes, she lay there watching as he seemed to take an actual pause in life itself. His eyes were closed, his dark face taut, his mouth flattened into a single white-ringed line of unbearable tension.

Yet not sexual tension, but a different tension.

'Andreas?' she breathed, unsure what was happening.

When he didn't respond she went to take her hand away, a hot flush of mortification staining her cheeks. But his hand snaked down to stay her, long fingers trembling slightly as they kept hers tightly wrapped around him.

Then he let the air out of his lungs in a long, slow, measured way, and his eyes fluttered open, revealing those dark, dark irises where that awful, wretched, pained vulnerability was back again.

He didn't say anything, though, and when he came to lean over her the tempo changed—the man changed, turning from ravaging hunter into devastatingly rich and sensual lover.

Still greedy, he was greedy—but then, so was she. She couldn't get enough of him, her teeth biting deeply into powerfully bunched muscle, her lips and tongue hungry to taste, to acquaint herself with this body that was giving her such untold pleasure.

It was as if nothing else in the world existed but each other. The party, the people, the anger—everything had been cast aside for this soul-filling journey into sensuality. He was heavy on top of her but she didn't care; her long and slender legs were parted while his hips thrust softly against her.

He wasn't inside her yet—but the experience was magical, the expression on his dark face so deeply intense that her heart swelled in her breast with a joy she could barely cope with.

I do love you so, she wanted to whisper. But just didn't dare in case she spoiled the magic.

So she did the next best thing and parted her legs that bit wider, smiled provocatively into the dark beauty of his impassioned face, arched her spine towards him—and invited him inside her.

His response was stunning. His dark face grew taut, his eyelids drooping over what she'd glimpsed as a flare of unbelievable emotion. Then, with a shudder that seemed to rip right through him, he buried himself in the deep, dark liquid heat of her body.

The small sting of pain she experienced at his entry barely registered, his short pause when he realised just what he had taken from her an acknowledgement of his prize. Then the passion coiled its hot, needy talons around them again, and the moment was forgotten—for the time being anyway.

No one said that making love had to be an earth-shattering experience. Only the lucky few reached those kind of peaks time after time.

They reached those peaks—surpassed them, rose onwards to another place where reality was suspended and the senses took over. When she began to flip over into that final climactic finish, Andreas wrapped her tightly to him, binding her there with his arms. Then, with each new measured thrust of his body, he watched as she shattered just that little bit more for him, her soft sounds of pleasure growing in strength, in volume, in vigour.

A sob broke from her—not a gasp, but a wild, bright electric sob of surrender that shook her body and kept on shaking it. And on a rasping growl he too surrendered to his own needs with driving thrusts that shattered what was left of both of them.

Coming down to earth again afterwards took a long, long

time, Claire discovered as she felt herself drifting gently through layer upon layer of sweet sensual fulfilment.

When she did eventually find the strength to take a small peek at reality, she found Andreas still lying heavy on her with his face pressed up against her throat, and his heart thundering against her breast.

He was still inside her. She could feel the exotic fullness of his manhood pulsing against the walls of her newly sensitised sex. It was wonderful. From hurt to anger to a blistering passion to this, she listed—this exquisite sense of supine contentment.

For the first time in months—maybe even years—she felt true happiness flood through her. 'I'm in heaven,' she whispered.

Andreas jerked away from her as if she were a poisonous snake. Taken by surprise by his abrupt withdrawal, her eyes flicked open to watch, in a state of bewildering confusion, him not only withdraw from her body but jackknife to his feet.

But worse than that was the expression on his face as he did it. He looked utterly devastated. Big and strong and god-like as he was in his full naked glory, when his eyes clashed briefly with her startled eyes he actually shuddered, his dark head wrenching to one side as if he couldn't bear to so much as look at her.

Hurt quivered through her, forcing her to sit up and hug her knees protectively to her chest. 'What?' she whispered shakily.

'No,' she thought she heard him utter, though even that single word was almost quashed in the way he swallowed thickly. 'This should not have happened,' he tagged on hoarsely.

What did he mean—it shouldn't have happened? Claire wondered painfully. 'Well, it just did!' she cried, her blue eyes dark pools of anger and hurt at his cruel insensitivity.

He didn't even acknowledge she'd spoken—couldn't even bring himself to look at her again!

Instead he just turned and strode quickly towards his own room, wrenched open the connecting door then disappeared through it—leaving Claire staring after him, white-faced and with her flesh chilling in mind-stunning dismay.

It should not have happened...

Still sitting there long, lost minutes later, huddled over her own bent knees in the middle of a sea of tumbled white bedding, Claire was bitterly agreeing with him.

For if it hadn't happened, then she would not have had to be sitting here feeling so painfully used then ruthlessly rejected.

Or punished would probably be a better word, she thought dully as she listened to him dressing somewhere in his own bedroom. She had also sat here suffering the sounds of him showering her scent from his flesh, because in his eagerness to get away from her he had forgotten to shut the connecting door and it stood half open, allowing her a blow-by-blow account of his every movement.

She shuddered sickeningly. Hating him, despising herself. Her first love, her first lover, and now this terrible feeling of hurt and rejection.

It should not have happened...

She had a horrible feeling that those words were branded in fire onto her very soul for ever now.

She should have run when her instincts had told her to. How could she have lost control like that and let him do what he had done?

Great to work that out in retrospect, she mused bitterly.

'I am going back down to our guests,' a deep voice informed her from the connecting doorway.

Claire didn't even lift her head up. She felt soiled and tainted, and unbearably humiliated.

'I suggest you remain here,' he went on stiffly. 'I will

make your excuses for you, blame your early retirement on your recent accident, or bridal nerves or—something. Are you all right?' he then tagged on with enough clear reluctance to make her wince.

'I'm not going to be a bride,' she mumbled from the confines of the white sheet she had pulled around her. 'The wedding is off.'

'Don't be foolish,' he sighed.

Why does he always call me foolish when I am at my most sensible? 'I want to go home to England tomorrow,' she insisted. 'And I never want to set eyes on you again.'

A small silence followed that, then another sigh to precede a rasping 'Look—I'm sorry' that sounded tense and uncomfortable and just damned bloody irritable.

No grace in that apology, she noted acidly.

'It was entirely my fault and I am now thoroughly ashamed of myself. Does that make you feel better?'

To know you're ashamed? 'No, it does not!' she cried, lifting flashing blue eyes to find him standing there looking as if he'd never been out of those clothes all evening.

When in actual fact what he had done was simply replace the first lot with the same again from his wardrobe because the ones he'd been wearing earlier were still lying in a crumpled heap on the carpet by her bed where they'd landed after being wrenched off him.

Self-contempt rippled through her as she saw herself eagerly helping him to remove them. She shuddered again, and drew the sheet more closely around her.

'Just go away, will you?' she choked, realised the tears weren't far away, and swallowed angrily down on them. For she wouldn't cry in front of this man ever again! she vowed fiercely.

He went to say something, but a raucous laugh filtered into the room from the galleried hallway below, and whatever he had been going to say turned into a heavy, 'I have to go back down there. We don't have time to deal with this now.'

I don't want to deal with it at all! Claire thought wretchedly. 'I bet they all know by now how you dragged me up here,' she whispered as humiliation sank its teeth deeper into her. 'I'll be the running joke of the party by now. Have you any idea how that makes me feel?'

'Don't,' he said tautly.

Don't what? she wondered. Don't hurt, don't feel used and humiliated—when she had every right to feel all of those things?

'I hate you,' she whispered, feeling the threatening tears burn all the hotter in her throat. 'The deal is off. So instead of lying you may as well go and give them that little piece of juicy truth to joke about!'

Suddenly he wasn't looking so good either, she noted. Despite the clean skin and the fresh suit of clothes, his skin wore the pallor of a man who still was not comfortable with himself.

But his words didn't sound anything but grimly resolute. 'I'm afraid I can't do that,' he refused. 'Things have gone too far for you to pull out of our arrangement now.'

'I was not aware that I was giving you a choice here!' she responded.

'And I am not giving you the choice to pull out,' he coldly shot back as he began walking towards her.

And—surprise, surprise! Claire mocked herself caustically—the ice was back like the loyal little friend it had always been to him!

'So listen to me, Claire, because I mean what I say...' He arrived by the bed, his tone deep with warning.

She buried her face in her knees again because she just couldn't bear to look him in the face this close to. He sighed harshly as if he knew exactly why she was hiding away like that.

'Our arrangement still stands as formerly agreed,' he grimly insisted, sounding insultingly as though he were chairing a business meeting. 'And although I know this development has—complicated things between us slightly nothing has really changed.'

Nothing has changed? What about me? Claire wanted to yell at him. What about the wretched change you've brought about in me? 'If you don't stop talking to me like a damned computer, I am likely to start screaming,' she breathed in seething fury.

He swung away from her—then back again, the action seeming to ignite his own fury. 'For the love of God, Claire!' he rasped. 'I am trying my best to be sensible amongst all of this—'

'Carnage,' she supplied for him when he bit back whatever choice of word he had been going to offer.

'Yes,' he hissed, seeming to accept that this was indeed carnage—which only made her hurt all the harder. 'But I can absolutely assure you this is not going to happen again. So we will go on as agreed. The marriage of convenience stands. I will take Melanie as my daughter. And you will still be free to get on with your own life unhindered by me just as soon as you are ready to. But if you think,' he then added very seriously, 'that I am going to let you break my grandmother's heart in her final days, by walking away from our deal, then you are heading for trouble. For I don't take defeat on the chin like a gentleman. I fight back and I fight dirty.'

He meant it, too. Claire could hear the ruthless ice of intent threading every single word. She shivered; he saw it happen and seemed to take that as a gesture of acquiescence because he stepped back from the bed.

'Now I am going downstairs,' he announced less harshly—trying, Claire assumed, to defuse the tension simmering between them now he had made his point. 'Where I will make a very Greek joke about temperamental females with more spirit than any poor mortal male could possibly hope to deal with. And I will see you again in the morning.'

As he walked towards her door, Claire lifted her head to watch him leave with bitterness in her eyes. He turned unexpectedly, catching her looking at him, and she was trapped, caught by a pair of devil-black eyes that held knowledge of her no one else did. It hurt her, knowing that he now knew her so very intimately while she still felt she didn't know him at all, even after what they had just done to each other here in this bed.

'Will you be all right?' he questioned huskily.

'Yes,' she nodded, and wished he would just hurry up and go so she could curl up and weep her heart out.

Yet still he lingered with those dark eyes flickering restlessly over her. 'Shall I send Althea up to help you—do whatever it is you need her for?' he then offered, wafting a descriptive finger at her plaster-cast.

'I can manage.' She quietly refused the offer.

He nodded and turned back to the door then opened it while Claire held her breath in suffocating anticipation of his finally getting out of here.

But almost immediately he changed his mind and closed the door, though he did not turn to face her again. Stiff, tense, almost pompous in his delivery, he then had the gall to murmur gruffly, 'I would hate you to think that I do not appreciate the—honour you bestowed on me tonight. It was—'

'Will you just go?' Claire coldly interrupted, not wanting to know what *it* was.

He nodded, taking the hint. And this time when the door opened and closed again he was on the other side of it.

And at last Claire could do what she wanted to do, which was curl up in a tight ball on her side and sob her wretched heart out.

After the storm was over, she made herself get up, tape a plastic bag to her plaster-cast, then stood beneath the shower for long minutes, simply letting the heated sting of the water wash away the lingering pangs of emotion the tears hadn't cried away.

After putting on one of her new silk nightdresses, she began picking up his clothes and folding them neatly before taking them through to his room, reasonably sure she was not going to walk in on him.

Like her own room, his was lit by only a single small lamp left burning on the bedside table. In fact, in almost every way the room was a match to hers, she noticed—except his bed didn't look as if war had taken place in it, she thought with a small shudder as she laid the clothes down on the smooth pale grey counterpane then walked back into her own room to eye with distaste her tumbled bed.

An honour, he had called it. She called it a waste of something so very precious and she knew there was no way she could sleep in this bed again tonight.

Tears back and burning, with an angry jerk, she turned away from the wretched bed and walked across the room to the soft-cushioned sofa, where she curled herself up, then closed her eyes tightly in a grimly determined effort to shut the last dreadful hour right out of her head.

Surprisingly she slept, though she hadn't really expected to be able to switch her mind off as easily as that. Moreover, she slept long and heavily, and awoke the next morning vaguely aware of half surfacing only once during the night when she'd been dreaming that she was being carried.

It had been a disturbing sensation. Strangely painful though not in a physical way, she recalled as she lay there watching the morning sunlight draw patterns on the ceiling via the white voile drapes covering the windows.

'Don't cry,' an unbelievably gentle voice echoed inside her head.

Recognising that voice, she sat up with a start, saw she was back in her bed and knew exactly how she'd got there. It had been no dream last night! Andreas had come into her room and found her asleep on the sofa! He'd woken her up when he'd gathered her into his arms to carry her back to bed, and she even remembered the raw humiliation in starting to cry all over again!

Oh, how could you, Claire? she chided herself furiously. How could you let him see how hurt you are?

And there was worse—much worse, she recalled, closing her eyes in the hopes of shutting it all out again. But it would not be shut out. And she saw herself clinging to him. Saw him lay her gently on the bed then come down to lie beside her. She felt the light brush of his lips on her cheek and the way his hands had stroked her, quietly soothing her back into oblivion before he must have got up and placed the covers over her.

I hate him, she thought angrily. I really, really hate him for catching me out like that!

Too angry to just sit there tormenting herself, she got up and dressed quickly, needing to soothe her savaged ego by spending some time with Melanie.

She could even make herself a drink there, since the nursery came with its own fully equipped kitchen, which would save her having to face Andreas across the breakfast table.

The idea lifted her spirits, and as her brain fed that inspired thought to her stomach she realised just how desperate she was for some food and a hot cup of tea.

Dressed comfortably in a sage-green tee shirt and a pair of slim-fitting yellow Capri pants, she stepped out of her room to be immediately struck by how quiet the rest of the house was.

Early though she knew it was, she had expected the house to be a hive of activity by now as the staff cleared up after last night's party. But as she peered over the gallery rail at the huge hallway below she saw that the place had already been wiped clean of all evidence of partying.

The staff must have been working until the early hours, she realised, leaving them at liberty to have a well-earned lie-in this morning which probably meant that she was the only person up and around.

A prospect that suited her very well while she was still struggling to deal with what had happened last night, and she resolved to use their long day yesterday as an excuse for them to leave her to take care of Melanie today.

The nursery would give her somewhere to hide. Somewhere to lick her wounds and try to come to a decision as to what she was going to do. For the impulse to just pick up the baby and run before she dug herself even deeper into the mire her emotions were in was a gnawing ache that filled her brain.

If it hadn't been for Andreas's grandmother, she had a suspicion she would have done it already and stolen away in the dead of night like a thief running off with the family silver.

Also there was still Melanie to consider. Melanie who could gain so much from living this kind of luxury life—and so little from the life Claire could give her.

Not many pluses in favour of running, she heavily concluded, and she hadn't even taken into consideration the dire threat of retribution Andreas had laid on her last night.

Inside the nursery all was quiet, the early morning sunlight diffused by the pretty apple-green curtains still drawn across the windows. Claire quietly closed the door behind her, and was about to walk over to the crib to check on the baby when a sound in the other corner of the room had her head twisting round, expecting to see Althea—only to freeze when she found herself looking at Andreas.

Dressed in what looked like a white cotton tracksuit, he was sitting in the comfortable rocking-chair in the corner, cradling a sleeping Melanie in his arms.

His eyes were closed, his dark head resting back against the chair's cushioned back—though he wasn't asleep. The way one long brown bare foot was rhythmically keeping the chair rocking while the other rested across its knee told her that.

He was just too lost within his own deep train of thought to have heard her arrival.

Not pleasant thoughts either, she noticed, looking at the

grim tension circling his shadowy mouth. Then she had to suffer a vivid action replay of what that mouth had made her feel like last night and she unfroze with a jolt, her first instinct to turn and leave quickly before he realised she was there.

His eyes flicked open, catching her in the act of a cowardly retreat. The chair stopped rocking. They both froze this time. The fact that Andreas was as disconcerted to find her standing there as she was to find him was enough to hold them trapped as a new knowledge of each other raked through the silence in a whiplash so painful it seemed to strip Claire's tangled emotions bare.

Neither spoke; neither seemed able to. Her heart was pounding, her throat thickening up on a stress overload that was seriously affecting her ability to breathe.

What he was feeling was difficult to define with a man so good at keeping his own counsel, but something stirred in the unfathomable black eyes.

Regret, she wondered, or even remorse? Whatever it was it managed to hurt a very raw and vulnerable part of her, and she would have continued her cowardly retreat if he hadn't spoken.

Speaking softly so as not to awaken the baby, he said, *'Kalimera...'* offering her the Greek morning greeting that she had grown very used to over the last few days.

Slowly she turned back to him. *'Kal-Kalimera,'* she replied politely, not quite focusing on him.

'You are up early. It is barely six o'clock,' he remarked, trying, she knew, to sound perfectly normal but it was a strain and it showed in the slight husky quality of his voice.

She nodded, licked her dry lips and wished her heart would stop racing. 'S-so are you,' she managed, but that was all she could do.

'I haven't been to bed,' he replied, glancing ruefully at the baby. 'Melanie has had a disturbed night. Althea was exhausted so I sent her to bed around dawn and took over here.'

'Oh!' Instant concern for Melanie had her moving towards him on legs that were trembling with nervous tension. 'Someone should have come for me!' she protested as she peered worriedly at the baby.

'I was here.' That was all he said, yet it seemed to say it all. For he handled the baby girl as if he had been doing it all her little life. It was, in fact, the talk of the house how good he was with the baby. Claire already knew he spent time with her sister every morning before he left for Athens, and the same in the evening when he got home again.

Bonding was the modern term for it, and Claire supposed it described what Andreas had been doing since Melanie had arrived in his life.

'What has been the matter with her?' she asked now.

He smiled that brief smile—wry, though, not grim. 'I have been reliably informed by the experienced Lefka that babies do have restless nights.'

Claire nodded knowingly, her fingertips already stroking Melanie's cheek without even realising she was doing it. 'She hardly slept at all after Mother died,' she confided sadly. 'You wouldn't think someone so young could know, but I think she missed her dreadfully.'

'As you do?'

Her throat thickened at the gentle question. She answered it with another nod. 'I'll take her now, if you like,' she offered. 'Then you can go and get some rest...'

But even as she reached out to take the baby from him Andreas caught hold of her fingers.

The very fact that he was touching her was enough to bring the panic back. Her tension suddenly soared. Yet, though he had to feel it, he grimly ignored it. 'She is happy with us, Claire,' he said urgently. 'You must be able to see that?'

Which meant what? she wondered. That Melanie had never been happy with only her sister taking care of her?

As usual, he read her thoughts. 'No.' He renounced them. 'You misunderstand me. You have *both* been grieving—*both* of you, Claire. And although I know you may not be prepared to accept this right now you have *both* been happier in my care!'

She knew what he was saying. She knew *exactly* what it was he was getting at. He wanted her to agree to stay without him having to exert undue pressure on her. He wanted her to go on as before as if last night had never happened.

As if nothing had changed.

'Give this a chance,' he pleaded huskily. 'Give *me* a second chance to make this work for us—if only for Melanie's sake…'

For Melanie's sake. If this organ throbbing thickly in her breast was still a heart, she mused heavily, then she would have that phrase engraved on it.

I did this—for Melanie's sake.

She gave one last nod of her head in mute acquiescence.

It was enough. He let go of her fingers and silently offered her the baby. Melanie snuffled then settled into her arms. Andreas stood up, looking taller, leaner, darker in his all-white tracksuit. He was about to step around her so that she could sit down when he paused, touched her pale cheek with a gentle finger, and murmured, 'Thank you.'

Then he was gone, quickly, beating a hasty retreat now he had what he wanted.

Which wasn't Claire, she told herself in dull mockery.

CHAPTER NINE

IT WAS a retreat that had in fact taken him right out of the firing line, Claire discovered when she eventually emerged from the sanctuary of the nursery which had turned out to be no sanctuary at all in the end.

'A problem with one of his latest acquisitions,' she was told. But Claire knew the real problem was her and that he had simply taken himself away so as not to risk anything else going wrong before the wedding.

But then, she was his latest acquisition, she supposed. So she couldn't call the excuse a lie exactly.

The rest of that week slid by quickly. She spent the time sharing herself between Melanie and Andreas's grandmother, who was determined to make sure her precious grandson's bride walked down the aisle looking as perfect as she had looked herself all those many years ago.

She produced a wedding veil of the same heavy lace as the dress, and commanded Claire to put it on then presented her with two delicately worked diamond and gold hair combs which she then instructed her exactly where to position to hold the veil in place. Next day came the diamond necklace and earrings to match the ring Claire already wore on her finger.

'My husband gave me these the night before we married,' she said sighingly. And Claire didn't have the heart to protest at being given so many precious things to wear when the old woman's eyes looked so full of wonderful memories.

I'll hand them all back to Andreas straight after the wedding, she consoled her uneasy conscience. At least then I won't feel like a thief as well as a fraud.

After those uncomfortable visits she would steal her sister

138

and push her out in the gardens while she tried to re-convince herself that doing this was not so much deceiving a very old lady as trying her best to make her happy in her final days.

Sometimes it worked, sometimes it didn't, but having no Andreas around to bounce either feeling off meant she had to deal with the conscience-struck days herself.

So her wedding day arrived, and behind a protective haze of disassociation she went through with it, stepping into the tiny but beautiful candlelit church on the arm of Andreas's uncle Grigoris to be handed over to a man who had taken back the guise of tall, dark stranger in the days since she'd seen him last.

All those who had been at the betrothal party were here to watch them marry. Like a puppet responding to each pull on its strings, Claire repeated vows she didn't mean to a man who didn't mean them, his voice a dark and husky rumble that vibrated through her system like the growl of a hungry animal who saw her as its next meal.

Only this particular animal didn't really want to eat her. So that fanciful impression was just another deception she could add to a growing list of them.

A slender gold wedding band arrived on her finger. She was kissed—though she completely shut herself off from it. She caught a glimpse of his eyes, though, as he drew away again. They were narrowed and probing the strained white-ness of her face.

She looked away. That kind of intimate contact was just too much for her right now.

They arrived back at the house to find that the wedding breakfast was to take place outside on the lawn. But when she went to move in that direction, already armouring herself for the next ordeal of having to face again all those people who, in her mind, had somehow become indelibly linked with the night of her wretched leap into womanhood, Andreas stayed her with the light touch of his fingers on her shoulder.

Sensation ripped through her like a lightning bolt, straightening her spine and drawing the breath into her lungs on a stricken gasp.

Why it happened, when she had managed to disregard every other time he had touched her today, she didn't know.

But his fingers snapped back, his lean face freezing in what she could only believe was shock. 'I can accept it is a bride's right to look pale and interestingly ethereal,' he rasped out harshly. 'But do you think you could at least refrain from behaving as a lamb being led to her sacrifice?'

'Sorry,' she said awkwardly, but it was already too late for the apology.

He turned away from her, angry, tense. 'We have another ordeal to contend with before we can go out to greet our guests,' he then informed her grimly. 'My grandmother is waiting to meet Melanie.'

Of course, she thought as mutely she followed him towards the stairs. Melanie was no longer an illegitimate member of this family—which was the real point to all of this after all. So why hadn't she considered this eventuality?

Because it had been one lie that had become lost within all the other lies. She answered her own question.

The amber eyes flicked over Claire then did the same to Andreas, who was standing beside her holding Melanie. And Claire knew the old lady was superimposing her own and her late husband's image over the top of them as she did so.

'Perfect,' she sighed out in eventual satisfaction. 'Except for the child, of course,' she then added censoriously. 'I would have been banished from the family and my dear Tito would have been whipped to within an inch of his life. Now, get me that soft cushion over there,' she went on impatiently. 'Place it on my knee then let me have my great-granddaughter.'

Eager now—almost greedy in her desire to hold the baby, Claire moved to her bidding, collecting the requested cushion and laying it on the old lady's lap. With infinite care, Andreas followed it with Melanie, then they both straightened to watch as the bony fingers of her only useful hand gently touched Melanie's cap of silky black hair then stroked her baby cheek.

As if she sensed a stranger around, Melanie's eyes flicked open and stared directly into the wizened old face leaning over her. It was an electrifying moment, though Claire didn't know why it felt like that. But a few seconds later Andreas's grandmother lifted her eyes up to his, and static was suddenly sparking between them.

'You devil,' she said.

That brief grim smile of his appeared. 'And you are just too shrewd for your own good sometimes,' he replied.

Then they both went on speaking in their own language while Claire stood by, utterly lost to the conversation, though she was aware that it took the form of a very sharp question-and-answer session that seemed to be including her because the old lady kept on glancing sharply at her.

The inquisition was concluded with a final thoughtful glance in Claire's direction and a brief nod of her head. 'Now send Althea to me,' the old lady commanded, and her attention was back on the baby lying wide awake now on her lap. 'And leave me to get to know my great-granddaughter in peace.'

'What was all that about?' Claire dared to ask after they'd left his grandmother with Althea safely ensconced to watch over Melanie.

'She likes to think she still has control over everything, you know that,' he drawled dismissively.

'She called you a devil.' And she'd meant it, Claire thought frowningly.

'Maybe I am,' he replied in a light, mocking vein that nonetheless still made Claire feel that, like his grandmother, he was being serious.

She was missing something here; she knew she was; she just didn't know what the something was.

Then Andreas was diverting her thoughts into a whole new area that completely dismissed everything else for a while. Because he took her to his study and produced a set of legal documents that were, he explained, a formal application to the British authorities for them both to legally adopt Melanie.

Yet another stage of his carefully thought out game-plan, she mused bleakly as she set her signature to each page as Andreas indicated. A game-plan that had gone very smoothly for him—if you didn't count that one small glitch in the middle when he'd given in to his baser instincts and seduced one of the expendable pawns.

'Don't look so worried,' he said. 'This will strengthen your claim on Melanie, not weaken it. Trust me.'

Trust me... It was quite a request when she was already being plagued by a feeling that there were things going on here that she didn't know about.

But then, expendable pawns did not necessarily need to know the overall plan of the main player, did they? she mocked herself. Or was she just overreacting and reading too much into light, throw-away remarks that probably held no hidden agenda?

It suited her better to believe the latter when she still had one last ordeal to get through—namely playing the happy bride throughout the rest of that day—for her own pride's sake, because her pride needed to remedy the poor impression she had given of herself in front of these people the last time they'd been together like this.

Maybe Andreas was of a similar mind because he never left her side for a moment and played the attentive groom to the hilt. And slowly—slowly Claire began to feel comfortable with him again; she even laughed once or twice at some smoothly whispered remark he made in her ear about one of his relatives.

It was nice. She even discovered that she was actually enjoying herself.

As the day softened into evening, people relaxed at white-linen-covered tables with champagne glasses chinking and the light-hearted conversation eddying softly all around.

The stars came out. Several tall torches mounted on wrought-iron stakes that had been driven into the lawn were lit to add yet another dimension to the rather seductive scene. Then, to top it all, a group of musicians arrived and set up in a shadowy corner of the garden. Classical Greek music began filtering into the evening air.

Without a word, Andreas drew Claire to her feet and walked her over to the terrace then pulled her gently into his arms. Feeling shy and self-conscious when everyone turned to watch them, she looked down at her plastered wrist, which felt very cumbersome suddenly, and wondered flusteredly where she was supposed to rest it while they danced.

He solved the problem for her, by lifting it up and around his nape as he set them moving slowly to the music. It brought her too close to his body—reminded her of when she had last placed her arm around his neck like this—and she tensed up accordingly.

'Stop it,' he murmured softly. 'Don't spoil it.'

Don't spoil it... She reinforced that remark, and made herself relax, made herself ignore that warm, hard body brushing against her own as they moved. She made herself pretend that the butterflies were not going wild inside her stomach. And she refused to so much as flicker a fleeting glance at the shadowy mouth that only required her to raise her head a half inch for her own mouth to be in burning contact with it.

'You make an enchanting and very lovely bride, Claire,' his dark voice inserted into the silence between them. 'Some day some man is going to be very fortunate to claim you as his prize.'

But not you, she made bleak note, understanding exactly why he felt the need to say that. He was reinforcing *his* position just in case she might be dreaming of a more romantic ending while she danced with him like this.

'I'll look forward to it,' she replied, wishing that her response could cut him as deeply as his words had done to her.

If he reacted at all Claire never found out because at the same moment Lefka appeared at Andreas's elbow, the look on her face enough to warn them that something was dreadfully wrong. Bending towards the housekeeper, Andreas listened to what she murmured in his ear. And, as Claire had witnessed many times during the short period she had known him, she saw his expression completely freeze.

'What's wrong?' she demanded anxiously when Lekfa melted away again.

'One moment,' he said, no emotion, no warning of what was to come showing in his flattened voice as he glanced around the people present and eventually caught the eye of his uncle Grigoris. The older man came hurrying over. By then Claire was trembling, though she didn't know why.

Andreas murmured something to Grigoris in Greek. The older man's face dropped in dismay. 'Take care of my wife for me,' he then added in English. And, without making eye contact with her once since Lefka had come to him, he turned and disappeared into the house.

'Please...' She turned her anxiety on Grigoris. 'What's happened? Where has he gone? Is it Melanie?' she then added on a sudden jolt of maternal anguish.

Grigoris shook his steely head, his dark eyes—usually full of laughter—looking unbearably sad. 'It is Yaya,' he murmured huskily.

Then, while Claire stood frozen herself as realisation began to wash coldly through her, Grigoris placed a hand around her waist for support and turned to the rest of the party.

'Attend to me, everyone,' he announced. 'Yaya Eleni has gone. The party is now over...'

Dressed in a long aquamarine silk nightdress and a matching robe, Claire had fallen into a fitful doze on her bed when a sound in the room woke her.

Opening her eyes, she saw Andreas standing by the long French window that led out to the veranda. He had pulled back the voile drape and was staring out at the moon-kissed evening. His jacket and tie had gone and the sleeves were rolled up on his white shirt, his hands lost inside the pockets of his iron-grey trousers.

Lying there studying him, Claire felt her heart give a wrench in aching sympathy—because though his broad shoulders were straight and his spine erect he still managed to emit a mood of utter dejection.

'What time is it?' she asked, smothering a yawn behind a hand.

He glanced at her—then away again. 'Late,' he replied sombrely. 'Very late. Go back to sleep. I had no intention of disturbing you. I just did not want to—'

Be alone, Claire silently finished for him with the pained understanding of one who knew. 'I wasn't asleep,' she said. 'Just dozing.'

He nodded in acknowledgement but that was all, his concentration seemingly fixed on some far-away point way out on the horizon when she knew he wasn't seeing anything but the darkened shadow of his own grief.

Sliding her feet off the edge of the bed, she sat up then stood up, ignoring the protest of muscles that had been slaves to tension for too long that day as she went to stand beside him.

'Did she feel anything?' she questioned softly.

He released a short laugh that almost strangled into a choke. 'She died in her sleep with a smile on her face,' he replied very dryly.

'She went happily, then, as you wanted her to,' Claire pointed out. 'You have to take some consolation from that.'

'Do I?' He smiled that brief smile and Claire couldn't bear it because although he was staring directly ahead the moonlight shone on the moisture in his eyes.

Without thinking twice about what she was doing, she

slipped round in front of him, put her arms around him and laid her cheek against his chest. For if anyone needed physical contact with another human being right now, then it was him.

His first reaction was to stiffen at the unexpected gesture. Then, when he came to realise what she was offering him, he muttered gruffly, 'You are too wise for your age.'

'Age is not a prerequisite to feel what you're feeling,' she countered. 'Believe me, I've been there, so I know.'

His answer to that was a heavy sigh, then he relaxed a little, and his hands left his pockets to link loosely around her. 'Grigoris said you disappeared as soon as he had told everyone. Where did you go?'

'I hid in Melanie's room,' she confessed, lifting her face up to wrinkle her nose at him in acknowledgement of her own cowardice. 'I didn't think I could have coped with their pitying looks if I'd stayed there in my bridal finery, looking about as out of place as anyone could look.'

'You could have changed into something more—suitable,' he suggested, refusing to let her off the hook for her desertion.

'After all the trouble your grandmother went to, to re-create herself in me?' she protested. 'She would never have forgiven me!'

He smiled—he actually managed to smile! Claire began to feel dizzy at her success in teasing away his melancholy, even if it was only temporary.

'But you changed eventually,' he made wry note, sliding his thumbs against the silk of her robe at the base of her spine, sending a sprinkling of static washing through her.

She tried not to respond to it by concentrating all her attention on the remark. 'After you took her to the chapel,' she nodded. 'I felt she wouldn't mind if I changed then—don't ask me why,' she added wryly. 'Because I don't really understand it myself.'

'It does not need explaining, Claire,' he murmured very

softly. 'You honoured her passing in the way you thought she would appreciate it the most. I—thank you for that.'

'No need,' she shrugged, and began to ease herself away from him as the moment when she could excuse her closeness to him as comfort began to fade.

But he didn't let her go. Instead his loosely linked arms closed just that little bit tighter around her. And out of sheer desperation she spun in his arms to face the window, so he couldn't see the kind of control it was taking for her not to show what his touch was doing to her.

'You know, I won't hold you to your commitment to Melanie now that your grandmother is no longer here,' she told him.

'I thought you understood that I want that commitment,' he replied.

'Yes,' she nodded. 'But it is no longer necessary, is it?' If it was ever necessary, she added silently. She'd never really understood his motives where Melanie was concerned. 'Which seems to make a mockery of the whole thing.'

'Things stay as they are,' he decreed. 'And I would prefer not to have this conversation right now.'

'Oh, of course.' Instantly contrite for bringing it up when naturally he wanted to think only of his grandmother, she spun around in his arms to offer him a small smile of apology. 'Sorry,' she murmured. 'I just thought I would...'

'Let me off the hook,' he inserted for her. 'When it still does not seem to have sunk in with you that I have no intention of being let off—or to let you off it either,' he added pointedly.

'Well, a sham of a marriage seems a bit of a wasted gesture now.' She grimaced.

'When is a sham not a sham?' he pondered curiously.

Glancing up, Claire stopped breathing when she saw the dark gleam inside the hooded sombre eyes. He wants me, she realised. It's the reason why he came in here, why he broke the rules and crossed my threshold without first gaining my permission. He did not do it to talk about his grandmother but because he needs a woman to lose himself in tonight and that woman is me!

So, what are you going to do about that? she asked herself. But even as the question was filtering through her brain she was going up on tiptoe to brush her mouth against his.

His reply was a shaky sigh against the gentle pressure of her lips. 'What was that for?' he asked as she drew away again, trying to sound mocking and only managing to sound dreadfully needy.

'It's my wedding night,' Claire reminded him softly. 'And I want you. Will you make love to me, Andreas—please?'

Had she said it to protect his pride so he didn't have to lower it to ask her the same question? Claire wondered later. Or was it just that she was responding to her own needs?

Whichever it was, at least he didn't reject her—as she knew he was very capable of doing. Instead he released a muffled curse then was fiercely claiming her mouth.

Standing there with the moonlight shining in on them, he caressed and stroked and kissed the nightdress from her body, then stood back a little to sombrely rid himself of his own clothes.

He wasn't happy with himself for wanting her like this, and Claire wished she had the experience to remove his clothes for him in a way that would make him lose touch with himself, never mind his reservations. But she was no *femme fatale*, and with one near-useless hand she knew she wouldn't be able to pull it off with any grace. So she had to content herself with watching his moon-kissed, satiny flesh appear as his shirt was removed before he bent down to remove his shoes and socks.

Yet he stopped right there. Claire frowned at him as he reached for her again. 'You haven't finished,' she whispered.

'I will,' he promised. 'But later...'

Later turned out to be after he had carried her to the bed and laid her down on it. Later was when he had driven her

into a mindless state of unbearable arousal that left not a
single inch of her flesh untouched by his touch. Later was
after she had driven him almost over the edge by trailing her
mouth over his chest and had learned the intense pleasure in
toying with a small, tight male nipple.

Later was when she had grown bold enough to move on
downwards, utilising the expertise with which he had aroused
her to arouse him. But when her sensual journey was halted
by the waistband of his trousers he stopped her from taking
them from him by pulling her beneath him, and, ignoring her
small cry of protest at his frustrating tactics, he began the
whole wildly erotic process of arousing her all over again.

So by the time his idea of later arrived she was so lost in
the sensual haze he had created that she didn't even notice
him ridding himself of the wretched trousers until he came
over her and she felt the power of his naked arousal just
before he pushed urgently inside her...

This time, it really should not have happened.

'Don't say anything,' she warned him.

She was sitting at Lefka's huge scrubbed kitchen table,
hugging a mug of hot coffee in her hands as if her life depended on it. There was no colour in her face whatsoever,
and her hair was a tangled mess around her shoulders, her
body cloaked in a towelling bathrobe that covered her from
neck to feet.

He, by contrast, was fully dressed in fresh trousers and a
polo shirt. He looked neat, clean, perfectly presented. But
then, he'd shot off into his bathroom so damned fast that he
could have had ten showers before Claire had recovered
enough to move!

After he had lifted his weight from her, of course—
quickly, like the last time. Body still shuddering—like the
last time.

'I—'

'I said don't!' she choked out.

The silence screamed. The tension, the bitterness. Like an action replay of last time.

Then he sighed and moved away, walking wearily across the kitchen. Checking the coffee-pot with his hand, he poured himself out a cup then came to sit down at the table.

Claire flicked him a glance. He was staring down at his drink and his shoulders were hunched over. The strain of the last twelve hours was so severe in his face now that he looked like a man who was having to carry the weight of the world on his shoulders.

She looked away before she started feeling sorry for him again. He might look like Atlas, but he isn't, she reminded herself brutally. He is just a man—an ordinary man with ordinary appetites. And an extraordinary way of dealing with the aftermath.

'Do you have a mistress?' she shot at him.

His head came up, dark eyes very guarded. 'What?' he murmured warily.

'Desmona did warn me that you had a mistress tucked away somewhere, but with everything else I forgot to ask. So I am asking you now.'

'Desmona said that?' He frowned. 'When?'

'At the betrothal thing.' She refused to call it a party. 'She pointed out a couple of candidates and suggested I choose.' Her eyes flicked up again, catching him without his guard, and his expression was—

She looked away again quickly, not wanting to acknowledge what that expression was telling her because it had the power to shatter the brand-new shell of protection she was hugging closely around her.

'You haven't answered the question,' she prompted huskily.

'There is no one,' he said.

Eyes fixed on her cup, she tried to decide if she could believe him when the man found it so easy to be economical with the truth.

'There is no one, Claire,' he repeated in the kind of tone that forced her to believe him. 'I would not do that to you. Desmona was talking like a loser, that was all.'

Which was what Claire had told herself when Desmona had fed her the poison, she remembered. 'Good,' she said, deciding to believe him. 'That means I have one less guilty sin to carry around with me.'

'What we did just now was not sinful,' he denied.

'No?' she mocked. 'Well, it certainly feels as if I've just done something dreadful.'

'We made love!' he husked.

'No—we had sex!' she burst out. 'Just the same as we did a week ago. W-we had sex, then you walked away—just like you did a week ago. And I f-feel unclean,' she added painfully. 'Just like I did a week ago.'

'I did not walk away from *you* just now,' he asserted heavily. 'I walked away from   '

The words stopped.

Sitting there with bated breath, Claire waited for him to continue. But he didn't. Instead he ran a tired hand through his perfectly combed hair—and added nothing.

'May you burn in hell,' she murmured succinctly.

To her surprise he laughed—albeit cynically. 'I have been burning away in that place for years,' he drawled with an irony that flew right by her. 'You will have to come up with a better curse than that to hurt me.'

And why do I get the impression that he knows exactly what that curse would be? she wondered, seeing a flash of something almost haunted pass across his eyes.

'Whatever,' she said, dismissing the look—because she had to do that if she was to remain strong. 'Burn in hell or laugh at it. It doesn't really matter to me. I don't want you to come near me like that ever again—do you hear?'

With that she got up with the intention of leaving him—but his next words stopped her. 'I'm sorry if I let you down,' he said very huskily. 'I didn't do it to hurt you, Claire. I just didn't think.'

'You mean—you always walk away from a woman directly after making love to her?' she asked derisively.

There was a distinct pause—more a guarded hesitation—before he sighed out, 'Yes.'

'The man on a mountain,' she murmured softly, aware that the cryptic remark would mean nothing to him. She shivered inwardly. 'I understand now. It's yourself you feel the need to walk away from.'

She had been throwing out words haphazardly with the specific need to hurt him, but as she stood there watching his face grow white beneath his olive skin before it closed up altogether Claire realised, with a small shock, that she had hit the nail right upon its head!

'You know me so well,' he drawled, offering her that grim brief smile again in an effort to cover his reaction up.

And she wanted to hit him—probably would have done if she hadn't noticed the tremor in his fingers as he reached for his cup. He was more affected by all of this than he wanted her to believe.

What was it with him, Claire wondered furiously, that he hated wanting her as a woman so much that he kept his wretched sexuality hidden inside his trousers until the very last moment? As if he had still been praying for deliverance right up until then, she realised with a shudder.

And on a muffled sob she turned and ran from the kitchen—kept on running, across the hall and up the stairs, desperately needing to get to her room before she broke down and wept.

Panting and sobbing together by the time she reached her bedroom, she barely had a chance to close the door before it was thrust open again.

'Go away!' she cried.

'Don't...' he groaned, reaching out to pull her into his arms.

To her horror she pressed her face into his chest and sobbed all the harder.

It wasn't fair! she told herself pitiably. He loved his grandmother. He could love Melanie. Why was it so terrible for him to try to love her?

His first wife, she then remembered with a sudden chilling of her flesh. She must have been quite something to have locked his heart up as totally as this.

Fighting for control of the tears now, she tried to push away from him.

'No,' he refused, his arms only tightening around her.

Her face lifted away from his chest, blue eyes awash with so many painful things that it was impossible to pick which was hurting her the most. 'Oh, please,' she pleaded helplessly. 'Please, Andreas, let me go.'

For some unfathomable reason, hearing her use his name in that pained, wretched way unlocked something desperate inside him. His chest expanded on a tense draw of air, his eyes flashing with some awful emotion—then he lowered his head and crushed her mouth to his with a hunger so fierce that it caught her utterly blindsided.

Once again Claire discovered that she didn't stand a chance. Not with emotions running as rife inside her as they were doing right now. And his mouth was hot, the taste of her own tears mingling with the moistness of his tongue. It was a seductive combination. The passion ignited like a fork of lightning that exploded to smithereens all hope of control. She didn't even notice when her robe fell apart, or hear his muffled curses as he struggled with the zip on his straining trousers.

He entered her with a thrust that brought him to his knees with her straddled across him with his hands clamped to her hipbones.

'Oh, dear God,' she groaned against his devouring mouth as her body went wild for him.

But he lost it first, shooting into her like a man experiencing his first release. He couldn't control it, could not control the gasping pants that shot from his pulsing body. When she joined him his grip on her hips was locked tight. And as she went limp against him he crumbled sideways, his arms shifting upwards to control her fall as they landed in a tangle of trembling limbs on the bedroom floor.

What now? Claire wondered as she reached rock-bottom of the slow slide back to wretched sanity. Another quick withdrawal followed by a walk-out? She even tensed herself in preparation for it.

'I'm still here.'

His voice sounded like gravel, vibrating against her cheek where he had her face pressed against him. He hadn't let go of her, and she was still lying with her limbs locked around him.

'I'm going nowhere.'

'Why not?' she whispered.

'You were right about me,' he said. 'I do prefer to stand alone. I don't find it easy to be open with my feelings. But— as God is my witness, Claire, I want you. I want *this* with you!' His arms tightened round her. 'And if that means I must change then I will damn well change!' he vowed. 'And I will start by holding you like this for as long as you want me to.'

He meant it—he really meant it! The tears came back, but she wasn't sure what they were for any more.

'Say something,' he prompted huskily, and she felt the tremor in his lips as they brushed her brow.

Say something, she repeated to herself. But what dared she say? Could she take a chance on this actually meaning something? The trouble was, she loved this man—had known that for quite a while now—while he seemed to only lust after her. How long did lust last? Especially with a man as self-contained as Andreas?

'I want to go to bed,' she said.

There was a short, sharp pause, then a heavy sigh as he went to get up.

'Your bed,' she added, lifting her face out of his shirt-front so she could look warily into his equally wary eyes. 'I want to sleep in your bed, in your arms all night and wake up still there in the morning,' she told him huskily.

'Then what?'

Claire gave a helpless little shrug. 'I don't know,' she answered honestly. 'What do you want?'

'You,' he said gruffly, then repeated it. 'I want you.'

Her poor heart fluttered, attempting to reach out and grab those words because they were the closest thing she'd had to a declaration of caring from him.

CHAPTER TEN

DEATH was a strange thing. It brought some people closer together and pushed others wide apart. In Claire's own experience, she had lost more than a father when he'd passed away; she'd also lost lifelong friends who could not deal with the tragedy of the situation.

But when she stood beside Andreas as they buried his grandmother she found herself being drawn closer to the last person she would have expected, when Desmona suddenly broke down and began weeping so desperately that Claire didn't think twice about going over and gently placing her arms around the other woman.

'You were very kind to her, considering the circumstances,' Andreas remarked much later as they were preparing for bed.

They shared a room now. They shared a life. Claire was even daring to think that they were sharing a marriage.

'She needed someone,' she answered simply. 'It had never occurred to me until Desmona broke down like that that she and your grandmother must have been close.'

'Desmona has been a member of this family for many years,' he reminded her. 'We all—care for her, though sometimes she makes it difficult to do so,' he added dryly.

'Is that why the family wanted you to marry her?' she asked curiously. 'Because they care for her?'

'No.' He laughed, a softly mocking, sexily husky sound that curled up her toes. 'Wanting me to marry Desmona was an act of expediency. She owns rather large blocks of shares in some of our most lucrative companies and they wanted to keep them in the family.'

'But she is in love with you,' Claire pointed out. 'Or why would she agree to marry you?'

'Desmona loves Desmona,' he murmured sardonically. 'But she loves money even more. Marrying me would have given her relatively free access to the Markopoulou fortune once again. A very worthy cause in her eyes, believe me.'

'You're so cynical sometimes,' Claire sighed.

'Then reform me,' he invited, and covered her mouth, effectively ending the discussion when other, far more important things demanded her attention: mainly this man, who had become the centre of her universe so quickly that she didn't dare let herself consider just how deeply she had let herself fall in love with him.

So the next few weeks went drifting by without her giving a single thought to their original agreement. The plaster cast came off her wrist, and with Andreas looking indulgently on, she celebrated by jumping fully clothed into the indoor swimming pool with a shriek of delight because she had been so looking forward to being able to do that. They visited London a couple of times to appear in front of an adoption panel who wanted to reassure themselves that they were, indeed, fit parents for Melanie.

But there was no problem there. For they were lovers. They were husband and wife. They were a couple in every sense of the word, which showed in the way they responded to each other.

Life was wonderful, life was great. Claire had never been so happy. And the only blot on her otherwise perfect existence was the way her aunt Laura still hadn't bothered to get in touch with her.

'I have to be in Paris for a few days from tomorrow,' Andreas informed her one morning over the breakfast table. 'Would you like to come with me?'

'Yes!' she agreed, thinking, Paris! The most romantic city in the world, and she was going to go there with the most wonderful man in the world. 'Will my aunt be there?' she questioned impulsively.

It was so many weeks since she'd watched his face close up that seeing it happen now came as a bad shock. 'We will not discuss your aunt,' he said coldly.

'But why?' Claire demanded. 'Why are you so determined to keep the two of us apart? It isn't as though she can hurt me, you know. I understand her better than you think I do.'

He got up from the table. 'We will not discuss her,' he repeated, and walked arrogantly away.

'Then I'm not coming to Paris,' she threw after him. Childish, she knew. Petty, she knew. But she felt childish and petty at that moment.

And Andreas responded accordingly—by not even faltering a single step in his retreat. She sulked for the rest of the day and he retaliated by treating her as if nothing was the matter. But when he reached for her in bed that night it was Claire who surrendered to a power much greater than her will to stand aloof from him.

The next morning she awoke to find him gone to Paris, and she felt so angry and hurt that he hadn't once attempted to change her mind about going with him that she paid him back by telephoning her aunt's London apartment. She got her answering service, which, Claire realised belatedly, she should have expected if Aunt Laura was in Paris with Andreas.

So she left a message asking her aunt to call her, then spent the next few days missing Andreas so badly that when he did arrive home she fell on him like a puppy dog who thought it had been deserted by its adored master.

A few more weeks went by. Melanie was changing fast now, becoming a real little personality with squeals and smiles, who liked to kick her legs on a blanket in the warm winter sunshine, as if her Mediterranean blood demanded it of her.

The day they received official notification that Melanie

was now their legal daughter, Claire had also begun to suspect that she might be pregnant.

That evening Andreas took her out to celebrate. Decked out in one of her elegant evening gowns and with Andreas in dinner suit and bow-tie, they spent a wonderful evening dining at a very exclusive restaurant he knew in the hills behind Rafina, where they ate food that tasted like a dream and laughed and teased and talked a lot. And as they danced close together to music composed exclusively for lovers there was a point where Claire almost confided her suspicion that she could be pregnant. Only an unwillingness to overshadow the real reason why they were out celebrating like this stopped her.

Plus the fact that she wasn't sure that she was just experiencing a small glitch in her usual smoothly running cycle.

But she was so happy. So lost in this all-encompassing love that she felt for this man of hers that by the time they drove home again that evening she was weaving delicious fantasies around the two of them that involved passionate declarations of love and a life spent making babies and growing old together. And she made love with him that night as if there were no tomorrow—sublimely unaware that, indeed, tomorrow was so very close.

The next morning, Nikos drove them into the busy sea port of Rafina. Claire had shopping to do and Andreas had several business appointments, so Nikos was to drive her back home when she was ready.

Andreas kissed her deeply before climbing out of the car and leaving her to Nikos's indulgently smiling care.

'You have made him very happy,' he replied to the questioning look he caught her giving him via the rear-view mirror. 'It is a delight to all of us who have known him for most of his life to see him like this again.'

He meant since the death of his first wife, Claire realised, and felt the tiniest suspicion of a cloud begin to shadow her little bit of clear blue sky. Then she firmly dismissed the sensation as she too clambered out of the car a few minutes later.

For this was now, not six years ago. The sun was shining. Life was great. And she wasn't going to let anything spoil it!

With the confidence of youth and a determination that it was she, Claire, who counted in his life now, she went about her shopping with her metaphorical chin high and her shining blue eyes set clear ahead—just asking to be tripped up by someone or something.

It happened sooner rather than later, too. Unexpected and unprepared for it, she walked out of the chemist shop armed with her only purchase—and stopped dead in her tracks as she came face to face with her aunt.

'Aunt Laura?' she gasped in delighted surprise.

Dressed to her usual sharp, immaculate standard, Aunt Laura looked so thoroughly disconcerted to see Claire standing there that there was a heart-stopping moment when Claire actually suspected she was going to turn away as if she didn't know her!

'Aunt Laura? It's me—Claire,' she inserted hurriedly, feeling just a little stupid for declaring herself like that.

Her aunt must have thought so too, because her expression was derisive. 'I know it's you,' she sighed. 'I'm not blind.'

But she *had* been going to turn away from her; Claire was certain about that now. And it hurt. Hurt almost as much as the realisation that if her aunt was right here in Rafina, then Andreas knew about it but hadn't bothered to tell her.

Her aunt was looking her over now, the derision more pronounced as her cool grey eyes took in the quality of Claire's casual linen jacket worn with a simple straight skirt and skinny top that still managed to shriek designer at her.

'Well, you certainly fell on your feet,' she commented tightly. 'You've caught yourself a rich man with a rich lifestyle—so who the hell can blame you for not caring if it is all just one big sham?'

'It isn't a sham,' Claire denied, stunned by the bitterness filtering through her aunt's voice. 'We're in love with each other.'

'Love?' Her aunt made a scoffing sound. 'A man like Andreas Markopoulou doesn't fall in love, Claire. He makes clear-cut, coldly calculating business decisions.'

'Stop it,' she responded, not understanding why her aunt was being so nasty. Besides Melanie, they were the only living relatives either of them had left in the world. Surely it had to count for something? But then, it never had before, had it? Claire reminded herself heavily. 'Andreas is your boss,' she said a little shakily. 'I thought you admired and respected him.'

'My—what?' Aunt Laura gasped, staring at her niece as if she'd grown an extra head. 'He isn't my boss,' she denied. 'Where the hell did you get that idea from?'

It was like standing on the edge of a precipice; Claire felt a frightening tingling sensation slither through her body right down to her toes. 'Don't play games with me.' She frowned. Why else would they bump into each other here, in Andreas's home town of all places? 'You were both on your way abroad on a business trip the first time I met him!'

'Is that what he told you?' Claire's own confused expression gave her aunt the answer to that question, and she huffed out a tightly sardonic laugh. 'You have to give it to the ruthless swine,' she allowed. 'He doesn't miss a trick. Has he told you anything, Claire?' she then asked cynically. 'Or has the smooth, slick devil managed to con you into his life and into his bed, *and* get what he really wanted from you—which was really only ever Melanie—without having to let a single family skeleton out of the family closet?'

She fell off that precipice. Standing there beneath the Greek winter-blue sky and with her feet planted firmly on solid earth, she felt herself beginning to fall a long, long way into a cold, dark place as she heard herself whisper, 'What are you talking about?'

Aunt Laura's angry gaze shifted restlessly away as if she was trying to decide whether to say any more. Then she looked back at Claire—and her face hardened. 'Why not?' she decided. 'He deserves his come-uppance, and I owe him one. So, come on...' she urged. 'Let's find somewhere less public for this, because you're in for a bad shock, and by the look of you it may be better if you receive it sitting down...'

Nikos kept sending her strange glances via his mirror as he drove her home. Claire didn't really blame him for looking at her like that. For the bright-eyed, happy person he had dropped off at the shops only an hour before had gone, and in her place was someone else entirely: a sad, pale, haunted-looking creature he had once seen before, lying in a road after she had been knocked down.

'Are you all right, *kyria*?' he enquired concernedly.

Claire's eyelashes flickered in an attempt to bring her glazed eyes into focus, but she wasn't very successful. 'Yes,' she nodded, and tried to swallow the huge lump that was blocking her throat—she wasn't very successful there either. 'A small headache, that's all. I'll be fine once I get back and take something for it.'

But she wasn't going to be fine. She knew it—and perhaps Nikos knew it, because she saw him lift his mobile phone to his ear and begin talking in Greek just before she shut herself away inside her own head again.

He was calling Andreas, she was sure. In a way she was glad. For the quicker Andreas was brought back to the house to find out what was the matter with her, the quicker she could leave it.

It wasn't far from Rafina to the house. Fifteen minutes at most. As Nikos drew the car to a stop, Claire climbed out, walked in through the front door and up the stairs without so much as glancing sideways.

In her room—*her* room, not the one she had been sharing with Andreas for the last few months or so—she came to a stop in the middle of the carpet, then coldly and precisely began stripping off the casual but chic clothes she was wearing. Leaving them to lie where they fell, she then walked naked into the dressing room hung with the kind of clothes most women only dreamed of owning. When she came back out again a few minutes later, she was wearing her old jeans and a tee shirt. In her arms she carried the rest of the clothes that she had brought with her from London and never worn since.

Now she was shutting the door on the extravagant dressing room knowing that she would never be wearing a single garment in there again.

For he could pay through the teeth for the privilege of having Melanie for his daughter, but he would never pay for the privilege of having Claire again!

She heard a car come racing up the driveway as she placed the stack of clothes on the bed, ready for packing. It was Andreas, she was sure of it, though who he had got to bring him home she had no idea—nor cared. By the time he swung in through her bedroom door, she was just placing her rings in the little velvet jewellery box where she kept all of the things his grandmother had given her.

She didn't bother to turn and look at him, but could sense him taking in at a glance the mound of discarded clothes on the floor and what she was now wearing. Only a fool would have missed the significance in the change, and Andreas was no fool.

'OK,' he said. 'Explain to me what this is about.'

'I'm leaving,' she said. Not, I'm leaving *you*, for she no longer acknowledged there was a *him* to leave. The man wasn't human. He was cast from some hard, impenetrable metal that gave him the will to do unspeakable things just to get his own way.

She heard the bedroom door close as she was rummaging in the dressing-table drawers, picking out the bits that belonged to her and leaving behind the ones that no longer did.

'Why?' he asked quietly.

She didn't answer—couldn't. It was all stopped up inside her as if someone had ground a cork into a fizzing bottle. But what really bothered her was what would happen if that same person came along and shook the damned bottle.

'Something happened in Rafina,' he prompted when she didn't say anything.

Naturally he would presume that because that was where she had been when she'd altered into a different person. Or went back to being the person she used to be, she corrected grimly.

'You saw someone...'

She could feel his footsteps vibrate through the carpet as he came towards her. Her hands began to shake badly as she pulled open another drawer.

'Desmona, perhaps. Has Desmona been stirring up trouble again, Claire?' he demanded. 'Is that what this is about?'

Try again, she thought bitterly. She picked up a framed photograph of her mother holding Melanie in her arms and made as if to edge round him.

His hand came out to touch her shoulder. 'Claire...!' he rasped out impatiently. 'This is—'

The cork blew. In a fountain spout of bitter fury, she turned on him and let fly with her hand to the side of his wretched, deceiving face. 'Don't touch me ever again—do you hear?' she spat at him.

His hand was already covering the side of his face where she'd stung him. He should have been angry—Claire would have preferred him to get angry so she could feed off it, build on what was bubbling up inside her.

But those black eyes of his just looked bewildered. And she couldn't cope with that. 'You lied to me,' she accused him thickly. 'Ever since the first day that we met you've lied and you've lied and you've lied...'

With that she managed to step around him. On trembling

legs she walked across to the bed and placed her mother's photograph on the stack of things already assembled there.

'You've seen your aunt Laura,' he realised belatedly. 'I did wonder if there was a risk of that when she turned up at my office today.'

Claire said nothing. She just stood tautly, with a white-knuckled grip on each side of the photo frame, and let the silence grow to suffocating proportions.

'What did she tell you?' he asked eventually, sounding flat and weary, like someone who knew he had been exposed without the ability to defend himself.

'She doesn't even work for you,' she whispered. 'She never did.'

'You made that assumption, Claire,' he murmured. 'All I did was allow you to go on thinking it.'

That was his defence? Claire didn't think much of it, then.

'But why?' she demanded, spinning around to lash the question at him, and so hurt by her own wretched gullibility that she couldn't keep it out of her voice. 'Why should you want to deceive me and trick me and manipulate me like this—when the truth would probably have given you the same results?'

He released a heavy sigh. His hand fell away from the side of his face and as it did so Claire felt a tiny pinch of remorse when she saw the imprint of her fingers showing white against his olive skin.

'I could not afford to take the risk that you would not fall in with my—plan,' he answered.

'Your plan to take Melanie away from me.' She spelled it out clearly.

'That was the original idea, yes.' He freely admitted it. Then his eyes flicked her a searching look. 'Your aunt told you about my brother and your mother?'

For an answer, she wrapped her arms around her slender body, her eyes closing as her mind replayed her aunt's wretched story of her mother's brief affair in Madrid with the hugely wealthy but very married fifty-year-old Greek merchant banker, Timo Markopoulou, which had resulted in Melanie.

'I'm sorry,' she heard him mutter.

What for? she wondered. For being responsible for making her feel like this, or was he apologising on behalf of his brother and her mother?

'Did you know about their affair while it was happening?' she whispered threadily.

'I knew about an affair—yes,' he confirmed, turning away from her to go and stare grimly out of the window. 'But I did not know who the woman involved was,' he went on. 'Or the fact that she had borne him a child, until almost a year after Timo's death and I was in London on business when your aunt came to see me.'

Claire's eyes flicked open, the blue bright with a derision she speared at his profile. 'You mean you went to see my aunt,' she corrected him. 'To get her to bargain with me for possession of Melanie!'

'Is that what she said?' His dark head turned. 'Then she lied,' he declared, holding her sceptical gaze with a grim demand that she believe him. 'Your aunt Laura approached me, Claire,' he insisted. 'It was she who told me that my brother's mistress had given birth to his daughter. It was she who wanted to bargain—not for Melanie,' he made succinctly clear, 'but for your silence about the affair. *Your* silence, Claire,' he sombrely repeated. 'Your aunt placed herself in the role of mere mediator between myself and her *niece*—the niece she swore had been my dead brother's mistress!'

'M-me?' she stammered in shocked confusion. 'My aunt told you that *I* was your brother's mistress?'

Her sense of horror and dismay was obvious. Andreas acknowledged her right to feel like that with a tight-lipped grimace. 'Apparently you were threatening to sell the story to the papers if I did not pay for your silence,' he explained.

'But how could you think such terrible things about me?' Claire cried.

'I had not met you then,' he reminded her. 'So I gained an impression of a grasping young woman who saw her child's wealthy Greek relatives as a pushover for a bit of lucrative blackmail.'

It made a kind of sense. Claire felt sick suddenly. Sick with shame at her aunt's mercenary cunning.

'I could not afford to risk such a scandal breaking in the press when my grandmother was so frail,' he continued, whilst, white as a sheet now, Claire stared blindly at the floor. 'The one thing your aunt could not have known was my grandmother's dream to hold her great-grandchild before she died. But it was only a dream,' he sighed, turning back to the window. 'Both she and I knew she didn't have a chance of fulfilling it...'

He meant because his grandmother's days had already been numbered, Claire realised sadly. 'Learning about Melanie must have seemed like a heaven-sent opportunity, then.'

The dark head nodded. 'I offered to take the child off your hands for a—certain amount of money,' he told her. 'Your aunt led me to believe that you would not be averse to the idea of giving up the burden of caring for Melanie—for the right price.'

Nice of her, Claire thought bitterly. The whole thing was a macabre circle of deceit, betrayal and greed, she acknowledged with a terrible shudder.

'So you drove her over to my flat then sat outside it in your big limousine, and waited for her to buy your brother's child for you,' she concluded, beginning to feel more than a little sick now as the rest fell into place without needing to be dragged out and pawed over.

She'd come running out of her flat and got herself knocked over in front of him. He had then been given the opportunity to see where she lived and how she lived, and eventually learned that not only was she innocent of any charge of extortion, but that he would have a hell of a job convincing her to give her sister up to him!

So then came the next round of lies, she continued while he remained silently staring out of the window, perhaps doing the same as she, and replaying the whole thing scene by miserable scene! The proposition, the coercion, the sob story gauged to tug at her tender heartstrings about a grandmother who wanted to hold her only great-grandchild before she passed away.

The only bit of truth in among all the lies, she noted cynically.

'Did your grandmother know whose child Melanie is?' she asked huskily.

He didn't answer for a moment, and there was something very—odd about his hesitation. It smacked at another lie on the way, Claire judged, eyeing him suspiciously.

'She—guessed,' he said in the end.

Truth or lie? Claire wondered. 'You devil,' his grandmother had said to him, she recalled, and got to her feet as an icy chill went washing through her.

What a waste of all his efforts, she mused acidly. For by then the wedding had taken place, otherwise he could have saved himself a whole lot of inconvenience. Then she remembered that Andreas had still needed to acquire legal control of his brother's illegitimate child. So—not such a waste of his time.

'Did you pay my aunt to keep away from me?' she asked.

'Yes,' he admitted. 'The reason why she started this was because she had lost her job, was in a terrible amount of debt, and she saw me as a quick way to get herself out of trouble. But she then proceeded to lose the money trying to double it by speculating on the markets.'

'So she came to your office today wanting more.'

'I kicked her out,' he stated flatly. 'She took her revenge.

I should have expected it—being a ruthless rat myself dealing with one of my kind.'

Which seemed to round it all off pretty well, Claire thought as the pain in her breast eased to a dull ache.

'I never did any of this to hurt you, Claire,' he murmured, as if he could sense what she was feeling. 'Though you probably find it impossible to believe right now, I acted with your interests at heart also.'

It was impossible, she agreed. People who had your interests at heart did not lie, cheat and plot to steal from you.

'Your aunt intended to give me Melanie, take the money and run,' he told her. 'I could not have done that to you,' he added huskily. 'I only had to know you for half an hour to realise I could not have done it. So I lied,' he admitted. 'I gave you what you seemed to need then, which was a reason worthy of you staying within my protection. Think about it,' he urged. 'When has anything I've done—lies or truth—actually been done to deliberately hurt you?'

Silence met that. The kind of silence that throbbed and pulled and prodded at the self-control she was having to exert over herself not to break down and cry all over him.

'Stay,' he fed gently into that silence. 'Don't let yourself be manoeuvred by a cold and embittered woman who has never done anything but hurt you...'

'I can't think straight,' she whispered, pushing a hand up to her aching eyes. 'I need time to come to terms with all of this before I make a decision as to whether I stay or go.'

Andreas seemed to draw himself up. 'Fair enough,' he agreed, and his tone altered, cooled, and became businesslike. 'Take your time,' he invited. 'There is no rush.'

With that he began to walk away. Making the tactical retreat, Claire recognised as she watched him with the tears already splitting her vision into a million fragmented parts.

Halfway to the door the toe of his shoe caught something that lay on the floor amongst the debris of her recently discarded clothes. Through the blur of tears she watched him pause and glance down, watched him go still for a moment before be bent to pick something up. It never occurred to her what that something was—until she heard the tearing of flimsy paper.

And, on a lightning shot of panic, she was galvanised into action, darting across the room in an effort to snatch the pregnancy testing kit out of his hands before he realised what it was he was looking at!

Too late. He spun to stare at her. Her heart sank to the soles of her feet. He'd gone white—perfectly, sickeningly white. 'Why have you bought this?' he demanded hoarsely.

He might be white, but Claire wasn't; she was blushing like a schoolgirl. 'Please give it to me,' she insisted, holding out a badly trembling hand.

'Why?' he barked.

The sheer ferocity of it thoroughly shocked her. Her blue eyes widened in surprise, and she began backing away, cautiously—bewilderedly. Not understanding the need for this depth of anger.

'Answer me,' he commanded forcefully. 'Answer me, Claire!'

'I w-would have told you,' she stammered shakily. 'If—if it w-was positive.' Was that why he was so angry—because he believed she'd intended to hide it from him? 'I would have told you, Andreas!' she repeated shrilly when he actually took a step towards her.

'I want you out of this house,' he hissed furiously at her. 'Within the hour, do you hear me? I want you gone from my sight and I never want to see you again!'

'But—why are you so angry?' Claire shrilled, still backing while he paced towards her like a wild animal needing to taste fresh blood. 'We haven't used protection once in all the weeks we've been making love! Surely you must have considered this a strong possibility?'

'And I used to get these damned things shoved in my face once a month by my first wife!' he rasped. 'For five hellish years, I used to listen to her sob her heart out once a month when the damn things told her what we both already knew! I am infertile, Claire!' he raked rawly at her—watched her face blanch in shock, and tossed the packet aside in disgust.

The dreadful words held her still and shaking, confusion and horror warring for dominance on her face. 'I know you said you never wanted children of your own,' she whispered. 'But...I *feel* pregnant, Andreas!' she cried out pleadingly.

'So did Sofia,' he growled. 'Every single wretched month.'

'No...' she breathed, refusing to take on board what he was saying here. 'I'm not like her—I'm not!' she insisted as those hard black eyes flicked her a contemptuous look. 'I love you!' she cried, saying the words out loud for the very first time in her desperation. 'I couldn't hurt you by playing on your feelings like that!'

'Sofia loved me,' he replied. 'She worshipped the ground that I walked upon! She leaned on me—lived for me!' A harshly grating sound of scornful laughter escaped him. 'And in the end she even decided to put me out of my misery by killing herself in the name of *love*!'

That was six years ago, and he still has not recovered from what that final act of rank selfishness did to his soul, she realised.

She was so white in the face now that she began to look like marble. 'I don't want to believe all of this...' she breathed as if in a crazed nightmare.

'Then make yourself believe,' he advised her coldly. 'For I am infertile and this marriage is over. I will not be put through that kind of hell again—not for you—not for any woman,' he concluded as he strode angrily for the door.

This time he passed through it without any hesitation. The door closed behind him, leaving Claire standing there, trembling from the top of her head to the soles of her feet as she tried desperately to come to terms with all the ugliness and horror that had been unveiled in this room today.

Infertile...

With her head turning on a neck that was too locked by stress to make the movement a smooth one, she stared dazedly at the flat packet now lying on the bed where he had tossed it. What to her had been a silly purchase made in the excitement of the moment was an instrument of torture to Andreas.

She shuddered, hating the very sight of it now, and was about to turn away from it in sickened distaste, when something he had said suddenly stilled her.

Make yourself believe, Andreas had said.

Make yourself believe…

Feeling her heart turn to stone in appalled dismay at what she was daring to consider, Claire picked up the packet.

The fierce roar of a car racing away from the house filled her head as she walked grimly into her bathroom.

CHAPTER ELEVEN

IT WAS very late by the time his car swung back into the driveway. Huddled inside a warm winter coat, Claire was sitting on one of the pale blue upholstered chairs on the front terrace, where she had been waiting for him for what seemed like hours now.

He had to have seen her sitting there because his car headlights had picked her out as he'd driven by on his way to the garages. Yet long, long minutes went by before his tall, dark figure loomed up at her from the inky darkness.

And her first response when she looked up at him was a cold little shiver. 'Still here, I see,' he drawled.

'I needed to ask you a question before I left,' she explained. 'So I decided to wait until you got back.'

'You mean there is a lie we forgot to rake over?' he mocked.

'Maybe.' She smiled a little sadly. 'I'm not sure... Will you at least sit down and listen?' she then requested. 'Only it's very difficult to talk to someone who is bent on cutting you to ribbons with their eyes while you speak.'

He smiled that smile she hated so much, and for a moment she thought he was going to tell her to go to hell. The tension soared, filling the cool winter night with a hostility that clutched at her throat.

Maybe it did something similar to him, because he released a taut sigh as if attempting to dispel the feeling, then in the next moment was reluctantly dropping down into the chair next to her.

'Fire away,' he grimly invited.

But now that she had his attention she found she'd lost the courage to say what she wanted to say. Ironic, really, she

173

mused, when you think how many hours I've waited so patiently for this moment.

'Nice evening?' she asked, merely as a cover while she got her courage back.

His dark head turned to look at her delicately drawn profile. She looked so pale, her skin seemed to glow ghost-like in the darkness. 'Is that the question?' he enquired. 'Or just an extra one you decided to throw in?'

In other words, he was not going to make this easier for her, Claire noted. 'I am not naturally a cruel or vindictive person, Andreas,' she murmured soberly. 'I did not set out to deliberately hurt you today.'

'Now that definitely was not a question,' he clipped.

And he *definitely* was not going to make this easy. At which point she decided to just hit him with it and wait to see what he did.

'Have you been making love to me for all of these weeks just for the hell of it because I was there and so obviously willing?' she asked. 'Or did you actually let yourself care something for me *before* you allowed things to go that far?'

He shifted restlessly, so his chair creaked on the tiled terrace floor. From the way his jaw clenched, he didn't like the question and liked even less having to offer an answer.

'I did not make love to you for the hell of it,' he said.

Claire sat there beside him and smothered the urge to sigh loudly in relief as she felt a huge weight lift from her shoulders because, if he had not done it for the hell of it, then he must care—even if he never actually said that he did.

'Then may I stay?' she requested huskily. 'Please?'

He made a jerky movement with his head that made her feel as if she'd hit him again. 'You said one question,' he gritted. 'That makes two.'

So she rephrased it. 'I'll go if you want me to, but I prefer to stay. I *need* to stay here with you.'

'And Melanie, of course,' he cynically mocked.

Claire's blue eyes flashed, glinting a warning at his hard

profile. 'Don't bring Melanie into this,' she admonished. 'What is best for Melanie is a separate issue. I am talking about *me* here. *My* needs.' She tersely pressed the point. 'What *I* am going to do!'

'And you want to stay,' he drawled with crushing derision. 'How very—saintly of you, considering who you would be staying with.'

'Do you think that by mocking both me and yourself in the same sentence you will force me to hate you enough to leave *without* you having to tell me to go?' she demanded.

'I thought I had already done that,' he remarked, saw her wince, and with a sigh relented in his acid tone a little. 'Listen to me, Claire,' he prompted heavily. 'You are generous and loving and selflessly kind,' he told her. 'But you are also young and extremely beautiful. If you leave here now, you will soon pick up the threads of your own life, eventually meet a lucky man one day who will fulfil your heart's desire in every single way. But I am not that man,' he stated gruffly. 'I am too old for you, too—flawed, and just too cynical for someone as fresh and perfect as you.'

'But you aren't saying that you wouldn't like to be that lucky man,' she said. 'Only that you don't think you can be him.'

His laugh was soft and rueful. 'I forgot to say stubborn, too,' he murmured—only to tag on harshly, 'Why can't you make this easier on both of us and accept that I am not going to let you stay with me?'

'Because I love you,' she replied. 'Though I don't think you deserve it. Or you couldn't be trying to hurt me like this. And if you dare to quote the cruel to be kind thing at me,' she added warningly, 'I will probably hit you again—old man.'

'Then I won't say it,' he promised. 'But neither will I change my mind.'

He sounded so strong, so—resolved, her heart gave a painful little lurch in response to it. 'So, if I get up right now and walk off into that darkness leaving Melanie behind—which is what you only ever really wanted—will that make you happy, Andreas? Will it?'

He didn't answer, but she could feel the sharp increase in his tension. On impulse she stood up—could have wept when his hand snaked out to capture hers and he muttered, 'No,' so rawly that it rasped over his throat like sandpaper, and his grip was intense.

In a flurry of shaking limbs she spun around to come and squat down in front of him. Her hair had grown longer over the last couple of months, grown thicker and glossier so that even here, in the darkness of the terrace, it shone like golden syrup around the tense pallor of her face as she tried to capture his eyes. Only he wouldn't let her do that—hadn't, in fact, since he'd appeared in front of her tonight. And that made her hurt for him, because she understood why he would not meet her gaze.

It was wretched—utterly wretched.

'OK,' she murmured shakily. 'New scenario—right?' Her free hand went up, ice-cold and trembling fingertips touching the white ring of tension circling his mouth. 'You meet a girl, you fall in love with her. You ask her to marry you. She turns round and tells you that she can't have children. Do you just walk away, Andreas?' she asked him gently. 'Does the fact that she can't give you children suddenly make her less worthy of your love?'

'This is a senseless exercise,' he gritted, dislodging her fingers with a tense movement of his head. 'Simply because it is not the case here.'

'How do you know?' Claire challenged. 'How can either you or I know whether I don't have my own flaw that will stop me from conceiving? When it has never been put to the test?'

'And never will be by me,' he uttered grimly.

'But that isn't the point I was trying to make,' she pressed. 'Are you saying that when this fantastic new man comes along to sweep me off my feet I have to have him checked out to see if he's fertile before I fall in love with him? And that he has to do the same with me?'

'Don't be foolish.' He began to scowl. 'And stop this line of argument right now. For I refuse to play mind games with ifs, buts and maybes. Why can't you simply accept that I am not going to let you stay here with me?'

'Then why are you holding so tightly to my hand?' Claire countered softly.

His hand snapped away from her, his hard face darkening with a sudden loss of patience. 'I've had enough of this,' he muttered, going to get up.

But Claire beat him to it. 'So have I,' she agreed, straightening away from him before he could stand up. 'So I am going to go to my lonely bed to dream of wildly exciting men with very high sperm counts,' she bitterly informed him. 'And you never know—if I dream hard enough, by the time morning comes around, I may have managed to purge my love for you right out of me! Then leaving here tomorrow could well turn out to be a pleasure!'

With that she stalked into the house, leaving him sitting there alone with only his stubborn pride to help him mull over what she had just said.

On reaching her room, she stripped off her clothes and climbed into bed, closed her eyes and, with gritted teeth, waited to see if her angry words managed to shock a reaction out of him.

Sure enough, a couple of minutes later, the door to his own room slammed shut, and a few more minutes after that the connecting door flew open. Claire refused to open her eyes.

'You asked for this,' he growled, coming to lean over her. 'You wanted to make me angry—well, I'm angry,' he confirmed as his naked body slid between the sheets. 'You wanted to make me jealous,' he added as he reached out for her. 'Well, I am damned well jealous!'

'Of my dreams?' she taunted, opening her eyes.

'Of everything to do with you!' he rasped, and imprisoned her very willing mouth.

It became a battle of wills as to who could arouse the other more. He kissed and licked and teased her, and shrouded her in the heaviest kind of sensuality. And she returned everything with interest, driving him out of control with the touch of her mouth and the caress of her fingers and the soft urgency with which she whispered her desire to him. 'Will my other men make me feel as good as this?' she dared to question curiously.

Her innocence before he came along added immense power to the question. But it was dangerous, it was reckless. He responded by entering her like a man who had lost touch with his sanity.

And as he drove her before him into the same wild place she thought she heard an anguished whimper, and realised with a sense of wretched guilt that the sound had come from him.

'I don't leave tomorrow, then?' she murmured when it was all over and she was lying curled close up against him, his arms still wrapped around her as if they couldn't let go.

'You stay until you are ready to go,' he replied. 'I refuse to accept more than that from you.'

Very magnanimous, Claire thought, and broke herself free from his arms to walk off to her own bathroom. When she came back she had something hidden in the palm of her hand—though he didn't notice that because he was too busy absorbing every nuance of her slender shape as she came back to him.

Straddling his lean waist, she sat looking thoughtfully down at his dark face. His eyes were hooded again—but lazily, their dark depths gleaming with a deliciously greedy possessiveness as they looked at her body.

'I have something to tell you,' she confessed. 'But I need you to promise me that you won't get angry.'

'Strange request, that,' he drawled, lifting up his arms to fold them beneath his head. 'I feel myself growing angry at the mere suggestion.'

'I thought you might.' She grimaced, sighed and then began. 'I've had a very bad day today,' she informed him. 'Almost the worst of my life.'

'My fault, I presume.'

'Hmm... Yes and no,' she replied. 'Meeting my aunt didn't help. Then you and I rowed and you took off like a maniac. I was feeling pretty miserable by then, I can tell you.'

'I'm sorry,' he sighed.

She shrugged the apology away. 'Then something really frightening happened,' she told him. 'So I got Nikos to take me back to Rafina so I could visit a doctor.'

His eyes sharpened, his arms dropped down so his hands could clasp her around her waist. 'Why?' he raked at her. 'What happened to you?'

'He examined me,' she explained as if he hadn't spoken. 'Confirmed my worst fears... You do trust me, don't you, Andreas, not to have ever been unfaithful to you?' she then asked carefully.

'Of course.' He frowned, impatient with what he saw as an irrelevance, coming as it did right in the middle of what she was telling him. 'Stop making a meal of this,' he rasped. 'And tell me what the hell is wrong with you!'

'M-my uterus is enlarged,' she said, not finding this as easy as she'd expected it to be. 'H-he did some tests.' She took a deep breath, then let it out again. 'I'm—I'm pregnant,' she announced.

It took a moment, while Claire sat there across him and waited with bated breath. Then he uttered a very rude word, and in an act of blind fury he toppled her off his chest and launched himself out of the bed. 'I thought you had agreed not to do this!' he bit out as he paced angrily away from her.

'S-six weeks to be exact,' Claire continued unsteadily. 'Andreas—I need you to—'

'How many times do I have to go through this hell?' he raged right over the top of whatever she'd been going to say. 'You cannot be pregnant!' he turned to blast at her. 'I am infertile, for goodness' sake! I am *infertile*!'

Trembling too much to dare try to stand up and go to him, Claire drew up her knees and hugged them to her chest. 'The doctor explained that,' she murmured shakily.

He went off in a fury of Greek.

Sitting there like that, Claire closed her eyes tightly and waited for the furious stream to stop before grimly forcing herself to continue. 'He said that research into male infertility is relatively new. That they are only just discovering that a man's sperm count can change virtually by the m-month.'

'I'm not listening to this.' Reeling almost drunkenly, he made for his own room.

'H-he said if you only did the test once,' she stammered after him, 'then you could have just chosen an unlucky day!'

'An unlucky day?' he repeated, coming to a taut standstill. Then he twisted his dark head to look at her. What she saw written on his face made her insides shrivel. 'I had five years of unlucky days, Claire,' he reminded her bitterly. 'Try talking your way around that.'

She nodded, and swallowed, her blue eyes determined even while they swam with tears. 'Ap-apparently he used to be Sofia's family doctor,' she explained. 'He...'

'No.' Andreas immediately denied that. 'Our family doctor is in Athens—'

'And *this* doctor was Sofia's family practitioner *before* she married you!' Claire inserted. 'He—he w-wants to talk to you—confidentially,' she told him. 'H-he says he has some information y-you may like to hear ab-about Sofia...'

Something happened, Claire wasn't sure exactly what, but something most certainly cracked that death mask he was wearing clamped over his face—before he turned and walked into his own room without a word.

She wilted like a dying swan, her long neck folding over her knees. Her heart was pounding heavily, her lungs almost completely locked inside the tension surrounding them. And her brain seemed to have closed itself down altogether, because she could not think of a single thing beyond that expression on his wretched face as he'd walked away.

Something landed on the bed beside her. Her head shot up, blue eyes despairingly vulnerable as they searched out his. But Andreas had shut off completely. 'Ring him,' he commanded.

'Ring who?' She frowned in confusion.

'This—doctor.' A long, taut finger pointed stabbingly at something beside her on the bed; glancing dazedly down, Claire saw it was a mobile telephone.

'But it's the middle of the night,' she protested.

'Then wake him up,' he insisted.

When she still didn't make a move to do his bidding, he bent to snatch the telephone back again. 'What's the bloody number?' he grated.

'I d-don't know,' she confessed. 'All I did was ask Nikos to take me to see a doctor and he drove me there...'

'His name, then,' he flicked tightly at her. 'You do at least know the name of this doctor you allowed to make an intimate examination of you?'

'An appointment card,' she suddenly remembered. 'Over there on the dressing table.'

Grimly he went to find it with hard fingers scattering things anywhere they fell. In that kind of tight, staccato way, he read the Greek symbols printed on the card, and stabbed them into his mobile.

Claire couldn't sit there and take any more. She climbed off the bed and escaped into her bathroom, where she sat on the toilet seat and shivered while she listened to his deep voice firing questions at the poor doctor in Greek.

Then the silence came back. She continued to sit there, not sure what to do, until her flesh grew so cold she had to get up and pull on her bathrobe. Shoving her hands into the cavernous pockets, she allowed herself a couple of deep breaths for courage, then let herself into the bedroom again.

Andreas was sitting on the end of her bed, slumped over with his face buried in his hands. In all her life she had never seen anything so wretched as this proud Greek man reduced to this.

Without a second thought, she went over there, climbed onto the bed behind him then simply wrapped her arms around him as tightly as she could.

'She lied to me,' he murmured hoarsely.

'I know,' Claire softly replied.

'She knew even before she married me that she was not able to conceive, yet she put me through all of that—torment. Month after month.' He laboured the point, dragging his hands away from his face so he could use them to help him. 'She made me feel useless and helpless and...'

It all came pouring out then. While Claire knelt behind him and held onto him tightly, Andreas drew a vivid picture of what it had been like to live with a woman whose obsessive need to bear a child had turned both their lives into a living nightmare. Not once had Sofia suggested the fault could be hers. Loving him and living in fear of losing him, she had created a web of deceit that involved cruel tricks and lies which kept him balanced on a knife-edge of failure and despair. By the time he had been driven into taking a fertility test himself, the sheer stress of it all must have lowered his count.

'She took a terrible risk, allowing you to take that test,' Claire pointed out soberly.

'Not really,' Andreas contended. 'Either way, the torment would have continued. With a strong count she would have merely increased her efforts to conceive. A low count gave her a similar excuse to—be lucky one day—as she loved to say to me.' A shudder ripped through him; Claire tightened her hold on him. 'In the end I couldn't bring myself to touch her, I felt such a pitiful failure,' he admitted. 'I think my withdrawal from her bed was what finally tipped her over the edge.'

And left him with yet another sense of failure he had to learn to live with, Claire realised sadly.

'I'm so sorry,' she murmured.

His shoulders flexed. 'What have you got to be sorry for?' he demanded. 'It should be me apologising to you for the way I behaved before!'

'I understood.'

'You're pregnant...' he husked suddenly.

'Mmm,' she softly confirmed. 'Are you pleased?'

He rubbed his hands over his face. 'Shell-shocked, I think,' he admitted, but some of the tension began to ease out of him.

'I have something for you,' she said, and, taking the pen-shaped tester out of her pocket, she gravely handed it to him over his shoulder. 'Our baby,' she confided. 'What do you think—boy or girl?'

She tried to keep it light, but she could feel the emotion come roaring up inside him as he sat there staring down at that silly little indicator that had been such a source of pain to him before now.

When he moved, he did it with a throaty growl as he twisted around and tumbled her onto the bed. 'From the moment you opened your lovely blue eyes on a dusty road back in London, I knew you were going to mean something special to me,' he told her deeply. 'But I never dared to so much as dream of anything *this* special.'

'Here,' Claire invited. 'Feel for yourself just how special...' And, taking hold of his hand, she fed it between their bodies so she could press his palm against her womb. There was nothing to show for the miracle taking place inside her, of course—it was much too soon—but the gesture itself was enough to have her drowning in the intense darkness of his wonderful eyes.

'I am going to love you until the day I die,' he vowed. 'And I am never going to let you go.'

'I've been trying very hard not to get away, please note,' she pointed out gently.

'Stubborn,' he accused her softly.

'In love,' she amended.

For that, he kissed her. Kissed her long and deep and with a heart-stirring tenderness that told her more than anything else could do just how much he loved to hear her say that.

Timo Markopoulou arrived in the world very early on a bright and hot summer morning.

His mother was exhausted, but she couldn't allow herself to fall asleep. She was too busy observing the way Andreas was sitting in the chair by her bed, with Melanie seated on one half of his lap while his small son occupied the other.

He was introducing them to each other, his voice softly reassuring though both babies were too young to understand. Yet, sitting there on his lap, gazing solemnly at her new brother who looked remarkably like herself when she was born, Melanie seemed to understand something of what her papa was saying, because she reached out with a small hand and touched the baby's cheek in just the same way Claire had always done to her.

The incredibly gentle act from one so young had a lump forming in Claire's throat. It affected Andreas too; she saw the waves of love and pride go washing through him as he caught the little girl's hand and carried it to his lips.

Lifting his head, he caught her watching them, and Claire sent him a soft, understanding smile, but he didn't smile back. There was just too much emotion at work inside him for him to smile right now.

'My cup runneth over,' he murmured deeply.

That was all; his feelings at that moment required no further explanation. Needing to make a physical link with those feelings, Claire reached out to rest a hand on one of his wide shoulders. He acknowledged it by brushing it with his cheek as his attention returned to his children.

And that was the image Claire took with her as she drifted into slumber. Her love. Her life, encapsulated in that one special moment. Her own cup of happiness was overflowing too.

THE PURCHASED WIFE

MICHELLE REID

CHAPTER ONE

GETTING from flight arrivals to the airport's main exit was like taking a long walk through hell. The whole route was lined with baying reporters, flashing light bulbs and a cacophony of questions aimed to provoke an impulsive response.

Xander kept his mouth clamped tightly shut and ignored provocations like, 'Did you have anything to do with your wife's accident, Mr Pascalis?'—'Did she know about your mistress?'—'Did she run her car off the road to kill herself?'—'Is there a good reason why you withdrew her bodyguard last week?'

With his eyes fixed directly ahead Xander just kept on going, six feet two inches of mean muscle power driving long legs towards the airport exit with no less than three personal-security men grouped around him like protective wolves guarding the king of the pack.

Through it all the questions kept on coming and the camera bulbs flashed, catching his severely handsome dark features locked in an expression of blistering contempt. Inside, his fury was simmering on the point of eruption. He was used to being the centre of media interest, speculation—scandal if they thought they could make it stick. But nothing—nothing they'd said about him before had been as bad or as potentially damaging as this.

He hit the outside and crossed the pavement to the waiting limousine where Rico, his chauffeur, stood with the rear door open at the ready. Dipping into the car, the door shut even before he'd folded his long frame into the seat, while outside his security people dispersed in a prowling circle that kept the reporters back until Rico had safely stashed himself back behind the wheel.

Ten seconds later the car moved away from the kerb and another car was pulling into its place to receive his men.

'How is she?' he lanced, rough toned, at the man sitting beside him.

'Still in surgery,' Luke Morrell replied.

The granite set of Xander's jaw clenched violently on a sudden vision of the beautiful Helen stretched out on an operating table, the object of a surgeon's knife. It was almost as bad as the vision he'd had of her slumped behind the wheel of her twisted wreck of a car with her Titian-bright hair and heart-shaped face smeared with blood.

His jaw unclenched. 'Who is with her at the hospital?'

There was a short hesitation before, 'No one,' Luke Morell answered. 'She refused to allow anyone to stay.'

Turning his dark head, Xander fixed his narrowed gaze on the very wary face of his UK-based personal assistant. 'What the hell happened to Hugo Vance?'

'Nell dismissed him a week ago.'

The simmering silence which followed that tasty piece of information began to burn up the oxygen inside the luxury car. 'And you knew about this?'

Luke Morrell swallowed and nodded. 'Hugo Vance rang to let me know what she'd done.'

'Then why the hell was I not told—?'

'You were busy.'

Busy. Xander's lips snapped together. He was always busy. Busy was a damned bloody way of life! 'Keep something like that from me again and you're out,' he seared at the other man with teeth-gritting intent.

Luke Morrell shifted tensely, wishing to hell that the beautiful Helen had remained locked away behind the gates of their private country estate instead of deciding it was time to venture out and take a look at life.

'It was an accident, Xander. She was driving too fast—'

A pair of wide shoulders shifted inside impeccable dark suiting. 'The point is—*why* was she driving so fast?'

Luke didn't answer. In truth he didn't need to. Xander could put two and two together and come up with four for himself. Yesterday his name had been splashed all over the tabloids alongside a photograph of him standing outside a supposedly discreet New York restaurant with the beautiful Vanessa DeFriess plastered to his front.

His skin contracted against tightly honed face muscles when he thought of the incident. Protecting Nell from embarrassing scenes like that was a duty from which he never shirked. But his bodyguard of the evening had been distracted by a drunk trying to muscle in on them, and by the time the drunk had been hustled away and the frightened Vanessa had been peeled off Xander's front, a convenient reporter had already got his sleaze-grabbing photograph and slunk away.

Nell would have been upset, angry—who the hell knew what went on inside her beautiful head? He'd stopped trying to find out a year ago when she'd married him to a fanfare of 'Romance of the New Century' then promptly refused to share his bed. By the time she'd finished calling him filthy names ranging from *power-driven fiend* to *sex-obsessed moron*, he no longer wanted her anywhere near him.

Liar, jeered a voice inside his head. You just had no defence ready when you were hit with too many ugly truths, so you backed off to hide behind your pride and arrogance.

Photographs of his relationship with Vanessa had been the catalyst then, he remembered. Tasty snippets of truth printed in with the lies that had made it impossible for him to defend himself. He *had* been with Vanessa the week before his marriage. He *had* wined and dined her at a very fashionable restaurant then taken her back to her apartment and gone in with her. The fact that he'd been doing it on the other side of the Atlantic made him stupidly—*naively* believe he was safe.

But back here in the UK, his young, sweetly besotted future bride had been avidly following his every move as it was recorded in the New York gossip columns via the internet.

The sneaky little witch had told nobody. His mouth gave a grim, uncontrolled twitch. She'd come to him down the aisle of the church dressed like an angel in frothy silk tulle and gossamer lace. She'd smiled at him, let him take her cool little hand, let him place his ring on her slender white finger, let him vow to love, honour and protect. She'd even allowed him that one traditional kiss as they became man and wife. She'd smiled for their wedding photographs, smiled throughout the long wedding breakfast that followed and even smiled when he'd taken her in his arms for their traditional bridal dance. If there had ever been a man more ready to be a willing slave to his lovely young bride then, by the time they reached the hotel suite where they were to spend their wedding night, he, Alexander Pascalis, was it.

She'd waited until then to turn on him like a viper. A cold, glassy-eyed English version of a viper, who'd spat words at him like ice picks that awoke this handsome prince up from his arrogant dream-world instead of the prince awakening his sleeping beauty with the kind of loving that should have made her his slave for life.

And sleeping beauty she was then—too innocent to be real. That same innocence had been her only saviour on their miserable wedding night. Still was, did she but know it.

Because his marriage might have turned into a disaster even before he'd got around to consummating it but his desire to possess the beautiful Helen had remained a strong, nagging entity amongst the rubble of the rest.

'I suppose you know why she dismissed Vance?' he queried now, dragging his mind back to the present crisis.

There was a tense shift beside him. Xander turned his dark head again and a warning tingle shot across the back of his neck when he saw the new guarded expression on his employee's face. Luke was wary—very wary. There was even a hint of red beginning to stain his pale English cheeks.

'Spit it out,' he raked at him.

Luke Morrell tugged in a breath. 'Hugo tried to stop her,' he claimed defensively, 'but Nell took offence—'

'Tried to stop her from doing what?'

Luke lifted up a hand in a helpless gesture. 'Listen, Xander,' he said in an advisory voice that sounded too damn soothing for Xander's liking, 'it was nothing serious enough to need to involve you but Hugo was concerned that it might…get out of hand, so hc…advised Nell against it and she—'

'Advised her against doing what?' Xander sliced right through all of Luke's uncharacteristic babbling, and by now every bone in his body was tensing up as his instincts shot on full alert. He was not going to like this. He was so damn certain of it that his clenched teeth began to sing.

'A man,' Luke admitted reluctantly. 'A—a friend Nell's been seeing recently…'

Nell felt as if she were floating. It was a really strange feeling, all fluffy and soft yet scary at the same time. And she couldn't open her eyes. She had tried a couple of times but her eyelids felt as if they'd been glued down. Her throat hurt when she swallowed and her mouth was so dry the swallowing action was impossible anyway.

She knew where she was. Had a vague recollection of the car accident and being rushed by ambulance to hospital, but that pretty much was the sum total of her recollection. The last clear thing she remembered was gunning the engine of her little open-top sports car and driving at a pace down the long driveway at Rosemere towards the giant iron gates. She could remember the wild sense of elation she'd felt when the gates had swung open with precision timing to let her shoot right through them without her having to drop her speed. And she could still feel the same sense of bitter triumph with which she'd mocked the gates' efficiency as she'd driven past them. Didn't the stupid gates know they'd just let the trapped bird escape?

Escape. Nell frowned, puzzled as to why the word had jumped into her head. Then she was suddenly groaning when the frown caused a pain to shoot right across the front of her head.

Someone moved not far away. 'Nell…?' a deep, darkly rasping voice said.

Managing to open her eyes the small crack that was all they would allow her, she peered out at the shadowy outline of a man's big, lean, dark-suited bulk standing stiffly at the end of her bed.

Xander, she recognised. Bitterness welled as her heart gave a tight, very painful pinch. What was he doing here? Had corporate earth stopped turning or something? Nothing less would give him the time to visit her sickbed.

Go away, she wanted to say but did not have enough energy, so she closed the slits in her eyes and blocked him out that way instead.

'Nell, can you hear me?'

He sounded unusually gruff. Maybe he had a bad cold or a sore throat or something, she thought hazily. How would she know? She'd barely set eyes on him for months—not since he'd turned up like a bad penny on her birthday and dragged her out to have dinner with him.

The candlelit-table-for-two kind of dinner with good wine and the requisite bottle of champagne standing at the ready on ice. Her fuzzy head threw up a picture of his handsome dark image, the way the candlelight had played with his ebony hair and the golden sheen of his skin as he'd sat there across the table from her with his slumberous dark eyes fixed on her face. Sartorial elegance had oozed from every sleek skin pore. The smooth self-confidence, the indolent grace with which he'd occupied his seat that belied his height and lean muscle power. The lazy indifference with which he'd dismissed the kind of breathless looks he received from every other woman in the room because he was special and he knew he was special, and there was not a person in that restaurant that didn't recognise it. Including Nell, though she was the only one there that refused to let it show.

'Happy birthday,' he said and used long, tanned fingers to push a velvet box across the table towards her. Inside the box was a diamond-encrusted bracelet that must have cost him the absolute earth.

If she was supposed to be impressed, she wasn't. If he'd presented her with the crown jewels she still would not be impressed. Did he think she didn't know that a bracelet like that was the kind of thing a man like him presented to his mistress for services rendered?

Where was his sensitivity? Where it had always been, locked up inside his impossible arrogance, as he proved when he dared to announce then that he wanted to renegotiate their marriage contract as if some stupid trinket was all it would take to make her agree.

She pushed the box back across the table and said no—to both the bracelet and the request. Did it faze him? Not in the slightest. He took a few minutes to think about her cool little refusal then nodded his disgustingly handsome dark head in acceptance, and that was basically that. He'd driven her back to Rosemere then drove away again to go back to his exciting life as a high-profile, globe-trotting Greek tycoon and probably given the bracelet to some other woman—the more appreciative Vanessa, for instance.

'I hate him,' she thought, having no idea that the words had scraped across her dry lips.

The sound of furniture moving set her frowning again, a pale, limp hand lifting weakly to the pain that stabbed at her forehead. Another hand gently caught hold of her fingers to halt their progress.

'Don't touch, Nell. You won't like it,' his husky voice said.

She opened her eyes that small crack again to find Xander had moved from his stiff stance at the bottom of the bed and was now sitting on a chair beside it with his face level with hers. A pair of dark eyes looked steadily back at her from between unfairly long black silk fringes, a hint of strain tugging on the corners of his wide, sensual mouth.

'How do you feel?' he asked.

Pain attacked her from the oddest of places—her heart mainly, broken once and still not recovered.

She closed her eyes, blocking him out again. He shouldn't even be here; he should be in New York, enjoying the lovely Vanessa with the long dark hair and voluptuous figure that could show off heavy diamond trinkets while she clung to someone else's husband like a sex-charged limpet.

'Do you know where you are?' Xander persisted.

Nell quivered as his warm breath fanned her face.

'You are in hospital,' he seemed compelled to inform her. 'You were involved in a car accident. Can you hear me, Helen?'

The *Helen* arrived with the rough edge of impatience. Xander did not like to be ignored. He wasn't used to it. People shot to attention when he asked questions. He was Mr Important, the mighty empire-builder aptly named after Alexander the Great. When he said jump the whole world jumped. He was dynamic, magnetic, sensational to look at—

Her head began to ache. 'Go away,' she slurred out. 'I don't want you here.'

She could almost feel his tension slam into her. The gentle fingers still holding hers gave an involuntary twitch. Then he moved and she heard the sound of silk sliding against silk as he reached up with his other arm and another set of cool fingers gently stroked a stray lock of hair from her cheek.

'You don't mean that, *agape mou*,' he murmured.

I do, Nell thought, and felt tears sting the backs of her eyelids because his light touch evoked old dreams of a gentle giant stroking her all over like that.

But that was all they were—empty old dreams that came back to haunt her occasionally. The real Xander was hard and cold and usually wishing himself elsewhere when he was with her.

How had he got here so quickly anyway? What time was it? What day? She moved restlessly then cried out in an agonised, pathetically weak whimper as real physical pain shot everywhere.

'Don't move, you fool!' The sudden harshness in his voice rasped across her flesh like the serrated edge of a knife—right here—and she pushed a hand up to cover the left side of her ribs as her screaming body tried to curl up in instinctive recoil. The bed tilted beside her, long fingers moving to her narrow shoulders to keep her still.

'Listen to me...' his voice rasped again and she arched in

agony as pain ricocheted around her body. He tossed out a soft curse then a buzzer sounded. 'You must try to remain still,' he lashed down at her. 'You are very badly bruised, and the pain in your side is due to several cracked ribs. You are also suffering from a slight concussion, and internal bleeding meant they had to operate. Nell, you—'

'W-what kind of operation?'

'Your appendix was damaged when you crashed your car; they had to remove it.'

Appendix? Was that all? She groaned in disbelief.

'If you are worrying about a scar then don't,' Xander clipped. 'They used keyhole surgery—barely a knick; you will be as perfect as ever in a few weeks.'

Did he really believe that she cared about some silly scarring? Down in A&E they'd been tossing about all kinds of scenarios from burst spleen to ovaries!

'I hate you so much,' she gasped out then burst into tears, the kind of loud, hot, choking tears that came with pure, agonising delayed shock and brought people running and had Xander letting go of her to shoot to his feet.

After that she lost sight of him when a whole army of care staff crowded in. But she could still hear his voice, cold with incision: 'Can someone explain to me, please, why my wife shares a room with three other sick individuals? Does personal dignity have no meaning here...?'

The next time Nell woke up she was shrouded in darkness other than for a low night lamp burning somewhere up above her head. She could open her eyes without having to force them and she was feeling more comfortable, though she suspected the comfort had been drug-induced.

Moving her head on the pillow in a careful testing motion, she felt no pain attack her brow and allowed herself a sigh of relief. Then she began to take an interest in her surroundings. Something was different, though for the life of her she couldn't say what.

'You were moved this afternoon to a private hospital,' a deep voice informed her.

Turning her head in the other direction, she saw Xander standing in the shadows by the window. Her heart gave a helpless little flutter then clenched.

Private hospital. Private room. 'Why?' she whispered in confusion.

He didn't answer. But then why would he? A man like him did not leave his wife to the efficient care of the National Health Service when he could pay for the same service with added touches of luxury.

As she looked at him standing there in profile, staring out of the window, it didn't take much work for her dulled senses to know his mood was grim. The jacket to his dark suit had gone and he'd loosened the tie around his throat. She could just pick out the warm sheen of his golden skin as it caught the edges of a soft lamplight.

For a moment she thought she saw a glimpse of the man she had fallen in love with a year ago.

The same man she'd seen on the evening she'd walked into her father's study and found Xander there alone. He'd been standing like this by her father's window, grimly contemplating what lay beyond the Georgian glass with its hand-beaten distortions that had a knack of distorting everything that was happening in the world beyond.

That was the night he had asked her to marry him; no fanfare, no romantic preliminaries. Oh, they'd been out to dinner a couple of times, and Xander tended to turn up at the same functions she would be attending and seem to make a beeline for her. People had watched curiously as he monopolised her attention and she blushed a lot because she wasn't used to having such a man show a desire for her company.

Twenty-one years old and fresh back from spending three years high up in the Canadian Rockies with a mother who preferred getting up close and personal with pieces of driftwood she found on the shores of the Kananaskis River than she did with living people. Nell had gone to Canada for her annual two-week visit with the reclusive Kathleen Garrett and stayed to the end when her mother had coolly informed her that she didn't have long to live.

Nell liked to think that her quiet company had given her mother a few extra years of normal living before it all got too much. Certainly they became a bit more like mother and daughter than they'd been throughout Nell's life when previous visits to her mother had made her feel more like an unwanted distant relative.

Coming back to England and to her father's busy social lifestyle had come as a bit of a culture shock. She'd gone to Canada a child who'd spent most of her life being shunted from one boarding-school to another with very little contact with the social side of her industrialist father's busy life. Three years' living quietly with her mother had been no preparation for a girl who'd become a woman without really knowing it until she met Alexander Pascalis.

An accident waiting to happen... Nell frowned as she tried to recall who it was that had said those words to her. Then she remembered and sighed because of course it had been this tall, dark, silent man looking out of the window who'd spoken those words to her. 'A danger to yourself and to anyone near you,' he'd rumbled out as he'd pulled her into his arms and kissed her before sombrely asking her to marry him.

She looked away from his long, still frame, not wanting to go back to those days when she'd loved him so badly she would have crawled barefooted over broken glass if that was what it took to be with him. Those days were long gone, along with her pride, her self-respect and her starry-eyed infatuation.

Her mouth was still dry, the muzzy effects of whatever they'd given her to stem the pain making her limbs feel weighted down with lead. When she tried to lift her hand towards the glass of water she could see on the cupboard beside her, she could barely raise her fingers off the bed.

'I need a drink,' she whispered hoarsely.

He was there in a second, sitting down on the bed and sliding an arm beneath her shoulders to lift her enough to place the glass to her lips. She felt his warmth and his strength as she sipped the water, both alien sensations when she hadn't been held even this close to him since the day of their marriage.

'Thank you,' she breathed as the glass was withdrawn again.

He controlled her gentle slide back onto the pillows then sat back a little but didn't move away. Something was flickering in his dark eyes that she couldn't decipher—but then he was not the kind of man who wanted other people to read his thoughts—too precious, too—

'Your car was a write-off,' he remarked unexpectedly.

Her slender shoulders tensed in sudden wariness. 'W-was it?'

He nodded. His firmly held mouth gave a tense little twitch. 'You had to have been driving very fast to impale it so thoroughly on that tree.'

Nell lowered her eyes on a wince. 'I don't remember.'

'Nothing?' he questioned.

'Only driving through the gates at Rosemere then turning into the lane. After that—nothing,' she lied huskily.

He was silent for a few seconds and she could feel him studying her. Her cheeks began to heat. Lying had never been her forte. But what the devil did not know could not hurt him, she thought with a stab at dry sarcasm that was supposed to make her feel brave but didn't.

'W-what time is it?' She changed the subject.

Xander sprang back to his feet before glancing at the gold watch circling his wrist. 'Two-thirty in the morning.'

Nell lifted her eyes to watch the prowling grace of his long body as he took up his position by the window again.

'I thought you were in New York.'

'I came back—obviously.'

With or without Vanessa? she wondered. 'Well, don't feel like you have to hang around here for my benefit,' she said tightly.

He didn't usually hang around. He strode in and out of her life like a visiting patron, asked all the right polite questions about what she'd been doing since he'd seen her last and sometimes even lingered long enough to drag her out with him to some formal function—just to keep up appearances. He occupied the suite adjoining her bedroom suite but had never slept in it. Appearances, it seemed, only went as far as delivering her to her bedroom door before he turned and strode out of the house again.

'It is expected.'

And that's telling me, Nell thought with another wince. 'Well, I hereby relieve you of your duty,' she threw back, moved restlessly, which hurt, so she made herself go still again. And her eyelids were growing too heavy to hold up any longer. 'Go away, Xander.' Even her voice was beginning to sound slurry. 'You make me nervous, hanging around like this...'

Not so you would notice, Xander thought darkly as he watched the little liar drop into a deep sleep almost before her dismissal of him was complete.

The night-light above her bed was highlighting her sickly pallor along with the swollen cuts and bruises that distorted her beautiful face. She would be shocked if she knew what she looked like.

Hell, the miserable state of her wounded body shocked him.

And her hair was a mess, lying in lank, long copper tangles across the pillow. Oddly, he liked it better when it was left to do its own thing like this. The first time he'd seen her she'd been stepping into her father's house, having just arrived back from taking the dogs for a walk. It had been windy and cold outside and her face was shining, her incredible waist-length hair wild and rippling with life. Green eyes circled by a fascinating ring of turquoise had been alight with laughter because the smallest of the dogs, a golden Labrador puppy determined to get into the house first, had bounded past her, only to land on its rear and start to slither right across the slippery polished floor to come to a halt at his feet.

She'd noticed him then, lifting her eyes up from his black leather shoes on one of those slow, curious journeys he'd learned to recognise as a habit she had that set his libido on heat. By the time she'd reached his face her laughter had died to sweet, blushing shyness.

What a hook, he mocked now, recalling what happened to him every time she'd blushed like that for him—or even just looked at him.

Xander looked away and went back to his grim contemplation of the unremarkable view of the darkness outside the window, not wanting to remember what came after the blushing look.

He should have backed off while he still had a chance then—right off. If he had done they would not be in the mess they were now in. It was not his thing to mix business with pleasure, and the kind of business he'd had going with Julian Garrett had needed a cool, clear head.

Sexual desire was neither cool nor clear-headed. It liked to catch you out when you were not paying attention. He'd had a mistress, a beautiful, warm and passionately sensual woman who knew what he liked and did not expect too much back, so what did he need with a wild-haired, beautiful-eyed *ingénue* with a freakish kind of innocence written into her blushing face?

A sigh ripped from him. Nell was right and he should leave. He should get the hell away from here and begin the unpalatable task of some very urgent damage control, only he had a feeling it was already too late.

The tabloid Press would already be running, churning out their damning accusations cloaked in rumour and suggestion. The only part of it all that he had going for him was the Press did not know what Nell had been in the process of doing when she crashed her car on that quiet country lane.

His pager gave a beep. Turning away from the window, he went to collect his jacket from where he'd tossed it on a chair and dug the pager out of one of the pockets.

Hugo Vance was trying to reach him. His teeth came together with a snap.

And so to discover the truth about his wife's new *friend*, he thought grimly, shrugged on his jacket, sent Nell one final, searing dark glance then quietly let himself out of the room.

CHAPTER TWO

FOR the next few days Nell felt as if she had been placed in purdah. The only people that came to visit her belonged to the medical staff, who seemed to take great pleasure in making her uncomfortable before they made her comfortable again.

The first time they allowed her to take a shower she was shocked by the extent of her bruising. If anyone had told her that with enough applied pressure you could achieve a perfect imprint of a car safety belt across your body she would not have believed them—until she saw it striking across her own slender frame in two ugly, deep bands of dark purple bruising. She had puncture holes and stitches from the keyhole surgery and her cracked ribs hurt like crazy every time she moved. She had bruises on her legs, bruises and scratches on her arms and her face due to ploughing through bushes in an open-top car—before it had slammed into the tree.

And the miserable knowledge that Xander had seen her looking like this did not make her feel any better. It was no wonder he hadn't bothered to come and visit her again.

Her night things had been delivered, toiletries, that kind of thing. And she'd even received a dozen red roses—Xander's way of keeping up appearances, she supposed cynically. He was probably already back in New York by now, playing the big Greek tycoon by day and the great Greek lover by night for the lovely Vanessa.

If she could she'd chuck his stupid roses through the window, but she didn't have the strength. She'd found that she ached progressively more with each new day.

'What do you expect? You've been in a car accident,' a nurse said with a dulcet simplicity when she mentioned it to her. 'Your body took a heck of a battering and you're lucky

19

that your injuries were not more serious. As it is it's going to be weeks before you begin to feel more like your old self again.'

The shower made her feel marginally better though. And the nurse had shampooed her hair for her and taken gentle care as she blow-dried its long, silken length. By the time she'd hobbled out of the bathroom she was ready to take an interest in the outside world again.

A world in which she had some urgent things to deal with, she recalled worriedly. 'I need a phone,' she told the nurse as she inched her aching way across the room via any piece of furniture she could grab hold of to help support her feeble weight. 'Isn't it usual to have one plugged in by the bed?'

The nurse didn't answer, her white-capped head averted as she waited for Nell to slip carefully back into the bed.

It was only then that she began to realise that not only was there no telephone in here, but the room didn't even have a television set. What kind of private hospital was it Xander had dumped her in that it couldn't provide even the most basic luxuries?

She demanded both. When she received neither, she changed tack and begged for a newspaper to read or a couple of magazines. It took another twenty-four hours for it to dawn on her that all forms of contact with the outside world were being deliberately withheld.

She began to fret, worrying as to what could have happened out there that they didn't want her to know about.

Her father? Could something have happened to him? Stunned that she hadn't thought about him before now, she sat up with a thoughtless jerk that locked her into an agonising spasm across her chest.

That was how Xander found her, sitting on the edge of the bed clutching her side and struggling to breathe in short, sharp, painful little gasps.

'What the hell...?' He strode forward.

'Daddy,' she gasped out. 'S-something's happened to him.'

'When?' He frowned. 'I've heard nothing. Here, lie down again...'

His hands took control of her quivering shoulders and carefully eased her back against the high mound of pillows, the frown on his face turning to a scowl when he saw the bruising on her slender legs as he helped ease them carefully back onto the bed.

'You look like a war zone,' he muttered. 'What did you think you were doing, trying to get up without help?'

'Where's my father?' she cut across him anxiously. 'Why haven't I heard from him?'

'But you did.' Xander straightened up, flicking the covers over her in an act she read as contempt. 'He's stuck in Sydney. Did you not receive his flowers and note?'

The only flowers she'd received were the...

Turning her head, Nell looked at the vase of budding red roses and suddenly wished she were dead. 'I thought they were from you,' she whispered unsteadily.

He looked so thoroughly disconcerted by the idea that he would send her flowers that being dead no longer seemed bad enough. Curling away from him as much as she dared without hurting herself, Nell clutched her fingers round the covers and tugged them up to her pale cheek.

'You thought they were from me.' He had to repeat it, she thought as she cringed beneath the sheet. 'And because you thought the flowers were from me you did not even bother to read the note that came with them.'

Striding round the bed, he plucked a tiny card from the middle of the roses then came back to the bed.

'Shame on you, Nell.' The card dropped against the pillow by her face. It was still sealed inside its envelope.

And shame on you too, she thought as she picked it up and broke the seal. Even a man that cannot stand the sight of his wife sends her flowers when she's sick.

Her father's message—brief and to the point as always with him—read: 'Sorry to hear about your accident. Couldn't get back to see you. Take care of yourself. Get well soon. Love Pops.'

Saying not a word, she slid the little card back into its envelope then pushed it beneath her pillow, but telling tears were welling in her eyes.

'He wanted to come back,' Xander dropped into the ensuing thick silence. 'But he is locked in some important negotiations with the Australian government and I...assured him that you would understand if he remained where he was.'

So he'd stayed. That was her father. Loving in many ways but single-minded in most. Money was what really mattered, the great, grinding juggernaut of corporate business. It was no wonder her mother had left him to go back to her native Canada. When she was little, Nell had used to wonder if he even noticed that she'd gone. She was a teenager before she'd found out that her mother had begun an affair with a childhood sweetheart and had returned to Canada to be with him.

Like mother like daughter, she mused hollowly. They had a penchant for picking out the wrong men. The duration of her mother's affair had been shorter than her marriage had been, which said so much about leaving her five-year-old daughter behind for what was supposed to have been the real love of her life.

'You've washed your hair...'

'I want a telephone,' she demanded.

'And the bruises on your face are beginning to fade...' He spoke right over her as if she hadn't spoken at all. 'You look much better, Nell.'

What did he care? 'I want a telephone,' she repeated. 'And you left me with no money. I can't find my purse or my clothes or my mobile telephone.'

'You don't need them while you're lying there.'

She turned her head to flash him a bitter look. He was standing by the bed, big and lean, taking up more space than he deserved. All six feet two inches of him honed to perfection like a piece of art. His suit was grey today, she noticed. A smooth-as-silk gunmetal grey that did not dare to show a single crease, like his white shirt and his silk-black hair and his—

'They won't let me have a newspaper or a magazine.' She cut that line of thinking off before it went any further. 'I have no TV and no telephone.' She gave a full list of her grievances 'If it isn't my father, then what is it that you are trying to hide from me, Xander?' she demanded, knowing now that her isolation had to be down to him. Xander was the only person with enough weight to throw about. In fact she was amazed that it hadn't occurred to her to blame him before now.

He made no answer, just stood there looking down at her through unfathomable dark eyes set in his hard, handsome face—then he turned and strode out of the room without even saying goodbye!

Nell stared after him with her eyes shot through with pained dismay. Had their disastrous marriage come down to the point where he couldn't even be bothered to apply those strictly polite manners he usually used to such devastating effect?

It hurt—which was stupid, but it did and in places that had nothing whatsoever to do with her injuries. Five days without so much as a word from him then he strode in there looking every inch the handsome, dynamic power force he was, looked at her as if he couldn't stand the sight of her then walked out again.

She wouldn't cry, she told the sting at the backs of her eyes. Too fed up and too weak to do more than bite hard on her bottom lip to stop it from quivering, she stared at the roses sent by that other man in her life who strode in and out of it at his own arrogant behest.

She hated Alexander Pascalis. He'd broken her heart and she should have left him when she'd had the chance, driven off into the sunset without stopping to look back and think about what she was leaving behind, then she would not be lying here feeling so bruised and broken—and that was on the inside! If he'd cared anything for her at all he should not have married her. He should have stuck to his—

The door swung open and Xander strode back in again,

catching her lying on her side staring at the roses through a glaze of tears.

'If you miss him that much I will bring him home,' he announced curtly.

'Don't put yourself out,' she responded with acid bite. 'What brought you back here so quickly?'

He didn't seem to understand the question, a frown darkening his smooth brow as he moved across the room to collect a chair, which he placed by the bed at an angle so that when he sat himself down on it he was looking her directly in the face.

Nell stirred restlessly, not liking the way he'd done it, or the new look of hard intensity he was treating her to. She stared back warily, waiting to hear whatever it was he was going to hit her with. He was leaning back with his long legs stretched out in front of him and his jacket flipped open in one of those casually elegant attitudes this man pulled off with such panache. His shirt was startlingly white—he liked to wear white shirts, cool, crisp things that accentuated the width of his powerful chest and long, tightly muscled torso. Black handmade shoes, grey silk trousers, bright white shirt and a dark blue silk tie. His cleanly shaved chin had a cleft that warned all of his tough inner strength—like the well-shaped mouth that could do cynicism and sensuality at the same time and to such devastating effect. Then there was the nose that had a tendency to flare at the nostrils when he was angry. It wasn't flaring now, but the black eyes were glinting with something not very nice, she saw.

And his eyes weren't really all black, but a dark, dark brown colour, deeply set beneath thick black eyebrows and between long, dense, curling lashes that helped to shade the brown iris black.

Xander was Greek in everything he thought and did but he got his elegant carriage from his beautiful Italian mother. And Gabriela Pascalis could slay anyone with a look, just as her son could. She'd done it to Nell the first time they'd met and Gabriela had not tried to hide her shock. 'What is Alexander playing at, wanting to marry a child? They will crucify you the moment he attempts to slot you into his sophisticated lifestyle.'

'He loves me.' She'd tried to stand up for herself.

'Alexander does not do love, *cara*,' his mother had drily mocked that. 'In case you have not realised it as yet, he was hewn from rock chipped off Mount Olympus.' She had actually meant it too. 'No, this is more likely to be a business transaction,' her future mother-in-law had decided without a single second's thought to how a statement like that would make Nell feel. 'I will have to find out what kind of business deal. Leave it to me, child. There is still time to save you from this...'

'Finished checking me out?' The mocking lilt to his voice brought her eyes back into focus on his face. She wished she knew what he was thinking behind that cool, smooth, sardonic mask. 'I am still the same person you married, believe me.'

Oh, she believed. Nothing had changed. His mother had been right but Nell hadn't listened. Not until Vanessa DeFriess had entered the frame.

'Want do you want?' She didn't even attempt to sound pleasant.

He moved—not much but enough for Nell to be aware by the way her senses tightened on alert to remind her that Xander was a dangerously unpredictable beast. He might appear relaxed, but she had an itchy suspicion that he was no such thing.

'We need to talk about your accident,' he told her levelly. 'The police have some questions.'

Nell dropped her eyes, concentrating her attention on her fingers where they scratched absently at the white sheet. 'I told you, I don't remember anything.'

'Tell me what you do remember.'

'We've been through this once.' Her eyebrows snapped together. 'I don't see the use in going through it a—'

'You would rather I allow the police to come here so that you can repeat it all to them?'

No, she wouldn't. 'What's to repeat?' Flicking him a guarded look, she looked quickly away again. 'I remember driving down the driveway and through the gates then turning into the lane—'

'Left or right?'

'I don't remember—'

'Well, it might help if you said where it was you were going.'

'I don't remember that either.'

'Try,' he said.

'What for?' she flipped back. 'What does it matter now where I was going? I obviously didn't get there.'

'True.' He grimaced. 'Instead of arriving—wherever it was—you left the road at speed on a notorious bend we all treat with respect. You then proceeded to plough through a row of bushes and concluded the journey by piling head-on into a tree.'

'Thanks for filling in the gaps,' she derided.

'The car boot sprang open on impact,' he continued, unmoved by her tone. 'Your possessions were strewn everywhere. Sweaters, skirts, dresses, underwear...'

'Charity!' she declared with a sudden burst of memory. 'I remember now, I was taking some of my old things to the charity shop in the village.'

'Charity,' Xander repeated in a voice as thin as silk. 'Well, that explains the need to drive like a maniac. Now explain to me why you dismissed Hugo Vance...'

Nell froze where she lay curled on her side, her moment of triumph at her own quick thinking fizzling out at the introduction of her ex-bodyguard's name. She moved, ignoring the creases of pain in her ribs to drag herself into a sitting position so she could grab her knees in a loose but very defensive hug, her hair slithering across her slender shoulders to float all around her in a river of rippling Titian silk.

'I don't need a bodyguard,' she muttered.

'I have three,' Xander replied. 'What does that tell you about what you need?'

'I'm not you.' She sent him an acrid look. 'I don't stride

around the world, playing God and throwing my weight around—'

His eyes gave a sudden glint. 'So that is how you see me— as a god that throws his weight around?' The silken tone gave her no clue as to what was about to come next. 'Well, my beautiful Helen,' he drawled in a thoroughly lazy attitude, 'just watch this space—'

In a single snaking move he was off the chair and leaning over her. The next second and he was gathering her hair up and away from her face. A controlled tug sent her head back. A stifled gasp brought her startled eyes flicking up to clash with his.

What she saw glowing there set her trembling. 'You're hurting—'

'No, I'm not,' he denied through gritted teeth. 'But I am teetering, *cara mia*, so watch out how many more lies you wish to spout at me!'

'I'm not lying!'

'No?' With some more of that controlled strength he wound her hair around his fingers, urging her head back an extra vulnerable inch so as to expose the long, creamy length of her slender throat.

'You were leaving me,' he bit at her in hard accusation. 'You were speeding like a crazy woman down that lane because you were leaving me for another man and you got rid of Vance to give yourself a nice clean getaway, only that damn tree got in the way!'

Caught out lying so thoroughly, she felt hot colour rush into her cheeks. His eyes flared as he watched it happen. Defiance rose in response.

'So what if I was?' she tossed back at him. 'What possible difference was it going to make to the way you run your life? We don't have a marriage, we have a business arrangement that I didn't even get to have a say about!' Tears were burning now—hot, angry tears. 'And I dismissed Hugo a week ago, much that you noticed or cared! I have a right to live my own life any way I want—'

'And let another man make love to you any time that you want?'

The raking insert closed Nell's throat, strangling her breath and the denial she could have given in answer to that. Her angry lips followed suit, snapping shut because she didn't want to say it. She did not want to give him anything that could feed his mammoth ego.

The silence between them began to spark like static, his lean face strapped by a fury that stretched his golden skin across the bones in his cheeks as their eyes made war across a gap of barely an inch. Then his other hand came up to cover her throat, light-fingered and gentle but oh, so menacing.

'Say it, *yenika*,' he encouraged thinly. 'Live dangerously…'

He thought she was holding back from admitting she had taken a lover, Nell realised, and felt the triumph in that tingle all the way down to her feet. She moistened her lips—tempted, so desperately tempted that she did not know how she managed to keep the lie back. Their eyes continued to war across several taut, suffocating seconds. It was exciting, knowing that she had the power to shatter his precious ego with a single soft word like *yes*.

The tips of his long fingers moved on her throat, locating a wildly beating pulse. Nell needed to take a breath, her ribs were hurting under the pressure she was placing on them, and in the end she managed a short, tense tug of air into her lungs before improvising shakily, 'If you want to strangle m-me then go ahead; I'm in no fit state to stop you.'

Surprise lit his face. He glanced down to where his fingers curved her throat, dark lashes curling over his eyes before lifting again to view the way his other fingers were knotted into her hair. There was yet another second of taut, breathtaking stillness in which the entire world seemed to grind to a halt. Then the fingers began to slide again, moving almost sensuously against stretched, smooth, creamy flesh as they began to make a slow retreat.

Relief quivered through her, parting her lips on a small, soft gasp. The fingers paused, she held her breath again, felt a different kind of excitement erupt as she flicked a look into the deep, dark, swirling depths of his eyes and saw what she'd always seen there.

Xander had always desired her and Nell had always known it. Whatever else had motivated him into marrying her, the desire had always been the added incentive that made the deal worthwhile.

'You remind me of a sleeping siren,' he murmured. 'It is the only thing that has kept you safe for the last year. Give me one small hint, *cara*, that you have given to someone else that which I have resisted and you will spend the rest of your days regretting it.'

It was just too tempting to resist this time. Defiance back in her eyes, she opened her mouth 'I—'

His mouth arrived to stop whatever she had been about to utter. Shock hit her broadside, sheer surprise at the unexpectedness of it holding her utterly transfixed. He hadn't kissed her once since their wedding night and then he'd been so angry—hard and punishing with frustrated desire. This was different, the anger was still there but the rest was warm, deep and sensually tantalising, the way he used his lips to prise hers apart then stroked the inner recesses of her mouth.

It was her very first tongue-to-tongue experience and the pleasurable sensations it fed into her tapped into one of her many restless, hopeless dreams about moments like this. The warm, clean, expensive scent of him, the smooth, knowing expertise with which he moulded her mouth to his, the slight rasping brush of his skin against her soft skin, the trailing, sensual drag she could feel on her senses that made her relax into him.

He drew back the moment he felt her first tentative response to him. Eyes too dark to read watched the soft quiver of her mouth before he looked deeply into the swirling green confusion mirrored in her eyes. Then he smiled.

'There,' he murmured with silken huskiness. 'I have just saved you from yourself. Aren't you fortunate to have a caring husband like me?'

As she frowned at the comment, he brushed a contemptuous kiss across her still parted mouth then drew right away, fingers trailing from her throat and untangling from her silken hair while she continued to puzzle—until she remembered what she had been about to say before the kiss.

She shivered, horrified at how easily she had let herself be diverted. Resentment poured into her bloodstream. 'I still intend to leave you the moment I get out of here,' she said.

'You will not.' He was already on his feet and replacing the chair back from where he'd got it. 'And I will tell you why.' He sent her a cold look down the length of his arrogant nose. 'We still have a contract to fulfil.'

Nell lifted her chin to him, green eyes wishing him dead now. 'I signed under duress.'

'You mean you signed without reading it.'

Because she'd loved him so much she was blind! 'How many women would expect to be duped by both their own father and their future husband?' she defended her own piece of stupid folly.

Xander nodded in agreement. 'I offered to renegotiate,' he then reminded her. 'You turned the offer down, so the contract stands as written and signed.'

'And all for the love of money,' she said bitterly.

'A loan of fifty million pounds to haul your father out of trouble is a lot of money, Nell. Have you got the resources to pay me back?'

He knew she hadn't. The only money Nell had even a loose connection to was tied up in trusts left by her grandmother for any children Nell might have. And what her mother had left would not even pay back a tenth of what was owed to Xander.

'But I was not referring to the money,' he slid in smoothly. 'I was referring to the other clause—the one which involves me protecting my investment by you providing me with my son and heir to inherit from your father.'

Effectively putting Nell right out of the inheritance loop! 'Not with my permission.'

'With your permission,' he insisted. 'And at my time of choosing...'

He came back to the bed to lean over her again, ignoring her defensive jerk as he began plumping up the pillows behind her back. 'I have been very patient with you until now, *yenika mou*—'

'Because you had more—interesting things to do.'

As a direct shot about Vanessa, it went wide of its mark.

'Because,' he corrected, 'when we married you were nothing but a wounded babe in arms only a monster would have forced himself upon. The arrival of another man on the scene tells me I may well have been too patient with you.' Taking her by the shoulders, he gently urged her to lie back. Then his eyes were pinning her there, relentless and hard. 'Your growing time is up, Nell. I want a proper wife. Renege on the contract we made and I will take you, your father and your boyfriend to the cleaners and hang you all out to dry.'

'And cause yourself a nasty scandal involving yourself, your mistress and your lousy unfaithfulness?'

'Is that why you thought you could leave and get away with it?' Black silk eyebrows made a mocking arch. 'You think that because Vanessa has suddenly arrived back on the scene it gives you a tasty weapon to wield? I will let you into a little secret,' he murmured, a taunting fingertip making a swipe of her full bottom lip before he replaced it with the casual brush of his mouth. 'Vanessa has never been off the scene,' he informed her smoothly. 'I am just very discreet—usually.'

It was like being kicked while she was already down on the ground. It didn't help that her lips had filled with soft, pulsing heat. 'I hope you both rot in hell,' she breathed thickly.

'But you still want me, as that beautiful, quivering, hungry mouth is telling me.' He smiled a very grim smile. 'And if you were not so battered and bruised I would show you how much you want me.'

'I—'

He saw the lie coming, the tight repudiation of his arrogant confidence, and he swooped, claiming her parted mouth and pressing her back into the pillows. The long length of his torso followed, exerting a controlled power that stopped just short of crushing her beneath his weight. Nell felt taken over, overwhelmed, besieged. The scent of him, the heat, the way he used this kiss to demonstrate the difference between taunting and a full sexual onslaught. Hot tingles of sensation flared up from nowhere with the stabbing invasion of his tongue. Fierce heat rushed through her bloodstream, desire like she'd never known before set her groaning in protest and lifting up her hands to push at his chest.

But Xander was going nowhere, the unyielding contours of his body remaining firm as he deepened the kiss with an unhidden hunger that had Nell stretching beneath him in a wild sensual act that arched her slender shape from breasts to toes. He moved with her, a very male thigh finding a place for itself between her thighs. The bedcovers should have lessened the coiling spring of intimacy she was experiencing but did nothing of the kind.

She tried to drag in some air but found that she couldn't. She tried to separate their mouths but he had control. His tongue slid across her tongue and set it quivering as it hungrily began to follow his lead. Nothing had prepared her for a kiss like this. A kiss that sparked senses alive in every intimate place she had. When his hand covered the arching thrust of one of her breasts she almost shattered into little pieces, writhing and gasping as the rosebud nipple stung as it tightened to push into his palm.

He muttered something, went to move away, her hands stopped pushing at his chest and slid up to bury themselves in his hair so she could hold this amazing, sensational mouth clamped to her own. She didn't know she had the ability to behave like a wanton, but wanton she felt and wanton she acted, writhing beneath him, ignoring the many twinges of physical agony because everything else that was happening to her was oh, so much more important. When his thigh pressed into greater contact with the apex of her thighs she went up like tinder, a thick cry of pleasure coiling in her throat.

A knock sounded at the door. Xander drew back like a man bitten. Eyes like burning black coals scorched her a blistering look. Two hot streaks raked his high cheekbones; his mouth pulsed visibly even though it was suddenly stretched taut. She was panting and still clinging to his hair, the green of her eyes glazed by the stunning shock of her own loss of control.

'This had better be your awakening, *cara*, or you're dead,' he blasted down at her, voice rusted by jealous desire.

Before she could construct any kind of answer he had moved away, landing on his feet beside the bed. He did not look at her again until he'd stridden to the door and grasped the handle. The pause he made then sang between them, stretched taut and raw by that final rasping threat.

He was angry—*still* angry. The kiss had been delivered in anger, the deliberate assault of angry passion that left her lying here hot and trembling, shaken to her core by her own response, her mouth, her body, her deserted breast with its stinging nipple feeling utterly, shamefully bereft.

'Hypocrite,' she heard herself whisper across a throat thickened by the bubble of tears to come.

The charge swung him round to lance her with a hard, glinting look. 'And primitive with it,' he extended grimly. 'Forget the lover,' he warned thinly. 'You will not be laying eyes on him again.'

The note in his tone brought Nell upright. 'Why—w-what have you done to him?' she demanded in alarm.

'As yet—nothing.' His eyes blackened dangerously. 'His fate rests in the future when I have more time to discover if he taught you more than just how to kiss.'

Nell blinked then blushed at his thinking behind that revealing comment. He thought it was Marcel who'd taught her to kiss as she'd just done! Her kiss-numb lips parted to speak a denial then closed again. Let his primitive side twist his gut, she thought angrily, lowering her gaze from the piercing hardness of his. Let him learn what it felt like to imagine her locked in naked passion with another man as she had spent the last year imagining him with Vanessa the tramp!

'I will be away for the next few days but will be back in time to collect you from here on Saturday.'

This final piece of news brought her eyes flickering up again as he opened the door and left without another word, allowing whoever had knocked on the door earlier to come into the room.

It was one of his personal bodyguards, his polite greeting spoiled by the tough look on his face. He placed something down on the bedside cupboard. 'Mr Pascalis gave his permission for you to have these,' he said, then went to leave the room.

'H-how long have you been standing out there?' she asked, horrified that he might have heard or—worse—seen what had been going on in here through the little window in the door!

'Since you arrived in this hospital,' Jake Mather replied.

Nell stared at the door closing behind Jake Mather's bulky frame. She'd been under guard without even knowing it. She was in prison. She had been completely surrounded and isolated from the outside world. A shiver shot through her. It was like being back at Rosemere only worse.

Mr Pascalis gave his permission... She turned her head to look at what Xander had kindly given his permission to.

It was a neat stack of papers—tabloids—broadsheets—magazines. Reaching out to pick the top one of the stack, she let it unfold so she could see the front page in all its damning glory. 'Greek tycoon's wife tries to kill herself after he flaunts his mistress.'

No wonder he saw no threat in a scandal—it was already here!

She plucked up another paper and another, swapped them for the magazines. Scandal galore was splashed across the pages. There were even photographs of her wrecked car! She turned the page on those pictures quickly as nausea swam up inside.

But there was no mention of Marcel anywhere, which told her exactly what Xander was doing. Her imprisonment here had nothing to do with contracts or primitive demonstrations of ownership—but with damage control, pure and simple damage control!

He didn't want it reported that his wife had been leaving him for another man when she crashed her car!

He would rather they report that she was attempting to kill herself. What did that say about the size of his ego?

Kill herself? Where had they dragged up that big lie from? Had Xander himself put it out there?

She hated him. Oh, God, she hated him. No wonder she was being so thoroughly isolated. He didn't want her retaliating with the truth!

Leaving him for another man... Oh, how she wished she'd managed to go through with it. She would have written her own headline. 'Wife of philandering Greek tycoon leaves him for Frenchman!'

CHAPTER THREE

STANDING unnoticed in the doorway, Xander watched Nell's trembling fingers grapple with the intricacies of fastening the tiny pearl buttons on the silky white blouse he'd had delivered to her along with a blue linen suit that did amazing things for her slender shape.

Someone had fixed her hair for her and it lay in a thick, shining, sandstorm braid to halfway down her back. She looked very pale, though the bruising on her face had almost disappeared. But it was clear to him that even the simplest of tasks still came as an effort.

She was not recovered, though the doctors had assured him that she was fit to travel and for now that was all he cared about: getting her away from here and to a place void of tabloid gossip—and the temptation to contact her lover the first opportunity she was handed.

His blood began to boil when he thought about the elusive Marcel Dubois. The Frenchman had disappeared into the ether like the scarlet pimpernel, and maybe showed some sense in doing so—sense being something he had not shown when he'd decided to make his play for the wife of Alexander Pascalis.

Wife... He could almost laugh at the title but laughing was not what was lurking inside him. His hooded eyes took on a murderous glitter as he watched Nell struggle with those tiny pearl buttons. Had his wife in name only lain with her Frenchman and allowed him to touch what Xander had not touched? Had Dubois seen power in her soft, willing body and those little confidences a woman like the love-vulnerable Nell would reveal to a lover about the emptiness of her marriage?

She turned then and noticed him standing there. His libido instantly kicked in to join the murderous feelings as her eyes

36

began to make their rise up from his shoes to the casual black brushed-cotton chinos covering his legs and the plain white T-shirt moulding his chest. No other woman had ever looked at him the way Nell looked at him, with a slow, verdant absorption that drenched him in hellishly erotic self-awareness. She could not help herself, he knew that, which made the idea of her giving those looks to another man all the more potent. When she reached his shoulders, covered by the casual black linen jacket he was wearing, he could not halt the small recognising shift of muscle that sent a shower of pleasurable static rushing through his blood.

One day soon he was going to give this awareness true substance, he promised. He was going to wipe out all memory of her other man and introduce her to his power with all its naked, hot passion.

He was no neanderthal; he did not need a woman to be a virgin to enjoy her. But this one, this beautiful freak of modern living with her innocence steeped in womanly desire for him that she still did not have the tools to hide whatever the Frenchman had taught her, was going to open up like a chrysalis under his guidance and fly with him into ecstasy. She owed him that much.

She'd reached his face at last and Xander lost the murderous look to give her the benefit of a slow, easy smile, which she dealt with by flicking her eyes away. Nell was no fool. The last time he was here he had thrown down the sexual gauntlet and the smile was to remind her of it.

'Ready to come with me?' he enquired with the kind of soft challenge that had her breath feathering a quiver across the thrust of her breasts.

'I have no make-up,' she complained. 'You forgot to send it.'

'You don't need make-up. Your beautiful skin does not need it.'

'That's a matter of opinion.' Her chin lifted, eyes pinning him with an arctic green look. 'I've seen the waiting Press out there,' she said with a flick of a hand towards the window.

'Witnessing me leaving here looking black and blue won't help your cause, Xander.'

'And what cause is that?' The sexy smile was beginning to fade, Nell noticed.

'Damage control,' she replied. 'I presumed you would want me to look utterly love-blind and radiant for the cameras.'

'Your tongue is developing an aspish tone that does not suit it,' he drawled, moving further into the room with his graceful stride. 'Can you manage that last button on your blouse or do you need assistance?'

'I can manage.' Her chin dipped, her fingers moving to quickly close the button. 'The fact that I'm unhinged and suicidal does not make me totally useless.'

Xander hooked up her jacket from where it lay on the bed. 'You must admit, Nell, it made hilarious reading.'

'You think it's a big joke?'

'You clearly don't.'

Neither did he by the look on his grim face. The jacket arrived around her slender shoulders, held out absolutely perfectly for her to slide her arms into the sleeves without needing to strain herself.

'They presented me as a spiritless fool.'

'And me as the ruthless womaniser.'

'Better that than a man that cannot keep his wife happy—hmm?'

Nell turned to face him with that aspish challenge, but it was the first time she'd actually stood in front of him in goodness knew how long and it came as a shock to be reminded of his overpowering six feet two inches of pure masculinity compared to her own five feet five inches' more diminutive build.

Black eyes glinted narrowly down at her. 'Are you deliberately goading me into proving you wrong?'

Remembering the kiss of a few days ago, she felt her stomach muscles give a hectic quiver. 'No,' she denied and lowered her eyes in an attempt to block him out as his long fingers smoothed the jacket fabric into place.

'Then take my advice and hold back on the barbs until we can achieve guaranteed privacy.'

As if on cue, the door swung open and the doctor who'd been overseeing her recovery strode into the room. He and Xander shook hands like old friends then proceeded to discuss her as if she wasn't standing right beside them.

So what was new there? Nell asked herself as she stood with her eyes lowered and said not a word. From the moment he'd stepped into it, Xander had been arranging her life for her as if she wasn't a part of it. Their very odd courtship, the contract he had discussed with her father but not with her that she didn't bother to read. The marriage that had taken place in her local church but was put together by his efficient team with very little input from her. So why bother to make a fuss that he was discussing her health with the doctor he'd probably hand-picked to go with the private hospital he'd moved her to without her approval?

The only time he'd ever really listened to her was on their wedding night, when she'd refused to make their marriage real. She might have been upset, angry—hysterical enough to be a turn-off for any man, but she also knew that when he agreed to leave her alone, the final decision had been his. He could have changed her mind. He could have seduced her into weakening to him.

But no, what Xander had done was walk away—easily. Nell cringed inside as she thought it. He'd gone back to his life as if she was not in it, other than for those few token visits aimed to keep up appearances.

As the discussion about her needs went on around her Nell began to feel just a little light-headed because she'd been standing up for longer than she'd done since the accident. Her legs felt shaky and the solid prospect of the nearby chair was almost too tempting to resist. But if she showed signs of weakness now they might decide to keep her here and the risk of being incarcerated for another single hour was enough to keep her stubbornly on her feet.

By the time the doctor turned to say his farewell to her, her fixed smile was wavering though. Xander reached out to take her arm, had to feel the fine tremors shaking her and abruptly cut the goodbyes short.

Two minutes later she was walking down the corridor with his grip like a vice and his grim silence ominous. They entered a lift, the doors closed behind them. Xander propped her up against the wall then remained standing over her as they shot downwards, his grim face strapped by tension. The moment the doors slid open again, he was taking her arm and guiding her out of the lift.

Nell showed a brief start of surprise when she realised they had not arrived in the hospital foyer but in a basement car park and she had never felt so relieved about anything. Not only had Xander pre-empted the Press pack but his black Bentley stood parked right there in front of them with Jake Mather standing to attention by the open rear door.

Nell sank with trembling relief into soft leather. The door closed as another opened. Xander arrived at her side and within seconds they were on the move.

So what came next? she wondered wearily when, a short minute later, Xander was on his mobile phone, lean dark profile wearing its power mask as he talked in smooth, liquid Italian then switched to rich, sensual Greek for the second call he made.

Uttering a small sigh, she closed her eyes and just let the sound of his voice wash over her—only to open them again with a start when her door came open and she found herself blinking owlishly at Xander, who was leaning into the car and unlocking her seat belt.

She must have fallen asleep. As she was too disoriented to do more than let him help her out of the car, it took a few more seconds for her brain to register that she was not standing outside Rosemere.

'What's going on?' she questioned.

'Nothing.' With a coolness that belied the alarm that was beginning to erupt inside her, he turned her round so she could see the sleek white private jet standing on tarmac a few yards away. 'We are going home, that's all.'

'By air?' She blinked again as he drew her across those few yards towards the waiting flight steps. 'But it's only an hour by car back to Rose—'

'Greece,' he corrected. 'I need to be in Athens on Monday morning, and if you think I am leaving you alone at Rosemere to plot assignations with your Frenchman then think again.'

Greece, Nell repeated and stopped dead at the entrance to the plane. Her heart gave a punch against her sore ribs. 'No,' she refused. 'I don't want to go—'

'Don't make a fuss, *agapita*.' The flat of his hand at the base of her spine gave her a gentle push forward. Before she knew it, she'd been hustled inside the plane and the door was being closed.

Staring bemusedly at her luxury surroundings, she turned suddenly to make a protest and cannoned right into Xander's chest. The breath left her body on a tense little whoosh and she tried to take a defensive step back, but his arms came around her, strong and supportive. It was like being surrounded by the enemy, frightening and suffocating.

She breathed in anxious protest. 'Please…'

'Please what?'

His voice had deepened and roughened. Glancing up, Nell saw the dark, simmering spark in his eyes and tried one final breathless, 'No…'

But his mouth found hers anyway, moulding her lips and prising them apart to allow his tongue to make that slow, sensual slide against moist inner tissue that made her breath quiver as her senses tingled with pleasure. She wanted to pull away but instead her mouth crushed in closer. She wanted to deny this was happening at all but once again her mind was not in control. He murmured something, she didn't know what. But his tongue when it delved deeper sent her hands up to clutch at his chest and, as strong male muscle rippled beneath her fingers, he eased her even closer to him.

His thighs pressed against her thighs, the solid evidence of his desire pushing against the tense flatness of her lower stomach. Damp heat sprang out all over her and on a very masculine growl he deepened the kiss some more. Dizzily she clung to him, her breathing coming faster as the intensity of the kiss increased. Her head tilted backwards, arching her breasts into the solid wall of his chest. Her nipples sharpened like stinging arrows against him and she could feel the uneven thump of his heart and the fine tremor attacking him as he used long fingers to draw her more tightly against the sensual movements he was making with his hips. It was all so sexual, so overwhelmingly physical and exciting. A shimmering, quivering shower of desire dragged at inner muscles that seemed to scoop out the strength from her legs.

Then the plane's engines gave a sudden roar, breaking them apart with an abruptness that left Nell staring dizzily up at his face. She saw the tension there, heat streaking across his cheekbones, the flaring nostrils, the predatory burn in his eyes, and quivered out a constricted gasp.

He dipped his dark head and caught the sound, burnt this kiss onto her pulsing lips—then without warning took hold of her shoulders, turned and dumped her unceremoniously into the nearest seat then spun away in an odd jerky movement that kept her eyes fixed on him in giddy fascination.

He really wanted her. Badly. Now. The knowledge ploughed a deep furrow of heat down her front and held her utterly, breathlessly entrapped. When he suddenly twisted back round to look at her his eyes were so black she didn't even try to look for the brown. That one glance at her expression and he was growling out some kind of harsh self-aimed curse and coming down on his haunches to grimly belt her in. Her eyes clung to his taut features as he did so. She didn't even breathe when he moved away to take a seat on the other side of the aisle and strapped himself into it.

Nothing going on inside was making any sense to her any more; everything was just too new. The plane engines gave another roar then they were shooting forward with rocket propulsion that only helped to heighten the awareness pulsing back and forth.

'If you ever let another man touch you again I will kill you,' he rasped into the charged atmosphere.

Kill her—kill Marcel. The primitive man in him was beginning to take on a life of his own. Is this what untrammelled lust did to men—turned them all into angry, murderous, primeval beasts?

'Speak!' Xander lashed out, stopping her thought processes stone dead as he seared a blistering look across the aisle.

He wanted her to retaliate. To spit something back at him about Vanessa so he could shoot her down with some cruel remark. It was all to do with a need to finding an alternative release for all of this tension, but she turned her face away and refused to respond.

Couldn't respond; she was too locked up inside with what she was feeling herself.

They were already in the air and still shooting higher; the pressure in the cabin hummed in her head. Lifting a set of trembling fingers, she touched the place above her nose where the last and worst bruise on her face still lingered. She thought it would be throbbing, it felt as if it was but it was all over that was throbbing.

A click followed by an angry hissing sound came at her from across the aisle and she dropped the fingers back to her lap—only to find that Xander had moved with the speed of light, unfastening his belt to come to squat down in front of her again, his own long, cool fingers coming up to cover where her own had just covered.

'You are hot and in pain,' he muttered angrily. 'I apologise for my—thoughtlessness.'

Sounding stiff and very foreign to her now, 'I'm all right,' she managed on a shaken breath.

'You are not.' His fingers moved to one of her burning cheeks. 'Don't give me that stiff upper-lip stuff, Nell. I treated you roughly. You now think I am crass and uncivilised,' he brusquely pronounced. 'Did I hurt you anywhere—your injured ribs?'

Nell reached up to curl her fingers around his wrist to pull it away from her cheek so she could give a negating shake of her head and was instantly assailed by the sensation of strong bone and warm skin peppered with crisp dark hair. This was mad, she tried to swallow, found her eyes lifting to clash with his. Darkened emerald-green showing a complete helplessness as to what was happening to her. She'd spent so many months blocking out what she used to feel for him; now it was all pounding about inside her and she didn't like it.

She tugged her hand down again. 'Let me go home to Rosemere,' she whispered unsteadily.

'No.' It came out hard and gruff. 'Where I go you go from now on. I want you with me.' Eyes no longer black with passion but dark—dark brown and swirling with feelings that shattered the breath she tried to take.

'So you can protect your investment?' she hit out. 'Your bodyguards can do that just as well in England.'

'So I believed. You proved me wrong.' He sprang to his feet. 'We will not discuss this again.'

She only had herself to blame for what was happening to her now, in other words. She looked away from him, and had never felt so trapped in her life.

They landed in Athens to a blistering heatwave that almost sucked her of her remaining strength as they transferred to a waiting helicopter and immediately took off again. Three and a half hours on a plane, too much tension and stress, and she was beginning to feel so wiped out she could barely sit up straight.

'Where to now?' she asked as they swung out over a glistening blue ocean with this now daunting man at the controls.

'To my private island.'

Spoken like a true Greek billionaire, with an indifference that suggested that all Greeks owned their own island. Nell was too tired to do more than grimace at his arrogance.

But she couldn't stop the tip of her tongue from running an

exploratory track across her still warm and swollen full bottom lip, unaware that Xander witnessed the revealing little gesture and the way he had to clench hard on a certain part of his anatomy to stop the hot response from gaining in strength.

The island turned out to be a tiny baked brown circle of land floating alone in a crystal blue ocean. Nell caught sight of two white crescents of sand, a fir-covered hill in the middle, and a beautiful two-storeyed whitewashed villa with a swimming pool nestling in between the two sandy beaches.

They landed in an area close to the pool. Jumping out, Xander had to stoop as he strode round to the other side of the machine to open her door, then held out his hand to help her alight. She stumbled as he hurried her from beneath the rotors. A sharp frowning glance at the exhaustion wrenching at her pale face and he was scooping her off the ground.

'I can walk—'

'If you had to,' he agreed tersely. 'Which you don't.'

With a sigh, Nell gave in because she didn't have the energy to argue with him never mind the strength to put up a physical fight. Her head lolled onto his shoulder, his warm breath brushed her face as he carried her past the glinting blue pool and up a set of wide, shallow steps towards the house. A wall of plate-glass stood open ready for them and a tiny woman dressed in black waited to welcome them with a warm, crinkly smile.

She said something in Greek. Xander answered in the same language, his tone short and clipped. The old woman lost her smile and turned to hurry inside ahead of them, tossing long sentences over her shoulder that sounded to Nell as if Xander was being thoroughly scolded, like a child. He seemed to take it without objection, allowing the woman to lead the way across a cool hallway and up a flight of stairs.

They entered a beautiful room with pale blue walls and white drapes billowing at the floor-length windows covered by blue slatted shutters that helped to keep out the worst of the afternoon heat. Setting Nell down on the edge of a pale blue covered soft, springy bed, Xander clipped out an order and the woman hurried away, leaving him squatting down in front of Nell, whose head was just too heavy to lift off his shoulder.

'The journey was too much,' he hissed. 'I apologise.'

Again? Nell thought. 'I just want to go to bed.'

At any other time Xander would have jumped on such an appealing statement. But not right now, when it was clear she was totally wasted and he was worried and feeling as guilty as hell for putting her through such a journey before she had recovered her strength.

Reaching between them, he unbuttoned the lightweight blue summer jacket and slid it carefully from her shoulders then tossed it aside. The white blouse was silky, the tiny pearl buttons more difficult to negotiate from this position and he frowned as his fingers worked, the frown due more to her silent acquiescence. It was a good ten seconds before he realised that she'd actually fallen asleep.

The blouse came free and landed on top of the jacket, working by stealth, he gently laid her down against the pillows then shifted his attention to removing her shoes then the slippery silk-lined skirt and lace-edged stockings that covered her slender legs. Leaving her dignity intact with her lacy bra and panties, he was just grimacing to himself because this was as naked as he had ever seen his wife of a year—when he saw what he had missed while he'd been busy undressing her and it straightened his spine with a stark, rigid jerk.

She was so badly bruised he could not believe the doctor had dared to say that she was fit to travel! One whole side of her ribcage was a mass of fading purple and yellow, and he just stared in blistering horror at the two thick seat-belt lines, one that ran from her left shoulder diagonally across her body to her waist, where the other took over, strapping straight across her hips.

What the hell kind of speed had she been doing when she hit that tree to cause such bruising?

Had it been deliberate?

His blood ran cold at an idea he dismissed instantly. But the cold shock of the thought lingered much longer than that. And the guilt he had been feeling at the rough way he'd handled her on the plane grew like a balloon in his chest.

Someone tutted beside him. 'Oh, poor wounded child,' Thea Sophia murmured. 'What kind of man have you become, Alexander, that you bring her this far in this state?'

It was not a question he cared to answer. He was struggling enough with it for himself. Setting his mouth, he bent down to gather Nell into his arms again with as much care as he could manage.

'Pull back the covers, Thea,' he instructed gruffly. Ten seconds later he was resettling his wounded bride against the cool sheets of their marriage bed.

Did she but know it, he thought as he straightened a second time and stepped back to allow Thea to gently fold the covers back over Nell's limp frame. Her hair lay in a thick braid beside one of her cheeks and she had never looked so pale—or so vulnerable.

God give me strength, he thought grimly, glad that only he knew what plans he'd made for the beautiful Helen involving this island, some serious seduction, this room and this bed.

Shelved plans. He turned away, grim face mask-like as he watched Thea fuss around picking up Nell's discarded clothes and folding them neatly on a chair.

He made a decision. One of those quick-thinking, business-minded decisions he was more familiar with. It was called a tactical retreat.

Nell slept on through the sound of rotor blades stirring up again, slept through the whooshing din the helicopter made as it took off. She had no idea at all that while she slept Thea Sophia sat in the chair beside the bed, quietly working her lace with gnarled, nimble fingers while a maid just as quietly unpacked and put away Nell's clothes. The afternoon sun slowly turned the room golden. She only stirred when the sound of rattling crockery made her dry throat and her empty stomach demand she take note.

Opening her eyes, she took several long seconds to remember where she was, and a few more seconds' sleepily watching the old lady in black as she fussed around a table by the window across the room. Then the old lady turned.

'Ah, you are awake at last!' she exclaimed and came across the room with her crinkly face full of olive-toned smiles. 'My name is Sophia Theodora Pascalis,' she introduced herself. 'I am Alexander's great-aunt. You may call me Thea Sophia and I will call you Helen—such a proud Greek name.'

Was it? Nell had never given much thought to her name's origin.

'Of course, if Alexander were here he would have made the formal introductions,' Thea Sophia continued. 'But welcome— welcome to our beautiful island and our beautiful home, Helen.' Nell found her face being clasped between two hands in a warm, affectionate gesture, and released again.

'Th-thank you. I'm very happy to meet you, Thea Sophia,' Nell returned politely and it was impossible not to smile back in response.

'Ah, it is I who is happy to see you here at last.' The old lady stood back to beam a very satisfied smile then turned to walk back to the table by the window. 'We will become very good friends, you and I, *ne*? You will like it here,' she promised. 'When that stupid boy Alexander decides to get his priorities right and come back here you will makes lots of babies between you in that bed as is Pascalis tradition and we shall be a very happy family, *ne*?'

The baby part floated right by Nell, pushed out by the much more disturbing part of Thea Sophia's chatty speech. 'Xan— Alexander has…gone?' she prompted unsteadily.

'He took one look at your poor bruised body and took to his heels,' his aunt informed her in disgust. 'You would not believe that such a big strong man could be so squeamish, but there you go.' She added a very Mediterranean shrug. 'It will be his guilty conscience taunting him, of course. He was brought up to protect his loved ones. In this, with you, he failed. He will come back when he has come to terms with his…'

Nell had stopped listening. She was pushing the covers away from her body and staring down at her near-naked flesh. Hot

colour poured into her cheeks then paled away again when she
saw what Xander had seen.

'W-who undressed me?'

'Alexandor, of course.'

'Then he left...'

'Ne.' China chinked against china.

Nell sat up with a jerk and drew her knees up to her chin
so that she could hug herself. Tears were burning, hurt tears,
angry tears.

Xander had brought her to this island to seduce her—he'd
left Nell in no doubt whatsoever about that. One glance at her
miserable body and he'd seen his plans thwarted so he'd done
what he always did.

He'd walked away. Left her. Marooned her on this tiny island with this sweet but *old*, old lady, while he returned to his
busy, important life, the seduction of his wife shelved—again.

'You ready for a nice cup of English tea now...?'

CHAPTER FOUR

NELL stepped barefooted onto the sand, dropped her book and her sunglasses down at her feet then removed the wide-brimmed straw hat Thea Sophia had insisted that she wear to shade her face from the fierce rays of the sun.

Using the hat as a fan, she wafted it to and fro as she stood looking around the small cove she'd found during her first week here and since then made it her very own. It meant a stiff climb up and down the tree-covered hill to get here but it was worth it. The sand beneath her feet was sugary soft and hot, the sea a crystal-clear, smooth as glass, glistening blue, and in between the two lay a strip of cooler damp-silk sand kept that way by the flow and ebb of a lazy tide.

It was the stillest day since she had arrived here two weeks ago. Hot, breathlessly calm, exotically pine-scented and so exquisitely hush-quiet you could hear an ant move a leaf fifty feet away.

A wry smile played with her mouth as she stooped over again to place the hat over the book and sunglasses, paused long enough to scoop up a handful of warm sand then straightened again, green eyes fixed thoughtfully on her fingers as she let the sand filter through them while she tried to decide what she was going to do.

She was being watched. Not only was she very aware of that pair of eyes fixed on her, but she also knew to whom they belonged. She'd heard the helicopter fly overhead as she'd been strolling up the path that led over the pine-shaded hill on her way here. She also knew how he had found her so quickly. Yannis, the bluff, gruff odd-job man on the island and her latest guard would have told him where to look.

It made her curious as to whether it had ever occurred to

Xander that having her watched for every waking hour of the day meant that Yannis often saw what he was seeing right now as he stood beneath the shade of one of the trees that edged the little cove.

If her instincts were sending her the right messages, that was, and she knew that they were. Only one man had ever filled her with this tingling mix of anger, resentment and excitement just by looking at her.

There were two things she could do next, she pondered thoughtfully. She could turn round and confront him or she could ignore him and continue with what she'd come here to do.

The smile on her lips stretched wider. It was not a pleasant smile. The first option had never been a real contender, Nell had known it from the moment she'd heard his first footfall on the woodland path behind. There was no way that she was going to turn and let him know that she knew he was standing there.

It did not suit her purposes because she was about to show him just what it was he had been consistently rejecting for the last year. Show him how she looked without the bruises he'd turned his back on in favour of Athens and probably Vanessa's perfect, unblemished, *willing* charms.

Her fingers shook a little, though, as she began to untie the knot holding her sarong in place across the warm rise of her breasts. Her heart pumping a bit too thickly as she let the fine white Indian cotton slide away from her body to land softly on the top of the hat.

Underneath the sarong the new honey-gold tan she had been carefully cultivating shone softly beneath a protective layer of high-factor oil. Exercising three times a day by swimming in the pool or here in the sea had toned her up quite impressively—not that she'd been a slouch before the accident, but physical injury had taken a toll on her weight and her muscles.

Now, as she stood looking down at herself, a lazy finger absently rubbing in a previously missed smear of oil across the flat slope of her stomach, she was quietly impressed with how she looked even if it was vain to think it about herself. Whoever it was who'd packed her clothes for her in England must have been in romantic mood because they'd more or less picked out everything she'd bought for her non-starter honeymoon, like this bikini for instance, bought along with several others to seduce a husband who should have been her lover by the time she'd worn one of them.

The bikini consisted of a tiny white G-string that made only a scornful play at covering what it should, and a skimpy top made of two tiny triangles of silky fabric held together by two bootlace straps, one knotted around her neck and the other around her back. If she swam too energetically she came out of the top but—who cared? she thought with a large dose of defiance. She felt slinky and sexy and the G-string wasn't going to go anywhere because of the way it was held in place in the tight cleft of her buttocks.

So eat your heart out, Alexander Pascalis, she told him as she tilted her face up to the sun. Because here stands the unbattered version of the woman you turned your back on two weeks ago. And on that rebellious thought she moved into a long, slow, sensual stretch that accentuated every slender line of her figure from arms to spine to smoothly glossed buttocks and long, slender legs, held the pose for a few seconds then released it and began running lightly down to the sea.

In the shade of the tree, Xander watched the start of her little exhibition from a lazy, relaxed stance with one shoulder resting against the tree trunk.

She knew he was here, he was almost certain of it. She had to have heard his footfall on the path on such a still day. So, what was she thinking about as she stood there sifting sand through her fingers? Was she contemplating how he would react to a handful of the sand thrown in his face?

He knew she was angry with him. He knew she felt dumped and deserted when he'd left her here the way that he did. But what other choice had he had at the time? He had a wife who was not yet a wife and a marriage bed that was not yet a marriage bed that his aunt fully expected them to share.

Playing the loving husband who'd had a whole year to lose the edge to his sexual desires for this woman had not been an option he had been able to take. Put him in a bed next to Nell and despite the bruises he would not have been able to keep his hands to himself.

She was beautiful—look at her, he told that nagging part of his conscience that kept on telling him he could have sorted something out which had not involved shifting himself across the Aegean in a bid to put temptation out of reach.

The long, slender legs, the slender body hidden beneath the white sarong she had tied round the firm thrust of her breasts. The pale copper hair left free to ripple across slender shoulders tanned to a smooth honey colour since he'd seen them last.

Turn to look at me, *yenika*, he urged silently. Give me that slow, sensual glide with your eyes that turns up my sexual heat. I don't mind paying the price of the sand in my face.

But she didn't turn. Leaning there against the tree while willing the little witch to turn, Xander watched through eyes narrowed against the sunlight as she untied the knot holding the sarong in place then allowed the scrap of fine white Indian cotton to slide away from her body and fall on top of the hat.

His heart stopped beating. His shoulder left the tree trunk with a violent jerk. He could not believe what he was seeing. In fact he refused to believe it. It was the sun playing tricks with his eyes, he decided as he watched her move into a long, lithe stretch, which lifted her arms up as if in homage to the sun.

'*Theos*,' he breathed as his senses locked into overdrive. He'd seen many women in many different stages of undress. He'd seen them deliberately playing the temptress in an effort to capture his interest but he never expected to see this woman do it—never expected to see her wearing anything so damned outrageous!

Maybe she did not know of his presence. Maybe she was playing the siren like this because she truly believed there was no one to see!

Then he remembered Yannis—warned to follow her every

move because he did not trust her not to find some way to flee again. The idea of any other man enjoying the sight of his wife parading herself in what could only be called a couple of pieces of string had a red-hot tide of primitive possessiveness raking through him and sent his head shooting round, glinting black eyes flashing out a scan around the area, hunting out places a silent guard could watch unseen.

Then she dropped out of the stretch and his attention became riveted on Nell again as she began to run down to the sea, light steps kicking up soft, dry sand then leaving small footprints in the wet as she went. She hit the water at a run, her beautiful hair flying out behind her. In a smooth, graceful, curving dive, she disappeared beneath the smooth crystal water, leaving him standing there hot, damp in places, feeling as if he had just imagined the whole thing!

Nell swam beneath the surface until her lungs began to burst then she bobbed up like a seal, took in a deep breath then struck out with a smooth, graceful crawl towards the edge of the little cove where the rocky landscape on this side of the island rose up in a sheer slab for several feet she'd always thought would be great to dive from but had not yet found a way to reach the edge up there.

The tiny cove was perfect for swimming in because its two flanking outcrops gave her something to aim for when she swam across the cove. Making a neat racing turn, she started back in the other direction. She loved swimming, always had from being small. She'd swum for her school and won a few gold medals too. In Canada she'd scared her mother by swimming in the Kananaskis River, and before getting married had been a regular visitor to the local public swimming pool. When she'd married Xander, he had changed all of that by closeting her at Rosemere, which had its own pool, so she did not have to leave home to swim. On the rare occasions he'd turned up at the house unexpectedly to find her using the pool, she'd glimpsed him standing by the bevelled glass doors watching her cut a smooth line through the water—not that she'd ever let him know that she'd known he was standing there. When you hated and resented someone you ignored them as much as possible then they could never know what was really fizzing around your insides.

She made sure she did not look his way now, though the fact that she knew he was there watching her filled her with a mad, crazy, excited exhilaration as she cut through the water with smooth, darting strokes that barely caused a ripple on the ocean surface.

She was halfway across the cove when he struck, swimming beneath her and closing his hands around her waist. Nell let out a shrill, high-pitched scream and almost drowned as she gulped salt water into her lungs just before Xander lifted her high out of the water, rising like a big, black-eyed Poseidon out of the sea with his catch gripped between his hands.

'You shameless, ruthless provocateur!' he bellowed at her, then brought her sliding down the length of his body until her face was level with his.

Still coughing and choking, and almost hyperventilating with shock, Nell felt her skin slither against hard, tough, hair-roughened skin, legs, breast—*hips*! 'Oh, my God,' she gasped out. 'You've got no clothes on!'

'*I* have no clothes on?' he bit out angrily. 'What the hell do you think it is that *you* are wearing?'

Clutching at his satin-tight shoulders because she had to clutch at something, Nell lowered her eyes from the fury burning in his, then wished she hadn't when she saw to her horror that the two wet triangles of silk that should be covering her breasts had shifted and now two tight pink nipples were pouting at her like reckless taunts. Colour pouring into her wet cheeks, she flicked her wide eyes back to his blazing eyes and opened her mouth to retaliate with something—but he got there first, slamming his mouth onto hers with all the angry passion that had driven him through the water, submerged and unseen until he could grab her from underneath.

It was a kiss like nothing she had ever experienced. Open-mouthed, hot, frenzied and deep. It didn't help that they were both still panting from their energetic swim, both hearts pounding like thunder, both straining wildly against each other, her fingernails digging into his shoulders, his like clamps around her slippery waist.

The rough sound of masculine desire ground from his throat and he broke the kiss to lift her high again, eyes like burning black coals as he dipped his head and latched his mouth onto one of her breasts. The greedy suck dragged a shocked cry of pleasure from her, and sent him in search of the other breast.

When he lowered her to recapture her mouth he moved his hands to her wriggling hips, used long, sensually sliding fingers to urge uselessly flailing legs apart then wrapped them firmly around his hips. She took the new intimacy with a breath-gulping quiver, felt the bold thrust of his penis, rock-solid and probing against her flesh. The G-string was no barrier. She was going to lose her virginity right here in the ocean to a man balanced on the edge between violence and passion, and what was worse, she didn't care.

His hands were moulding the tight curve of her bottom now, her fingers buried in the wet silk of his hair, fingernails clawing at his scalp. The kiss was so wild and hot and urgent she felt dizzy from it, then it was gone.

With an angry growl he thrust her from him, sending her floundering into the sea. She dropped beneath the surface. By the time she'd gathered enough sense to make the push back to the surface he was already pounding his way back to the beach.

It was the worst, most devastating rejection he had ever dealt her. For a horrible few seconds Nell thought she was going to faint. If she could she would be turning and swimming out to sea just to get away from the fresh burn of rejection she was feeling but he'd sapped her strength, taking it with him like some lethal, heartless virus, leaving her with this hot, sensual, dragging feeling that was so new to her she didn't know what to do to ease herself out of its grip.

She watched him rise out of the water, a beautiful, wide-shouldered, long-bodied, bronze-skinned male without a hint of shame in his own nakedness. Toned muscles that moved and flexed in lithe coordination were caught to perfection by the water clinging to his flesh and the loving glint of the sun. He did not look back, and Nell could feel his anger emanating towards her back across the calm ocean and she hated herself for responding to him. Her breasts felt heavy, their tips tingling and tight. Even as she trod water in an effort to keep herself afloat her thighs had clamped together as if to hold in their first experience of a fully aroused man thrusting against the hidden flesh.

It took every bit of will-power she could drum up to make herself follow him, dipping beneath the water in an effort to cool the heat from her face and her body then angrily resettling her bikini top before she allowed herself to surface again then make deeply reluctant strikes for the shore.

By the time she reached it he'd pulled on a pair of smooth-fitting trousers, muscles clenching tightly across his glistening back when he heard the splash of her feet as she waded through the shallows to the beach.

Bending down, he scooped up her sarong, half turned and tossed it to her. It landed in a floaty drift of white on the damp sand at her feet, and he was already snatching up his shirt and dragging it on over his glinting wet skin.

Xander thought about apologising but he'd played that hand before and too often to give the words any impact. Anyway, he was not sorry. He was angry and aroused and he could still feel her legs wrapped around him, could still taste her in his mouth. He had an ache between his legs that was threatening to envelop him.

'You will not flaunt your body in get-ups like that excuse for a bikini,' he clipped out, heard the words, realised he sounded like a disapproving father, hated that, uttered a driven sigh that spun him about.

She was trying to knot the sarong with fumbling fingers. Her beautiful hair was slicked to her head. She had never looked more subdued or more tragic.

'And when we get around to making love it will not be out in the open for anyone to watch us,' he heard himself add.

'Behind a locked bedroom door on a bed, maybe,' she suggested. 'How boringly conventional of you.'

Subdued but not dead, Xander noted from that little piece of slicing derision. He could not help the smile that twitched at his mouth. It eased some of the passion-soaked aggression out of his voice.

'More comfortable too,' he agreed drily. 'I was treading water out there. I don't know how I kept us both floating. Add some of the really physical stuff and I would likely have drowned us in the process.'

'I can swim.'

'Not with me deep inside you, *agape mou*,' he drawled lazily. 'Trust me, you would have lost the will to live rather than let me go.'

She managed the knot. He had a feeling it cut off the circulation, it appeared so tight. And her cheeks went a deep shade of pink. He liked that. However, the look she sent him should have shrivelled his ego like a prune. It didn't though. The physical part of his ego remained very much erect and full.

'Such confidence in your prowess,' she mocked, stalking past him to scoop up the rest of her things. 'Don't they always say that those who boast about it always disappoint?'

'I will not disappoint,' he assured with husky confidence.

'Well, if you wait until it's dark to prove that, I can always pretend you are someone else, then maybe you won't.'

And with the pithy comment to cut him down to size where he stood she put the hat on her head and walked off towards the path.

A lesser man would react to such an insult. A lesser man, Xander told himself as he watched her walk away, would go after her and drag her down in the sand and make her take such foolish words back.

The better man picked up his socks and shoes and followed her at a leisurely pace, while he plotted his revenge by more—subtle methods.

Then a frown creased his smooth brow when he remembered something and increased his pace, only becoming leisurely again once he'd caught up with her and tempered his longer stride to hers.

Hearing him coming, Nell pushed her sunglasses over her burning eyes and increased her pace. She received a glimpse of sun-dappled white shirting, black trousers and a pair of long brown bare feet as he came up beside her, but her mind saw the naked man and her tummy muscles fluttered. So did other parts.

'I grew up on this island,' he remarked casually. 'As a small boy I used to walk this path each morning to swim in the cove before being shipped across to the mainland to attend school. Diving from the rocks is an exhilarating experience. The snorkelling is good out there, the fishing too—though I do not suppose the fishing part is of any interest to you.'

'You, used to fish?' Nell spoke the words without thinking then was angry because she'd been determined to say nothing at all.

'You think I arrived on this earth all-powerful and arrogant?' He mocked her lazily. 'In the afternoons I used to fish,' he explained. 'Having been transported back here after my school day was finished, with my ever-present bodyguard as my only playmate.'

Now he was playing on her sympathies by drawing heartstring-plucking pictures of a small, lonely boy protected and isolated from the world because of his father's great power and wealth.

'My parents were always off somewhere doing important things so I rarely saw them,' he went on. 'Thea Sophia brought me up, taught me good manners and the major values of life. The fishing taught me how to survive on my own if I had to. I used to worry constantly that something dreadful was going to happen to those who lived here on the island with me and I would be left alone here to fend for myself. I knew that my father had powerful enemies that might decide to use me in their quest for revenge. Before the age of six I had all my hiding places picked out for when they came for me...'

'Is there a point to you telling me this?' She would not feel sorry for that small, anxious boy, she wouldn't.

'*Ne.*' He slipped into Greek, which didn't happen often.

Xander was a man of many languages. Greek and Italian both being natural to him, the rest because he was good at them, and in the cut-throat, high-risk world he moved in it paid to know what the people around you were saying and to be able to communicate that fact.

'You think that you are the only one to have lived a strange, dysfunctional, sheltered life but you are not,' he stated coolly. 'I have lived it too so I can recognise the person you are inside because I am familiar with that person.'

Nell clutched her book in tight fingers and tried hard not to ask the question he was prompting her to ask, but it came out anyway. 'And what kind of person is that?'

'One who hides her true self within a series of carefully constructed shells as a form of self-defence against the hurts, the fears, the rejections life has dealt her from being small and vulnerable—like myself.'

Well, he certainly knows how to top up my feelings of rejection! Nell thought angrily. 'What rubbish,' she snapped out loud. 'And spare me more of this psycho-babble, Xander. I have no idea where you're going with it and I don't want to know.'

'Towards a deeper understanding of each other?' he suggested.

'For what purpose? So you can eventually get around to bedding me before you fly off to pastures new—or old,' she tagged on with bite. 'In case you didn't notice, I was easy prey out there in the water.' God, it stung to have to admit that. 'That means you don't need to achieve a greater understanding of me to get what you want.'

'You have always been easy prey, *cara*,' he hit back. 'The point at issue here is that I have always managed to avoid taking what has always been there to take.'

Nell pulled to a simmering stop. The hat and the sunglasses

hid her expression from him but there were other ways to transmit body language. 'I think you're into humiliation.'

'No,' he denied that. 'I was trying to…'

She walked on again, faster, her breath singing tensely from between her clenched teeth as she pumped her legs up the final stretch of the hill.

'Will you listen to me?' He arrived at her side again.

'Listen to you spelling it out for me that you married me because you saw your perfect soul mate? One you can pick up and drop at will and she won't complain because she's used to rejection, and all of this rotten isolation you prefer to surround her with?'

'I married you,' he gritted, 'because it was either that or take you to bed without the damned ring!'

Her huff of scorn echoed high in the trees above them. 'I was a business deal!' She turned on him furiously, brought her foot down on a sharp piece of gravel and let out a painful, 'Ouch!'

'What have you done?' he rasped.

'Nothing.' She rubbed at the base of her foot with a hand. 'And we've never shared a bed!' she flashed at him furiously. 'We've never even shared a bedroom!'

'Well, that's about to change,' he drawled.

I'm not listening to any more, Nell decided and dropped her foot to the ground to turn and start walking again, her legs and her body trembling with fury and goodness knew what else while her eyes still saw a tall, dark, *arrogant* man with tousled wet hair and a sexy damp shirt, dangling his shoes from his long brown fingers.

Topping the peak of the hill, she started down the other side of it. Below through the trees she could see the red-tiled roof of the house and the helicopter standing in its allotted spot by a glinting blue swimming pool.

All looked idyllic, a perfect haven of peace—sanctuary.

Sanctuary to hell! she thought. Her sanctuary had been in the isolation, not the place itself. Now Xander was back and the comfortable new world she'd created here was shattered.

She hated him so much it was no wonder her blood was fizzing like crazy as it coursed through her veins.

He did it again and took her by surprise, hands snaking around her waist to spin her round to face him. The shoes had landed with a clunk somewhere, her book went the same way. Next thing her hat came off, followed by her sunglasses, and were tossed aside. She caught a fleeting glimpse of a lean, dark, handsome face wearing the grim intent of what was to come, her breath caught on a gasp then that hard, hot mouth was claiming hers again and she was being kissed breathless while his hands roamed at will.

Her thighs, her hips, the smooth, rounded curve of her naked bottom beneath the covering sarong. He staked his claim without conscience, her slender back, her flat stomach, the still thrusting, pouting shape of her nipple-tight breasts. She was dizzy, narcotic, clinging to him, fingers clawing inside the shirt to bury into the tightly curling matt of hair on his chest.

It had all erupted without a warning gap now, as if one erotic encounter led straight into the next. He drew back from the kiss, face hardened by a burning desire that was no longer held in check.

'You want that we do it right here and now, Nell—up against the nearest tree maybe?' he gritted down at her. 'Or shall we go back to the ocean and complete what we started there? Or would you have preferred it if we had done it two weeks ago in the bed down there where you lay injured and weak? Or we could have whiled away the hours doing it on the flight over here. Or let us take this back to our wedding night, when you were so shattered only a monster would have tried. No,' he ground out. 'You will not turn away from me.'

His hands snaked her closer, cupping her behind to lift her into even closer contact. 'Do you understand now what I am trying to say to you? Look at us, *cara*,' he insisted. 'We are not what you would call passive about this. You hide your true self. I hide my true self. But here they are out in the open, two people with more passion for each other than they can safely deal with.'

'Only when you have the time to feel like it.'

'Well, I feel like it now!' he rasped. 'And if you refuse to listen to reason then maybe I will take you up against a tree, with your knees trapped beneath my arms and your heels digging into my back!'

Such a lurid, vivid picture made her push back from him, all big, shocked green eyes. 'You've done it before like that!'

Xander laughed thickly, so thoroughly disconcerted by the attack that he discovered he had no defence.

The whooshing sound of a helicopter's rotor blades suddenly sounded overhead, saving him from having to defend himself. They both looked up then Xander uttered a thick curse.

'We have a visitor,' he muttered.

'Who?' Nell shot out as they watched the helicopter swoop down the side of the hill then come to a hovering stop beside the other one.

There was a moment of nothing, a moment of hovering stillness in Xander that brought her eyes back to his face. He didn't look happy. He even sent her a grimace.

'My mother,' he said.

CHAPTER FIVE

HIS mother...

Nell's heart sank to the soles of her bare feet. The beautiful, gorgeous, always exquisitely turned out Gabriela Pascalis was paying them a visit and Nell looked like this—wet, bedraggled, and more than half-ravished.

Her voice developed a shake. 'Did you know she was coming here?'

There was a sighed-out, 'No,' before he changed it to a heavy, 'Yes... She said she was coming. I told her not to bother. I knew she would ignore me—all right?'

Nell flashed him a killing look. 'You didn't think to warn me about that?'

'We were busy talking about other things—I forgot.'

He forgot...

'And I suppose I was hoping she would listen to me for once...'

Nell didn't even grace that with the spitting answer sitting on her tongue. Turning, she began striding down the hillside, leaving Xander cursing colourfully as he gathered up their scattered things.

She knew that mother and son did not enjoy a warm relationship, in fact the best she could describe it as was cool. They met, they embraced, they threw veiled but heavily barbed comments at each other; they embraced then parted again until the next time. It was like standing in the middle of a minefield when they were together. One step out of line and Nell had a feeling that they would both ignite and explode all over her, so she'd tended to keep very quiet and still in their company.

Not that it happened often. It wasn't as if with a relationship like that mother and son lived in each other's pockets. Xander had his life and Gabriela had hers—par for the course with Xander's relationships, she tagged on acidly. The very few times that Nell had come into contact with both of them together was usually at one of those formal functions Xander would drag her to occasionally—to keep up appearances while Vanessa hovered around somewhere in the murky background, awaiting her lover's return.

Her skin turned cold as she thought that.

A shriek of delight suddenly filled the hillside, dragging her attention down the hill towards the house. She saw that the helicopter had settled next to the other one and Gabriela was now standing by the pool with her arms thrown wide open while Thea Sophia hurried towards her clapping her hands with delight.

To witness the dauntingly sophisticated Gabriela dressed in immaculate lavender silk fold the little black-clad bundle that was Thea Sophia to her in a noisily loving hug came as almost as big a surprise as the way Nell had just behaved with Xander up on the hill.

Where had all the warmth and affection come from? She would never have believed Gabriela capable of it if she was not seeing it with her own eyes.

The two faces of the Pascalis family, she thought grimly as she maintained a brisk pace downwards. Behind her was a man who had been as cold as ice for ninety-nine per cent of their marriage, suddenly showing her he had passion hot enough to singe layers from her skin! Now here was the drop-dead sophisticated mother putting on a demonstration of childlike adoration that would shock her peers—though anyone would love Thea Sophia, she then had to add with a brief softening inside. The sweet old lady would make the devil want to give her a loving hug.

As the two embracing women dropped out of sight behind the red-tiled roof of the house, Nell felt the silly burn of tears sting her eyes. It was stupid to feel hurt by such an open display of affection from Xander's mother for his aunt, but that was exactly what she did feel. Gabriela had never greeted her like that, never welcomed her with open arms and shrieks of delight. On those few tension-charged occasions they had met just the brief air-kissing of Gabriela's perfumed cheeks had always made Nell feel as if she were desecrating holy ground.

Or was it the other way around and she was the one who repelled deeper displays of affection? Had those defensive shells Xander talked about kept her mother-in-law at arm's length? She didn't know. She didn't even know if Gabriela knew the full truth about the true disaster that her son's marriage was.

The two women had gone from the pool area by the time Nell reached it. Making directly for the rinse shower that occupied a corner of the patio area, she switched it on and began washing the dust from her feet. The bottom of her foot still stung from its contact with the sharp stone, but as she was about to lift up the foot to inspect it she saw Xander arrive a few paces behind her and her full attention became fixed on him.

He had gathered up their things and was now placing them on one of the tables, tall, dark, uncomfortably alluring with his shiny wet hair, loose clothes and bare feet. Nothing like the man she was used to seeing—nothing. The other Xander was all skin-tingling, sophisticated charisma; this one was all—sex.

She looked away as he turned towards her, stiffened like mad when his hands snaked around her waist to gently crush fine muslin against her skin. A long brown foot with long brown toes appeared next to her foot so he could share the water sprinkling down on them.

Next the smoothness of his cheek arrived against her cheek. 'We are being watched, *agapita*,' he warned huskily as she tried to pull away from him.

It was all he needed to say to halt her attempt to escape. So she clamped her teeth together, kept her chin lowered and swapped one cleaned foot for the other and felt the intimacy deep in her trembling bones in watching Xander do the same thing.

'You're trembling all over. I like it,' he remarked in a sexy, husky groan by her ear, felt the heat mount her cheek and laughed softly as he brushed his lips against that tell-tale heat.

'I'm trembling because I'm angry with you,' she said. 'Look at me, Xander,' she then said heavily. 'I'm all wet and salty and now I have to go in there and meet your mother looking like this. You should have given me more warning then at least I could have found time to shower and change before she arrived...and she will know, won't she,' she then added unhappily, 'what the papers have been saying about us?'

'And that bothers you.'

'It bothers you too or you would not have brought me here and hidden me away like you have.'

His foot disappeared and she sensed a new grimness in him as he reached over her shoulder to turn off the shower. 'I did not bring you here to hide you,' he denied.

'Yes, you did. The same as you've been hiding me away all year.'

'So you thought you would make me wake up and take notice by involving yourself with another man?'

'Isn't that just typically arrogant of you to think I was trying to grab your attention?' She tried to move away again but he still would not allow it, the flat of his hand resting lightly but firmly against her stomach to keep her trapped in front of him. She sucked in a short, tense breath. 'I was leaving you, Xander,' she stated bluntly. 'And I was going, hoping never to set eyes on you again.'

'You did more than set eyes on me a few minutes ago, Nell, and I don't recall you turning away. In fact...' He turned her to face him. His eyes wore a hard glitter. 'I would say that you could not get enough of what you saw.'

'That was just sex.'

'And you know so much about it to sound so dismissive?'

Nell didn't answer. She was glaring at the ribbon of hard brown skin dressed with crisp dark hair showing between his gaping shirt and wishing with all her heart that her tongue didn't tingle with a desire to taste.

'We were talking about your mother.' She slewed her eyes sideways to stare at the glinting pool.

'She's here to discuss some family business.'

'Well, maybe she will be kind enough to give me a lift off this island when she leaves.'

'You think I would allow it?'

Green eyes flashed into contact with his. 'Would you like to repeat that bit about not hiding me?'

He went several steps further and lowered his dark head and kissed her, not hot and driven like before but slow and gentle with just enough passion to elicit a response. 'That is why you're here, *agape mou*,' he murmured as he lifted his head again. 'We are going to kick-start this marriage. *Then* let us see if you still wish to leave.'

Xander could say this in *that* tone of voice because she'd responded. He could say it because her fingers were already in contact with his brown skin. This beautiful, defiant, contrary creature might not want to want him but hell, she did want him, Xander thought grimly.

Letting go of her, he strode off, leaving her standing there knowing that he had won that little battle without her putting up much of a defence.

Waiting in the coolness of the foyer, he viewed Nell's arrival in the open doorway through carefully hooded eyes and had to lock his jaw to keep other parts of him under control. Lit from behind by the sunlight, she looked like a sea nymph standing in the jaws of a hungry shark.

He was the hungry shark. If they had been alone here he would be closing those jaws and carrying her off to finish what he'd started out there. He'd laid down the gauntlet as to where this marriage of theirs was going to go from here and by the way she was hovering in the doorway he would say that she knew she did not stand a chance of changing that course.

She began walking forward. As he watched her come closer his head played a tempting little scene that involved him carrying her up the stairs and laying her on the bed then stripping away the few scraps she wore.

Though maybe he would leave the G-string in place, he thought darkly, seeing his mouth tracing its skimpy white lines with a chain of tongue-tipped kisses that would have her begging him to take it off.

That was how he wanted her—begging. He wanted her spreading those slender golden thighs and inviting him in. He wanted her arms around his neck and her eyes pleading and—

A frown clipped his brows together. 'Go and make yourself presentable while I entertain our—guest,' he instructed.

'But your mother will think it rude if I don't—'

His eyes made a glinting sweep over the now damp strip of Indian cotton that was doing so little to hide the brevity of what was beneath. 'Trust me, you will feel better if you take time to change.'

A self-conscious flush mounted her cheeks. 'You don't look so presentable yourself,' she still had the spirit to hit back as she walked by him.

Xander just grinned. 'The difference being that I don't care what other people think when they look at me.'

Only because he still managed to look fabulous even with bare feet and his damp shirt lying open down his hair-tangled, muscle-contoured, bronzed front, Nell thought as she took to the stairs without further argument.

If she'd looked back she would have caught him quickly fastening buttons and combing long fingers through his hair. And the expression on his face had changed from lazily indifferent to grim.

He could have done without this intrusion from his mother today of all days. When she had rung his apartment in Athens this morning with an urgent request to see him, only to be told he was coming to the island, the last thing he had expected was for her to promptly invite herself and he'd told her not to come.

Though in truth, now she was here, he had some things of his own he needed to thrash out with his mother, things he preferred to get out of the way before his single-minded seduction of his beautiful wife continued along its present course.

Thinking about that exciting creature he'd met in the cove an hour ago set his nerves on edge. Nell had turned the tables on him with her provocative performance, and what was bothering him was why she had done it.

As the aggravating witch had just pointed out, three weeks ago she had been leaving him for another man.

A man, no less, that she'd been trying to contact via the telephone in his study here ever since she'd arrived on the island, but, like himself and the small army of people he had out there looking for him, Nell had discovered that Marcel Dubois had effectively disappeared from the face of the earth.

Scared of the repercussions when he heard of Nell's accident and knew that her husband was about to find out about them? If so, the Frenchman should have thought about those repercussions sooner—before he lured Nell into taking flight.

But that was not the point that was troubling Xander right now as he stood outside the salon door, grimly tidying himself. Nell was still trying to contact the cowardly swine yet she'd responded to him like a woman who'd been suppressing her desires for too long.

Hedging her bets? Using him as a substitute for her new love? Had that bastard woken her up to her own sexual desires and after three weeks without him she was hungry enough to let any man have her—even the one she believed was having an affair with another woman?

Anger bit its sharp teeth into him at the mere idea of another man taking what belonged to him. He threw open the salon door and stepped inside to the smell of his mother's perfume and to see an aunt who was all beaming smiles because her favourite person had come for a visit.

Shame that the son did not feel the same way. 'OK, Madre, let us make this brief. I have more important things to do than listen to your business troubles today.'

'I think you have already been dealing with your—business, *caro*,' his mother drawled with a swift up-and-down glance of his dishevelled state despite the attempt to tidy up. 'And there was I, thinking as I flew here that at last Alexander will know what it feels like when a marriage flounders on the rocks...'

'Your marriage did not flounder; you scuppered it,' he incised.

'If you two are going to fight I will leave you,' Thea Sophia put in and headed for the door, her beaming smile lost. 'You might also like to embrace each other *before* you tear each other to pieces,' she added sternly before she walked out.

Fifteen minutes later and Nell was coming down the stairs again after the quickest shower on record and with her freshly washed hair rough-dried by an urgent towel then left to do its own thing while she scrambled around for something suitable to wear. The fact that whoever had packed for her in England had chosen almost all of the clothes she'd bought for her non-existent honeymoon did not make the choice a simple one. One, the clothes had been bought with Xander and romance in mind. Two, they were now a full season out of date. So to have to put on one of the slinky off-the-shoulder short dresses in last season's rich jade colour did not give her confidence a major boost as she hovered outside the salon door, running nervous fingers down a mid-thigh-length dress that might do good things for her eyes and her figure but was going to look out-of-date to her super-elegant, fashion-guru mother-in-law.

That she'd stepped into a war zone took Nell about two seconds to register. Xander was lounging in one of the chairs, looking for the world like the king of all he surveyed even with bare feet—while he shot angry sparks at his mother.

Gabriela was sitting opposite him, giving the cool appearance that she did not notice the sparks. Heaven had left nothing out when they made this beautiful woman, Nell thought enviously. The sleek black hair, the sensational dark eyes, the long, slender figure which could pull off any fashion statement with panache.

As he turned his head to look at her, Nell felt a blush coming on as Xander let his eyes narrow then linger on her shining hair with its still damp, spiralling ends touching the hollow of her back. She'd tugged the dress up onto her shoulders as far as it would let her but it still looked low-cut at the front and slinky—as those too expressive eyes had already assessed.

'Ah, Helen, there you are.' Her mother-in-law's smooth voice brought her eyes swinging in her direction as Gabriela rose gracefully to her feet. 'You look delightful, *cara*,' she smiled as she came towards her, her expression revealing nothing as she swung her eyes down over Nell's dress, but the criticism was there, Nell was sure that it was. 'Enchantingly clean and fresh as you always look,' Gabriela added, then they air-kissed while Nell tried not to cringe at the 'clean and fresh' bit. 'And such hair! I am sure it grows two inches longer each time I see you. You know,' she eyed Nell shrewdly, 'with the touch of a gifted stylist I know in Milan it could be the most—'

'You will leave Nell's hair alone,' Gabriela's son interrupted as he rose to his feet. 'I like it exactly the way it is.'

'Don't be snappy, *caro*,' his mother scolded. 'I was only going to suggest that if you gave me a week with Helen in Milan I could truly turn her into—'

'I will extend on that,' Xander put in. 'You will leave Nell alone altogether. I like *all* of her exactly the way that she is.'

'Well, of course you do,' his mother agreed. 'But—'

'*Exquisito, mi amore.*' Placing his mouth to Nell's cheek, Xander spoke right over whatever Gabriela's but was going to be. 'Don't listen to her,' he advised. 'I do not need another fashion slave in this family.'

'I am not a slave to fashion!' his mother protested.

'The couture houses of Europe wipe their feet on you, Madre, and you know what makes it so crazy?' He looked down on her from his superior height. 'You would look amazing in whatever you chose to wear, be it sackcloth. They should be paying you to wear their clothes.'

'They do,' Gabriela informed him stiffly. Then because, like Nell, Gabriela clearly did not know if he was teasing or being cruel, 'Oh, go away and put some dry clothes on,' she snapped, wafting a slender white hand at him. 'You make a compliment sound like an insult and confuse me.'

Xander made no attempt to enlighten her as to which had

been his intention. He was angry, Nell noticed, so she had to assume the insult was what he'd meant.

He went obediently enough though, pausing long enough to assure Nell that he would be back before Thea Sophia arrived with refreshment for them all. The door closing behind him left Nell and Gabriela alone with a small silence to fill.

Gabriela did it. 'We were arguing when you came in, as I am sure you noticed. Alexander likes to have things all his own way but cannot always have it.'

The way her eyes slid away from Nell made her wonder if the argument had been about her.

Or the ugly rumours about their marriage seemed likely.

'Strong men are like that,' Nell found herself saying—as if she knew much about them.

'You think him strong?' Gabriela quizzed thoughtfully. 'I think him arrogant to believe that I should sacrifice my... Ah, but let us not talk about it.' She cut herself off from saying what she had been about to say right at the intriguing point, as far as Nell was concerned. 'Tell me about your accident and how you are recovering,' she invited. 'A much more interesting subject...'

By the time they'd done to death the scant details Nell was prepared to give about her accident and her ensuing recovery, which she suspected by the far-away expression Gabriela barely heard, Thea Sophia arrived and the odd mood lightened as Gabriela found a true smile as she went to take the heavy tray from the older woman.

There was a small tussle, which Thea won, as Nell knew from experience that she would.

'Leave me be, Gabriela,' she said. 'I must feel useful or I may as well take to my bed and wait for God to come and get me.'

'Wait for God indeed,' Gabriela mocked as she went to sit down and the older woman crossed the room to set down the tray. 'What you need, Thea, is to be taken out of yourself. When was the last time you left this brown dot of an island?'

'This brown dot is Pascalis land,' the old lady responded. 'And you might not have liked it here, but I love it.'

'Which did not answer my question.'

'I do not recall when I last left it.'

'Then it is high time that you did. Since Alexander refuses to let me make-over his wife, I think I will take you to Milan, Thea, and we will give you a complete make-over then find you a passionate man who will stop you talking about waiting for God.'

To Nell's surprise the old lady let out an amused chuckle. 'He will be too old to fulfil my hidden passions.'

'Not these days, *carisima*,' Xander's mother came back. 'Today the old men have the Viagra to maintain their flagging passions and will be very useful indeed to you. No, don't sit down right over there, Helen. Come and sit here beside me.'

'Wicked creature.' Sophia spoke over Gabriela's command while Nell meekly did as she had been told. 'If my nephew were still alive he would lock you in your room for speaking so disrespectfully to me.'

'Ah, four years and I still miss Demitri,' Gabriela sighed wistfully.

'I was twenty-three when the war took my Gregoris and made me a widow but I still miss him every single day.'

It was news to Nell that Thea Sophia had been married!

'You miss his *passions*, Sophia?' Gabriela prodded teasingly.

'Of course!' the old lady declared. 'He was a big, strong, handsome man—as with all the Pascalis men. My bed felt cold for years.'

'I understand the feeling,' Gabriela sighed. 'Maybe we should go to Milan to find ourselves a new man each. A cold bed is no pleasure, Thea. You would have liked my husband, *cara*.' She turned to include Nell in the conversation. 'Alexander is just like him—hewn from rock on the outside and deliciously protective by nature, but so jealously possessive of me that he rarely let me out of his sight. Yet what did he do but go and die in two short seconds while I was out of the room!'

'What is this—a wake?' Xander strode in on the conversation, wearing pale chinos and a fresh white shirt.

'Your father was my one abiding love,' his mother said sadly.

'Maybe he was, but you...'

The rest of the 'but' was completed in some cutting Italian that literally froze the discussion and turned Gabriela pale.

Thea Sophia recovered first, bursting into a flurry of chatter as she handed out the small cups of strong black Greek coffee and Nell puzzled over what Xander could he have said this time to destroy his mother as effectively as that.

She cast him a hateful look, which he returned with a grimace that seemed to say he was already regretting whatever he'd said. But no apology was offered and after giving him as long as it took him to lower himself into the chair he had been occupying earlier, Nell flicked him another hard look then turned to Gabriela.

'A trip to Milan sounds very exciting,' she said. 'I've never been there and I've had a yen to have my hair cut—short and spiky,' she added for good measure while Gabriela's eyes began to glow. She knew what Nell was doing and it was working. Xander shifted in his chair. 'Perhaps I could come with you,' she suggested. 'It would be fun to spend lots of money on new clothes and things, try out a new image—'

'Try for a full recovery before you make any plans,' Xander grimly put in.

'I am recovered,' Nell insisted. He was eyeing her narrowly, warning sparks glinting at her now instead of his mother. 'I've had two whole weeks under Thea Sophia's tender care to aid my recovery.'

'You were the good patient,' Sophia put in, bending to pat Nell's cheek fondly as she handed her a cup of coffee. 'You should have seen the extent of her bruising, Gabriela,' she declared in dismay. 'No wonder Alexander could not bear to look at them. Where were his protective instincts when this poor girl drove her flimsy car into a tree? She was bruised from here to here.' A gnarled hand drew a slashing left-to-right diagonal line in the air across Nell's chest then added the other line across her stomach.

Nell saw Xander's brows shift into a sharp frown as he watched the vivid demonstration take place.

'Car seat-belt burns, Helen called them,' his aunt continued in disgust. 'I call them criminal. Who would want to ever wear a seat belt again if they had suffered such damage?'

'Think of the damage without the belt, Thea,' her great-nephew pointed out. 'Nell lost her appendix, cracked her ribs and got off lightly into the bargain, if you want the truth.'

'While you were on the other side of the world getting your name in the newspapers and—'

'That is enough, Sophia…'

It was Gabriela's quiet command that brought a halt to it, her dark eyes flickering from Nell's suddenly pale face to her son's cold, closed one. The old lady resorted to mumbled Greek as she bustled back to her coffee tray, leaving a tense silence in her wake.

It screeched in Nell's head like chalk across a blackboard— a white chalk that had scraped itself across her cheeks. She wanted to jump up and run out of the room but she didn't think her trembling limbs would make it. So she stared down at the brimming cup of strong black coffee she balanced on its saucer and tried to swallow the lump of humiliation that was blocking her throat.

She'd known that her useless marriage was public property so why should she feel so upset that Thea Sophia was so willing to remark on it?

Xander shifted in his chair and she flinched a look at him from beneath her eyelashes. His eyes were fixed on her, narrowed and intense.

The lump in her throat changed into a burn as tears decided to take its place. In desperation she turned to Gabriela.

'How—how long do you plan on staying?' she asked in a polite voice that came out too husky.

Her mother-in-law was looking at her in dark sympathy, which hurt almost as much as Thea's thoughtless words had done. As Gabriela opened her mouth to answer, Xander got there before her.

'She will not be staying.' It was blunt to the point of rude.

Nell ignored him. 'It w-would be nice if you could stay a few days,' she invited. 'W-we could get to know each other better—'

'My mother does not do getting-to-know-you, *agape mou*,' Xander's hateful voice intruded yet again. 'She lives a much too rarefied life, hmm, Madre?'

Gabriela's lips snapped together then opened again. Like Nell, she was grimly ignoring her sarcastic son. 'I am afraid I cannot stay,' she murmured apologetically. 'I came because I need to discuss some business with my son.'

'Just business?' he mocked.

Nell couldn't take any more, ridding herself of the coffee-cup, she jumped to her feet. 'What is it with you?' she flashed at the sarcastic devil. 'Trying to have a polite conversation with you around is like living inside a tabloid newspaper—full of sarcasm and innuendo!'

'That just about covers it,' Xander agreed.

'Oh, why don't you just shut up?' she cried, making Thea Sophia jerk to attention, and Gabriela's eyes opened wide. 'You know what your problem is, Xander? You are still that resentful little boy who swam alone in the sea. You forgot to grow up!'

'*I* forgot to grow up?' Xander climbed to his feet. 'Where the hell have you been for the last year?'

'Right where you put me until I decided I'd had enough of it,' Nell answered fiercely. Cheeks hot now, green eyes alight with rage.

'So you decided it would be fun to drive you car into a tree?'

Fun? He thought she had done it for *fun*? 'Well, we all know what you were doing because you featured in the newspapers so prominently,' she tossed back. 'Would you like me to tell them what I was doing while I was having *fun* crashing my car?'

'Watch it, Nell.'

Now he was deadly serious. You could cut the tension with a knife. Nell's chin shot up. Xander towered over her by several intimidating inches but she faced up to his threatening stance.

Shall I tell them? her angry eyes challenged him while their audience sat riveted and the desire to unlock her aching throat and shatter his impossible pride to smithereens set the blood pounding in her head.

His face did not move, not even by an eyelash, hard, handsome and utterly unyielding like a perfectly sculptured mask. The cold eyes, the flat lips, the flaring nostrils—he was warning her not to do it—*daring* her to do it.

The pounding changed to a violent tingling. Taking Xander on was becoming a drug that sang like a craving she just had to feed. Her lips parted, quivering, and that stone-like expression still did not alter even though he knew it was coming—he *knew*!

Then another voice dropped cool, calm, curiously into the thrumming tension, 'Helen, darling, did you know you are bleeding from the base of your foot...?'

CHAPTER SIX

NELL broke vital eye contact with Xander to glance dazedly down at her foot, where, sure enough, blood was oozing onto the base of her strappy mule. The sharp stone on the hillside, she remembered, and was about to explain when Xander struck, seizing the opportunity to scoop her up off the ground!

'Get off me, you great brute!' she shot out in surprised anger.

'Shut up!' he hissed as he carried her from the room.

'I have never seen such fire,' Thea Sophia gasped into the stunned space they left in the tension behind them. 'The child has been as quiet and as sweet as a mountain stream all the time she has been here.'

'She's certainly found her voice now,' Gabriela drily responded.

'She's found more than her voice,' Xander bit down at her as the salon door swung shut behind them and he strode across the foyer, heading straight for the stairs. 'She's found a compelling desire for a death wish!'

'Not feeling so sarcastic now?' Nell hit right back, still fizzing and popping inside with fury.

He stopped on the stairs, blazing black eyes capturing sparking green. His wide, sensual mouth was tight with fury, nostrils flaring like warning flags. The cold mask had broken, she saw, and felt the hectic sting of a dangerous excitement vibrate just about every skin pore.

'You are goading me for some reason,' he ripped down at her. 'I want to know why!'

'Death wish?' Nell answered in defiance, only to bury her top teeth in her bottom lip when his glittering eyes narrowed for a moment, widened—then flared.

He caught that bottom lip with his own teeth and robbed it

from her. As she drew in a startled gasp he held on and sucked, turning the whole crazy thing into a very erotic kiss.

Downstairs in the salon Thea Sophia made a jerky move to follow them. 'They will need—'

'Stay where you are, Thea,' Gabriela murmured quietly. 'I don't think they will appreciate the intrusion right now.'

'Oh.' Thea stopped.

'Mmm,' Gabriela agreed with the older woman's dawning expression. 'Your calm mountain spring is about to turn into a raging torrent, *cara*,' she said thoughtfully. 'And our angry, high-principled boy is about to learn what it is like to be caught up in such an uncontrolled flood.'

'You sound pleased about that.'

'Pleased?' Gabriela considered. 'I suppose I am. He never forgave me my raging torrent. Let him learn and understand how I felt.'

'Those two are man and wife. Your torrent took place out of wedlock and devastated more people than you care to recall,' Thea said curtly.

The sighed-out 'Yes,' took place as Gabriela came to her feet then walked restlessly over to the window, where she stood staring out at the glinting swimming pool, beyond which lay a crescent beach and an ocean of glistening blue.

'I've had enough of this place,' she decided suddenly and, turning back to the room, went to collect her purse. 'Tell Alexander we will deal with our business some other time—'

'Oh, I did not mean to chase you away, Gabriela,' Sophia said anxiously.

'I know.' Gabriela kissed the old woman's worried cheek. 'But I should not have come. Alexander did warn me he had no time for my problems and now I know why.'

'They've been apart for two weeks, Gabriela.'

'They've been apart for much longer than that, Thea.' Gabriela smiled ruefully at the older woman's rose-tinted view of life. 'Those two might be married, my sweet darling,' she broke the news gently, 'but they are not yet man and wife...'

The kiss lasted all the way up the stairs and into the bedroom. Nell only thought to pull back from it when she heard the door slam behind them with the help of a foot. Xander watched the liquid bewilderment darken her beautiful eyes as she stared up at him. He could feel her heart racing beneath the flat of his palm.

'I'm going to ravish you senseless until you tell me what it is you are up to,' he bit out thinly.

The heart rate speeded up. 'I'm not up to anything!' she denied.

But her cheeks began to heat—a sure sign that she was lying, the little witch. 'You have been playing me hot and cold since I arrived here! Do you think I cannot tell when someone has a hidden agenda? And don't blink those innocent eyes at me,' he rasped. 'I know when my strings are being pulled!'

'*Your* strings are being pulled?' Nell tried to wriggle free of his arms but he was having none of it, strong muscles flexed in a show of pure male strength. 'You've been threatening to ravish me since you turned up at my sick-bed!'

'What a good idea,' he gritted out with a teeth-clenching smile and headed for the bed.

Oh, my God, Nell thought and started to tremble. 'My foot!' she jerked out in the wild hope it would pull him up short.

It did. He stopped in the middle of the bedroom, cleft chin flexing, tiny explosions of angry frustration taking place in his eyes. Without a word he changed direction, carrying her into the bathroom, where he slotted her down on the marble top between the his-and-hers washbasins.

Her hair stroked Xander's face as she straightened away from him, her fingers trailing a reluctant withdrawal from around his neck. Her heart was still racing, the fine tremors attacking her slender frame, making his teeth grit together because he couldn't decide if they were tremors of anger or desire.

It was novel; he didn't think he'd ever been in this kind of situation before in which he was having to out-guess the confusing signals he was being sent. Women usually fell on him— wholesale. Having this beautiful, contrary creature try her best to tie him in knots was stinging to life senses he'd had no idea he possessed.

A taste for the fight. A deeply grudging willingness to play the game for a while just to see where she thought she was going with it. He knew where it was going. Hell, he was already there. She might have earned herself some respite with the injured foot but that was all it was—a brief time-out while the rest of it throbbed and pulsed in the quickened heat of his blood.

Reaching above her head, he opened a cupboard and fished around for a clean cloth and some other bits and pieces he kept up there. He was standing between her legs, her thighs touching his thighs and she wasn't moving a muscle. Yet another surge dragged on his senses as he dropped his arms and saw the way she was staring at the flexing muscles beneath his shirt. Narrowing his eyes, he watched as the tip of her tongue sneaked out to moisten her upper lip as he ran his fingers lightly down her thighs to go in search of the offending foot.

Mine, he thought as he watched that nervy pink tongue-tip, and let his hands pause so his fingers could draw some light, experimental circles across the soft skin behind her knees. She jolted as if he'd shot her. Her chin came up, their eyes clashed, his carefully unfathomable, hers as dark and disturbed as hell.

'Foot,' he said.

Her teeth replaced the tongue-tip, burying into the full bottom lip as she lifted her knee so he could grasp her ankle and remove her shoe. One glance down and he realised she'd offered him the wrong foot.

'The left not the right,' he said then began to frown. Something was niggling him about the left and the right side of this aggravating woman. What could aggravate him when they both looked more or less the same?

Beautiful, perfect, ripe for seduction.

She offered him the other foot. Removing the shoe, he dipped his head and used the cloth to wipe away the blood so he could check out the cut.

'You did this on the hill,' he recalled and she nodded.

'It didn't bleed then. The hot shower I took must have aggravated it—ouch,' she added when he pressed the pad of her foot around the small cut in search of foreign bodies.

Her toes wriggled, small, pink, slender toes with a shading of gold across their tops from the sun.

Xander's tongue moistened. 'Feel anything in there?'

'No. It's just stinging a bit.'

'Clean cuts do.'

'Speaks the voice of experience,' she mocked huskily.

Swapping the cloth for a packet of antiseptic pads, he ripped a sachet open with his teeth.

'I wet-shave,' he answered, bringing those incredible eyes flickering curiously up to stare at his lean, smooth chin. That pink tip of a tongue returned to replace the teeth as she studied him with a fascination that set the skin all over his body tingling. If this wasn't the most intimate she'd ever been with a man—not counting the interlude in the cove—then he did not know women as he thought he did.

'I cut myself sometimes. Usually when I'm—distracted.'

The colour bloomed in her cheeks as she caught his meaning. 'Hence the antiseptic pads.' She sounded breathless.

'And wound strips.' He ripped the protective cover off a small plaster next and bent to press it over the cleaned cut.

But he didn't let go, his gaze recapturing hers as his thumb began lightly stoking the smooth, padded flesh at the base of her foot in the same circling action he had used on the backs of her knees. Silence followed. He didn't think she was even breathing. No two people had ever been more aware as to where this was leading and any second now she was going to disappear in a shower of her own prickling static.

'Xander...' His name feathered helplessly from her.

He responded by releasing the foot so he could run his hands back up the length of her legs—only this time he slid them beneath the clingy little dress.

'You are gorgeous, you know that?' he murmured softly.

'You don't have to say—'

'Gorgeous eyes, gorgeous hair, smooth, satin skin...' His

hands moved higher in a slow, sensual glide. 'You have the heart-shaped face of an angel and the mouth of a siren, the blush of a virgin and the teasing skills of a whore.'

'That isn't—'

With a controlled tug he slid her towards him across cold marble until she fitted neatly to his front. Her eyes widened when she felt the hardening thickness at his crotch. He felt her revealing little quiver, watched her breasts shift on a stifled little gasp. Then her thighs tightened against him, narrowing his eyes on her very—very expressive face.

'You like this, don't you?' he taunted lazily.

Nell dragged her eyes away. 'I don't know what you're talking about.'

'Sex, *agape mou*,' he named it. 'You are quivering with delight because you love to know you can affect me like this.'

'For all I know you're like this with any woman you come into contact with,' she tossed at him, making a jerky shift in an effort to move back.

His hands held her clamped to him. His hips gave a slow, smooth, sensual thrust. She quivered like a trapped little bird as damp heat spread across the exposed and vulnerable centre of her sex.

'Do I apply the same reasoning to your response?'

He knew what was happening to her, Nell realised. How could he not when she was so burning hot? A stifled gasp shot from her when he bent his head, his lips moulding hers and taking control of them, his tongue darting into her mouth. Each time they did this it got worse, she thought dizzily as she fell into it with a hopeless groan and let her slender arms snake up and around his neck.

She felt strong muscles flex in his shoulders as he lifted her up from the marble, felt the hard and pulsing sexual promise in his body as he flattened her to his chest. Her legs had wrapped themselves tightly around him and they might as well have been back in the ocean with no clothes on because she could feel everything that was happening to him.

It was only when he tipped her down onto the bed that she

realised where they were now. With a gasping drag on her unwilling lips she broke the kiss to look around her. With a swimming sense of disorientation noticed for the first time that since she'd taken her shower earlier someone had been in here and closed the shutters over the windows to keep out the fierce heat of the afternoon sun. The room had a warm, soft, sultry feel to it as if it had been deliberately set for making love.

Even the bedcovers had been drawn back, she realised. Her gaze flicked back to the man lying in a languid stretch beside her on the bed, lazily reading each expression as it passed across her face. He offered her a mocking smile. The air went perfectly still in her lungs. He'd done it. When he'd come up to take his own shower he'd come in here and made this room ready for seduction as if it had always been a forgone conclusion that it was going to happen this afternoon.

'No,' she pushed out across taut throat muscles.

He merely held on to the smile and brushed a stray lock of Titian silk from her suddenly pale cheek. 'I've spent a whole year imagining you lying here with your beautiful hair splayed out around you and your beautiful mouth warmed and pulsing as it awaits the pleasure of mine.'

Sensation trickled right down the front of her. 'We are not going to do this,' she insisted shakily.

For an answer he began to unbutton his shirt. Nell stared as warm, bronzed skin roughened by dark hair began to make its appearance. Everything about him said man on a course he would not be moved from. Real alarm struck her with a frightening clarity.

She drew in a taut breath. 'Y-your m-mother,' she reminded him. 'W-we—'

'I don't need her permission to do this, *agape mou*,' he drawled.

'But she—'

He moved, long fingers leaving the shirt to come and frame her heart-shaped face from pale cheek to trembling chin. Pinpricks leapt across the surface of her skin as he bent to brush his mouth across hers. 'No more reprieves,' he murmured very softy. 'This is it, my beautiful Helen. It is time to face your fate because it is here…'

Her fate. Nell stared at him. He was deadly serious. To her horror he began to stroke the hand down her throat and across her shoulder, fingertips pushing stretchy jade fabric out of his way.

'Stop it!' she choked out and at last found the sense to put up a fight.

Dark eyes lit with a kind of cold amusement that chilled her as he captured her flailing fists and flattened them to the bed above her head. 'The little game you've been playing with me is over,' he said grimly. 'Accept it, for you are about to get your just desserts.'

'You're angry,' she gasped in shocked realisation.

His tight grimace confirmed it.

'But—why?'

The innocent question locked his lean, handsome face. 'I've done nothing but treat you with respect since we married and you paid me back by leaving me for another man.'

With his free hand he went back to undoing shirt buttons in a grim display of intent.

'Just thank your lucky stars that you did not make it, my beautiful Helen,' he glinted down at her. 'Or you would not be about to enjoy Alexander Pascalis the lover, but the other Alexander Pascalis—the one that makes big men quake in fear!'

'How do you know I didn't make it?' she prodded recklessly, staring as more and more of that muscled, bronzed, hair-roughened chest appeared. 'How do you know I didn't *make it* a dozen times during the week Hugo Vance wasn't around to stop it from happening?' she choked up at him. '*Before* I decided to leave you for good!'

The fingers stopped working the buttons. Nell heaved in a wary breath of air as a *frisson* of alarm shot across her heaving breasts.

'But you didn't, did you?'

It was a very seriously driven warning to be careful what

she said next, making her wish her mouth would just shut up—
but it wouldn't. He might already be wearing the face that made
big men quake, but she had a whole year's-worth of unfairness
pounding away inside her, and it needed to be heard.

'Y-you left me alone on our wedding night,' she reminded
him, beginning to struggle again to get free. He subdued her
by clamping a leg across her thighs. 'You refused to make
excuses or defend yourself—you couldn't even be bothered to
lie! I've had to live with that, Xander, not you. Y-you just went
back to your life and didn't care what you left behind!' Tears
were threatening, making her soft mouth quiver and turning
her eyes into deep green pools of hurt. 'W-well, you left me
behind w-with a twenty-four-hour guard to do the caring for
you! If I went to the local village shop Hugo Vance came along
with me. He had to do—he was in charge of the remote control
for the wretched gates!'

'He was there for your safety,' he bit back impatiently.

'He was there to control your limp rag of a wife!' she cried.
'You said that you and I are alike; w-well, tell me, Xander,
would you have lived my life for the last year without doing
something about it?'

'But I repeat—you didn't, did you, Nell?'

Nell lay there beneath him heaving and panting, his leg
heavy across her legs and her shining hair caught beneath the
hands he still pinned above her head. She glared hotly into a
face that was coldly mask-like, reminding her of that rock his
mother had talked about. And the stinging pinpricks attacking
her flesh were the sparks of her mutiny bouncing right off him.

Hewn, hard, handsome and so threatening she shivered. Yet
backing down now just wasn't an option she was prepared to
take. 'Do you think you are the only one that can be discreet
about their lovers?' she heard herself dare to challenge. 'Do
you think that because you didn't want me I should think myself unfit for anyone else?'

Maybe she did have a death wish, she thought tensely as a
new level of stillness locked his hard eyes on her face with an
expression that was too frighteningly inexplicable to dare to

read. He was eleven years older than Nell and at that precise moment she felt every one of those years boring holes into her head.

'Are you telling me—without the guts to make the full statement,' he pushed out finally, 'that you have taken lovers since you married me?'

Nell's quivering upper lip had to fight to break free from her bottom lip. 'Would it make me a lesser person in your eyes if I said yes?' she quavered huskily. 'Perhaps totally unfit for you to touch?'

It was living on the edge, Nell knew that as she said it, feeling more afraid of what she was prodding here than she dared let herself think. But she needed to know. She'd lived the last year loving a man who'd locked her up in a glass bubble marked, 'Virgin. Sole possession of Alexander Pascalis', as if it was the only thing about her that made her worthy of the place she held in his life, while he blithely continued to bed his mistress as if that was perfectly OK.

But the real point she was making was, would he still want to be here with her without the provenance?

A stifled gasp escaped when his hand came to rest beneath her breast, where her heart was racing madly. It began a gentle stroking as he lay stretched out, half beside her, half on top of her, a look of grim contemplation taking charge of his face. She'd stop fighting to get free and had never felt more vulnerable because she just didn't know what he was going to say or do next. His eyes weren't telling her, his expression wasn't telling her, even the light stroke of this hand wasn't telling her anything because she wasn't sure that he was aware it was doing it.

It was a test, Xander knew that. He was not so blinded by those beautiful flashing eyes and this sensational body he had pinned to the bed that he could not recognise a challenge when it was being tossed at him.

What he could not decipher was if the reckless little witch was talking like this because she wanted to hit him hard with the truth or because she was taunting him with the possibility of it being the truth.

Was it the truth?

He still did not know. She had still not made that *yes* a full-blown, bloody statement of fact.

Did it make a difference to how he felt?

To wanting to make love to her? Not the slightest difference to the desire pounding away in his blood.

To this creature he had respected more than anyone else in his entire life? Hell, yes, it made a difference there. Nell belonged to him. She wore his ring on her slender white finger. She had loved him so much once that he refused to believe that she was capable of making love with any other man but him.

But he discovered he was scared that in a fit of rebellion she might have done.

He pulled in a deep breath. The atmosphere was so thick with his long silence that he could taste it on his tongue as he slid his hand up to cover her breast. Its receptive tip stung to life to push into his palm and another strangled gasp escaped her soft, quivering mouth.

He looked at her hair spread out across the cover like a burnished copper halo. Then at her face, heart-shaped, exquisite but wary as hell. His eyelashes glossed over his gaze, dipped lower, across the smooth-as-silk shoulder he had exposed that looked so sexy and inviting, then further to where his long fingers cupped her breast over sensually moulding jade-coloured fabric. The tips of his fingers were in tantalising contact with smooth flesh just above the dress, where a little pulse was beating wildly. He stroked, she quivered, his body tightened in response.

Then came the rest of her, slender, flat-planed yet deliciously curvy inside the hugging dress. She was stretched out beneath him like an offering. But what exactly was on offer? Experienced lover or the beguiling innocent he'd walked away from on their wedding night and since suffered so many hot dreams about?

He slid his eyes back to her eyes, capturing a deep look of anxiety that pricked the hairs around his groin. The sultry heat of the afternoon shifted around them as he released a hissing sigh.

Time to find out. 'The answer is—no,' he stated very huskily then before the next stifled gasp could escape her he trapped it with his hungry mouth.

Nell felt herself go up in a plume of sharp static. The wait, the breathtaking silence, the scouring inspection of her body followed by his answer had shattered her tension and sent her spiralling out of control. Sensation latched on to every nerve-end, making each muscle she possessed stretch in long, sensual response then collapse into the driving power of his kiss.

He responded without hesitation, taking that kiss even deeper. It was as it had been in the water only far more de-manding, a wild, escalation of pleasure that would not let her be still and had her fighting to free her trapped hands so she could touch him as he was touching her.

He let the hands go, sliding his own hand over her hair to the side of her neck then the smooth skin of the shoulder he had exposed for himself. His mouth followed, pressing small kisses to her skin that had her fingers clutching at his head. Smooth, dark silk hair filtered through her fingers. The kisses reached the soft, pulsing mound of her breast. She released a tight groan then pulled at his hair, caught his mouth and began kissing him back so desperately it was almost frightening.

'Want me?' It was so harshly spoken that Nell thought he was still angry; opening her eyes, she expected to see the cru-elty of rejection about to hit her once again, only to find herself drowning in the smouldering, dark depths of desire.

'Yes,' she breathed.

His masculine growl scored her cheek as he plundered that soft, breathy answer. His hand returned to her shoulder, took a grip on the dress and pulled it down to her waist.

No bra—had he known that? The next masculine growl said yes, of course he had known it and long before he'd cupped her breast. He'd known from the moment she'd walked into the salon that she'd dared to come there wearing less than she should. Even her nervousness towards his mother had not been able to quieten the little devil at work inside her that wanted to torment him as she had been doing since he arrived in the room.

His mouth took possession of one pouting nipple while his fingers took possession of the other. The wet and dry rasping of tongue and fingers sent her into a paroxysm of gasping jerks and quivers. He knew what he was doing. He knew this was torture.

'Xander.' She groaned out his name in an anxious plea for mercy and received it when his warm, damp mouth came back to hers.

After that she lost touch with everything but her senses and him. He was an expert at this and so incredibly ruthless about it she barely had time to absorb one new exciting experience before he was overriding it with something else. Her flesh sang where he caressed it, her restless fingers digging into satin-tight flesh that rippled in response to the sharp edges of her nails.

His shirt had gone. Nell had no idea that she had removed it. Her dress lay in a discarded heap on the floor. He was kissing her breasts again, her stomach, her navel, tongue-tip sliding sensual moisture across her acutely alive and sensitised flesh. When he suddenly rose to his feet, she let out a cry of pained protest because she saw rejection coming yet again. When she realised what he was doing, she moved on her side to watch him unashamedly as his fingers worked to free himself of the rest of his clothes.

Eyes black with promise, he watched her watch him. Every movement he made was hard and tense—packed with sexual motivation that curled her up with excitement. The trousers were stripped from his body and deep green eyes made a slow, shy sweep of him that couldn't help but linger on the bold thrust of his erection. Arrogant, she thought, and, on the tight little sensation of alarm mixed with excitement, she gave it the right to be.

'The way you look at a man is going to get you into trouble one day,' he ground roughly into the tension.

'I only do it with you.'

It was an admission that brought him back to her side, his superior framework rolling her onto her back so he could cover her. Then the real seduction of his bride began. It was hot and it was deadly serious, an intoxicating journey into a dark new world that explored all her senses and tuned them to a thick, throbbing, aching pitch. No tormenting of her breasts now but long, deep suckling, hands stroking her everywhere, the knowing movements of his body keeping her floating on a desperate high. When he finally eased the briefs down her legs then stroked his fingers along her thighs she began whimpering uncontrollably because she knew what was coming, her body clenching and unclenching in a mad mix of uncertainty and need.

He took her mouth in a deep, drugging kiss as if he knew what she was feeling and was trying to soothe her fears as he reached that warm, damp, untouched place. Her head suddenly filled with dark noises, a swirling, whipping, throbbing pulsation that had her fingers clutching at him. He was hot, damp, tense and trembling, his breathing all over the place.

'Nell.' He said her name, hoarse and husky, then made that first gentle intrusion inside.

She went wild in a second, it was that devastating. Had her gasping and crying out as shocking, hot pulses of pleasure rushed into her blood. He was touching her in ways that sent her mindless, smooth, slick, knowing fingers dragging feelings from her she would not have believed could be as powerful as this. And she could feel the heat of his own desire feeding from hers with the plundering depth of his kisses and the shuddering pleasure he was getting from this.

'*Theos,*' she heard him utter in a deep, rasping growl, then he stretched, the length of his sleek, muscled frame sliding damply against her. '*Nell...*' He breathed her name like a caress, trying to reach wherever it was she had gone off to. 'I need to know if this is the first time for you.'

The first time, Nell repeated hazily, and lifted heavy eyelids to see the intensity burning in passion-glazed eyes and the savage control locked into his beautiful face.

'Of course it is,' she answered softly as if he should know that—and smiled.

His response was dynamic, the heated power of his kiss and the return of his caresses that drew her like liquid into thick, melting heat. She was lost and she knew it, blown away by sensation and the power he possessed to make her feel like this.

'Xander,' she whispered, feeling oddly as if he was slowly shattering her into tiny pieces.

He moved again, overwhelming in his maleness as he slotted himself between her thighs then made that first careful thrust with his hips. She felt his heat, his probing fullness. The shuddering strength with which he controlled the slow force of his entry was an experience in itself. Nell opened her eyes, found herself trapped once again by the spellbinding intensity carved onto his lean, dark features. He was big and bronzed and glossed with perspiration. The scent of his desire permeated the air. Sweat beaded his tautly held upper lip, his black eyelashes heavy over the bottomless black glaze of his eyes.

'You tell me if I hurt.' His voice was hoarse and husky.

She nodded, soft mouth parted, breathing reduced to small, thick gasps of quivering anticipation.

She felt the increased burn of his slow intrusion, the hunger, the reined-in control. Silken muscles flexed and he was trembling. She lifted her head to crush a kiss against his parted lips.

'Take it,' she whispered and the potent flare of masculine conquest lit his eyes when he made that final long, smooth stab that sent her arching against the bed in a moment of hot, stinging agony.

He caught the sound in his mouth as if it belonged to him, lips fusing like their bodies as she tensed and clawed at his hot, damp flesh that rippled with each helpless dig of her nails. His breathing was ragged, the tension holding him showing in the tremor of his fingers as they did their best to soothe the moment of discomfort away with gentle strokes of her face.

Yet, 'Mine,' he still breathed in rasping triumph, then the pain was dispersing and she was shifting restlessly beneath him. With a groan that lost him the final grip on control, he began to move again, plunging ever deeper while she made the wild leap into a mindless pleasure, clinging not clawing, riding the ever-increasing pace of his passion as it grew and grew until it exploded in a sense-shattering whirl of electrifying release. He followed her into that amazing place with convulsive rasps, which tore from his chest.

Too stunned by it all to do more than listen to the pounding of his heart as he lay heavily on her, Nell lay quietly beneath him while he laid languid kisses across her face.

'You surprised me,' he murmured.

'In what way?' She couldn't even find the energy to open her eyes as she asked the question.

His tongue teased her kiss-swollen bottom lip. 'You put me out of my misery when you could have damned me forever by letting me take you without knowing the truth.'

'Whether you are my first lover or not should make no difference.' She could not resist sliding her tongue across the tip of his.

'I am not built for innocence, *agape mou*.' He made a move with his hips so she could understand what he meant. He was still inside her, a thick, pulsing entity that filled her. 'I hurt you anyway, but not as much as I would have done without your generosity to keep me in check.'

'And your arrogance is showing again.'

'*Ne,*' he acknowledged lazily. 'But admit it—I did not disappoint.'

The remark was to remind her of her cutting little quip at the cove. Nell gazed up at him, watched him return the gaze with a dark-eyed, warm-lipped, wryly knowing smile. Beautiful, she thought helplessly, so indolently masculine and sure of himself. Her heart gave a hopeless little squeeze to let her know how much she still loved him despite every attempt she'd made to shut the feeling out.

Did he have any idea that the sex wasn't enough for her?

No, she was sure of it. He saw power in his undoubted physical prowess but wouldn't think to look beyond it for something deeper than that.

So what had she gained here?

Nothing, the hollow answer came back. If, that was, she didn't count intimacy wrapped around the kind of physical pleasure she never knew it was possible to experience.

For that alone she reached up to kiss him on the mouth. 'You didn't disappoint.' She was willing to grant him that much. 'Now all we have to do is wait to see if *I* disappoint…'

A frown grabbed his eyebrows, muscles flexing as he levered himself up on his forearms so he could narrow a questioning look into her face.

'You did not disappoint.' It was rough-toned declaration that vibrated across the walls of his cavernous chest and set her breasts tingling.

He was about to recapture her mouth when she added, 'I was talking about your other goal…'

'Goal?'

'To make me pregnant.' She spelt it out gently.

The comment acted like a cold douche on his lingering passions. He withdrew then rolled away from her. 'That was not my intention,' he denied.

'No?' Sitting up, Nell came gracefully to her feet then walked towards the bathroom on legs that felt too trembly and weak to carry her there, leaving that questioning little *no* hanging in the sultry air she left behind.

CHAPTER SEVEN

WATCHING her go, with her hair tumbling down her slender back helping to hide her nakedness from him, Xander wondered grimly how the hell she had walked him into that silken trap.

His body responded to tell him how. He hadn't used anything. He had not so much as glimpsed the distant idea of using anything to protect her from the risk of pregnancy—and not because of some fixed agenda he had been working towards, though he allowed Nell the right to believe that had been his ultimate motive. No, for the first time in his long sexual history he'd found himself too locked in the thrall of how she'd made him feel.

And if anyone from now on ever dared tell him that a condom did not stunt the pleasure of sexual intercourse then he would know they had never experienced what he had just experienced.

'*Theos,*' he breathed, turning it into a sigh as he threw himself flat against the bed then glanced down at his body, where the length of his shaft lay tight and proud against the flat of his abdomen, impatiently demanding more of the same.

It knew the difference. *He* knew the difference. He turned his head to glance at the closed bathroom door and wondered what Nell would say in response if he went in there and informed her that she had not been the only one enjoying a virgin experience in this bed.

Not one of his better ideas, he thought ruefully as that highly active part of his body gave another impatient tug. A confession like that would still not alter the fact that his intoxicating wife might be a virgin no more but her cynical view of him was still very much in tact.

And—hell, what could he say to make her believe that he'd harboured no deliberate intentions but had simply lost his head? The way his body was acting, it was not going to back him up. *It* wanted more—and more of what they'd just had. Prolific, rampantly free and potently unprotected sex shared with the beautiful, excitingly responsive woman who'd just left this bed.

Not just any woman—his woman.

His wife...

Sensation flipped a running ripple down his body. Turning his head on the pillow, he stared up at the ceiling where the lines of sunlight reflected on it filtered in through the slatted shutters then released a deep sigh of satisfaction at how good those two words sounded and felt.

His wife in fact and at last now in body. Why not enjoy sowing the seeds of that union? Why not tie the beautiful if cynical Helen to him so tightly she would never be free to attempt to leave him again?

See her walk away from their child-to-be with her Frenchman, he challenged grimly and felt hot, grinding jealousy stir in his chest. Who the hell was the guy that he believed he could poach his wife from him in the first place? *What* the hell did he have that made Nell want to go away with him so badly that she planned her escape a whole week before she crashed her car?

Then worse came, shifting him restlessly on the bed. Had the lily-livered swine chickened out at the last minute and Nell had been driving so fast because she'd been nursing a broken heart?

Did she love the guy?

Had she only let him make love to her here because she was thinking, what did it matter now?

It did not matter, he told himself. The Frenchman did not get her. He, Alexander Pascalis, did. Their marriage was consummated at last and whatever else came after this day, the one thing that would never change was that Nell now belonged to him right down to the last silken strand of hair on her beautiful head.

He settled back against the pillows, a look of grim calculation glinting behind his slowly drooping eyelids. The agenda was real. His cynical wife would have to get used to it because he was going to keep her barefooted and pregnant and too damn busy making love with him to pine for some fickle Frenchman who'd dared to break her heart.

That decision made, he relaxed his body, the sunlight glinting through the slats soothing in the soft, drowsy heat. In a second or two he would get up and join her in the shower he could hear running—consolidate his place with some very passionate seed-sowing and at the same time he would make Nell fall in love with him again. He could do it. She had loved him once. All it would take was some of his famous, single-minded ruthlessness to make her love him again...

Wrapped in a bathrobe, Nell stepped back into the bedroom to find the man of her dreams lying spread out on the bed and fast asleep. Her tummy muscles quivered at the picture he presented of bronze-muscled abandonment with his quietened sex still very much a daunting sight.

She'd half expected him to barge into the bathroom and demand she believe him that he had not deliberately set out to make her pregnant just now. Well, of course he hadn't. Any fool—even this fool called Helen Pascalis—could tell when a man was being ruled by his desires and not his intelligence.

Take note, darling Vanessa, she thought grimly. This man wanted me so badly that he couldn't stop himself from having me without the protection he stops to apply with you in bed. Now he sleeps on *my* bed with *my* kisses still moist on his skin and wearing the scents of *my* body on his warm golden flesh.

You're out, Vanessa, and I am most definitely in and with no intention of ever letting go. What I have right here, this time I keep.

It had taken her a whole year to recognise and understand that she had to fight for what she wanted instead of hiding away like some distant shadow waiting for Xander to remember that she lived.

Well, now she had him and she had no intention of letting

him go. A man who could tremble in her arms the way Xander
had trembled was hooked and she knew it with every single
fibre of her female being. And if she had to learn sensual wiles
that were probably going to get her him on end only to imagine
them, then she was willing to use them to keep her man.

Before too long, Xander was going to find himself chained
so tightly to her that he wasn't going to be able to take in a
breath without her knowing about it. Instinctively her hand
went to her cover her abdomen, inside which the seed of her
lover was busily performing its potent magic—or if not yet it
would be before too long.

A baby. Their baby. The next Pascalis heir. Eat your heart
out, Vanessa, because this is one thing you will never have,
she thought with grim satisfaction.

Ex-lover, she then corrected as she moved quietly towards
the bed with a new deeply felt sensual pulse to her movements
as she began to remove the bathrobe to begin her very first
seduction of any man.

A sound coming from beyond the shutters diverted her attention; dropping the bathrobe to the floor, she crossed to the
window to press a gap between two wooden slats and glanced
down to see that Yannis was carrying out one of his daily duties
and cleaning the pool.

Something else caught her attention. For a few short seconds
she stood frowning, trying to decide what was different out
there. Then her eyes alighted on Xander's helicopter where it
stood anchored to its concrete deck—and alone.

A strangled gasp broke from her. She suddenly remembered
the swirling, whipping noises as she'd lain in Xander's arms.
Those sounds were not the sounds of the whirring, pulsating
heat of their loving—they had been the sounds of his mother's
helicopter leaving the island!

'Oh!' A blast of mortification at the way they'd left Gabriela
kicking her heels downstairs while they made love up here had
her whirling round to run to the bed.

'Xander...' It was necessary to put a knee on the mattress
so she could reach his shoulder to give it an urgent shake.

'Wake up!' she insisted. 'Your mother has gone! You have to call her up and bring her back here. You—'

The snaking hook of a long, muscled arm toppled her onto him. 'Mmm,' he murmured sleepily. 'I was dreaming about you.'

'Will you listen?' she insisted, trying to fight him off and not to respond to the seeking warm brush of his mouth. 'I said your mother has gone!'

'I know.' The arm curved her closer. 'I heard her leave—didn't you?'

Nell flushed at what she'd believed the helicopter noise had been. 'You have to go and invite her back,' she said anxiously. 'She must be terribly offended to just go off like that.'

'You cannot offend my mother.' He was kissing her shoulder, the tip of his tongue gliding a sensual pathway towards her throat. 'Beneath the perfect gloss beats a heart of pure steel.'

Like the son; Nell frowned at the cool way he'd said that. 'Don't be cruel...'

'You taste of fresh water and soap.'

'I showered,' Nell mumbled distractedly.

'And removed my scent from your skin. Now I will have to put it back again.'

'But you need—'

'You,' he said. 'Again,' he added on a lusty growl as he leaned over to claim her mouth.

'Mmm,' Nell mumbled out a dizzy protest. 'Don't do that. Your mother. We have to—*What are you doing?*' she choked as his hand made a shockingly intimate dive between her legs.

'Making sure that you don't disappoint,' he returned smoothly, then laughed when her eyes widened in shock that he'd dared to actually admit it. 'A deal is a deal,' he said smoothly and flattened her to the bed.

Nell was caught in her own trap and she knew it.

When Xander had come back to the island to stake his claim on his bride, he did it by unleashing the full power of his sensual repertoire upon her that by far outstripped any ideas her naïve imagination she could have come up with.

He was amazing.

Any attempt to get him to talk about anything serious was thoroughly quashed by—sex. The kind of sex that could mercilessly slay her senses even when she was only thinking about it. He just had to look at her and she wanted him. He just had to say, 'Come here', in that rough-toned, desiring voice and she went like an eager lamb to the slaughter of her own common sense.

They played together, in the pool or in the ocean. He showed her how to reach the top of the rock flanking the little cove so they could dive into crystal-clear water beneath. He taught her how to fish from the selfsame rock then laughed himself breathless as she screamed in horror when she actually caught a fish.

And of course they made love—all the time, anywhere. Xander could not get enough of her and in truth Nell learned to use the newfound power over him with a feline ruthlessness that kept him forever and delightfully on his guard.

'I knew you would be dangerous once you discovered how to do this to me,' he complained late one afternoon after she'd spent the whole day taunting him with teases and half-promises and now rode him with slow and sinuous moves with her body that kept him pitched right on the edge, fighting not to give in because giving in before she did would fill her green eyes with so much triumph.

His skin was bathed in sweat and his hands were clamped to her supple hipbones. When she leant down to capture his mouth a whole new set of sensual muscles joined the torment. She caressed his taut cheekbones, the rasping clench of his jaw. She brushed the hard tips of her breasts against him and rolled her tongue around the kiss-softened contours of his lips before whispering, 'My lover,' then drew in every sensitised, beautifully tutored muscle to send him toppling over the edge.

As role reversals went, Nell knew she had cornered the market. She had him hanging on every flirtatious word and look and gesture like a besotted slave. On the occasions he grabbed back power just to remind her that he could do if he so desired to, she became the tormented one, the hopeless, helpless, besotted slave.

One week floated in perfect harmony into two then a third. Thea watched them and smiled a lot, and began crocheting an intricately patterned gossamer-fine christening shawl with a serene complacency that made Nell blush.

This was what she'd wanted, wasn't it?

Frowning as she bent to pick up a stray piece of driftwood off the shoreline, she sent experienced fingers gliding over its undulating ocean-smoothed contours the way her mother had taught her to do, while her mind drifted elsewhere.

She suspected she was pregnant. It was very early days yet to allow the suspicion to grow too large in her head, but her regular-as-clockwork period had let her down three days ago, and if Xander's virility was as potent as the rest of him then she knew, deep down, what it meant.

It changed everything. From believing she wanted to conceive his baby she now discovered that she didn't. Not yet, not like this. Not while they still hid from the real world on this tiny island where she felt more like a very indulged mistress than she did a wife.

A sigh broke from her, sending her chin tilting up so she could stare bleakly at the blue horizon. Xander could not remain hidden here for very much longer. As it was he needed to spend more and more time in his state-of-the-art study here dealing with business.

And Nell had pressing things of her own she needed to do— if she could only get to a telephone that did not have every call made on it carefully monitored.

Marcel. She was worried about him. She needed to know how he was and what he was doing. If he was cutting himself up with guilt and remorse or too angry with her to care that she was worrying about him.

When Xander did find it necessary to leave here, did he intend to take her with him this time or was she, in effect, still his prisoner whether it be behind the gates of Rosemere or here in this beautiful place?

He evaded the question each time she asked it. He evaded any discussion about life beyond here. Their honeymoon, he called it. A time to enjoy now, not what tomorrow had to bring.

But even a honeymoon as idyllic as this one had to come to an end some time.

She released another sigh. Xander watched it leave her as he stood in the window with the phone pressed to his ear. She was wearing a blue sarong today. Beneath the sarong would be a matching-coloured bikini, and her hair was up, looped into one of those casual knots she had a way of fashioning that always tempted him to tug it free.

His fingers twitched, so did other parts as he saw himself unwrapping the beautiful package that was his sensational, warm and willing wife.

Wife. *His wife.* As soon as he thought the words a blanket of seemingly unquenchable possessive desire bathed his flesh. He wanted to be out there with her, not standing here talking business on the telephone.

'I know I have to attend,' he snapped out, sudden impatience sharpening his tongue. 'I merely asked if there was any way it could be put back a week.'

No chance. He'd known it even before he suggested it. Wishful thinking was a useless occupation out there in the real world. And that was his biggest problem. Nell and this incredible harmony they had come to share did not belong in the real world. Nell, he'd come to realise, never did. Not in his world anyway. For the last year he'd kept her safely locked up inside a pair of iron gates, waiting, he'd told himself, for her to grow up before he attempted to redress the mess their marriage had become. In his arrogant self-confidence, he had not seen that she'd done the growing seething inside with resentment at the way he treated her. If she had not crashed her car, she would have been long gone with her Frenchman before he'd known anything.

And the way the guy had disappeared so completely turned

his blood cold when he thought of Nell disappearing with him like that.

'What of that other business?' he clipped into the telephone.

His frown deepened when an unsatisfactory reply came back.

'A man cannot drop from the face of the earth without leaving some trace, Luke,' he rasped out in frustration. 'I need you to find him. I need you to interrogate him. I need to know what his true intentions had been towards my wife!'

'And if it was a subtle form of kidnap?' he lanced back at whatever Luke Morell said. 'I will continue to think of her as in danger until I have answers... No, I will not leave her safety to the hands of bodyguards again. What use was Hugo Vance? Helen is my wife, my responsibility... Then let an empire crumble.'

Grimly he slammed down the phone, knowing he was being unfair, unwise—irrational. But how the hell else could he behave around a woman as unpredictable as Nell?

He'd spent three weeks in her constant company—had sunk himself into her more times than he cared to count! But did he know what made her tick? No more than he did a year ago when he'd wrongly believed he had her tagged and labelled—my beautiful, besotted wife.

She'd turned the tables on him that time. Then she'd done it yet again when she'd tried to leave him for her elusive Frenchman. OK, so this time he had managed to breach the damn citadel of her physical defences, but with Nell he could not afford to let the sex count for anything. He did not trust her, or that strange, glinting look he'd glimpsed in her eyes now and then. The little witch still had her own agenda, he was damn sure of it. She might love what he could make her feel, but did she love him...?

When you've had your fingers burned by complacency not once but twice, unless you are a complete fool you do not take chances on it happening again.

And what was she doing with that piece of driftwood? he questioned suddenly. The way she was caressing it was almost erotic. Was she imagining it was him—or someone else?

Jealousy. Uncertainty. He did not like feeling like this! With a grim clenching of every bone in him he spun away from the window, wondering what the hell he was going to do. He had to go to London. He did not want to take Nell with him. But was she going to accept that?

Not a chance in hell, he thought as he began gathering together papers that littered the top of his desk. Papers that were important to running an empire—yet all he wanted to do was hide away here with his wife!

A black scowl darkened his face as he strode into the hall-way. Seeing Nell stashing the piece of driftwood by the open door, he pulled to a stop as he made one of those clean-cut, uncompromising decisions that usually made him feel better about himself.

'We need to talk,' he announced brusquely.

'We do?' Surprise lit her tone as she walked towards him, a sensational, wand-slender, Titian-haired woman wearing a halo of sunlight all around her. 'Well that makes a change,' she drawled teasingly.

He was wearing white, Nell noted. Xander liked to wear white, white, loose, fine muslin shirts that allowed the gorgeously tight, bronzed shape of his body show through, and white linen trousers that fastened with a tie cord low on his lean waist. One tug at the cord and she would reveal the real man, she thought temptingly, felt the hot secretion of desire sting her senses and wished she had more control over herself.

But she didn't and her mouth quirked into a rueful smile that acknowledged her weakness as she came to a halt in front of him and lifted her face for a kiss.

It didn't arrive. She focused her eyes on his hard, handsome face. He was cross, she realised. Her smile died.

'What was the smile for?' he demanded suspiciously.

'Well, it was for you but I've taken it back. What's the scowl for?' she countered.

He made an impatient flick with a long-fingered hand. 'I have to go to London today,' he told her abruptly.

London. Her eyes lit up. 'OK,' she said. 'So you don't have to sound so cross about it. I'll go and pack and we can—'

'No.' Xander used the refusal as if it were a landmine he was setting down in the small space between them. 'You will stay here.'

Nell's chin shot up again, green eyes making full contact with grimly uncompromising brown, then for the space of ten taut seconds she gave no response. Not with her steady gaze or her closed, perfectly formed mouth—or any other part of her, yet some inner body language had to be speaking to him because Xander tensed every muscle he had.

'It's business,' he clipped out as if that justified everything. 'I can be back here in two days. No need for both of us to uproot.'

'Do you want sex before you leave?'

It was not an invitation. In fact it was more like a cold slap in the face. The provocative witch, Xander thought heavily. 'Not if you are going to turn it into a punishment,' he returned drily, then grimaced because he was aware by the tingling of his flesh that he'd take the punishment if it was all that he was going to get.

'Goodbye, then,' she said and abruptly turned about.

She was going to walk away! Shock lanced through him. Didn't she care one way or another if he took her with him or not?

'Nell…' He rasped out her name not sure if it was said in anger or appeal. Then he took a step forward to catch her arm and the explosion erupted. She swung back, green eyes alive now and flashing with rage and biting contempt.

'What do you want from me, Xander?' she lashed out at him. 'Do you expect me to smile happily as I wave you off? Do you think I *like* knowing I'm a prisoner here, that I can only leave this island at your behest?'

'It's for your own safety.' He frowned darkly.

'For your peace of mind, you mean.'

'I have enemies! How do I know that your Frenchman isn't one of them until I locate him so that I can find out?'

'You mean—you're actually looking for him?' Her eyes went wide with shock.

His hooded. 'My people are.' He made yet another terse gesture with a hand. 'Your fate lies in what he has to say for himself.'

But his people hadn't found Marcel yet, Nell surmised from that and could not keep the relief from showing on her face.

Xander saw it. His own face hardened. 'You know where he is!'

She went to turn away again but his grip on her arm spun her back round. Defiance roared through her system. 'Don't manhandle me,' she protested angrily.

'Tell me where he is,' Xander hissed.

'Where's Vanessa?' she retaliated.

'This is not about Vanessa!'

'Well, I'm making it about her!' she flashed. 'Tit for tat, Xander,' she tossed back. 'You tell me all about your mistress and I'll tell you about my—'

'He was never your lover,' he derided before she'd even got the final word out.

But he wasn't denying that Vanessa was his! 'Not physically,' she conceded. 'But emotionally? How would you know if I love him? You wouldn't know about emotional love if it jumped up and bit you!'

The scorn in her voice had him tugging her towards him. Even as she landed hard up against his chest she was registering that something inside him had snapped. With ruthless intent he caught hold of the silken knot holding her hair up and used it to tug her head back then capture her angry mouth.

Titian silk crackled when it tumbled over his fingers as they strained against each other right there in the hall. Thin cotton beachwear was no barrier to hide what was happening to him but Nell was determined she was not going to give in to it. He was equally determined that she would.

A sound somewhere close intruded on the struggle. With an angry growl Xander scooped her up and swung her into his study, kicked the door shut behind them as he strode across the room to drop her on the soft leather sofa then followed her with his weight.

There the struggle continued. She plucked at his skin through his thin clothes with angry fingers, he forged a path with urgent fingers between her thighs.

'Stop it,' she gasped as his touch set her sobbing because she could feel herself responding even though she hated herself for it.

'Why?' he breathed tensely. 'This is not emotional enough? You think I go crazy like this for anyone? You think that you would feel hot and as willing as this for your Frenchman's touch?'

That he did not want an answer showed in the way he crushed her mouth open and plundered its sensitive interior. He was jealous of Marcel. He was doing this from the burning depths of a jealous rage. If she didn't stop him he was going to take her like this with none of the preliminaries then hate himself for it afterwards.

Closing her fingers in his hair, she pulled his head back to free her burning mouth. 'I think I'm pregnant,' she told him shakily, and watched as shock totally froze him, the colour draining out of his face.

In the pin-drop silence that followed neither of them took a single pounding breath, then Nell's mouth gave a vulnerable little quiver and he jackknifed away from her, landing on his feet by the sofa with his back towards her, muscles flexing all over him as he came to terms with what he had just been about to do.

Nothing like a good shock to turn the heat down, Nell thought bitterly and sat up, shaking fingers pulling her sarong back into place.

'Sorry to spoil your farewell,' she heard herself add with the slicing cut of embitterment.

His dark head jerked as if she'd hit him. In many ways Nell wished that she had. She had never felt so shocked and shaken. Without saying a word he just walked from the room.

Nell couldn't move. She thought he'd taught her everything

there was to know about making love but now she knew differently. A soulless slaking of lust that he dared to call emotion had not shown up in his repertoire before.

Nor had it prevented her from almost toppling into its cold, murky, thick depths. She started to shiver she was so cold suddenly, hating herself—despising him.

On the other side of the door Xander had frozen again, eyes closed, face locked into a taut mask of self-contempt. He did not want to believe that he had just done that. He did not want to remember the pained look on her face when she'd said what she said.

Pregnant. He flinched. What had he done here? How had he allowed three weeks of damn near perfection sink as low as this?

Marcel Dubois. The name arrived in his head like a black taunt.

No excuse, he dismissed. No damned excuse for doing what he had. The hand he used to scrape through his hair was trembling. Grimly he made for the stairs with a sudden dire need to wash the shame from his skin.

Nell was just trying to find the strength to stand up when the telephone on Xander's desk began to ring. She thought about ignoring it but something stronger than good sense pulled her like a magnet towards it and had her lifting the receiver off its rest.

When your life shatters, it really shatters, she thought blankly as a soft, slightly husky female voice murmured, 'Xander, darling? Is it all right for us to speak?'

The receiver clattered as it landed back on its rest. Pale as a ghost, Nell turned and walked to the door and out of the room then out of the house.

The piece of driftwood stood where she'd left it. Why she picked it up she hadn't a single clue but she hugged it to her front as she walked around the side of the house and took the path that would take her up the hill.

CHAPTER EIGHT

Two hours later, dressed for his trip to London in tailored black trousers and a crisp white business shirt, Xander gave up trying to locate Nell on foot and decided to take to the air instead. His mouth was tense, his lean face set and severe. He left an anxious-looking Thea standing by the pool, wringing her hands.

'Why did you have to fight with her?' she'd scolded him earlier. 'She's a good girl, Alexander. A trip to London to see her *papa* would not have put you out.'

The 'good girl' part was still cutting into him. The fact that Thea had overheard just enough of their fight to draw her own conclusions did not help his riddling feelings of guilt as the helicopter blades wound up, disturbing the hot morning as he took to the air.

Sat huddled on a rock hidden beneath the deep shade of a tree close to the spot from the one they usually dived from, Nell listened as the helicopter flew overhead.

He was going—leaving her here despite everything. Why she thought he might have a change of mind now he knew her suspicions about the baby she didn't know—but she had thought it.

Her eyes flooded with hot, helpless tears.

Vanessa. She shivered, feeling cold despite the fierce heat of the day. Perhaps his urgent business in London was really urgent Vanessa business. No wonder he'd become so angry when she wanted to go with him. What man wanted a wife along when he was looking forward to enjoying his long-standing mistress?

She hated him for treating her like this. She hated herself for falling so totally under his spell when she had known—

known that Vanessa was always there, hovering like the black plague in the background. A sudden husky, tear-thickened laugh broke from her aching throat. Face it, Nell, she told herself, You are the one he hides away like a mistress while Vanessa gets to play the very public wife!

Sweeping around the rocky headland, with deft use of the controls Xander swung the helicopter round to face the island then began to search the tiny cove.

She had to be here somewhere, he told himself grimly. Where the hell else could she go?

Dark glasses shading the brightness of the sun from his eyes, he checked the water first for sight of her but there was no sign of a Titian-haired mermaid swimming alone down there.

Teeth flashing white on a hiss of relief because if she was feeling anywhere near as bad as he was feeling she was in no fit state to swim alone, he switched his attention to the shore. He'd already checked the other side of the island, checked the paths through the trees without a single sighting of her. A viscous curse aimed at himself for introducing her to his boyhood collection of hiding places had led him on a wild-goose chase on foot. From up here it was like looking for a butterfly in a forest. If he did not spot her soon then he was going to panic. He could already feel it clawing at the inner tissues of tension racked across his chest.

What if she had decided to swim? What if she had been crazy enough to strike a direct line right out to sea? He swung the craft around, eyes scanning the glistening blue ocean for a sign of one wilful idiot with a desire to drown herself just to make him feel worse.

Don't be stupid, he then told himself. *Nell* isn't that stupid. And he uttered another curse as he swung the helicopter back to face the island then set it crabbing along the shoreline. She might hate him right now but not enough to risk killing herself—and their unborn child.

Their unborn child. A baby! He was still struggling to come to terms with the shock. His beautiful Helen was going to have his baby and he had never felt so wretched about anything in his entire life!

What had he done? *Why* had he done it? Jealousy was not an emotion he was used to. Women were jealously possessive of him, not the other way round!

Women, he repeated and let out a scornful huff of a laugh. *Woman* in the singular, he corrected. One tough, teasing, exquisite creature that fell apart in his arms on a regular basis yet still protected her bloody Frenchman!

What was he doing out there? Nell wondered as she watched him hover then move and hover again. Then enlightenment dawned. Why it took so long to sink in that he was looking for her she had no idea but, hugging the piece of driftwood to her, she lowered her head over it and squeezed her eyes tight shut and willed him to go away.

As if her wish was his command she heard him move further along the coast and for some totally indefensible reason the tears flooded again. She wouldn't cry—she wouldn't! she told herself forcefully as she listened to the dying whoosh of the rotor blades until only stillness filled the air.

Tomorrow she left here, she decided. She could do it and she knew exactly how. All it required was for her to feign illness and frighten poor Thea Sophia into calling in the air ambulance. She knew it could be done because she'd witnessed it happening when one of the maids had been taken ill suddenly during her first week here. The air ambulance had swooped in with a full complement of medical crew and efficiently carried the maid away.

Once she was away from this island she would disappear as thoroughly as Marcel had apparently done and to hell with Xander. She never wanted to lay eyes on him again.

Then, without warning, the helicopter was back and suddenly so close that her chin scraped the driftwood as her head shot up. By then Xander had inched the machine in so close to the edge of the ledge that for a horrible moment she truly believed he was going to crash!

Leaping to her feet, she ran to the edge on some crazy idea that she could make him stop!

For a hellish kind of moment Xander thought she was going to take to the water. Icy dread bathed his flesh as he looked down at the sea where the ebbing tide had uncovered the razor jutting peaks of some lethal rocks.

'Get back, you fool!' he heard himself bellow at the top of his ragged voice, almost lost control of the helicopter and, by the time he'd wrestled with it and looked back at her, she was already teetering on the edge and caught up in a whirlwind of dry, stinging dust and flying debris, her slender frame cowering as she stared at him in abject horror.

Teeth lashed together, he pushed in closer, herding her backwards step by unsteady step until she was safely back from the edge. Then he stayed there, hovering so dangerously close that if he didn't harness nerves of steel he had a feeling it would be him tumbling to his death.

Shaken, severely shaken when she realised what Xander was doing, Nell began to back away, so terrified for him she took the stinging whip of dust full in the face while she screamed at him to move back!

The whole mad, nerve-slaughtering incident could only have used a few seconds but by the time she saw him begin his retreat she was close to fainting with relief.

Xander kept his jaw locked tight as he swung the machine away. If he could he would land on the damn beach so he could run up there and strangle life out of her for being so stupid, but there were too many overhanging branches covering the narrow crescent of sand to make it a safe place to land.

Biting out a thick curse, he flew back round the island to land by the house. Having settled the machine down, he then just sat there, bathed in sweat and shaking too badly to move. What if she'd jumped? What if the rotor blades' fierce downdraft had toppled her over the edge?

He climbed out of the cockpit. His legs felt hollow as he walked. The sun was hot but his skin wore the chill of stark, mind-blowing fear.

What next? What now…?

He knew what now, he told himself grimly as he set his feet walking in the direction of the pathway that would take him up the hill.

Nell saw the helicopter was safely back on its pad as soon as she crested the peak of the hill and her footsteps stilled. She'd thought Xander had gone. She'd *hoped* he had gone. Now she could see that he hadn't, her instincts were telling her to flee back into the woods and find a new place to hide from him.

Then the man himself appeared, rounding a bend in the path below, sunlight filtering through the trees to dapple his long frame dressed in smooth black trousers and a crisp white business shirt with a slender dark tie knotted at his brown throat. When he saw her he pulled to a stop.

He looked every inch the lean, dark Greek tycoon, Nell thought sinkingly. Hewn from rock, and twice as hard.

Lowering her eyes, she hugged the piece of driftwood even tighter to her chest then took some short, shallow breaths to help her feet to move.

He waited, watching her from behind the shade of his silver-framed sunglasses, the rest of his face caught by a stillness that worried her more than if he'd come charging like a bull up the hill. She'd always known that Xander could be tough, cold, ruthless. She'd always been aware of that streak of danger lurking inside him that was sensible to be wary of. But even on those few occasions when she'd sensed the danger had been threatening to spill over she'd never really expected him to give in to it. Now he had—twice in as many hours. First back at the villa then up there on the rock ledge when he'd driven the helicopter right at her without a care for his own safety.

Now she did not know what to expect from him—didn't want to know. If she possessed the luxury of choice she would not even want to be even this close to him again.

As it was her feet kept her moving down the path until she drew to a halt about six feet away from him. Tension sparked in the sun-dappled silence, and kept her eyes focused on a point to the right of his wide, white-shirted chest.

Xander felt the muscle around his heart tighten when he saw the chalky pallor nosting her cheeks. He knew he'd frightened her with the helicopter manoeuvre. Hell, he'd frightened himself! *She'd* frightened him. Now all he wanted to do was gather her into his arms and just hold her close, but what had come before the fright on the rocky ledge had lost him the right to do that.

'I thought you'd gone.' She spoke first, her voice distant and cool.

'No.' He, on the other hand, sounded raw and husky. 'Are you OK?'

She gave no reply as if the answer spoke for itself. She was not OK. Looking into those carefully lowered, beautiful eyes set in that beautiful face, he thought it was as if a light had gone out. He'd switched it off. Now he didn't know what to do or say that would switch it on again.

Dragging off his sunglasses, he pushed them into his trouser pocket then gripped them in a strangling clinch. 'What's with the piece of driftwood?' he asked out of a need to say something, however inane.

The bewildered way she glanced down at the piece of sun-bleached wood hugged close to her chest, he had a suspicion that she'd forgotten it was there.

'N-nothing,' she mumbled. 'I—like it.'

She liked it…

This was crazy! They'd almost killed each other not ten minutes ago; now here they were, standing halfway up a hill discussing bloody driftwood when they should be—

'Shall we go down?' he suggested on a thick, driven rasp.

She nodded, lowered her eyes all the way to the ground and pushed her feet into movement again. When she drew level with him he fell into step beside her and the tension inside him pounded in his chest as they walked side by side without uttering another damn word.

When they reached the house, Thea was standing anxiously in the doorway.

'Oh, there you are!' She hurried forward to close Nell's pale face between gnarled fingers in a gesture of relief. 'Alexander was so worried when he could not find you. The foolish boy went crazy, upsetting everyone by turning the whole house upside down and searching the wood before he jumped in his helicopter to look for you from the air.'

The *foolish boy* stood by in grim silence while Nell quietly soothed the old lady's anxious nerves. 'I was walking on the other side of the island,' she said gently.

'This explains why you did not hear us calling to you.' Thea nodded. 'Now you must hurry and change out of those beach clothes or he will grow truly impatient and go without you.'

Nell started frowning. 'Go where?' she asked.

'With Alexander to London, of course!' Thea exclaimed in beaming triumph. She turned to her great-nephew. 'Did you not tell her that you have changed your mind?' Then before he could answer she was hustling Nell inside. 'Come—come. Your case has been packed for you. All you need to do is choose something to wear to travel in, then we...'

Nell was glancing back over her shoulder, a puzzled frown on her face. Xander was saying nothing—nothing, and his grim, dark stance did not encourage questions.

What was going on? Why had he changed his mind? 'Xander—'

'Do as Thea says,' he cut in. 'We must leave in ten minutes if we are to make our air slot out of Athens.'

With that he spun and strode away.

Bewildered and confused, Nell allowed herself to be hurried upstairs. Xander had to have decided to take her with him before he started looking for her but—why?

'You must not get so upset when he lets off the anger, *pethi mou*,' the old lady murmured beside her. 'He loves you. That makes him jealous and possessive. All Pascalis men are the same. He worries that you might meet some other fine young man in London and leave him—as if you would be so cruel...'

Nell felt a blush stain her cheeks at Thea's faith in Nell's loyalty to her great-nephew, because she knew that she could be so cruel—*would* be so cruel if she was given the opportunity.

This marriage was over as far as she was concerned.

The flight to Athens airport was quick and smooth and trouble-free. As they flew across the island before heading towards the mainland, Nell didn't even bother to glance down.

She'd come to love that little island but she would not be coming back to it. And her only regret at leaving it behind was having to leave a tearful Thea behind too.

'You will come and see me soon,' the old lady made her promise. Nell didn't have the heart to say no, never again.

Landing in Athens was like being dropped from heaven into hell. The moment they began the transfer from helicopter to waiting plane, people stopped to stand and stare. Xander didn't seem to notice. Nell had a feeling he didn't see anything beyond his next target, which in this case was his private plane waiting on the tarmac.

With only a few minutes to spare to hit their slot, they boarded the plane and were taxiing towards the runway only moments after they'd strapped themselves into their seats.

And the whole shift from island to plane had been achieved in an empty hollow of perfect silence. It was awful. Neither spoke, neither attempted to, neither looked at the other. Body language did it all for them. Dressed in a razor-sharp business suit, he was grim, tight-lipped and supremely contained within himself.

Nell, on the other hand, had nothing she wanted to say. She was wearing the same clothes she'd travelled to Greece in— mainly because they were hanging in the closet and she hadn't cared what she wore so long as she got back down the stairs within the allotted time. The only difference being that her hair had been left loose because she didn't dare waste time in braiding it in case he left the island without her. As she'd walked out into the sunshine where Xander was waiting for her, he'd taken one look at her from behind those miserable sunglasses, his mouth had compressed then he'd just turned and stridden away.

She'd suffered his help into the helicopter without flinching and kept her gaze fixed directly ahead as he settled himself in his seat. Tension had fizzed all around them throughout the short hop to Athens Airport—making it almost impossible to breathe.

Now they sat surrounded by the kind of luxury travel most people only read about, yet they could have been two strangers on a packed package flight, the way they sat across the aisle from each other, ignoring the other's presence. As soon as the plane levelled out Xander was climbing to his feet. The sunglasses had gone but it made no difference; his long, glossy eyelashes had taken their place and Nell refused to look up at him anyway.

He disappeared into his custom-built office area towards the back of the plane and a smiling Greek stewardess brought Nell refreshment—at Xander's instruction, she presumed, because no one had asked her if she wanted anything.

Still, the freshly brewed tea was like manna from heaven after her having drunk nothing for hours. And she even managed to nibble at the selection of freshly made sandwiches before she gave up and pushed the tray away. After that she spent some time flipping through a couple of magazines without focusing on a single page. Then, in the end, because she felt so utterly dragged down and exhausted by all the emotional stresses, she rested her head back against the seat and went to sleep.

When she eventually opened her eyes again she found Xander standing over her. Her nerve-ends leapt on edge, her defences shooting back into place so violently that what she'd gained by managing to fall asleep was lost in that instant.

A nerve ticked in his jaw as she glanced warily up at him. He quickly flicked his eyes away. 'We will be landing at Heathrow in twenty minutes,' he informed her then strode away, his body language still speaking loud and clear.

The walk through Heathrow was like being placed beneath a microscope. As had happened in Athens, people stopped in their droves and stared. Nell wanted to curl into a tight chrysalis and just disappear. With a trio of tough-faced bodyguards hustling around them, they must look like one of those celebrity couples you saw splashed across the tabloids. She hated it and kept her eyes lowered and was actually grateful for the protective arm Xander placed around her as he paced beside her like a sleek, prowling cat that wanted to leap off and savage a couple of those staring faces—keeping up appearances, she thought again with a tiny grimace. And wondered curiously why she hadn't been treated to this kind of walk down the concourse when they'd left London for Greece. But didn't ask; neither the man nor the moment nor the throat-clutching pump of her heartbeat encouraged speech.

Rico was waiting outside with the Bentley, its rear door held open wide. She was hustled inside the car's luxury interior, Xander followed, the door shut, silence clattered around them with the same ear-twisting quality of a full string orchestra tuning their instruments.

They sped away with all the smooth efficiency Xander clearly took for granted. Nell would have smiled if she'd had the will to but she didn't. She had never felt as cold and unhappy or as isolated—and that was saying something, she mused as she stared out of the car window.

'Do you actually like living like this?' The words were out before she could stop them.

'I beg your pardon?' That she had surprised him with real speech showed in the huskiness of his voice.

'Like you're a beast living in a zoo,' she enlightened and watched him stiffen. 'Or maybe you're the star in the quintessential TV reality show,' she went on, wishing she'd kept quiet, but unable to stop herself from going on. 'Everything you do, wherever you are in the world, is watched and discussed and pored over. The Press love you. Those people back there love you. Paths appear in thick crowds so you can pass through unhindered while they stand and goggle and gasp.'

She dared to flick a look at him then wished she hadn't. He was sitting like a block of rock, no reaction whatsoever. It infuriated her; she didn't know why but it did.

'Is there a weekly vote on who gets kicked out of your life next?' she prodded recklessly. 'Do big companies fall to a million or two phone calls? Mistresses get dumped—bodyguards that don't fit the tough-guy bill?'

'Shut up, Nell,' he advised very quietly.

She wished she could but she was on a roll here. 'If I don't please the masses, do I get to go too? Vote out the nagging little wife so our wonderful hero does not have to listen to her any more!'

She saw his hands curl into two fists on his lap. 'You are going nowhere, so don't build your hopes up.'

'Because I might be pregnant?' she flashed at him with acid bite. 'Well, that event should boost the ratings. Do we produce your son and heir in front of a blaze of cameras and maybe have your mistress watching from the sidelines just to add a bit of spice?'

The snakelike twist of his body came without warning. For such a big man he struck with stunning, lithe grace. Before she even knew what was happening he had her trapped in the corner of the seat with a hand at her nape and the other clamped across her reckless mouth.

'Now listen…' he hissed out in thin warning.

Nell stared at him over the top of his clamping hand—really stared, and for the first time took in his pallor, the tension cutting deep grooves around his wide, sensual mouth. But it was his eyes that held her, eyes like black crystal that pierced her so sharply they hurt.

'I give you the right to mock me and my lifestyle,' he bit out tautly. 'I will even admit that I probably deserve to feel the acid whip of your tongue. But you will not mock yourself in the same manner and you will *not* degrade our unborn child!'

Is that what she'd done? Oh, yes, that was what she had done, Nell acknowledged. Her lips trembled beneath his hand.

'And don't cry,' he added on a driven mutter. 'I have enough torment to contend with without you adding your tears!'

Her breasts heaved on a tightly suppressed and tremulous shudder. Some of that torment he'd admitted to flashed across his eyes. He bit out a couple of thick foreign curses then, with the same unpredicted lithe movement, let go of her and snaked back into his own seat.

'You have no idea what you do to me,' he said then in rough-toned fury while Nell just sat there and trembled. 'You have no idea of your own damn power to draw breathless gasps from the masses!'

Shocked by that, she blinked at him in bewilderment. Turning his dark head, he caught the surprised blink and his lean face hardened into cynicism.

'You have the wild, waving hair of a fantasy mermaid, the face of an angel and the body of a natural sensualist!' he ripped out as if in contempt. 'Your sensational legs are so slender and long there isn't a man alive that would not have hot dreams about them wrapped around him. Other women look at you and *wish* they possessed a small fraction of what you've got! *I* wish I'd never set eyes on you, then I would not be sitting here feeling hard and hot and bloody frustratingly impotent to do anything about it!'

'Trust you to drag it all down to your lower-body level,' Nell responded, too shaken by what he'd thrown at her to care that her voice quivered with the onset of fresh tears. '*I* wish you'd never set eyes on me too, then I would not have spent the last year being shipped from one luxury prison to another by a money-motivated brute with sex on the brain!'

'So what would you rather have been doing?' he questioned curiously.

'Getting on with my life!'

'Life with the Frenchman perhaps?'

Turning a tight-lipped profile to him, she refused to answer. Let him think what he liked about Marcel, she thought mutinously—especially if it annoyed the hell out of him!

'Tell me, Nell, because I'm genuinely curious. Did the elusive pimpernel have the fifty million to bail your father out?'

'Marcel is not motivated by money,' she stated haughtily.

'Ah, so he's dirt poor with a sensitive heart but no balls,' he said crudely.

Nell flashed him a disgusted look. 'You know nothing about him so don't pretend that you do.'

'Are you so sure about that?'

'Yes!' she insisted. 'Or you would have had him beaten up by your mob and be throwing it at me by now.'

'Clever girl,' he drawled.

'Shut up.' She hated him.

'Are you going to tell me where he is?' he persisted.

'You must be joking,' she scoffed.

'No,' he denied. 'In fact I have never been more serious. Where is he, Nell?' he repeated levelly. 'And before you answer me with some whipping comment I think I should warn you that your freedom will continue to be restricted until you do tell me…'

Nell sizzled on a seething breath of air. 'I wish I'd never married you.'

'As if your choices were crowding at your father's begging door,' he mocked. 'As far as I am aware, it was either me or some short, ugly guy in his forties with fat lips and three pairs of hands.'

Stung, she flicked him a sharp glance. 'What's that supposed to mean?'

'Nothing—forget I said it.' Frowning, he leant forward to press a button, which brought a miniature drinks bar shooting out of the car's central bulkhead.

Feeling a bit as though she was about to be slaughtered where she sat, Nell watched him select a bottle of whisky then pour himself a measure into a squat crystal glass. He relaxed back into the seat, downing some of the whisky as he went, his lean face turned to stone again with just the merest hint of self-contempt.

Nell's upper lip trembled as she parted it from her stiff lower lip. 'Xander, y-you—'

'Don't ask,' he clipped out.

But it was too late. He had not pulled that nasty remark out of a bag at random just to get at her. There had been hard meaning behind every deriding word.

'I n-need to know what you meant.'

'You married me, therefore it meant nothing.' He stared grimly into his glass.

'Tell me!' she cried.

A burning blast of annoyance racked his face. 'Your father had overstretched his resources. He was sinking very fast. He needed bailing out but there are not many people out there with fifty million pounds sterling to spare on a very bad risk. I was one such person willing to take the risk—for a price.'

Julian Garrett's daughter and his risky investment protected as much as it could be with the production of a son and heir from the union who would claim the daughter's inheritance!

'You already know all of this, so why drag it all out again?' Xander flicked harshly into the strumming tension holding Nell pale and still.

Because he was still missing out one vital detail—the man with the fat lips. The weekend before Xander came to stay at her father's house, Clive Benson had come to stay—short, overweight, constantly smiling. At first she'd suffered his over-friendly attitude towards her out of good manners and because she thought he was just doing it in a fatherly way—until he'd become just a bit too friendly, and dared to touch her thigh. She'd taken refuge by spending as much time as she could outside with the dogs, aware that her father had some heavy business going with the man—aware that she could not afford to offend.

'You're trying to imply that my father put me up for auction,' she whispered.

'You will please make note that I am trying hard *not* to say those ugly words, *agape mou*,' he returned.

But they were there—they were there!

'My father wouldn't do such a h-horrible thing to me.'

Silence. All Xander did was toss the rest of his whisky to the back of his throat. Nell felt the churning surge of nausea in her stomach.

'I w-wouldn't have Clive Benson touch me w-with a barge-pole.'

'I am so relieved that I did not encourage such feelings of objection,' Xander drawled. 'But take a moment to consider what you would have done if I had not offered a rescue package. Without me or—someone else to bail him out, your father's company, his employees and countless other subsidiaries would have gone under and sunk without a trace. He would have been in debt to his eye-teeth. His bullish pride would have been shattered. His home would have gone and his beautiful daughter would have found herself tossed out on the street. Suddenly wealthy men like Clive Benson don't look so bad, hmm?'

'Stop the car,' Nell breathed thickly.

He looked utterly incredulous. 'We are travelling on the motorway!' he laughed, then he saw her milky pallor and his voice roughened. 'For goodness' sake, Nell, it's too late for you to run away from—'

'Stop the car!' she all but shrieked at him just before her hand jerked up to cover her mouth.

To give him his due, when he realised what was about to happen he moved like lightning, wrenching forward to snatch up the internal telephone and snapping out the order to Rico. Nell all but fell out of the car, staggering on wobbly legs across the hard shoulder of the motorway before she was thoroughly and violently sick onto the grass verge.

The arms that came to take her weight and keep her hair back at the same time were a godsend. She didn't even care that he had to stand there watching her bring up the full contents of her heaving stomach. She'd never felt so wretched— or so distressed. Everything he'd said and *not* said was pulsing and throbbing inside her.

When it was over she folded at the knees. In grim silence

Xander picked her up and resettled her on the back seat of the Bentley with her feet still out on the tarmac. He began snapping out orders while Nell desperately wanted to gulp in some deep lungfuls of fresh air but didn't dare do it in case she set the nausea off again. She was shaking like crazy. Even when Xander squatted down in front of her and gently urged her to sip the cool water that had appeared from nowhere, she still couldn't stop shaking like a leaf.

'My bag,' she managed to push out thickly.

He didn't question the request, just reached inside and found her bag where she'd placed it on the car floor and silently laid it on her lap. Her trembling fingers fumbled with the catch as she tried to open it. She could *feel* Xander wanting to take it and do the clasp for her but he didn't give in to the urge. Maybe he knew that even a small thing like that was going to tip this awful situation right over the edge.

The clasp sprang open; fingers scrambling inside, she found the little plastic envelope of damp freshen-ups she always carried, and managed to peel one away from the rest. Her hair was hanging all over her face and she was glad to have it hide the ravages she knew were there. I will never look at him again, she vowed sickly as she used the damp tissue to wipe her face, then she took the cool glass of water from him and began sipping sparingly while he continued to squat there with his hands clenched in fists between his spread thighs.

'OK?' he questioned her huskily after a few more minutes.

She nodded, offering the glass back to him, but didn't attempt to lift her head. Other things began to impinge on her consciousness, like the sound of other cars roaring past them on the motorway and the other car pulled up bumper to bumper with theirs. The three tough bodyguards had positioned themselves at a discreet but protective distance around the car.

She couldn't even be spared the dignity of privacy while she was sick.

'Nell, I'm sorry. I didn't say all of that to—' One of his hands was lifting towards her.

'Don't touch me.' She withdrew from him like a tortoise retracting into its shell.

Swivelling her legs into the car, she just sat motionless while he remained squatting there, the pull on the air so taut it felt as if it could wrench her in two.

He stayed like that for a few more seconds then rose to his full height. The car door closed, Nell used the few seconds it took him to stride around the car to comb her hair away from her face with trembling fingers. He arrived in the seat beside her, Nell turned her face to the side-window. The bodyguards dispersed. Car engines fired and the journey towards London continued in perfect—perfect—silence.

She must have dozed off, though she didn't remember doing it, but the next thing she knew the car had pulled to a stop outside a row of London townhouses sporting polished brass plates on the walls by the doors.

'Where are we?' she questioned. But Xander was already climbing out of the car. By the time he opened her door for her then stood there in grim silence waiting for her to get out, Nell had worked out exactly where they were.

'I don't need a doctor,' she protested.

The hand that took a grip on her arm said everything as he all but lifted her with it out of the car. He walked her up the steps and in through a doorway, where she glimpsed the word 'Gynaecologist' on one of the plaques with a sinking heart.

'It's too soon to consult anyone about…'

Half an hour later, with her grim-faced companion's hand like an electric charge to the hollow of her back, she was walking out again feeling washed-out and wasted and close to tears.

It was confirmed. She was pregnant. About three weeks along, at a considered guess. Potent didn't even cover it. He'd managed to achieve his goal at first try, knowing him, she thought bitterly.

'Mission accomplished,' she said in a voice that dripped ice, then stepped away from that proprietary hand and walked alone to the waiting car.

CHAPTER NINE

XANDER sat beside her as the car swept them onwards and wished to hell that he knew what to do to break this bloody grip guilt had on his conscience. In one short day he had managed to obliterate three weeks of total heaven.

He didn't want to feel like this!

He didn't want to look at her only to see that pained expression she'd worn on her pale face when the doctor had confirmed her pregnancy. He'd seen the same expression once already today when she'd been forced to tell him her suspicions about their baby because she knew it was the only way she would have stopped him taking her like a rutting beast!

In a zoo.

Theos. She had never spoken a truer word to him. How do you approach a woman who saw you like that?

How did you look her in the face when you'd just bludgeoned her with the ugly truth about her father?

You don't, came the tough but true answer. You back right off if you have a drop left of civilised blood. You put your stupid, juvenile burn of jealousy over the bloody Frenchman back under wraps, then take up the happy task of slowly and painfully trying to rebuild trust.

He turned his face to the side-window. Everything inside him felt as if it was carved in stone. One minute more of this God-awful silence and he was going to explode!

Relief arrived when he saw the front of his super-modern smoked-glass office building loom up beside the car. Rico got out and opened his door for him. Xander climbed out then moved round the car with the *civilised* intention of assisting Nell to alight, but she did that on her own.

He said nothing, took her arm, she flinched then settled. In a strained way he thanked her for that, and kept his own flinch-ing contained inside. As they walked together through the smoked-glass doors into the vaulted foyer he saw the zoo anal-ogy come up and hit him in the face like a bloody great tank.

Glass everywhere, cold tungsten steel. People—*employees*, for God's sake—stopping what they should be doing to turn and stare. He felt Nell quiver, his fingers twitched on her slen-der arm. Behind his grim lips his teeth were biting together so tightly they hurt as he walked her across the foyer and into the executive lift. The doors closed. They were transported up-wards with ultimate speed. She stared at the floor, he stared at the wall half an inch to the side of her head.

And the hell of it was that he was willing her to look at him, *willing* her to make that slow, sensual journey up from his polished shoes to his face.

It didn't happen. He'd never felt so bloody bereft.

The doors swished open. Nell had to steel herself to accept the return of his hand on her arm. Inherent Greek manners demanded that he hold her like this but she wished he were walking ten feet away.

She had never been inside this building before, definitely never been up here in his spacious and plush executive domain. More glass and steel met her gaze, interspersed now with pan-els of rich walnut and yet more curious faces that kept her eyes glued to her shoes.

The murmured greetings delivered with respect echoed the length of the long walk down the corridor. Xander said nothing. He was like a mechanical machine delivering a package.

Then his hand moved from her arm to the centre of her back as he leant forward to open a pair of huge walnut doors. She felt his fingers slide into the weight of her hair and for a mo-ment—a brief, sense-grabbing moment—his fingertips curled then straightened on a sharply compulsive sensual stroke.

Her breathing froze. She looked up at him. She hadn't wanted to do it but now it was too late and he was looking down. Everything stopped—*everything*! The door, only half pushed out of its housing, the sea of faces they'd left in their wake. He stood at least six inches taller than her and she wished—wished—*wished* she hated that handsome dark face!

Her eyes began to blur with stupid tears, her mouth started to quiver.

'Nell, don't,' he murmured thickly then turned like a whip on the sea of faces. 'Have you nothing better to do than to watch me make love to my wife?'

Shocked by the sudden outburst, Nell drew in a sharp breath. Muffled sounds erupted behind them. Xander bit out a curse then pushed the door wide and propelled her inside.

She found herself standing in a huge walnut-panelled office with a wall of glass, a steel-legged desk and a vast expanse of polished floor. The door shut with a controlled thud. As soon as it happened Nell spun around.

'What made you shout that out?' she demanded shrilly.

'Even zoo animals get sick of being stared at,' he rasped.

He had a grip on her hand now and was trailing her behind him across the room towards another set of double doors while, in a near-dizzy state of too many shocks in a single day, Nell found herself struggling with pangs of remorse.

'Look, I'm sorry I said that,' she said stiffly.

'It was only the truth. I do live in a zoo.'

A telephone started ringing somewhere. In a state of complete disorientation, Nell found herself being trailed in a different direction, towards the desk, where whole rows of paperwork stood lined up in thick, neat stacks. In amongst the stacks was the ringing telephone. Xander hooked it up with his free hand and began a clipped conversation in Greek.

She tried to slip her hand free but he refused to let go of it. The moment he replaced the receiver it started ringing again. Keeping her firmly anchored to him, Xander embarked on a series of conversations as one call led to another then another.

As one call stopped and before another started, Nell drew in a deep breath. 'Look, you're busy. And I need...' to lie down, she had been going to say but changed her mind because lying down meant a bed, and she didn't want to think about beds. 'If you'll let me use the limo, I'll go down to Rose—'

'You stay with me.' It was not up for argument. 'We are not—'

The phone shrilled out its demand for his attention. On a growl of annoyance Xander snatched it up. 'Hold the calls until I say otherwise!' he instructed, the bark of his voice rattling the windows.

Nell winced. 'I *hate* bullies.'

'Tough.' She was being trailed across the floor again. 'The vote's still out on your fate, so you stay.'

It took Nell a few seconds to get his meaning. 'Will you stop throwing my words back in my face?'

By then he'd taken them through that other pair of doors and her attention was seized, because this was no office but some kind of beautiful sitting room decorated and furnished to Xander's impeccable high standards and luxurious good taste.

'What is this place?' she asked curiously.

'My apartment.'

'You mean *this* is your City place?' She sounded so surprised that he sent her a wry look.

'What did you expect—some purple and red velvet-lined pad in atmospheric Soho specifically designed for bedding my women?'

The bedding-of-his-women bit brought the lovely Vanessa right into full focus. Instantly her face turned to paste.

He saw it and bit out a sigh. 'When I'm in town I work, I crash out here, I work,' he enunciated abruptly. 'I also keep a place in the country but have never got to sleep there yet.'

His sarcasm was really on a roll, Nell noted heavily, and was suddenly fighting yet another battle with tears... The next thing she knew she was being engulfed by a pair of arms, her face pressed to his chest.

'Idiot...'

The husky tone of his voice rumbled right through her. She wasn't sure who was the idiot, her or him, but she did know she wanted to be right where she was right now, and that had to make her a complete idiot.

The small haven of comfort didn't last long though. 'Come on,' he said gruffly, and turned her beneath the crook of his arm to guide her through yet another set of doors into a— bedroom with a huge, smooth coffee and cream covered bed on which he urged her to sit down on the edge.

'Now listen,' he said, coming to squat down in front of her. 'It's been a hell of a day and you're exhausted. The wise doctor advised rest so you will obey him and rest—alone *agape mou*,' he added severely at the protest he'd already predicted was about to shoot from her lips. 'I have work to do, consisting of a mountain of paperwork to plough through before I chair a meeting in...' glancing at his watch '...less than an hour.' Grimacing, he sprang lithely to his feet. 'There is a bathroom through that door,' he indicated. 'And a kitchen adjoining the other room if you feel the need for sustenance...'

He was already over at the window and drawing the curtains, so disgustingly invigorated by the prospect of work, while all Nell wanted to do was crawl into this bed and sleep.

'If you need me for anything,' he said as he walked back to her, 'there is a telephone in every room. All you have to do is hit the one button and you will reach me. OK?'

Locating the telephone on the bedside cabinet, Nell looked at it wistfully. 'Can I ring out on it?'

'No, you cannot!' He was suddenly in front of her and taking her shoulders to pull her upright. 'Now, listen, you aggravating bundle of controversy. I am in no mood to fight with you any more today, but if you attempt to contact your ex-lover I'll fight hard and dirty—got that?' He gave her a gentle shake.

'Yes,' she said.

He let go of her with an impatient hiss. 'Go to bed, get some rest and stop wishing for miracles.'

With that he strode out of the room with his dark head held high and his wide shoulders straight, leaving Nell wilting wearily back onto the bed.

Less than ten minutes later, stripped to her underwear, she crawled between the cool Egyptian cotton sheets. Feeling utterly bulldozed, she simply closed her eyes and dropped into sleep.

Pregnant, was her last memorable thought. I really am pregnant...

Pregnant, Xander was thinking as he stood in the doorway, following the streaming cascade of Titian hair spread out on the pillow until his gaze settled on her pale, pinched, sleeping face.

Was he pleased?

Hell, he didn't know. He wanted to be pleased. He wanted to shout it from the rooftops. But when he looked upon the face of this—impossible woman, he had a sinking suspicion that the cost he was going to pay for the pleasure of impregnating her was going to be much too high.

Smothering a sigh, he eased himself away from the doorframe and stepped back into the sitting room, pulling the door quietly shut.

Time to stop playing the lovelorn idiot, he told himself, and time to play the hard-hitting, go-getting business tycoon.

A role he was much more familiar with. A role he wished he felt an ounce of enthusiasm for right now but he didn't, which did not go down with his proud Greek ego very well.

Greek tycoon slain by a Titian-haired witch, he mentally wrote his own tabloid headline. Grimaced then braced his shoulders and went into his office, firmly closing that door behind him too.

Nell came drifting awake to the sound of rattling crockery. It reminded her so much of Thea Sophia that she lay there in smiling contentment, imagining herself to be on the island—until a lazy voice said, 'I hope that smile means you're dreaming about me.'

She opened her eyes to find Xander standing over her, looking lean and mean in his sharp business suit, and reality came crashing in. 'Oh,' she said. 'We're in London, aren't we?'

Yawned and stretched then looked back at him. 'What time is it?'

'Refreshment time,' he said lightly, turning away then turning back again with a tray in his hands.

Nell slithered up the pillows, dragged the sheet up to cover her breasts then yawned again, rubbed her eyes then swept her tumbled hair back from her face.

'Didn't know you did Room Service,' she quipped as a tray arrived across her lap.

'Anything for you, my love,' he responded in the same light vein as he sat down on the bed and removed the cover from a plate of fluffy scrambled eggs piled on a bed of hot toast.

Nell glanced at the half-light seeping through the drawn curtains. 'Is it morning already?' she asked in surprise.

Xander smiled. 'Not quite.' He handed her a glass of freshly squeezed orange juice. 'You've been asleep for hours while I've been chairing the meeting from hell. If the world were flat I would be taking great pleasure in pushing one half of a room of ten off the end of it. Is that OK?' he added questioningly as she sipped at the juice.

Nell nodded. 'Lovely.'

He sent her another smile then forked up some scrambled egg. 'Here, try this and tell me what you think.'

'It's only scrambled eggs,' she derided as she took the forkful into her mouth.

'Yes, but very special scrambled eggs, since they were prepared by my own gifted hands.'

'You?' Nell almost choked. 'I didn't think you knew what an egg looked like in its shell.'

'Shame on you.' He forked up another heap. 'I am very self-proficient when I have to be. Drink some more juice.'

Nell frowned. 'Why did you feel the need to be proficient at this particular moment?'

'Because I decided to leave the ten squabbling in my boardroom and came in here to see you. You were out for the count. I noticed that you must not have woken up to get yourself something to eat and, since you haven't had anything since you threw up on the motorway, I decided that it was time that you did. You can go back to sleep when you've eaten this...'

Another forkful was offered to her. Nell looked at his smooth, lean, totally implacable, super-relaxed face, said nothing and took the fork from him so that she could feed herself. For several minutes neither spoke while Nell ate and he seemed content to watch.

Then it came, the real reason he was sitting there looking at her like that. 'Nell—what I said about your father—'

'Is he still in Australia?'

'Yes,' he frowned. 'You knew he'd committed himself to overseeing the whole project,' he reminded her.

'Yes.' Her sigh was wistful and rather sad.

'I want you to know that I gave you the wrong impression about your father's involvement in our—'

'Oh, I don't think so,' she said as she laid down the fork. 'I think you made your point perfectly. You took me as assurance for your investment. We even have a contract that says so. You also saved me from a fate worse than death.'

A frown pulled his eyebrows together across the bridge of his nose. 'I'll rip the contract up if it will make you feel better.'

'It's so sweet of you to offer,' she mocked him. 'But the gesture would only have some weight behind it if you'd offered to do that *before* I got pregnant.'

'I did offer once before, if you recall.'

'On my birthday?' She looked up at him. 'Before my father had managed to scoop the Australian deal and put his business back on track? Bad timing, Xander,' she said. '*Not* what you're renowned for. You could have been asking to renegotiate yourself right out of the whole deal for all I knew. Still know,' she added when he opened his mouth to deny it.

The fact that he was going to have to pull rabbits out of the proverbial hat to make her believe otherwise now held him silent while he took that on board.

Nell hunted around for something trite to say to fill in the gap.

But what came out was miles away from trite. 'There,' she said. 'Plate cleaned. Baby adequately fed.'

'I did it for you, not the baby!' he snapped.

That she didn't believe him showed. He uttered a sigh, his indulgent manner disappearing without a trace. 'Does it actually matter what motivated me?' he posed curtly. 'Am I not allowed to be concerned for you both?'

He glanced at his watch then and stood up to remove the tray. 'I have a meeting to return to. I'll see you later.'

With that punishing slice of ice, he left. Nell threw herself back against the pillows and wished she knew how she should feel about him, but she didn't. Everything she had come to love and trust about him over the last three weeks had been shattered by a day-long series of hard knocks.

The telephone call from Vanessa being the hardest knock.

Restless now, she got up, feeling an instant chill on her skin because of the difference between a hot Greek summer and a cooler English one. Rubbing at her bare arms, she wandered around the bedroom, aimlessly picking things up, putting them down again, and would have gone and done the same in the sitting room but she couldn't be absolutely sure that someone might not come in from the office and catch her half-naked, and Xander seemed to have forgotten to have her suitcase brought up.

In the end she escaped to the bathroom and decided to indulge in a long, hot soak in the invitingly huge bath. A few carefully placed candles would have been nice to help her relax, but she had to make do with selecting a couple of soft downlighters. She found no sign of any female soapy things hanging around, which mollified her restless mood somewhat.

So Xander didn't indulge his women here, she mused as she lay submerged in hot, steamy water liberally laced with Xander-scented bath oil. Maybe he did have a purple and red velvet-lined pad in Soho. With a mirrored bed and flying cupids embroidered on the velvet, she extended with a soft laugh.

'Cheered up at last?'

'Oh!' She flicked her eyes open to find him casually propping up the doorframe. Sheer surprise had her slithering into a sitting position, causing a minor tidal wave to slosh around the bath. 'You were quick,' she said disconcertedly.

'I didn't like the company,' he drawled, dark eyes glossed by silky eyelashes as he looked her over from loose topknot to water-slicked breasts being caressed by steam.

It was stupid to feel shy after spending three weeks mostly naked around him, but telling herself that did not stop the blush from mounting her skin. Nell tried to make it look casual when she drew her knees up and looped her arms around them. The action did not change that look she knew so well on his lean, dark face.

He'd lost his jacket and his tie, she noticed. His shirt collar was undone and the shirt cuffs too. And if ever a man knew how to lounge sexily in a doorway then Xander had the pose down to a finely tuned art. Long legs relaxed, hands loosely looped in his trouser pockets, silk dark hair finger-ruffled just enough to add that extra brooding appeal.

Her body responded, breasts growing heavy, nipples peaking where she crushed them against her thighs. Even her lips felt as if they were filling and pulsing.

'You forgot my suitcase.' To Nell, it was an inspired stab at the prosaic.

It didn't alter his hungry look one iota. 'Stashed in the sitting room five minutes after we arrived,' he said. 'Didn't you bother to look?'

'No.' She added a grimace. 'Maybe you could get it for me?'

'Why?'

'So I can put something clean on?' she suggested ever so sarcastically to what she thought a stupid question to ask.

Xander clearly didn't. He straightened up and began approaching the bath. 'You can wear me instead,' he murmured huskily and began to undo the rest of the buttons on his shirt.

'Don't you dare try to get in here!' she cried, causing a floor-sloshing wave as she shifted up the bath. 'I'm still angry with you! I don't even like you any more! I will *not* be your sex slave just because you need—'

'Watch it...' His hand darted out, capturing her hair just before it tumbled out of the topknot into the bath.

Shaken by panic, utter confusion and a rotten desire to finish the job with his shirt, she glared at his hair-roughened breast-plate while he re-knotted her hair with an infuriating finesse.

'There,' he said. 'Now you won't have to spend half an hour drying it before we get to bed.'

'I'm not sleeping with you ever again.'

'Did I mention sleep?'

Nell tried to calculate if she had enough room to make a run for it while he was busy stripping off his clothes.

'Not a cat in hell's chance,' he teethed out, reading her like an open book.

Stark, blinding, beautiful naked, he stepped into the bath.

'We are not going to let this war continue,' he informed her as he came down on his knees to straddle her. 'You are my wife and you are having my baby.' His hands took possession of her warm, wet, slippery breasts with their tightly distended, lush pink nipples. 'As these beautiful things tell me you want me, *agape*, and as I am so majestically displaying I most certainly want you, why fight it?'

Why indeed? Nell thought helplessly as she, like a captured rabbit, watched him lower his head. It was like being over-whelmed by Poseidon again she likened helplessly as he took charge of her mouth, her body and the rest.

A few minutes later and she was slithering beneath him into the water with her arms clinging to his neck. They'd made love in a bath many times but for some reason this hot and steamy, oil-slicked occasion that was permeated with his scent tapped into another dimension. Water sloshed as they touched and ca-ressed each other, she was so receptive to everything about him that she found she didn't care if her face sank beneath the surface and she drowned like this.

His arms stopped it from happening. The way he was smoothing small, soft, tender kisses over her face kept her breathing slow and deep. His eyes kept capturing hers and fill-ing her with dark liquid promise, when he slipped a hand between her thighs she arched her body in pleasure and captured his mouth.

They kissed long and deep, they moved against each other slowly and sensuously. When with a lithe grace he changed his position, stretching out above her and murmured huskily, 'Open your legs,' she even made the move with a slow erotic invitation that set him trembling as she clasped his face in her hands so she could pull his mouth back to hers as he entered her with a long, smooth, silken thrust.

And the whole thing continued to a slow, deep, pulsing rhythm. His supporting arms stopped her from drowning in the water, while inside she drowned in a different way. When she fell apart she even did this slowly and deeply and the pulses of pleasure just went on and on and on.

When he lifted her out of the bath she clung to him weakly. Even when he dried them both she didn't let go. She was lost, existing in a place without bones or muscles; the only solid thing was him and the thickly pumping beat of his heart beneath her resting cheek.

'If you *ever* let another man see you like this you won't live,' he rasped out suddenly.

Nell just smiled and pressed a silky kiss to his hair-roughened, satin-tight chest. 'Take me to bed,' she breathed.

With a muffled groan Xander lifted her up and carried her into the bedroom, still clinging. She was still clinging when he settled them both in the bed. She fell asleep like that—clinging. Xander lay beside her wondering how long he should wait before he woke her up again.

He used up the time recalling the looks on the faces of the ten men in his boardroom when only half an hour after battle recommenced he'd stood up and brought the whole thing to an abrupt end.

'When you are ready to negotiate like adults let me know. Until then this meeting is over.' He smiled as he saw himself making that announcement because—there he was, being the hard-hitting, cool-headed, totally focused, ruthless dictator. Wouldn't they like to know that beneath the incisive veneer he'd brought that meeting to a close because he'd been aching so badly for this…

His wife. This sensational woman with a silken thigh lying across his legs and her slender arms still looped around his neck. On a sigh because he knew he should not give in yet, he reached up to claim one of her hands then carried it down his body to close it gently around the steel-hard jut of his sex.

'You're insatiable,' she murmured, letting him know that she was already awake.

'For you,' he agreed. She stroked him gently and the whole deep, drugging experience began all over again.

Afterwards he went off to raid the fridge and came back with a bottle of champagne and two glasses, one of which he handed to Nell—already filled.

'What's this?' she demanded, frowning into the glass when it became obvious it wasn't champagne because he was only now easing the cork from the bottle.

'Sparkling water,' he supplied. 'Pregnant women don't drink alcohol.'

'What would you know?' she protested.

About to take a sip at the water, since it was all that was on offer, she found her eyes pinned instead to the way he'd suddenly turned into a concrete block. The lean face, the black eyes—nothing moved.

'What have I said?' she gasped in surprise.

'I just remembered something I needed to do.' He seemed to need to give himself a mental shake before he could bring himself to pour out his champagne. 'Here,' stretching out beside her, he offered his glass up to her lips, 'a sip can't hurt, and a baby is something to celebrate…'

The odd little moment slid by.

Maybe she shouldn't have let it. Maybe Nell should have listened to the little voice inside her head that told her he was hiding something. If she had done then what happened the next morning would not have come as such a crushing blow.

Xander was already in his office and working at his desk by the time Nell sauntered out of the bathroom wrapped in a fluffy white towel. She was aching a little because Xander had been so unquenchable last night. Gentle though, she recalled with a soft smile, unbelievably gentle, as if his knowing about the baby had brought out in him a whole new level of tenderness.

Her inner muscles quivered, her expression taking on a far-away look as she allowed herself the luxury of reliving some of those long, deep, drugging kisses they'd shared, the fine tremor of his body and the look in his dark eyes just before he'd allowed her to take him inside.

If that look didn't speak of love then she'd been dreaming it, she thought as she went over to her suitcase, which Xander had thoughtfully placed open on a low cabinet by the window.

There again it could be just that, having forced herself to accept that since she did not have the power to resist him she might as well stop trying to fight him, maybe she was justifying that by misreading the look.

Oh, shut up, she told that cynical side of her nature. Do you want to spoil it? They were man and wife in every which way you wanted to look at it now that they'd conceived a baby between them, which in turn meant that they were now so deeply committed to this marriage that the Vanessas of this world could take a hike, because no other woman would ever have what Nell now had of Xander.

His first child growing inside her. A child that Xander had spent the rest of the night protecting with the gentle spread of his hand. Did it matter if this had all started out three weeks ago with him determined to achieve that goal?

At least she did not disappoint, she mocked with a grimace. And turned her attention to sifting through the clothes one of the maids on the island had packed for her. One day, she thought ruefully, she might get to pack her own suitcase; then she might find something she wanted to wear.

They'd awoken to a cold, grey day this morning. Even with the temperature in here maintained by an air-conditioning system with climate control, her skin was wearing a distinct chill. The suitcase contained a choice of lightweight short white cotton skirts and a couple of white strapless tops or the turquoise dress.

On a sigh she selected some underwear, dropped the towel and slipped into bra and panties followed by the turquoise dress, then looked around her for something to cover her chilly shoulders and goose pimpled arms. The suit she had travelled here in lay across the back of a bedside chair but the thought of putting on the travel-limp jacket did not appeal.

On impulse she walked over to the wide walnut-faced wardrobe and opened the doors. Xander's clothes hung in clear plastic from their hangers. Business suits, dinner suits, shirts, ties. Nothing there she could borrow that would keep her warm, she thought ruefully and flipped her search towards the column of deep drawers built into the wardrobe. She found socks, men's undershorts, even a neatly stacked drawer of plain white T-shirts. A foray into the final drawer offered up a better prospect of neatly folded sweaters made out of the finest cashmere. It was probably going to drown her but as she dipped down to near the bottom of the pile to remove a black one she'd spied there, she decided that beggars couldn't be choosers and at least she would be adequately covered.

Then her fingertips came up against the sharp corners of something. On a softly yelped, 'Ouch!' she withdrew her fingers, checked she hadn't managed to draw blood, then frowningly began carefully lifting out the sweaters layer by layer until she'd uncovered the guilty object.

After that she seemed to lose touch with reality. The stack of soft sweaters she held in the crook of her arm fell unnoticed to the floor. She didn't even attempt to pick up the silver-framed photograph she'd uncovered but just stared into Vanessa's beautiful smiling face then at the miniature-sized version of Xander standing laughing in front of her then finally—most painfully—she read the hand-scrawled inscription. 'To Papa Xander,' it said. 'Love from your Alex.'

His son even had his name...

CHAPTER TEN

GLANCING up as Luke Morell stepped into the office carrying a manila file, Xander took one look at his PA's sober expression and sat back in his seat with a smile.

'Did you have to mop blood up off the floor last night after I left?' he quizzed drily.

'You know as well as I do that your shock tactic sent all ten into freefall.'

'Good. Let us hope they learned what it feels like to lose their only parachute.'

Managing a small grimace at the quickness of his employer's wit, 'They want another meeting today,' Luke informed him. 'Perhaps you could try to be a little more—tolerant?'

'For what purpose?' Xander asked. 'I am not into salving other people's egos.' Losing all hint of his own smile, he sat forward again. 'They would not want to meet with me at all if they had done their own jobs better so don't ask me to feel sorry for them. What's with the folder?' he prompted. 'Yet another set of impossible proposals from them?'

'This has nothing to do with the takeover.' Luke walked towards him, his grim expression more keenly in place. 'I suppose I should add that you are not going to like this, so I suggest you take a deep breath before you take a look inside.'

Curiosity piqued, Xander was about to accept the file when a quiet knock sounded at the door through to his private apartment. As he was about to flick his attention from the file to the door he saw Luke stiffen jerkily and his eyes narrowed and remained riveted where they were. He didn't like that telling bit of body language. He didn't like the way his assistant's face had closed up tight. A sudden warning prickle shot across the

142

back of his neck, the kind his instincts had taught him never to ignore.

Then the door-handle began to turn and he was forced to shift his attention to Nell as she stepped into the room. He frowned when he saw that she was wearing the blue suit she had travelled in yesterday, and her hair had been contained in that braid he didn't like. But it was her face that held him. She wasn't smiling, her vulnerably kissable upper lip stuck in a downward curve to its fuller lush partner, and even the light layer of make-up she was wearing could not disguise her odd pallor beneath.

'What's wrong?' he asked instantly, springing to his feet. 'Do you feel ill again?'

He was already striding out from behind his desk as Nell fluttered an unhappy glance at Luke then quickly away again.

'Y-yes—n-no,' she replied in confusion, clearly disconcerted to find Luke Morrell standing there.

'Well, which is it?' Xander demanded, coming to a halt directly in front of her then frowning down at her when she hooked in an unsteady breath of air before focusing her eyes on a point between his tie knot and his chin. 'Nell...?' he prompted huskily when she still didn't speak.

'I'm—fine,' she told him. Then her gaze made another sliding glide towards the very still Luke.

Xander took the hint. With a twist of his long body sent an impatient glance at the other man. 'Later, Luke,' he dismissed him.

Luke hovered, seeming undecided as to whether to walk out with the file or place it on the desk before he left.

'Leave it.' Xander made the decision for him. And after another moment's hesitation, the file was relinquished and Luke was letting himself back out of the room.

'OK.' Xander swung back to Nell the moment they were alone again. 'Now tell me.'

He'd barely got the command out when one of those wretched telephones on his desk started to ring. On an impatient apology he spun away and strode back to the desk, leaving

Nell standing there feeling dazed and dizzy, hating him so much yet hurting badly at the same time.

'Xander—'

He snatched the phone up, cutting short what she had been going to say as he snapped his name into the mouthpiece.

It was like a replay of the day before, Nell thought as she stared at the long, lean length of his dark-suited figure standing in profile against a backcloth of an unrelieved grey English sky.

Beautiful, she observed helplessly, and with an almost masochistic need to feed the ache throbbing inside her began absorbing every elegant inch of him from handmade shoes to the breadth of his wide, muscular shoulders dressed in the best silk tailoring money could buy.

The man with everything, she thought, and had never felt so bitter than she did at that moment. The sensation crawled along her flesh like icy fingers and she knew suddenly that she had to get away—from him, from this raw feeling of utter betrayal, from the sound of his deep velvet voice that was twisting her up inside because she loved that sound even while she hated him.

'I'm going out,' she announced in a breath-shaking whisper and headed jerkily for the outer office door, not caring if he'd heard her, not caring if he would have the usual objections ready to voice at her going anywhere without his say-so.

The telephone crashed with a slam. He moved so fast she'd barely taken two steps before he was catching hold of her wrist and swinging her round. The whole quick manoeuvre brought back memories of the way he'd done the same thing on the island only yesterday.

Her face paled, lips trembling as she released her breath. 'Don't manhandle me.' She yanked her wrist from him.

That he was totally taken aback by the venom in her voice showed in his shock-tautened face. 'What's the *matter* with you?' he bit out.

'I am not some object you can push and tug around as your mood takes you,' she hit back.

He stiffened up. 'I never meant—'

'Yes, you did,' she cut in. 'You think you own me right down to my next thought. Well, you don't.'

'This is crazy,' he breathed in total bewilderment. 'I left a beautiful, warm and contented woman only an hour ago, now the shrew is back.'

Nell deigned not to answer that. She had been warm and contented. She had been nicely, carefully, *patiently* seduced into being that pathetic creature again. She despised herself for that.

'And why are you wearing the same clothes you had on yesterday?'

The sudden flip in subject sent her vision oddly blank as she stared down at the summer-blue suit. It took a really agonised effort to make herself reply without flinging the *why* at him. But she didn't want to tell him. She did not want him to start explaining and excusing his rights over her rights.

'It's all I've got to wear unless you want me to wander around in the turquoise dress,' she said. 'Whoever packed for me at the island packed for the Greek climate, not this one. So I am going out—to shop.'

It was thrown down like a challenge. Xander's dark head went back as he took that challenge right on his cleft chin. He knew what she was saying. He knew which particular gauntlet was being handed out this time. As the tension built and he fought to hold back the instinctive denial that was lodged in his throat, Nell stared fixedly at nothing in particular and hoped to goodness that the fine tremors attacking the inner layers of her skin were not showing on the outside.

'Wait for me,' he said, cleverly couching that denial in a husky dark plea that, in spite of everything, touched a tingling weak spot. 'We will go together. Just give me a couple of hours to free myself up and we can—'

The telephone began to ring. His dark head twisted to send the contraption a look of angry frustration but his fingers twitched by his sides and Nell almost managed a mocking laugh because she knew he was itching to answer that call. His priorities were at war. She twisted back to the door. Behind her she heard Xander hiss out a curse about irritating women.

'Have you any money?' he sighed out then, work winning over his marriage, though to be fair to him he didn't know that—yet.

'I have credit cards.' A dozen of them linked to his accounts.

'Nell…!' he ground out as her hand caught the door-handle. She turned her head to find him already back at the desk with his hand covering the shrilling phone. 'Don't be long,' he husked.

She nodded, lips pressed together to stop them wobbling, then she let herself out of the room. As she braced herself for the walk down the long corridor towards the lift, she said a silent goodbye to him.

Back in his office, Xander was ignoring the ringing phone and snatching up his mobile phone instead. He hit fast dial. 'My wife is just leaving. See that she's protected,' he instructed.

Then he was stepping to the window, hands dug into his pockets, fingers tightly clenched into fists while he grimly waited for Nell to appear on the street below while the telephone continued to ring off its rest.

He did not understand any of that, he decided tightly. He'd thought last night that they'd called a pretty effective truce. Suddenly she was back to sniping at him and evading eye contact. He missed the eye contact. He didn't like the tingling feeling that was attacking the back of his neck.

He saw her step out onto the busy pavement, continued to watch as she paused and looked around as if she had no idea where she wanted to go. His heart gave him a tug, yanking at his gut and contracting it because even from way up here she looked so—lost!

As she seemed to come to a decision and struck out to the left Xander watched Jake Mather slip into step behind her. He remained where he was with his eyes fixed on the top of her shining head until she had disappeared out of sight with her bodyguard safely in tow. Then he turned away from the window and stood grim and tense, feeling unfathomably like a man who'd just made the biggest error of judgement he was ever likely to make.

The phone had finally given up though, he noted, and, straightening his wide shoulders, he stepped up to the desk, hovered on another few seconds of inner restlessness, then the manila file Luke had brought in caught his eye.

Recalling his PA's grim words of warning did not ease the tension singing inside him as he sat down, picked up the file then drew in the advised deep breath.

A breath that froze even as he opened the front flap. A breath that he did not release for the several long minutes it took him to scan the pages set in front of him. By the time he'd finished he felt as cold as death.

She was away for three hours and in that time Xander was in touch with every step that she took. Grim, cold—face stretched taut by the burning pulse of anger he was keeping tamped down inside.

Work had ceased. *Life* had ceased, he mused harshly. Beyond the four walls of his office a series of instructions was being carried out to the letter while he sat in grim isolation, telephones, people, everything shut out but for his mobile link to Jake Mather.

If she bolted she would not get five paces before Jake would have her in his grasp. If she was foolishly letting herself believe that safety lay in the heaving crowds she was trying to lose herself in then she was in for a hard knock of truth. Jake had been joined by his other men, one of which was in the process of tracing the call she had just made from a public call box. Xander had not enquired as to how this could be done. He did not want to know. But behind the cold mask he was wearing on his face he knew that the name Marcel Dubois was about to be quoted at him.

It was.

'Where is she now?' he scythed at Jake Mather.

'To be truthful, boss, I think she's on her way back to you.'

To be truthful, Xander mimicked acidly, he knew that Nell must know by now that she did not have another choice.

She thought he lived in a zoo? Well, now she knew what it felt like, having been swarmed all over by his security people since she'd stepped onto Oxford Street.

Though he now had to accept that he was going to be disappointed that she did not require bundling into the back of the limo that was loitering in a side-street, ready and prepared to receive its protesting package.

Satisfaction coiled around his tense chest muscles when Jake's voice arrived in his ear with, 'Turning into the street now...'

He was out of the chair and swinging to the window before the final word left his security guard's lips. Something hard hit him in the chest as he caught sight of her head with all of its glorious, bright Titian hair shimmering around her face and shoulders instead of being neatly contained in the braid she'd left with.

Xander found himself gritting his teeth as he absorbed her purposeful stride. She was angry. Good, because so was he. If she wanted all-out war he was ready for it.

She was carrying the distinctive yellow and black bags from her wild buying spree in Selfridges. She'd changed her clothes too. The summer-blue suit had gone and in its place tight designer jeans that moulded her long, sensational legs and a soft brown suede jacket that hung loose across a creamy coloured top.

If she'd deliberately chosen the clothes to make him sit up and take notice then she could not have done a better job, because he was seeing her exactly as he had first seen her when she'd walked through her father's front door, wild and windswept. As she turned to walk up the grey marble steps to his building she paused and looked up and, as if she knew he was watching her from up here, her green eyes suddenly sparked and tossed up bolts of burning fire.

'Well, come on up, my fiery witch,' he invited beneath his breath.

Turning, he broke the connection with Jake Mather then reached out to flip a key on his computer keyboard to bring his glass and steel foyer up on to the screen. As he watched his wife stride purposefully across the foyer via the in-house CCTV system he was lifting his jacket from the back of the chair and smoothly shrugging it on. Her barely concealed patience as she rode alone inside the steel-cased lift held his attention while his fingers dealt with his shirt-collar button and straightened his tie. By the time she began the long walk down the corridor towards his office, his finger-ravaged hair had been neatly smoothed and he was ready for her.

Nell pushed open the door and stepped into the room, green eyes flashing like emerald storms. The door slammed back into its housing and she dropped the bags then speared those eyes on Xander, who was casually swinging in his chair behind the desk, looking as crisp and as sharp as he'd looked when she left him—and of course he was holding a telephone to his ear.

Her fury hit boiling point. 'Would you like to explain to me where the heck you get the stone-cold arrogance to believe that you own my life?' she shrilled.

Without so much as a flicker in response from those long dark eyelashes, he murmured some very sexy Italian into the phone's mouthpiece, then gently replaced it on its rest.

'If you have a yen to argue the finer points of ownership then by all means do so,' he invited. 'But before you begin you will explain to me please why you needed to spend thirty minutes in the ladies' room in Selfridges. Were you feeling ill again?'

Oh, so casually asked. Nell felt a sudden trickle of ice run right down her spine. 'How many men did you have following me?' she gasped.

'Seven,' he supplied. 'Including Jake Mather, whom I presume you spotted quite quickly—mainly because he was not instructed to hide,' he seemed compelled to add.

'He tried to stop me using a public telephone,' she said tightly.

With the calmness of a coiled snake, he reached out and

picked up the phone then offered it to her. 'Try this one. All calls are free.'

The green eyes sent him a withering look. 'Don't be so obnoxious,' she condemned. 'You have no right to have me tagged, tailed and guarded like some—'

'Animal in a zoo?' he suggested when words failed her. 'Or, more appropriately in this case,' he then added thinly, 'like an untrustworthy wife!'

'*I* can't be trusted?' Nell launched back at him. 'That's rich coming from the most twisted and devious—*Machiavellian* swine it was ever my misfortune to meet!'

'Oh, you met a worse one, *cara*,' Xander drawled.

'What's that supposed to mean?'

Without any warning he lost his relaxed posture to shoot to his feet. 'You were leaving me for him—again!'

With the backcloth of grey Nell could not see his face but she could feel the anger bouncing off him.

'On the first opportunity you were presented with you rang *him*!' he all but snarled.

'You traced that call?' she gasped out in disbelief.

'You make me sick,' Xander announced, then gave a contemptuous flick of a long-fingered hand when Nell just gaped. 'I don't even want to look at you.'

On that damning indictment he swung away to the window, leaving Nell standing there shaking and quivering—not with hurt but in disbelief!

'How dare you speak like that to me?' she shook out furiously.

'Easily.' Twisting back, he picked up a manila file from his desk, brandished it at her then dropped it again. 'The police report on your accident,' he incised. 'You may read it if you wish.'

But Nell did not wish. Nell was already striding across the office and pushing open the doors to his apartment.

'You were not driving that car!' he flung after her. 'The angle of your seat belt burns proves it! You were sitting in the left seat, not the right—and if I drove myself more frequently in England I would have realised that as soon as I clapped eyes on your bruises and you would have been dead!'

Her face white, her lips clamped together in a flat line of disgust that was ripping her apart inside, without a pause in her stride she threw open the next set of doors, aware that Xander was tracking right behind her. Aware that in one small, satisfied way she had taken him by surprise by walking away.

'You are so in love with the guy that you told nobody that salient fact!' he rasped out from the bedroom doorway. 'You have been protecting him from taking any blame even though the lily-livered coward slunk away from the scene, leaving you lying there badly injured and in need of help!'

All the time he was tossing his accusations at her Nell was throwing the doors open wide on his wardrobe and dragging open his sweater drawer. The soft cashmere garments landed in a discarded scatter. If Xander had been in a more sensible state of mind he might have been forewarned as to what was about to hit him.

As it was he strode forward, gripping the manila file as if it was some kind of weapon. Now she spun on him and it was so *nice* to watch his breathing still when he saw the expression of icy distaste on her face.

'He did not slink away. I sent him away,' she corrected. 'As you say, I protected him from you and your lynch mob and what you might do to him.'

'Because you love him.' He sounded hoarse.

Nell nodded. Why deny it? 'In the same way you have been protecting your family—because you love them?'

The sarcastic tilt in her questioning tone floated right by him. 'You are my family,' he ground out.

'No—here is your family, Xander,' Nell said quietly, and placed the framed photograph down on the bed. 'Goodness knows why you didn't marry Vanessa and give her and that—little boy who looks like he loves you very m-much the right to use your name.' She sucked in a dreadful, choked breath. 'But don't ever dare refer to me as your family again because

I'm not—they are. I think it's time that you got your priorities right and owned up to that.'

He seemed to be having difficulty taking it all in. Nell stared up at his blank, taut face and waited for some kind of response. But all she did see was his eyes shifting from her white face to the sweaters scattered on the floor before slowly, almost unseeingly moving to the bed. As understanding did begin to dawn she watched his face slowly leech of its rich golden colour then his eyes turned black.

'I can explain this—'

'No.' Nell shook her head. 'Explain to *them* why you dared to marry *me!*'

'But this is crazy!' He suddenly exploded back to life again. 'I *can* explain this—!' he insisted.

'But I don't want to hear!' she all but screamed at him.

His eyes flashing black with rage now, he stepped round the bed, slamming the manila file down as he came towards her. The file landed right on top of the framed photograph, Nell saw in dismay.

'You did that on purpose,' she shook out accusingly.

He didn't even bother to deny it. 'I would love to know,' he gritted, 'how you've managed to turn this into a fight about them instead of one about your bloody lover!'

'I h-hate you for that.' Nell wasn't listening. 'How could you do that to that poor little boy?'

Taking hold of her shoulders, he gave them a small shake then pulled her hard up against his chest. 'Listen to me when I speak,' he ground out. 'They are not important. You—your Frenchman is!'

'He isn't French, he's Canadian,' Nell mumbled, still staring at the way he'd covered the photograph as if he'd committed some mortal sin. 'He's also my—'

'Canadian...' Xander repeated as if a whole load of pennies had just dropped into place. 'You stupid fool, Pascalis,' he growled furiously at himself. Then those expressive black eyes flared Nell a look of blistering contempt. 'What did the two of you do—make love on a mountain while your mother lay dying in her bed—?'

The crack of her hand landing against the side of his face made a whiplashing echo around the room. Nell stood locked within his iron-hard grip, panting, breasts heaving as she watched her finger marks rise on his cheek. There was a horrible moment while she stared into those black eyes when she thought he was going to retaliate.

Then he let go, his fingers unclipping from her shoulders before he took a step back. The moment he did Nell began to shiver. Pale as death now and still shocked by her own act of violence, a cold chill shook her, bringing her arms up to hug her body, tense fingers clutching at the soft suede sleeves of her jacket.

She took in a slow breath. 'As I was about to say before you said w-what you said, Marcel is not my—'

'Well, I know he did not taste the main treat, *yenika*,' he drawled insolently. 'But there is more to sex than a—'

'He's my *brother*, you filthy-minded beast!' Nell flung at him.

It was as if someone had plugged him into an electric socket, the whole of his posture racked up with a jerk. '*Theos,*' he husked. 'That was a joke—yes?' Then as he stared into her angry face, '*Theos,*' he breathed again. 'You are serious.'

'H-half-brother,' she extended in a trembling voice.

Violently, he twisted his back to her, lifted up a long-fingered hand and grabbed the back of his neck. Blistering tension was scored into every bone and sinew.

'You should have told me.'

'Why?' Nell quavered.

'*Why...?*' He swung round to spear her with a piercing glare. 'I did not know you even had a brother! Don't you think such a thing warranted a mention some time in the last year?'

'If you'd cared enough about me to want to *know* about me you would have found it out!' she shrilled. 'And anyway...' she pulled in a deep breath '...I enjoyed watching you squirm. It made a pleasant change from squirming myself.'

'What is that supposed to mean?' he demanded stiffly.

Nell felt the sudden threat of wounded tears. 'I was in love with you when you asked me to marry you. I don't think you even noticed or cared!'

'I cared,' he grunted.

'So much that you were with your mistress a week before you married me! Now I find out that she has your child!'

White-faced now, 'No,' he said. 'Listen to me...' He took a step towards her, one hand reaching out, but Nell backed away.

'I w-was going to leave you today.' She shook out the confession. 'If it hadn't been for your men dogging my every step I would have disappeared and you would not have found me.'

The way his jawline gave a tense twitch made her wonder if he was biting back the desire to argue with her about that.

'You play with people, Xander. You like to be in control and when you're not you react as if we have no right to pull on your strings! I've seen you do it with your mother. You did it with those ten men last night. You're *always* doing it with me. You did it today when you set your hounds on me—'

'You said it yourself you were going to disappear—'

'That was my choice!' she launched at him, felt the tears start to come and had to tug her fingers up to cover her quivering mouth. At the same time her other hand went to her stomach because it was beginning to feel strange, kind of achy and quivery and anxious.

'Nell...'

One hand covering her mouth, the other her stomach, Nell was already spinning away. She made a dash for the bathroom with no idea that Xander was right behind her, so he took the full force of the door slamming shut in his face.

CHAPTER ELEVEN

FOR a few blinded seconds Xander just stood there with that solid wall of wood a mere hair's breadth from his face and the whole of his front vibrating from the force with which the door had shut.

Still reeling from the stuff that Nell had thrown at him, he spun to face the other way.

Her half-brother.

'Hell,' he muttered thickly.

His eyes went to the bed and the manila file and he went over there and snatched it up with some deep-ridden desire to toss that damn thing across the room only he saw the photo frame he'd uncovered and he froze as he stared down at the lovely smiling Vanessa and a laughing Alex.

'To Papa Xander, love from your Alex', he read and the oddest kind of laugh broke from his throat.

Then the sound of retching filtered out through the bathroom door and he was dropping the file again to stride back the way he had come. Even as he pushed open the bathroom door and saw her hanging over the toilet bowl guilt was dealing him a well-deserved punch to his gut because he had allowed himself to forget her delicate condition while they'd been fighting like cat and dog.

Nell heard him arrive just as she was shuddering into stillness. 'Go away,' she whimpered, only to discover that talking was enough to set the whole thing off again.

Two seconds later he was taking control of the situation with the same grim, silent efficiency he had used on the motorway the day before. When eventually it was over and she'd rinsed her mouth out with a mouthwash, he lifted her limp, wasted and hot body into his arms and she discovered she had no strength left to fight him off.

'I hate you,' she whispered instead.

'*Ne,*' he agreed, carrying her into the bedroom.

'I wish you'd never set eyes on me.'

'*Ne,*' he agreed again, reaching down to toss back the covers before bringing her gently down on the edge of the bed.

'My feeling like this is your fault.'

'Entirely,' he admitted. 'Relax your arms from my neck so I can remove your jacket...'

It was the most humiliating part of it all to realise how she was clinging to him. Her arms dropped heavily to her sides. He removed the jacket while she watched his totally expressionless face. No man should be that good-looking, she thought bitterly. It gave him unfair advantage in the jaws of a fight because she wanted so desperately to reach out and kiss him that she felt dizzy all over again.

Her new flat shoes came next, landing with a clunk on the floor. His sensual mouth set straight, eyes hooded by those glossy black eyelashes, he then laid her back against the pillows with extreme care before shifting down her body to unzip her new jeans; a second later and the denim was sliding off her legs with a deft expertise. As the cool air hit her clammy flesh she began to shiver and, with his lips now pinched back against his set teeth, he covered her with the duvet then stepped back and proceeded to yank off his jacket followed by his tie.

'Don't you dare!' she gasped in quivering horror.

'Don't be stupid,' he growled back. 'I might be a control freak but I am not a sadist.'

The next thing his shoes had been heeled off and he was stretching out beside her and tugging both Nell and the duvet into his arms. She curled herself right into him then burst into tears. It was like throwing open a floodgate; she just couldn't control it. With the top of her head pressed into his chest she sobbed her heart out while he lay there and held her and said absolutely nothing.

It was as if every hurtful thing he'd ever done to her came

out for an airing in those tears. The way he'd made her fall in love with him then asked her to marry him in that cool, grim tone she only noticed much later when it was too late. The way he'd stood over her while she signed his rotten pre-nuptial without batting an eyelid because she loved him and trusted him then discovered the painful way that love *was* blind! If Marcel hadn't emailed her urgently with a link to the gossip pages of an American tabloid, she would have sailed down the church aisle to him in a besotted haze.

'I h-had to marry you,' she sobbed into his shirt front, unaware that he hadn't been in on her first wave of grievances. 'I was scared you'd pull out of the deal with my father.'

'Shh,' he said, tangling his fingers in her hair and pressing her closer.

'I f-felt like a child-bride in a regency m-melodrama—s-sold to the unprincipled rake then dropped like a hot potato w-when he got more than he bargained f-for.'

She'd spent the next year pining for what might have been and wishing she'd stayed blind.

'Marcel wanted to come and get me then but I wouldn't let him. I *played* the child-bride in a regency melodrama, h-hoping you were going to turn up one day and realise you were head over heels in love with me but you didn't.'

'You saw me as a self-obsessed rat and I probably was then but you were so innocent and naïve you didn't have a clue what was happening around you. I was trying to protect you until you—'

'Enter the hero stage left,' she mocked thickly, rolling away from him and reaching out for the box of tissues that sat on the table by the bed. Fingers trembling, she plucked a tissue free and sniffed into it. 'Right in the knick of time he saves the innocent twit of a girl from the ugly guy with the f-fat lips.'

There was a shimmer of movement behind her that made her twist sharply to look at him. But if he was laughing at her it wasn't showing on his face. The tears clogged in her throat because it wasn't fair that he should have such liquid, dark, serious eyes that seemed to be trying to tug her right in-side him.

'Nothing to say?' she challenged.

'I will not answer these charges while you're so distressed,' he said flatly, then on a sigh when fresh tears welled he moved to pull her back to him again. 'Tell me about your half-brother,' he prompted huskily.

'He's the son my father wanted from my mother but never got.'

'So he's younger than you?'

She nodded. 'Nineteen. My mother was already pregnant with him when she left us. He lives with his father in Banff.'

'You were miserable being married to me. You needed a shoulder to cry on so you rang him up.'

'Someone I knew loved me.' She gave another nod, thereby missing Xander's infinitesimal wince. 'I didn't expect him to climb on the next plane to England to come and sort you out. He had no idea who he was dealing with. It was almost a relief when Hugo Vance refused him access to the house.'

'Why did he do that? If he's your brother of course he's welcome in our home!'

'Marcel wasn't on your very short accepted list.' Nell sat up and used the crumpled tissue to dab her eyes again. 'And he might only be nineteen but looks a lot older because he's big— six feet three already and built to suit—a heck of a sportsman; can white-water raft like you would not believe.'

'You're proud of him.'

'Mmm.' It was that simple and neat. 'I think Hugo Vance felt threatened by him.'

'How is it that you or your father have never so much as spoken his name to me?'

'My father refuses to have his name mentioned because he blames Marcel for stealing his wife away. He's still hurting. I've just got used to never mentioning him because that's the way it's always been. And anyway, you and I didn't have the kind of relationship that encouraged sharing secrets.'

A small silence followed while Nell dabbed at her eyes and

Xander lost himself in deep thought. Then he hissed out a sigh. 'The irony of it,' he muttered.

Nell didn't find anything ironical in what had been said. 'Why was he driving your car?' he asked suddenly.

She gave a small shift with her hunched shoulders. 'Because I let him,' seemed excuse enough because the hell if she was going to admit that once she'd escaped Rosemere she then had a stupid change of heart and got so upset about it, Marcel had to drive because she wasn't fit to.

'OK…' said with such slow patience Nell knew that he knew she was fobbing him off. 'Explain to me, then, if he's so into playing your hero, why he ran away from the accident scene.'

'He didn't—and don't you *dare* speak of Marcel in that nasty tone!' She swung on him angrily.

'Now I know why I'm jealous,' Xander said bluntly.

Nell looked away again, refusing point blank to take up that comment. 'He wasn't licensed to drive here,' she admitted grudgingly. 'He wasn't used to our narrow, winding lanes,' and he wasn't used to driving such a small but very powerful car. 'When he lost control on the bend I thought we were both going to die…'

A hand arrived at the base of her spine, long fingers rubbing in a strangely painful, comforting stroke. 'But you didn't…' he said gruffly.

Nell shook her head. 'Marcel wasn't wearing his seat belt.' It was just another thing she'd felt guilty about. She'd been so stupidly upset she hadn't noticed he hadn't belted himself in. 'If you want irony,' she mumbled, 'when he was thrown out of the car he suffered barely a scratch.' She grimaced into the tissue. 'When I realised how bad things were for me I was scared for him. I convinced him to lift me into the driver's seat then begged him to leave. He wouldn't go. He was upset, angry with himself, scared for me—and I've never seen him look so young and helpless…' The hand at her spine rubbed again, she quivered on a sigh and swallowed fresh tears. 'He used my mobile phone to call an ambulance then stayed beside me until we heard it arrive then he hid in the woods until I was safely inside the ambulance. I was so worried about him, I got a nurse in A&E to call his mobile and reassure him I was absolutely fine.'

'I didn't know that.'

'Don't sound so surprised,' Nell flung out. 'You might be the control freak around here but I know how to get my own way when I need to. I picked a young student nurse with her romantic ideals still intact. She thought she was calling up my lover—she adored being a part of my wicked tryst.'

'You amaze me sometimes,' he laughed though it wasn't really a laugh. 'I truly believed you were the most open and honest person I know but you can lie with the best of them!'

Her shrug told him she couldn't care less what he thought or believed.

'Where was he staying?' he bit out next. 'I had every hotel and pub for miles around carefully combed for him without getting back a single damn clue!'

'He was backpacking. He camped out in a farmer's field.'

'Enterprising of him.'

'He's very self-sufficient.'

'Matinée-idol material.' His hand left her back.

He really was jealous. Nell smiled into the now crumpled tissue. Then he uttered another one of those sighs and tried to pull her back down to him but Nell refused to go.

'I want to go to Rosemere,' she announced.

'I want you here with me.'

Just like that, quietly spoken but deadly serious. Nell turned to look at him and found those jet-glossed eyes roaming over her with blatant messages.

It wasn't fair. She looked away again as a whole gamut of weak sensations went sweeping through her. 'I'll stay married to you until the baby comes.'

'Thank you,' he said.

'But afterwards we get a divorce.'

'You need another tissue, *agape mou*. That one is just about done.'

'I'm being serious!'

'So am I. You are about to start weeping again and that tissue has mopped up too many tears as it is.'

And those tears just returned all the harder. 'I can't seem to switch them off,' she sobbed.

'Come here.' This time he refused to take no for an answer so she landed in the crook of his arm. 'You are just in need of some tender loving care right now.'

'Not from you.'

'Yes, from me. Who else have you got?'

It was so brutally frank that she winced.

'Tell me why the call you made to Marcel today was traced to Paris.'

'He's been staying with the French side of his family. I knew he was flying back to Banff today so I wanted to catch him and doubly reassure him that I was OK before he left.'

'Was he reassured?'

Nell nodded but kept her mouth clamped tightly shut as to how she had given that reassurance.

'I would like to have listened in on that call,' Xander drawled with lazy amusement.

He knew, the beast. He knew she'd convinced Marcel that she was gloriously, happily in love with her husband.

'I thought you had meetings to attend,' she prompted.

'I am attending to you.'

'Well, I can—'

'Remain right where you are.' Tightening the hold he had on her, he rose up until he had her pinned to the bed. 'I am the control freak,' he murmured huskily. 'Be controlled or watch me get upset.'

Green eyes searched gently mocking dark ones. He was gorgeous—irresistible. He kissed her—lightly on both corners of her vulnerable mouth, on the warm, soft, tear-swollen bottom lip then tracked a whole line of soft kisses along her jaw until he reached that sensitive spot by her ear. Things she did not want to happen started to happen. Nell quivered out a sigh of discontent. He caught it, tasted it with his tongue and she felt the blunt jut of his desire thicken against her thigh.

'No,' she said. 'I don't want—'

To do this, she was going to say but the moment she opened her mouth to speak the gentle dart of his tongue stole the rest away. With the arrival of his fingers across her cheekbones he deepened that kiss, making love to her mouth with a slow tenderness that had her shifting restlessly beneath his weight. Each time he paused he looked deep into the conflict taking place in her eyes, if she tried to say anything he returned to the kiss until eventually she forgot what it was she wanted to protest about. Her fingers shifted, relaxing out of the tense fists she had them clenched in to begin a slow foray across the leanness of his taut hips to his waist and eventually with a slow, shuddering sigh over warm flesh covered by cool white shirting to his shoulders, his neck and with a final convulsive move buried them in his hair.

She was lost, his for the taking. The duvet was pushed aside. The only time he allowed her to think was those few too brief seconds he required to remove the rest of her clothes and even then the moment she showed signs of protesting he was back again, smothering out everything but him and what he was doing and how he was making her feel.

His own clothes disappeared by degrees, she didn't even notice until the manoeuvre was over and she was being overwhelmed by the fully naked male. He made love to her breasts, so acutely receptive that she stretched into a lithe, sensual arch, toes and fingers curling in drowning pleasure that earned her yet another deep kiss to her mouth. And he was trembling, she liked that. Her restless hands crowded each muscular flex and quiver until, 'Touch me,' he groaned and she did, closing her fingers around smooth silk on steel and felt him throb and thicken then lost touch with her breathing when his long fingers tested the wetness between her thighs.

Bright rainbows of colour began to dance on her senses, and he answered them with a thick, hoarse growl. His heart was pounding, hers was pounding, as he eased his weight between her spread thighs then made that smooth drive into her, and she opened her eyes to look at his harsh look of hungry passion etched on his face.

'I don't want to love you this badly,' she confided on a sad little whisper.

He lost control. She'd never known him do it so thoroughly before so the difference between smooth, slick, sophisticated lover and a man lost in the wild, throbbing beat of his desire was startling. All she could do was hang on for dear life as he drove the two of them to the edge then over it in a wild, hot charge that threw him into a paroxysm of gasps and shudders that just seemed to go on and on.

Afterwards, exhausted, she thought she might have actually lost consciousness. She certainly didn't remember another thing until she awoke much later to find herself alone in the bed with the cringe-making knowledge that once again she had allowed him to whittle away at what bit of pride she had left by letting him make love to her.

And not only make love—which was bad enough—but she'd also let him twist her into such knots by getting her to confess her crimes to him while he got away without confessing a thing about his mistress and his son!

His son. The tears began to sting. Throwing herself onto her back, she stared fiercely at the ceiling in an effort to stem the threatening flood. How could she let him do this to her? How could she *go on* letting him do this to her? She had to get away from him, she knew that now, because she couldn't fight this sexual empowerment he had over her and each time she gave in to it she lost a bit more of herself.

She brought an arm up with the intention of covering her stupid watery eyes—but as she moved the backs of her fingers touched something and, turning, she saw a folded slip of paper lying on the empty pillow beside her head. With her heart lodged in her aching throat, she lifted the piece of paper up then lay there just staring at it.

She was afraid to read it. Really scared because he had never done anything like this before and all she could think was it had to have something to do with Vanessa and that little boy.

Mouth—fingers trembling, she made herself open it out.

'I love you', it said. That was all, nothing fancy, no hearts and flowers, or trumpeting fanfares, just those three words scrawled in bold black pen.

She curled into a tight ball beneath the duvet and cried her eyes out with the note pressed against her breasts.

Getting showered and dressed was an effort. She throbbed and ached and trembled too much to be efficient at anything. Back in the jeans and the cream top and her hair brushed, she pushed open the bedroom door with the intention of going to the kitchen and making herself a fortifying drink before she had to face him again—but it wasn't to be.

One of the doors through to his office had been left spread wide open and the first thing to hit her was the sound of Xander's voice tearing into someone in cut-throat Italian. As her feet drew her unwillingly towards that open door the next thing to hit her was Xander himself wearing one of his dark business suits and looking as razor-sharp as the sound of his voice.

The sun had come out since she'd last seen him standing behind his desk like this, and sunrays were playing across his jet silk hair and the deep bronze sheen of his skin. Angry as he was, he looked magnificent, all-powerful, all-masculine, all hard, dark lines of lean musculature. Animal, sexual, so utterly magnetic that her breathing feathered in her chest and brought her feet to a halt as a wave of helpless, hopeless love swept through her on a shimmering wave of anguished defeat.

Why him? she asked herself painfully. Why did I have to fall for a man like him? Why did he have to leave a note on her pillow spelling out words he had never once said to her face? Guilt? Remorse? Damage control? She couldn't believe those words. How could she believe them when Vanessa and that poor little boy stood in the way?

She went to turn, needing to slip out of sight before he saw her because she just wasn't ready to face him, but as she went to move another voice spoke angrily and her heart sank.

She'd thought he was talking on the telephone. He was *al-*

ways on the telephone! Maybe she uttered the strained little laugh she could feel clogging up her throat because Xander's dark head whipped round.

'Noll...' the hard, husky rasp of his voice scored a shudder right down her spine as still she tried to escape from this

'No, don't go...' He was already striding round the desk while she hovered reluctantly, several feet into the sitting room. The sound of his swift footsteps sounded in her head then his hand caught her arm just above her elbow. He tried to turn her but when she dug in her heels he stepped around her and reached for her other arm, holding her still in front of him. She could feel his tension, the hot simmer of his anger as his harsh breath scoured the top of her head.

'Look at me,' he husked.

But there was no way she was going to look at him. She stared at the knot in his silk tie instead.

His fingers flexed then began to slide upwards, they reached her shoulders and used them to tug her closer, then moved on to bury themselves in her hair at the defensive curve of her nape. It only took the light stroke of his thumbs beneath her chin to have it lifting.

Once again her breathing feathered as she found herself flickering a dancing glance over his face. Tension packed it, strain, the simmering anger glinting in his eyes. As she fluttered her eyes downwards again she was suddenly caught by the difference in his mouth. Held tight though it was, the fuller bottom lip still protruded more than it should. It looked darker—swollen; a hot tug deep inside her abdomen reminded her how urgently she'd sucked and bitten that swollen bottom lip—clung to it in the wild throes of—

A tense hiss of air left his throat. 'I know what you're thinking but I don't want you to think,' he said fiercely. 'I want you to stay calm and for both our sakes trust me, *agape mou*. I can explain myself—'

'With little notes left on pillows?' It was out before she could stop it.

'Little notes left on pillows can be read and reread,' he

pointed out. 'If I said those words out loud they would be swallowed up by too many conflicts rattling around in your head right now.'

Well, he was oh, so right about that. 'I can't do this any more,' she told his shirt front. 'You play games with me, Xander. You make me feel like your stooge.'

'You are not the stooge around here, *cara*. I am—someone else's stooge. But it is going to stop.' It sounded more like a threat than a promise. 'All I need from you is your patience. I *can* explain this.'

'Will you stop saying that? And don't you dare kiss me!' she protested when he started to lower his head. 'You think you can just kiss away every objection I put up against you but you can't. I—'

'If you two are going to start that again I may as well leave you to it...'

As if in a daze, Nell looked around, saw her mother-in-law—dressed goddess-style in wine-red silk—appear in view. She blinked, stunned that she could have so easily forgotten that Gabriela was even there! Then she became aware of other things, like the way she and Xander were standing in the door-way, almost wedged there by his rock-solid, unyielding stance. Her hands were on his chest, palms flat, fingers splayed. His still curved her slender neck. But worst of all her hips were resting against his hips. They didn't need to be pressing that close to him but they were as if they couldn't help themselves.

A rush of colour burned into her cheeks. As if he knew why it did, Xander slid his hands down her tense back to her hips and crushed her even closer, then did what she'd told him not to do and kissed her on the mouth.

'Don't so much as move another foot near that door, Madre,' he murmured with cool threat as he lifted his head again. 'It is judgement day, and you will not get out of this building until you have paid your dues to my wife.'

Judgement day? Pay her dues? Nell stared up at him with a mind gone blank.

He ignored the look, and suddenly he was all sharp and businesslike again. 'In here, I think.'

Looping an arm around Nell's shoulders, he turned her into the apartment then led her over to a chair then pressed her down into it.

'Don't tremble so much,' he scolded quietly.

'I...'

He kissed her fiercely—again.

'Oh, stop it, *caro*,' his mother snapped out impatiently as she appeared on the threshold of the apartment. 'Can't you keep your hands off her for five minutes? Helen is not going anywhere, as apparently I am not. *Dio*, Helen,' she added with a small shiver. 'How can you stay in this soulless place? I always hated it. Demitri never managed to get me to stay here once.'

'Did he ever get you to do anything you didn't want to do?' her son shot back at her.

'Oh, that's so unfair!' Gabriela protested. 'And so typical of you, Alexander, to always take your father's side!'

'You made him miserable—'

'I made him happy!' his mother angrily declared. 'How dare you, with your own marriage hanging in the balance by what I choose to reveal here, stand there and judge mine?'

They were suddenly back to fighting across the width of the sitting room, and doing it in English this time so Nell could at least understand the words if not the reasons for them. Looking from one face to the other, she couldn't decide which of them was going to catch light first. Xander was a proud Greek by birth but a hot-tempered Italian by nature, and she wondered if he had a clue as to how much like his mother he was?

'I can judge because I had to live with it.'

'Poor little rich boy, so badly treated,' his mother mocked. 'Helen, what is that top you are wearing?' Gabriela turned her attention away from her angry son to toss some derision her daughter-in-law's way instead.

'Leave Nell out of this,' her son hissed as Nell cringed into the chair feeling like a rag doll suddenly.

'I think she's already very much *in* it.'

The fact that her dry point hit home showed in the way Xander stiffened his elegant shoulders.

'Maybe you're right.' He took in a deep breath, then next thing Nell knew he had moved to stand behind her chair and his hands were settling on her shoulders in a possessive act no one could mistake. 'Congratulate us, Madre,' he then murmured dulcetly. 'Nell and I are going to have a baby, which means that you are going to be a grandmother...'

CHAPTER TWELVE

GABRIELA went so white that Nell thought she was going to faint on them and tried to rise to her feet to go to her.

'Remain where you are.' Xander's hands kept her seated. 'She will recover in a moment.'

'How can you be so heartless?' she gasped.

'I find it remarkably easy,' he answered coolly.

'But she's in shock—'

Gabriela gave a slow—slow blink of her beautiful eyes.

'I am all right.' Her pale mouth even managed to stretch into a wry little smile though her usual grace was missing as she walked to the nearest chair and slowly, carefully sat herself down. 'A *bambino*...' she whispered dazedly. 'Now, that, *mia caro*, was quite a blow even from you,' she admitted.

'As you can tell, my mother is not very enamoured with babies, *agape mou*,' Xander drawled lethally to Nell.

'It is not the *bambino* part that repels me but the *nonna* part,' Gabriela inserted surprisingly. 'Now I understand your desire to have me explain about Vanessa and her—son.'

Nell immediately began to stiffen. 'The desire for you to explain has always been there.' Xander's hands tightened on her shoulders in a gentle but determined squeeze. 'You simply chose to ignore it.'

'Until now...'

'Until now,' he agreed. 'So start talking or so help me, Madre, I will publicly denounce you as my mother and acknowledge them!'

Nell was beginning to feel sick, very sick. A hand went up to press against her mouth. Gabriela saw it and a look of what could have been remorse crossed her beautiful face.

'Our apologies, Helen,' she sighed. 'You have no idea what

169

we are talking about and therefore are thinking the very worst. Alexander, Helen needs a glass of water,' she concluded quietly.

With a soft curse he took his hands from her shoulders, his angry steps took him into the kitchen then seconds later brought him back again, then the man himself appeared in Nell's vision, squatting down in front of her to offer her a glass of cool water at the same time that he touched a concerned hand to her warm brow then was lifting her fingers from her mouth and carrying them to his lips.

'Sorry,' he said gruffly. 'This was not supposed to turn into a battle in front of you. I hoped that you would sleep a little longer so we could get this part out of the way before you needed to hear.'

'Hear what?' Nell tugged her hand free. 'That you have another family out there that is more important to you than your own mother—or me, come to that?'

'That just is not true.'

'You know about Vanessa and the boy?' Gabriela murmured in surprise.

Stupid fresh tears sprang into Nell's eyes as she sipped at the water. Robbed of her hand, Xander brought his to rest against one of her pale cheeks.

'Start talking, Madre,' he rasped out.

Gabriela flinched at the serrated edge to his voice. 'I had an affair with a man half my age,' she confessed in a reluctant rush.

'And broke my father's heart—'

'He broke mine too! Vanessa is only a few years older than Helen! He should have been shot for taking such a child to his bed!'

Vanessa? Nell's attention picked up. She glanced at Xander to find his gaze fixed on her, narrowed and intent.

'Both you and your father had an affair with Vanessa?' she breathed in stricken horror.

Anger reshaped his mouth. 'No, we did not,' he denied and

sprang up and spun away, angry tension racked across his shoulders.

Gabriela sighed. 'You are such a fool, Alexander,' she informed him. 'Have you never learned how to get your priorities right!'

'Like my father did?' he lashed back.

'Sì!' Gabriela cried. 'As we both did!' she impressed. 'You cannot pick between the two of us when you look for faults, Alexander. It just is not fair!'

'You took another lover before he did,' her son dismissed that line of defence.

'And he had his revenge.' Gabriela took in a deep breath and returned her attention to Nell. 'You cannot begin to know about middle age until you reach it, Helen. No one can—not even the great Alexander, who apparently has never put a foot wrong in his life!'

As a dig at his marriage to Nell, it hit the mark.

'Middle age eats away at your heart and your belief in yourself. You see lines where only smoothness had once been and a sagging figure where once everything had been tight. You see younger women receiving the admiring looks you used to receive.'

'You break my heart.'

'Be quiet!' his mother responded. 'You're a man,' she said in disgust. 'You do not fade like an ageing rose, you improve year by year! Your father did this! He improved and improved in his physical stature *and* he admired these younger women while assuring me I looked *nice*. Have you any conception at all how badly *nice* can hurt?' She swung on Nell again. 'If my son ever uses that word on you, *cara*, then take my lead and find yourself another man, preferably one a lot younger than he is—'

'You're careering from the point,' Xander incised.

'Feeling the vulnerability of your age difference to Helen's, *caro*?' Gabriela incised back. 'When you hit your fifties she will still be in her thirties—the absolute prime of a woman's life!'

'Get to the point!' The tension in him was close to snapping. Nell blinked at the sight of darkness scoring the rigid line of his cheeks.

'At least you chose the child for your wife, not your mistress,' his mother continued with the same cutting scorn. 'I am the same age as your father. I *felt* it deeply when his interest began to stray. You are built in his image—a true Pascalis male who will not lose his good looks and his sex appeal as he grows older.'

'So you jumped on the first man that showed you some admiration.'

'I did not jump, I *dived*,' his mother declared without conscience. 'I lost myself completely in the glorious flood!'

'You have no shame.'

Nell stood up. 'I think I should leave you two to finish this on your—'

'Sit down again!' Xander thundered.

Her chin came up. 'Don't speak to me like that.'

With a flare of rage he stepped up to her and forcibly made her sit. She'd never seen him like this, so controlled by his emotions that he was almost fizzing. She opened her mouth to protest. He covered it—hard. Yet even though it began as an angry way to subdue her, the kiss did not conclude that way and she could feel the effort it took for him to drag his mouth from hers.

'Listen to what she has yet to say—please,' he begged, and when she could only nod, he claimed her mouth again, soft with gratitude—then moved away.

Having watched the little interplay with interest, oddly, Gabriela went quite pale. 'My son loves you—'

'The point, Madre,' Xander curtly prompted.

'He made me come here because he said you would not believe a word he says about this—thing with Vanessa DeFriess.'

'Liars lose the right to be believed,' Xander inserted.

'I still don't understand why you felt you needed to lie!' his mother cried. 'What man with a beautiful wife to love would want to lay claim to that—*puttana*? Unless, of course, you were... Ah,' she said when he all but threw himself over to the window.

'Stop trying to interrogate me and spit it out,' Xander gritted.

'Well, he was lying.' She turned back to Nell again, and then took in a deep breath. 'It was *my* husband who had the affair with Vanessa,' she spelled it out at last. 'Demitri took that woman to his bed to get his revenge on me. When the madness was over for both of us and we decided we could not live without each other, we made a promise that neither affair would ever be spoken about again.' She paused to take in a breath. 'All was well for several months. Indeed, we enjoyed the bliss of a second honeymoon.' Her beautiful dark eyes took on a wistful glaze. 'Then Vanessa came to Demitri and told him she was pregnant with his child. Everything fell apart in that moment. After Alexander was born and I discovered I was unable have more children Demitri had assured me that it did not matter...'

'I didn't know that,' Xander murmured gruffly.

'No.' His mother looked at him. 'You believed I was a fashion plate with a thin figure to protect. And you are now thinking of your own lonely childhood when I was not a very good mother to the one child I did have,' she tagged on to his hard expression. 'Which I suppose does give you every right to look upon me with such cynicism. I *admit* that I am not the maternal kind.'

It was like listening to some bizarre rehash of her and Marcel's story, Nell thought as she listened, while her mind stung her with disbelief. Coincidences like this just didn't happen. It was reality gone berserk. She looked up at Xander to find his fierce gaze was fixed on her.

'I know,' he said tensely, reading what she was thinking. 'This is why I knew you would not believe me if I told you this myself.'

His mother looked from one to the other. 'What are you talking about?' She frowned.

'Nothing,' Xander said. 'Please continue.'

'Continue.' Gabriela laughed stiffly. 'What is there left to say? There was your father, about to become a father again and he could not disguise his delight. I was going to lose him again and I was so terrified I—took an overdose and had to be flown to hospital. By the time I was out of danger Demitri was a different man. I begged him to never see Vanessa and her baby and, to his word, they were never mentioned again.'

'How much more proof could he offer that he loved you?' her son put in. 'He handed responsibility for Vanessa and his unborn child to me with the instruction that I never speak of them because he would not have you distressed like that again.'

'And you never forgave me for being so spineless.'

'The child has rights,' Xander said. 'You gave him none. The mother had the right to be treated with respect if nothing else. You denied her that right. She was gagged so quickly by my father's lawyers that she was left without a single leg to stand upon.'

'For money,' Gabriela pointed out. 'Don't forget the millions you take care of for her. Or the huge trust set up in the boy's name.'

'Or the hours of emotional support both Vanessa and her son required once Alex was born. I became a father without taking part in the act of conception and I do not recall you ever feeling sorry for my plight.'

'You didn't have to take duty to such extremes—'

'He's my half-brother!' Xander expelled in hoarse-voiced fury. 'Half my own flesh and blood!'

'I know I am a very selfish woman,' his mother said shakenly. 'I know you see me as a spoiled, vain, useless waste of space. But it is happening again, isn't it?' She looked helpless suddenly. 'You are willing to sacrifice me for them just as your father was willing to do the same thing.'

'No,' Xander uttered gruffly.

'You already threatened it, Alexander,' she wearily reminded him. 'Your father did the same.'

'Hence the dramatic overdose aimed to pull him back into line again?' Xander said hardly. 'If that isn't extreme then I don't know what is, Madre. Now I've made you talk about this, am I to wait with bated breath for you to use the same emotional blackmail on me?'

His mother went white. On a gasp of horror at his cruelty Nell shot to her feet. 'Xan—'

But Gabriela got in first. 'I have my regrets, Alexander,' she told him stiffly. 'And I can now feel the cutting pangs of remorse for denying your father the right to know his other son. But if you believe I have not been punished very adequately for my sins then you're wrong. When Demitri died I lost a major part of myself. I still miss him so much...'

'You know,' Xander drawled, 'I would respond kindly to that blatant attempt to play on my sympathies if it was not for the fact that only minutes before Nell came in you were still refusing to sacrifice your ego for the sake of our marriage.'

Gabriela accepted this final indictment with a wry little smile. 'Ah, that sin called ego,' she drily mocked herself then turned to go.

'No—don't go,' Nell begged huskily. 'You both need to resolve this...'

Gabriela looked into her daughter-in-law's anxious face then at Xander's rock-like stance and offered up a grimace. 'You are a sweet person, Helen. You will make a good mother to my grandchild. Let us hope that my son will be a good father, for I think he forgets that I was not the only parent to leave him for another love.'

Then she walked away, leaving Nell staring helplessly after her while Xander continued to stand there like a cold, hard, *stubborn* fool!

'Go after her.' She swung on him urgently. 'She's your mother, for goodness' sake. You love her, you know you do— faults and sins alike!' When he still didn't move from his stiff stance, 'If you let her go now you will never see her again because the *both* of you are too stuffed full of pride to give a solitary inch! I thought you were bigger than this! Xander, please...!' she begged painfully.

But she didn't need to add the last part because with a tight, angry growl of blistering frustration he spun and strode after her, leaving Nell staring after him feeling very much as if she'd just been run over by a pair of trucks.

She watched his hands reach out to grasp Gabriela's narrow shoulders, watched through a deepening glaze of tears as he turned her into his chest. She caught the tones of thick, gruff, husky Italian, felt her heart quiver as the proud Gabriela broke her control on a muffled sob.

Then she turned away and began to shake like a leaf, still too befuddled by what she had been told to even attempt to sort it out in her head.

She made for the kitchen, leaving mother and son alone to mend their differences while she attempted to do something really normal like setting about making coffee but feeling so at odds with herself and with Xander that she didn't hear him arrive at the door.

'OK?' The husky question came from behind her.

Stiffening her spine, she pressed her lips together and nodded, not sure she wanted to look at him until she'd made up her mind if she hated him for putting his mother through that ordeal, or loved him for doing it for her.

'No more nausea?' he questioned when it became clear she wasn't going to speak.

'I'm fine,' she managed, fingers fiddling with the slender white china cup she'd set out ready for her coffee. 'Would you like a drink?'

'Not if you're planning to poison it,' he said drily, then hissed out a weary sigh. 'Nell, we need to—'

'Your telephone's ringing.'

And it was. They both listened to it for a few fraught seconds, Nell with her eyes squeezed tightly shut on a tense prayer that he would just go and answer the damn thing. Xander, she was sure because she could feel it, piercing the vulnerable tilt of her neck with grim intent in his gaze, wanted her to turn and look at him.

'Easy on the belladonna,' he instructed heavily after a moment and went back to his office, leaving her wilting though she didn't really know why.

A few minutes later she was bracing her shoulders and carrying two cups of freshly made coffee into his office. Xandar was still on the phone with his dark head resting back against the chair's leather upholstery, and his eyes were closed. He looked tired, she noticed, dragged down and fed up. As she walked across the expanse of floor towards the desk she saw his lashes give a flicker and quickly looked away.

'Efharisto,' he murmured as she put one of the cups of coffee down in front of him.

She managed a brief upward glance at his face before turning away again.

'Stay,' he husked, showering her in tingling tremors. 'Sit down, relax, drink your coffee. I will be only a few more moments here.'

Sit down, relax, drink your coffee, Nell repeated silently and sank into the chair by his desk and wondered why she was still feeling so at odds with him when everything had been explained—hadn't it?

He was talking in Greek, she noticed, sitting up now and swinging his chair slightly with his eyes lowered to where a set of long fingers hit intermittently at the computer keyboard lying on the desk. His deep voice was quiet, asking low key questions with no hint of sharp command evident, as if someone had switched off his normal incisiveness.

The phone went quietly back on its rest. Strumming silence followed. Nell felt it so deeply inside that she tensed.

He picked up his coffee cup and looked down into it. 'How much belladonna?'

'Two spoonfuls,' she answered.

'Still not forgiven, then.' He grimaced a wry smile at her then lifted the cup to his lips and drank. The way that he did it was so much like a man willing to take his poison that she shot like a bullet to her feet.

'Stop it,' she stabbed at him.

'Stop what?' He looked at her.

'Making a joke of it.'

'Of what?'

'All of that—stuff we've got through today.'

'Are we through it?'

She frowned at the question, her tightening nerve-ends forcing her to discard her coffee-cup before she spilled it down herself. 'Y-your mother is your mother.'

'Is that supposed to make some sense to me?'

'Sh-she is what she is and you have to accept that.'

'I do—as much as I can do,' he reminded her. 'Next problem.'

The way he said it as if she was in a business meeting made her start to seethe. She jerked round to face the other way. 'I don't like you.' That was a problem, she thought. 'Sometimes...' she then added grudgingly because it was crazy to deny that she liked him in bed—*loved* him in bed.

Loved him all the time, she extended unhappily, but loving didn't have anything to do with liking, did it?

'You hurt people and don't seem to care when you're doing it.'

'Are we still discussing my mother?'

'No—me,' she said huskily.

Silence met that announcement. Nell folded her arms beneath her breasts and stared down at her feet.

'You should have told me the truth about Vanessa.'

'You should have told me the truth about Marcel.'

'That was different.'

'Why?'

'Because he wasn't an issue when you married me. Vanessa was and once you knew it you should have told me the truth straight away instead of letting me spend the next twelve months imagining you in her arms instead of mine!'

A sigh sounded behind her. The next sound was the creaking of his chair as he came to his feet. Her chin hit her chest when he came to stand right in front of her. Without saying a word he clamped his hands to her waist and lifted her up to sit on the desk. Next her thighs were summarily pushed apart and he was wedging himself between them, then her arms were firmly unfolded and lifted round his neck.

'OK,' he said. 'Now that we are more comfortable I will explain.... I fell in love with you within about two seconds of you walking through your father's front door...'

Her chin shot up, green eyes wide with shock and disbelief.

'Got your full attention now?' he mocked. 'Ready to hang on my every word with bated breath?'

'You never did love me then, or you would not have left me on our wedding night believing what I did.'

'You are referring to that memorable time when you stood there in your bridal gown, shouting at me and looking so heart-breakingly beautiful, hurt and *young*?' He uttered a sigh. 'It was either leave you there or toss you on the bed and ravish you and—trust me, *agape*—you would not have survived the kind of ravishing I had in mind right then. I was mad with you for believing that trash—mad with myself for not seeing it coming. Do you think that Vanessa is the only skeleton a man like me has lurking in his closet? I've had women trying to foist their babies on to me and women trying to blackmail me. I've had them sneaking into my bed in the dead of night and crawling through windows in an effort to get to me.'

'Oh, don't be modest; do tell the rest,' Nell drawled acidly.

'You think I like being every greedy gold-digger's dream catch? Why do you think my security is so tight? Would you like a ballpark figure on how much it has cost me to keep such stories out of the Press over the years? Give any one of those grasping women a glimpse at more money and they would be singing to the Press today. Vanessa was the exception. She was not my skeleton, which made those computer printouts you showered at me all the more annoying because I did not feel I had the right to break the promise of silence and protection I had made to my father on his death bed.'

'Not even to me?'

'Don't look so hurt,' he chided. 'Do you think it didn't hurt me to realise that you were not equipped with the necessary defences to live my life? I already knew I'd been unforgivably selfish, crowding you into marriage so young. I saw in a single miserable flash of enlightenment as I watched you enact that little tragedy just how selfish I had been. I saw how every jealous woman out there was going to have a story to whisper in your ear. It would have been like leading a lamb into a slaughterhouse then standing back to watch it be skinned.'

'So you walked away.' Her soft mouth wobbled.

'Yes.' He kissed the wobble then sighed. 'When I left you at Rosemere I did it determined to set you free—but I could not. I kept on putting it off. Kept coming to see you, couldn't stay away! Kept trying to convince myself that while you seemed content with what you had then you were OK. The night I offered to renegotiate our contract was the one time I was ready to rip the damn thing up and let you go. I've never felt happier when you turned the offer down without even hearing me out. I was off the hook for another few months until my conscience got to me again. Then that second photo of me with Vanessa appeared and you crashed your car. I've never felt so bloody lousy in my entire life!'

'Good,' she said. 'It's nice to know that I wasn't the only one feeling like that.'

'Ah, but that was before I knew about the new man in your life.' He smiled. 'I switched from feeling lousy with remorse to a thirty-four-year-old lusty, cradle-snatching lecher in a single blink of an eye. You think you were jealous of Vanessa? You barely scratched the surface of jealousy, *agape mou*. But I did. I scratched it right down to its bloody, primitive raw.'

'I love it when you're primitive.' She moved a little closer in an effort to capture his mouth.

His head went back. 'I'm being serious!'

'So what do you want me to say—get away from me, you uncivilised beast? Shall I get your pack of bodyguards to string you up to a tree and tar and feather you for wanting me too much to let me go?'

'Loving you too much,' he corrected softly.

'And aren't you the lucky one that I loved you too much to drive away...?'

'What's that supposed to mean?' He frowned at her.

Nell gave a little idle shrug. 'Only that Marcel was driving me *back* to Rosemere when we crashed. I thought your police report would have told you that.'

'If it did, I never got to read that far,' he murmured dazedly. 'I just read the bit about you being in the passenger seat and went berserk.'

'I noticed,' she murmured feelingly.

'Forgive me for what I said?'

Nell shook her head.

Xander uttered a sigh then changed tactics. He lifted her up until she straddled him then strode across the room.

'Where are we going?' she asked innocently.

'Guess,' he drawled. 'If I am to pay a penance then I will do it in comfort.'

And he did.

The island was trapped in the sultry heat of the late afternoon when the helicopters began to arrive. From her place at the nursery window Nell watched as Marcel jumped down onto the ground then walked towards the glinting pool. He looked so absolutely gorgeous that Nell uttered a small sigh of sisterly pride. A sudden cry of delight went up, then a young boy in swimming shorts was racing to meet him. Marcel grinned lazily as he accepted this show of pure hero worship from the much younger Alex.

'My hero status has been eclipsed by the matinée idol,' Xander murmured with a regretful sigh.

'Never mind, your real son worships you,' Nell consoled. 'And look at your mother and my father watching them together. They're actually smiling. That has to be a first for both of them.'

'It's called bowing to fate,' Xander said. 'They either accept our family as a whole or they miss out.'

'And who'd have thought Gabriela would be so besotted?'

'Why should she not,' Gabriela's son defended loyally, 'when my son looks exactly like me?'

'Too like you,' Nell complained, turning away from the window to go and lean over the cot, where Demitri Pascalis lay kicking contentedly. 'Now, you know I love you,' she informed the wide-eyed baby. 'But I still don't think it's fair that you didn't even elect to have my green eyes.'

The baby let out a shriek of delighted laughter. He didn't care that he looked the absolute spit of his dark-eyed *papa*.

'Cruel,' she scolded. 'But I will get my own back,' she warned him.

'And how do you intend to do that?' Xander asked.

Straightening up to find herself slipping easily beneath his waiting arm, Nell smiled one of those wait-and-see threats at him as she let him lead her away.

'I see,' Xander murmured fatalistically. 'The wicked witch is mixing spells again.'

As they left the baby's room Thea Sophia slipped quietly into it, and took the comfortable chair placed by the cot. Out came her lacework and her gnarled fingers got busy while the baby chatted away to her. He would fall asleep in a few minutes, bailing out with a blink of an eye, but until that happened he had his ever-attentive *thea* to entertain.

Walking Nell into their sunny bedroom, Xander turned her to face him. He was dressed in one of his loose white shirts and casual trousers, but soon they would have to start getting dressed up for the party that was to take place tonight—which was a shame, in Nell's opinion, because she preferred to keep him in clothes she could strip off quickly.

'Mmm,' she said as she pressed her lips to the triangle of hair-roughened flesh exposed by the open neck of his shirt. 'You taste of sun and salt and sexy masculinity.'

'And you have a one-track mind,' he sighed.

'It's my birthday. I'm allowed a treat.'

'Several treats.'

'OK,' she shrugged, not arguing the point because it was oh, so much more interesting to discover how smoothly the shirt fell open to her lightest touch. She ran her fingernails down his front and watched taut muscles flex.

'You're so gorgeous,' she murmured helplessly—and received her reward with the hungry clamp of his mouth.

It didn't take much longer for them to be lost. Xander's muttered, 'We don't have time for this,' was ruined by the urgency with which he stripped her blue T-shirt dress off her and tumbled her onto the bed. They made hot, frenzied love while the rest of the family chatted by the poolside.

When they came downstairs two hours later you would be forgiven for thinking that Nell had spent the whole afternoon achieving that gloriously chic look she'd donned in a short half-hour. She was wearing aquamarine silk, smooth and slinky, a perfect set of blue diamonds sparkling at her creamy throat.

Her hair was up to show them off because Xander had given her them for her birthday. And if anyone wondered at the rueful grimace he offered when his mother congratulated his wife on how two hours' pampering could put such a wonderful glow to her daughter-in-law, no one would have thought to question whether he knew something that they did not. He looked far too smooth and sophisticated to be recalling what they'd been doing in the shower only half an hour ago.

They separated, they danced and circulated amongst their fifty-strong guests as goods hosts did. They laughed and teased and flirted and came together on the terrace to snatch a private moment or two gazing at the moon.

'Happy?' Xander asked, holding her in front of him.

'Mmm,' Nell murmured uncertainly.

'Something missing from your perfect day?'

'Mmm,' she nodded.

'You would like me to toss you into the pool perhaps?'

'Not tonight, thank you,' she answered primly, then took hold of one of his hands and slid it over her abdomen. 'I'm afraid it's tender loving care time again,' she softly confided.

Xander immediately stiffened like a man in shock. 'I hope you are teasing me!' he grated.

'No,' Nell sighed.

He swung her around, a dark glitter in his eyes. 'You mean you really are pregnant? But our son is only ten months old!'

'I want a red-haired, green-eyed girl child this time,' she told him. 'And you really are lousy at birth control.'

'Ah, so I am to get the blame again.'

'Of course,' she said then wound her arms around his neck and leaned provocatively into him. 'But then you never, ever disappoint…'

THE PRICE OF A BRIDE
MICHELLE REID

CHAPTER ONE

JANUARY had arrived with an absolute vengeance. Standing in the window behind her father's desk, Mia watched the way the wind was hurling the rain against the glass in fiercely gusting squalls—while behind her a different kind of storm was raging, one where two very powerful men pitched angry insults at each other.

Not that she was taking much notice of what they were actually fighting about. She knew it all already, so her presence here was really quite incidental.

Merely a silent prop to use as leverage.

'Look, that's the deal, Doumas!' she heard her father state with a brittle grasp on what was left of his patience. 'I'm not into haggling so either take what's on offer or damn well leave it!'

'But what you are proposing is positively barbaric!' the other man hit back furiously. 'I am a businessman, not a trader in white slavery! If you have difficulty finding a husband for your daughter try a marriage agency,' he scathingly suggested, 'for I am not for sale!'

No? Way beyond the point of being insulted by remarks like that one, Mia's startlingly feminine mouth twitched in a cross between bitter appreciation for the clever answer Alexander Doumas had tossed back at her father and a grimace of scorn. Did he truly believe he would be standing here at all if Jack Frazier thought he couldn't be bought?

Jack Frazier dealt only in absolute certainties. He was a rough, tough, self-made man who, having spent most of his life clawing his way up from nothing to become the corporate giant he was today, had learned very early on that attention to fine detail before he went in for the kill was the key to success.

He left nothing whatsoever to chance.

Alexander Doumas, on the other hand, was the complete antithesis of Jack. He was smooth, sleek and beautifully polished by a top-drawer Greek pedigree which could be traced back so far into history it made the average mind boggle, only, while the Frazier fortunes had been rising like some brand new star in the galaxy during the last thirty odd years, the Doumas fortunes had been steadily sinking—until this man had come on the scene.

To be fair, Alexander Doumas had not only stopped the rot in his great family's financial affairs but had spent the last ten years of his life repairing that rot, and so successfully that he had almost completely reversed the deterioration—except for one final goal.

And he was having the rank misfortune of coming up against Jack Frazier in his efforts to achieve that one goal.

Poor devil, Mia thought with a grim kind of sympathy, because, ruthless and unswerving though he was in his own way, Alexander Doumas didn't stand a chance of getting what he wanted from her father, without paying the price Jack Frazier was demanding for it.

'Is that your final answer?' Jack Frazier grimly challenged, as if to confirm his daughter's prediction. 'If so, then you can get out for I have nothing left to say to you.'

'But I am willing to pay double the market price here!'

'The door, Mr Doumas, is over there...'

Mia's spine began to tingle, the fine muscles lining its long, slender length tensing as she waited to discover what Alexander Doumas was going to do next.

He had a straight choice, the way she saw it. He could walk out of here with his arrogant head held high and his monumental pride still firmly intact, but put aside for ever the one special dream that had brought him to this point in the first place, or he could relinquish his pride, let his own principles sink to Jack Frazier's appalling level and pay the price being asked for that dream.

'There has to be some other way we can resolve this,' he muttered.

No there isn't, Mia countered silently. For the simple reason that her father did not *need* another way. The Greek had called Jack Frazier barbaric, but barbarism only half covered what her father really was. As she, of all people, should know.

Jack Frazier didn't even bother to answer. He just sat there behind his desk and waited for the other man to give in to him or leave as suggested.

'Damn you to hell for bringing me down to this,' Alexander Doumas grated roughly. It was the driven sound of a grudging surrender.

The next sound Mia heard was the creak of old leather as her father came to his feet. It was a familiar sound, one she had grown to recognise with dread when she was younger, and even now, at the reasonably mature age of twenty-five, she was still able to experience the same stomach-clutching response as she had in childhood.

Jack Frazier was a brute and a bully. He always had been and always would be. Man or woman. Friend or foe. Adult or child. His need to dominate made no exceptions.

'Then I'll leave you to discuss the finer details with my daughter,' he concluded. 'Get in touch with my lawyer tomorrow. He will iron out any questions you may have, then get a contract drawn up.'

With that, and sounding insultingly perfunctory now that he had the answer he wanted from the other man, Jack Frazier, cold, cruel, ruthless man that he was, walked out of the room and left them to it.

And with the closing of the study door came quite a different silence. Bitter was the only word Mia could come up with to describe it—a silence so bitter it was attacking the back of her neck like acid.

I should have left my hair down, she mused in the same dry, mockingly fatalistic way she had dealt with all of this.

It was the only way, really. She couldn't fight it so she mocked it. It was either that or weep, and she'd done enough weeping during her twenty-five years to know very well that tears did nothing but make you feel worse.

'Drink?'

The sound of glass chinking against fine crystal had her turning to face the room for the first time since the interview had begun. Alexander Doumas was helping himself to some of her father's best whisky.

'No, thank you,' she said, and stayed where she was, with her arms lightly folded beneath the gentle thrust of her breasts, while she watched him toss back a rather large measure.

Poor devil, she thought again. Men of his ilk just weren't used to surrendering anything to anyone—never mind to a nasty piece of work like her father.

Alexander Doumas had arrived here this afternoon, looking supremely confident in his ability to strike a fair agreement with Jack Frazier. Now he was having to deal with the very unpalatable fact that he had been well and truly scuppered—caught hook, line and sinker by a man who always knew exactly what bait to use to catch his prey. And even the fine flavour of her father's best malt whisky wasn't masking the nasty taste that capture had placed in his mouth.

He glanced at her, his deep-set, dark brown Mediterranean eyes flicking her a whiplashing look of contempt from beneath the glowering dip of his frowning black eyebrows. 'You had a lot to say for yourself,' he commented in a clipped voice.

Mia gave an empty little shrug. 'Better men than me have taken him on and failed,' she countered.

She was referring to him, of course, and the way he grimaced into his glass acknowledged the point.

'So you are quite happy to agree to all of this, I must presume.'

Happy? Mia picked up the word and tasted it for a few moments, before deciding ruefully, that—yes—she was, she supposed, happy to do whatever it would take to fulfil her side of this filthy bargain.

'Let me explain something to you,' she offered in a tone gauged to soothe not aggravate. 'My father never puts any plan into action unless he is absolutely sure that all participants are going to agree to whatever it is he wants from them. It's the way he works. The way he has *always* worked,' she tagged on pointedly. 'So, if you are hoping to find your redemption through me, I'm sorry to disappoint you.'

'In other words—' His burning gaze was back on her again '—you are willing to sleep with anyone if Daddy commands it.'

'Yes.' Despite the deliberate insult, her coolly composed face showed absolutely nothing—no hint of offence, no distaste, not even anger.

His did, though, showing all of those things plus a few others all meant to label her nothing better than a trollop.

Maybe she was nothing better than a trollop, allowing her father to do this to her, Mia conceded. Certainly, past history had marked her as a trollop.

'Did you do the choosing yourself?' he asked suddenly. 'Is that what this is really all about?'

Taken by surprise by the suggestion, her eyes widened. Then she laughed—a surprisingly pleasant sound amidst all the bitterness and tension. 'Oh, no,' she said. 'You said yourself that my father is a barbarian. It would go totally against his character to allow me to choose anything for myself. But how conceited of you to suggest it...' she added softly.

'It had to be asked,' he said, stiffening slightly at the gentle censure.

'Did it?' Mia was not so sure about that. 'It seems to me that you're seeing yourself as the only victim here, Mr Doumas,' she said more soberly. 'And at this juncture it may well help if I remind you that there tend to be different kinds of victims in most disasters.'

'And you are a victim of your own father's tyranny—is that what you are trying to tell me?'

His scepticism was clear. Her green eyes darkened. If Alexander Doumas came to know her better he would take careful note of that. She was Jack Frazier's daughter after all.

'I am not *trying* to tell you anything,' Mia coolly countered. 'I don't have to justify myself to you, you see.'

After all, she thought, why should she defend herself when his own reasons for agreeing to this were not that defensible?

Not that he was seeing it like that, she wryly acknowledged. Alexander Doumas was looking for a scapegoat on which to blame his own shortcomings.

'No,' he murmured cynically. 'You merely have to go to bed with me.'

And she, Mia noted, was going to be his scapegoat.

'Of course, I do understand that my lot is the much easier one,' she conceded, with that same dangerously deceptive mildness. 'Being a woman, all I need to do is lie down, close my eyes and mentally switch off, whereas you have to bring yourself to…er…perform. But God help us both,' she added drily, 'if you find me so repulsive that you can't manage it because we will really have a problem then.'

She had managed to actually shock him, Mia was gratified to note—had managed to make him look *at* her and *see* her, instead of just concentrating on showing her his contempt.

With a wry smile of satisfaction she deserted her post by the window at last to come around her father's desk and walk across the room towards the two high wing-backed leather armchairs that flanked the polished mahogany fireplace.

A log fire was burning in the grate, the leaping flames trying their best to add some warmth to a room that did not know the meaning of the word—not in Jack Frazier's house, anyway.

But the flames did manage to highlight the rich, burnished copper of Mia's hair as she walked towards them. Although she didn't look at Alexander Doumas as she moved, she felt his narrowed gaze following her.

Eyeing up the merchandise, she thought, cynically mocking that scrutiny.

Well, let him, she thought defiantly as she felt his gaze sweep over the smooth lines of her face, which she had been told was beautiful although she did not see any beauty in it herself.

But, then, she didn't like herself very much and they did say that beauty was in the eyes of the beholder.

Therefore, it followed that neither would this man be seeing any beauty in her right now, she supposed, as he was so actively despising her at this moment.

Oh, she was no hound-dog. Mia wasn't so eaten up with self-hate that she couldn't see that her hair, face, body and legs combined to present a reasonably attractive picture.

Whatever this man was feeling about her right now, she knew that he had looked at her before today and had wanted her so his expression of distaste simply failed to impress her.

Reaching the two chairs, she turned, felt his gaze dip over the slender curves of her figure—so carefully muted by the simple coffee-coloured pure wool dress she was wearing—and chose the chair which would place him directly in her sight so she could watch those eyes draw down the long length of her silk-stockinged legs as she sat and smoothly crossed one knee over the other.

Alexander Doumas was no hound-dog himself, Mia had

to acknowledge. In fact, she supposed he was what most fanciful females would have seen as ideal husband material—tall, tanned and undeniably handsome, with the kind of tightly contoured Greek-god body on which top designers liked to hang their very exclusive clothes.

Indeed, that iron grey silk suit looked very definitely top designer wear. He wore his straight black hair short at the back and neat at the front, and the rich smoothness of his olive-toned skin covered superb bone structure that perhaps said more about his high-born lineage than anything else about him.

He had a good mouth, too—even if it was being spoiled by anger and disgust at the moment—and his long, rather thin nose balanced well with the rest of his cleanly chiselled features.

But it was his eyes that made him special—deep-set, dark brown, lushly fringed, deceptively languid eyes that, even when they were showing disdain, could still stir the senses.

Her senses, she noted as she watched those eyes settle on the point where her slender legs disappeared under the hem of her dress and felt a warm, tingling sensation skitter along her inner thighs in response.

'Well,' she prompted, unable to resist the dig, 'do you have a problem there?'

He stiffened, the finely corded muscles along his strong jawbone clenching when he realised he had been caught staring. 'No,' he admitted on a rasping mutter.

At least he's being honest about it, Mia reflected ruefully. And so he should be, having spent the last month trying to get her into his bed!

'Then your only problem,' she went on coolly, 'is having to decide whether you want your lost island of Atlanta— or whatever it is called,' she mocked flippantly, 'badly enough to relinquish your single status to get it.'

'But it isn't just my single status I'm being tapped for, is it?' he threw back sourly.

'No,' she agreed, with another wry smile of appreciation at his wit, even in the face of all this horror. 'And you are going to have to...er...produce pretty potently, too, if you want this arrangement kept short-term.'

That had his gaze narrowing sharply on her studiedly impassive green eyes. He didn't like the tone of voice she had used but she didn't care that he didn't like it. She didn't *like* Alexander Doumas.

However, she would go to bed with him, if that was what it would take to get what she needed to gain from this dastardly deal.

'And what is the incentive that makes *you* agree to all of this?'

Mia didn't answer, wondering bleakly what his reaction would be if she told him the truth.

He was still standing by her father's drinks cabinet, his body tense and his expression tight with anger and contempt—for her, for himself, or even for both of them, she wasn't sure. And it really didn't matter because there was a whole lot more at stake here than his personal contempt— or even her own self-contempt, come to that.

Her father wanted a grandson to replace the son who had foolishly got himself killed in a car accident several months ago. Alexander Doumas had been chosen to father that grandson—Mia to be the vessel in which the poor child would be seeded.

This man's reasons for agreeing to any of this were based on his own personal ambitions. He wanted to get back the family island that lay somewhere off the Greek mainland, which his father had been forced to sell during the downfall of the family fortunes. Jack Frazier was the only person who could return it to him since he now owned the deeds to the island.

Mia, on the other hand, stood to gain far more than what amounted to a pile of ancient Greek rock. What was more, she was quite prepared to do anything to complete her side of the bargain she had made with her father.

'Like you, I get back something that once belonged to me,' she murmured eventually.

'Am I to be told what?'

Her eyes clouded over, her mind shooting off to some dark, dark place inside her that made her look so bleak and saddened it actually threatened to breach his bristling contempt.

Then her lashes flickered, bringing her eyes back into focus, and the bleak look was gone. 'No,' she replied, and rose to her feet. 'That, I'm afraid, is none of your business.'

'It is if we are going to be man and wife,' he claimed.

'And are we?' Mia raised her sleek brows in counter-challenge. 'Going to be man and wife?'

'Why me?' he asked suddenly. 'Why, if you did not make the selection yourself, did your father set me up for this?'

'Are you serious?' she gasped, her green eyes widening in scathing incredulity. 'Last week you virtually undressed me with your eyes right in front of him! The week before that you invited me to spend the weekend in Paris with you in front of a room full of people—including my father! And there wasn't a person present who misunderstood what your intentions were, Mr Doumas,' she informed him. 'You certainly were not offering to show the city sights to me!'

From the moment they'd met, he'd not even attempted to hide the attraction he felt for her!

'You set yourself up for it!' she told him. 'I tried to head you off, freeze you out as best as I could do in front of my father. I even told you outright at one point that you were playing with fire, coming anywhere near me! Did you take any notice?' Her green eyes flashed. 'Did you hell!' she snapped, ignoring the way his expression was growing darker the more she threw at him. 'You just smiled an amused little smile that told me you had the damned conceit to think I was playing hard to get with you—and kept on coming on to me!

'And I'll tell you something else,' she continued, while he stood there, stiff-backed and riveted to the spot by what she was tossing at him. 'Until you started pursuing me, you weren't even up for consideration for this deal! But as soon as my father saw the way you looked at me you went right to the top of his carefully collected short-list of men fit to father his precious grandson! So, if you need to blame someone for this predicament you now find yourself in, blame yourself,' she suggested. 'You looked at me, you wanted me, you were offered me—on my father's terms.'

'In other words, your father is really your pimp,' he hit back.

Oh, very good, Mia grimly acknowledged. She'd cut into him, and he had cut right back.

'If you prefer to think of your future wife as a whore, then fine,' she parried. 'Though what that makes you doesn't really bear thinking about.'

He jerked as if she'd stabbed him—and so he damn well should! He might not like what he was being dealt here, but it didn't mean he could ride roughshod over her feelings!

'As it happens,' she tagged on, simply to twist the knife, 'you also had to pass several other tests before you qualified. You were younger than the other candidates on my father's list, as well as being more physically attractive—which was an important factor when my father was creating his grandson and heir,' she explained. 'But, most important of all, your family has a reputation for conceiving male children.' There hadn't been a female born to the Doumas line this century.

'And, of course, you were hungrier than the rest, not only for me,' she emphasized, 'but for your precious island.' And, therefore, so much easier to capture than the rest, was the bit she kept to herself.

But he took it as said. She saw that confirmed as his mouth took on a wryly understanding twist.

'And what happens to this—grandson and heir once he arrives in this world?' he asked next. 'Does your father come and snatch him from your breast an hour after his birth and expect me to forget I ever sired him?'

'Good heavens, no.' To his annoyance, she laughed again. 'My father has a real abhorrence of children in any shape or form.' Despite the laugh, her own bitter experience showed gratingly through. 'He simply desires a male heir to leave all his millions to. A legitimate male heir,' she added succinctly. 'I am afraid I can't go out and just get one from anywhere, if that's what you were going to suggest next...'

It had been a half-question, which his shrug completely dismissed. 'I'm not a complete fool,' he drawled. 'I would not suggest anything of the kind to you when it would mean my losing what I aim to gain from this.'

'And the child would lose a whole lot more, when you think about it,' Mia pointed out, referring to the size of Jack Frazier's well-known fortune. 'But I get full custody,' she announced with a lift of her chin that said she expected some kind of argument about it. 'That is not up for negotiation, Mr Doumas. It is my own condition before I will agree to any of this, and will be written into that contract my father mentioned to you.'

'Are you saying that I will have no control at all over this child?' he questioned sharply.

'Not at all,' Mia said. 'You will have all the rights any man would expect over his own son—so long as we stay married. But once the marriage is over I get full custody.'

'Why?'

Now there was a good question, Mia mused whimsically.

'I mean,' he qualified when she didn't answer him immediately, 'since you are making it damned obvious to me that you are no more enthusiastic about all of this than I am, why should you demand full custody of a child you don't really want in the first place?'

'I will *love* it,' she declared, 'no matter what his beginnings. I will *love* this child, Mr Doumas, not resent him, not look at him and despise him for who and what he means to me.'

'And you think I will?'

'I know you will,' she said with an absolute certainty. 'Men like you don't like to be constantly faced with their past failures.' She'd had experience of men of his calibre, after all—plenty of it. 'And agreeing to this deal most definitely represents a failure to you. So I get full custody,' she repeated firmly. 'Once the marriage is dissolved you will receive all the visitation rights legally allowed to you— if you still want them by then, of course,' she added, although her tone did not hold any optimism.

His eyes began to flash—the only warning she got that she had ignited something potentially dangerous inside him before he was suddenly standing right in front of her.

Her spine became erect, her eyelashes flickering warily as he pushed his angry face close to hers. 'You stand here with your chin held high and your beautiful eyes filled with a cold contempt for me, and dare to believe that you know exactly what kind of man I am—when you do not know me at all!' he rasped. 'For my son...' His hands came up to grip her shoulders. '*My son,*' he repeated passionately, 'will be *my* heir also!'

And it was a shock. Oh, not just the power of that possessiveness for something which was, after all, only a means to an end to him, but the effect his touch was having on her. It seemed to strike directly at the very heart of her, contracting muscles so violently that it actually squeezed the air from her tightened chest on a short, shaken gasp.

'*My son* will remain under *my* wing, no matter who—or what—his mother is!' he vowed. 'And if that means trapping us both into a lifelong loveless marriage, then so be it!'

'Are we?' Despite his anger, his biting grip, the bitter hatred he was making no effort to hide, Mia's beautiful, defiant eyes held his. 'Are we going to marry?'

His teeth showed, gleaming white and sharp and disturbingly predatorial between the angry stretch of his lips, his eyes like hard black pebbles that displayed a grinding distaste for both herself and the answer he was about to give her.

'Yes,' he hissed with unmasked loathing. 'We will marry. We will do everything expected of us to meet your father's filthy terms! But don't,' he warned, 'let yourself think for a moment that it is going to be a pleasure!'

'Then get your hands off me.' Coldly, she swiped his hands away. 'And don't touch me again until it is absolutely necessary for us to touch!'

With that she turned and walked back to the window where she stood, glaring outside at the lashing rain, while she tried to get a hold on what was straining to erupt inside her.

It didn't work. She could no more stop the words from flowing than she could stop the rain outside from falling. 'You seem to think you have the divine right to stand there and be superior to me. But you do not,' she muttered. 'You have your price, just like the rest of us! Which makes you no better than my father—no better than myself!'

'And what exactly is your price?' he challenged grimly. 'Give me one good reason why you are agreeing to all of this and I might at least try to respect you for it!'

It was an appeal. An appeal that caught at her heart because, even through his anger, Mia could hear his genuine desire for her to give him just cause for her own part in this.

Her green eyes flashed then filmed over, as for a moment—for a tiny breathless space in time—the sheer wretched truth to that question danced on the very edge of her tongue.

But she managed to smother the feeling, bite that awful truth down and keep it back, then spun to face him with her eyes made opaque by tears that had turned to ice.

'Money, of course,' she replied. 'What other price could there be?'

'Money...' he repeated, as though she had just confirmed every avaricious suspicion he'd held about her.

'On the day I present my father with a grandson I receive five million pounds as payment,' she went on. 'No better reason to agree to this—no worse than a man who can sell himself for a piece of land and a pile of ancient stone.'

He wasn't slow—he got her meaning. She was drawing a neat parallel between the two of them—or three people if she counted her father's willingness to give away a Greek island to get what he wanted out of this rotten deal.

'So make this a marriage for life if it suits you,' she defied him. 'I don't care. I will be wealthy in my own right and therefore independent of you no matter how long the marriage lasts! But we will soon know how strong your resolve is,' she added derisively, 'once the marriage is real and your sense of entrapment begins to eat away at you!'

'Entrapment?' he picked up on the word and shot it scornfully back at her. 'You naïvely believe I will feel trapped by this marriage? That I am prepared to change a single facet of my life to accommodate you or the vows we will make to each other?'

It was his turn to discharge a disdainful laugh, and Mia's turn to stiffen as his meaning began to sink in. 'I will change nothing!' he vowed. 'Not my way of life or my freedom to enjoy it wherever the mood takes me!'

His eyes were ablaze, anger and contempt for her lancing into her defiant face.

'I have a mistress in Athens with whom I am very happy,' he announced, using words like ice picks that he thrust into her. 'She will remain my mistress no matter what I have to do to fulfil my side of this filthy bargain! I will not be discreet.' he warned. 'I will not make any concessions to your pride while you live with me as my so-called wife! I will hate and despise you—and bed you with alacrity at regular intervals until this child of the devil is conceived, after which I will never touch you again!

'But,' he added harshly, 'if you truly believe I will also let you walk away with that child then you are living in a dream world because I will not!'

'Then the deal is off,' Mia instantly retaliated, using her father's tactics to make her own point.

After all, he hadn't given in to the big one—namely, agreeing to marry her and produce Jack Frazier's grandchild in what amounted to cold blood—without being desperate! And she would have her way in this if only because she had to glimpse some light at the end of this long dark tunnel or she knew she would not survive.

'Try telling your father that,' he derided, his eyes narrowing as her cheeks went white. 'You are afraid of him. I saw that from the first moment I set eyes on you.'

'And you want what only he can give you *more* than you want a child!' Mia countered. 'So I am telling *you* that you agree to my having full custody or the deal is off! This may also be a good moment for me to remind you of the shortlist of other names waiting to be called upon at a moment's notice,' she added, playing what she saw as her trump card.

To her immense satisfaction, his handsome face fell into harsh lines of raw frustration. 'You are as cold-blooded about this as your damned father!' he spat at her in disgust.

Mia said nothing, her chin up and eyes cool, her defiance in the face of his disdain so palpable it could almost be tasted in the air between them. Air that seemed to sing with enmity, picking at her flesh and tightening her throat as she watched him turn and stride angrily for the door.

'I will speak to my lawyers,' he said in a clipped voice

as he reached it, 'and let you know tomorrow what I decide.'

'F-fine,' Mia said, not quite managing to hide the sudden tremor of anxiety in her voice.

He heard it, and read it for exactly what it was. 'Your father is going to be bloody furious with you for not clinching this here and now, isn't he?' he taunted.

She merely shrugged one finely sculptured shoulder. 'My father knew my requirements before you arrived here. Why else do you think he left us alone like this when he actually had you so nicely caught in the bag?'

Take that, you nasty swine, she thought, her eyes gleaming with her own contempt.

One set of long, brown, lean fingers was gripping the brass doorhandle in preparation to open the door, but that final taunt had them sliding away again, and on a quiver of real alarm, which made her spine warily straighten, Mia watched him turn and begin to walk slowly towards her. Her heart began to hammer, her tongue cleaving to the dry roof of her mouth as he came to a halt mere inches away.

He was tall—taller than herself by several daunting inches. It meant she had to tilt her chin to maintain that most necessary eye-to-eye contact bitter adversaries always used as a weapon on each other.

His eyes were black, hard and narrowed, the finger he used to stroke a feather-light caress down the arched column of her throat an electric provocation that had her teeth gritting behind the firm set of her lips as she fought to stop herself from flinching away from him.

'You know...' he murmured, super-light, super-soft, 'you are in real danger of provoking me one step too far. I wonder why that is?'

'I d-don't know what you're talking about,' she said tremulously, feeling that trailing finger make its electrifying journey back up her throat again.

'No?' he said quizzically.

Then he showed her exactly what he meant as that taunting finger suddenly became a hand that cupped her jaw then tilted her head as his mouth came down to capture hers.

It was not a passionate kiss or even a punishing one. He simply crushed her slightly parted lips against his own, tasted her, using his tongue to lick a lazy passage along the vulnerable curve of her mouth, then straightened, his eyes still like dark glass as they gazed into her own rather startled ones.

'W-why did you do that?' she gasped.

'Why do you think?' he replied mockingly. 'I wanted to know if I would taste the acid that drips constantly from your lips. It wasn't there,' he softly confided. 'In fact, you tasted so sweet I think I will have to taste you again...'

And he did, that warning all she had before he was crushing her lips again, only this time his exploring tongue was sliding sinuously along the edge of her own, and as she released a protesting gasp his free hand snaked round her waist and pulled her against the long lean length of his body—a body she could feel already tightening with an arousal that actually shocked her.

But what shocked her more was the way her own senses went absolutely haywire, slinging out all kinds of demands that had her simmering from head to toe. The static-packed build-up of sensual excitement set her quivering all over and it was an effort not to give in.

What was the matter with her? she wondered deliriously. She didn't even like this man!

Yet she was on fire already, and she had to admit he was good. He seduced her mouth with an expertise that had her groaning, the splay of his hands across her body holding her trapped so he could move against her in a blatant demonstration of what the friction between their two bodies was doing to him.

To her horror, her own inner thighs began to pulse in hungry answer, her mouth quivered, her breathing quickened and her hands came up to cling to his shoulders as, on another helpless groan, her defences finally collapsed, and she was kissing him back with a passion that held her totally captivated.

It was raw and it was hot and it was so utterly basic that his deep-throated laugh of triumph against her clinging mouth had to be the worst humiliation she had ever experienced.

'Now this is a surprise,' he murmured silkily as he drew away. 'I knew our sparring was arousing me, but I did not realise it was having the same effect upon you. That adds a little spice to my final decision, does it not?'

Mia took a shaky step backwards, her trembling fingers falling from his shoulders and her cheeks blooming with shock and a dreadful consternation.

'Lie back and mentally switch off?' He mocked her earlier remark. 'I think you will be doing a whole lot more than that, Mia Frazier.'

'I never said I was frigid,' she shot back stiffly.

'But your father must think you are or why else does he believe he has to pay to get a man to bed you?'

'Not just any man, but the man of his own choice!' Her chin was up again and, despite the quivers still shaking her body, her eyes still managed to spit out defiance. 'Please remember that while you make your decision—you are not my personal choice. I am simply willing to do anything for that five millions pounds.'

Which was about as good as a slap in the face for him. He stepped right away from her, his expression so utterly disgusted that she almost—almost—wished the words unsaid.

'I will call you with my decision tomorrow,' he said abruptly as he moved back to the door.

'It's my father you will be dealing with, not me.'

'You,' he repeated. 'I will deal personally with *you*. Your father will be dealt with through my lawyers.'

CHAPTER TWO

MIA was staring out of the study window again when her father entered the room. She had just watched Alexander Doumas take off down the driveway with enough angry force to forge a vacuum through the storm still raging outside. There were tears in her eyes, though she didn't know why—unless those tears had something to do with the awful person she had been forced to play here today who bore no resemblance to the real Mia Frazier.

'Well, how did it go?'

'He has until tomorrow to agree to my terms or the deal is off,' she replied, without bothering to turn.

In the small silence that followed she sensed her father's frown of irritation. 'Don't spoil this for me, Mia,' he warned her very grimly, 'or you will be spoiling it for yourself.'

'I was taught by an expert.' Mia's smile was bleak. 'He will come around to my way of thinking simply because he has no choice.'

'Neither do you.'

'He doesn't know that, though.'

'Ah.' Jack Frazier lowered himself into the chair behind his desk with a sigh of satisfaction. 'You didn't tell him.'

'You warned me not to.'

'So, what does he think I am holding up as your incentive to agree to all of this?'

'I get five million pounds from you on the day I produce your grandson,' she informed him.

'Five million?' he grimaced. 'A nice round figure.'

'I thought so, too,' Mia agreed. 'It makes me a really expensive whore, don't you think?'

24

'You've always been a whore, darling,' Jack Frazier murmured insultingly. 'Expensive or cheap, a whore is still a whore. Tell Mrs Leyton I'm ready for some coffee now that the Greek has gone.'

Just like that. His low opinion of her stated, he was now calmly changing the subject.

Moving over to the desk, Mia lifted the internal phone which would connect her to the kitchen and held tightly locked inside herself the few choice replies that rattled around her brain regarding this man whom she was so ashamed to have to call her father.

Which was why neither Jack Frazier nor Alexander Doumas would ever have any control over her son. They could lay legal claims as mere blood relatives—she didn't mind that. They could even leave him every penny they possessed when they both decided to make this world a better place by leaving it.

But they would not have any control over who and what her son grew into. She already had in her possession her father's written agreement to that. And when tomorrow came she would be getting the same written agreement from Mr Doumas.

And how could she feel so sure about that? Because she had his measure. She had watched her father carefully mark it when he got the arrogant Greek to agree to any of this in the first place. If Alexander Doumas was prepared to wed and bed a woman just to get his hands on his old family pile then he would give away his first-born child also.

'If he surprises us both and doesn't give in to your terms,' her father posed quietly, 'what will you do then?'

'Wait until you come up with someone who will agree.'

His eyes began to gleam. 'The next on the list is Marcus Sidcup,' he reminded her silkily. 'Can you honestly bring yourself to let him touch you, Mia?'

Marcus Sidcup was a grotesque little man several years

older than her father who turned her stomach every time she set eyes on him. 'I'm a whore,' she replied. 'Whores can't be too picky. I'll close my eyes and think nice thoughts, like what to wear at your funeral.'

He laughed. Her opinion of him had never mattered simply because she didn't matter to him, the main reason being that she reminded him too much of his dead wife's many infidelities. Her brother Tony's conception had been just as suspect as her own, but because he had been male her father had been willing to accept him as his own. Mia being female, though, her paternity was an entirely different matter.

'If all goes well with Mr Doumas tomorrow,' she tossed in as a mere aside, 'I intend to go and visit Suzanna at school. She will need to know why I won't be around much for the next year or so.'

'You will tell her only what she needs to be told.' her father commanded sharply.

'I'm not a complete fool,' Mia replied. 'I have no wish to raise her hopes, but neither do I want her to think that I've deserted her.'

'She will be making no trips to visit you in Greece, either,' Jack Frazier warned her, 'so don't go all soft and try to placate her with promises that I might agree to it because I will not.'

Mia never for one moment thought that he would. Her eyes bleak and her heart aching for that small scrap of a seven-year-old who had seen even less of this man's love than she herself had, she walked out of the room before she was tempted to say something really nasty.

She couldn't afford to be nasty. She couldn't afford to get her father's back up, not when she was this close to achieving her own precious dream.

And she couldn't afford to lose Alexander Doumas either, she admitted heavily to herself, because no matter how much she despised him for being what he was he was her best option in this deal she had made with her father.

Pray to God he was as hungry as her father claimed he was, was the final thought she allowed herself to have that day on the subject.

The call came early the next morning just as Mia was emerging from her usual twenty laps of their indoor swimming pool. Mrs Leyton came to inform her that a Mr Doumas was waiting to speak to her on the phone. Wringing the water out of her hair as she walked across the white tiles, she went to the pool phone extension and picked up the receiver.

'Yes?' she said coolly.

'Yes,' he threw right back with a grim economy of words that showed every bit of his angry distaste. 'Be here at my offices at noon,' he commanded. 'My lawyers will have something ready for you to sign by then.'

Click. The phone went dead. Mia stood and grimaced at the inert piece of plastic, then ruefully replaced it on its wall rest.

At noon exactly she presented herself in the foyer of the very luxurious Doumas Corporation. Dressed in a severely tailored black pin-striped wool suit and plain white blouse, she looked the epitome of cool business elegance with her long, silky, copper hair neatly contained, as usual, in a knot high on her head and her make-up as understated as everything always was about her.

But, then, Mia Frazier did not need to make dress statements to look absolutely stunning. She was tall and incredibly slender, with legs so long that even a conservative knee-length skirt couldn't diminish their sensational impact.

Her skin was wonderful, so clear and smooth and white that it made the ocean greenness of her eyes stand out in startling contrast and the natural redness of her small heart-shaped mouth look lush and inviting and unwittingly sensual.

Add to all of that the kind of feminine curves that promised perfection beneath the severe clothing, and men stopped and stared when she walked into a room—as if they could recognise by instinct that beneath the cloak of cool reserve hid an excitingly sensual woman.

Alexander Doumas had been one man who had looked and instinctively seen her like that. One evening, a month ago, he had been standing with a group of people at a charity function when Mia had walked into the room on her father's arm.

He had been aware of who she was, of course, and who her father was, and how important Jack Frazier was to his reasons for being in London at all. But, still, he had taken one look at Jack's beautiful daughter and had made the most colossal tactical error of his life, by deciding he would like to mix business with a bit of pleasure.

It had been his downfall, which was how Mia liked to remember that moment. He had seen, he had desired and had done nothing whatsoever to hide that desire from either herself or her watching father. Maybe he had even seen his own actions as a way to ingratiate himself with Jack Frazier. Flatter the daughter to impress the father—that kind of thing—she had never really been sure.

Whatever, he had signed his own death warrant that very same evening when he had detached himself from his friends so he could come and introduce himself to Jack Frazier. His words might have been directed at her father but his eyes had all but consumed Mia.

In her own defence, Mia had tried to head him off before he had sunk himself too deeply into her father's clutches. She'd remained cool, aloof, indifferent to every soft-voiced compliment he had paid her—had tried to freeze him out when he wouldn't be frozen out.

For her own reasons. Alexander Doumas was one of the most attractive men she had ever laid eyes on, but for what she already knew her father was planning for her the Greek was just too much of everything. Too young, too dynamic, too sensually charismatic. Too obviously used to handling power, and just too confident in his own ability to win—both in the boardroom and the bedroom.

She needed a weaker man, a man with less of an aura of strength about him—a man with whom she could carry out her father's wishes and then walk away, spiritually unscathed, once the dastardly deal was done.

She certainly did not need a man who could make her heart race just by settling his lazily admiring dark eyes on her, or one whose lightest touch on her arm could make her flesh come alive with all kinds of unwanted sexual murmurings. A man whose voice made her toes curl and whose smile rendered her breathless. In other words, a man with all the right weapons to hurt her. She had been hurt enough in her life by men of Alexander Doumas's calibre.

She'd tried very hard to freeze him out during the last few weeks when her father made sure they were thrown together at every opportunity, but the stupid, stubborn man refused to be pushed away.

Now he was paying the consequences—or was about to pay them, Mia amended as she paused just inside the foyer.

The Doumas name had once been connected exclusively with oil and shipping, but since Alexander Doumas had taken over the company had diversified into the far more lucrative business of holidays and leisure. Now the name was synonymous with all that was the best and most luxurious in accommodation across the world. Their hotel chain and fleet of holiday cruise liners were renowned for their taste and splendour.

And all in ten years, Mia mused appreciatively as she set herself moving across the marble floor towards the reception desk. Before that the Doumas family had been facing bankruptcy and, from what her father had told her, had only just managed to stave it off by selling virtually everything they possessed.

Alexander Doumas had managed to hang on to one

cruise liner and a small hotel in Athens, which no one had actually known the family owned until he had begun to delve into their assets.

But that one cruise liner and hotel had been all that had been needed for the man to begin the rebuilding of an empire. Now he had by far outstripped what the family had once had, and the only goal left in his corporate life was regaining the family island.

Quite how her father had come by the island Mia had no idea. It was his way, though, to pick the bones clean of those in dire straits. He bought at rock-bottom prices from the absolutely desperate then moved in his team of business experts, who would pull the ailing company back into good health before he sold it on for the kind of profit that made one's hair curl.

Some things he didn't bother to sell on—like the house they lived in now, which he'd acquired for a snip from a man who'd lost everything in the last stockmarket crash. Jack Frazier had simply moved into it himself as it was in one of the most prestigious areas of London. The yacht and the plane had been acquired the same way, and of course the tiny Greek island that he'd held onto because—whatever else her father was that she hated and despised—he was astute.

He would have watched Alexander Doumas begin to rebuild the family fortunes. He would have known that the proud Greek would one day want his island back, and he had simply waited until the price was right for him to offer it back.

'I am here to see Mr Doumas,' Mia informed the young woman behind the reception desk. 'My name is Mia Frazier.'

'Oh, yes, Miss Frazier.' The girl didn't even need to glance down at the large appointment book she had open in front of her. 'You'll need to take the lift to the top floor, where someone will meet you.'

With a murmured word of thanks, Mia moved off as gracefully as always, and so well controlled that no one would have known how badly her insides were shaking or that her throat was tight with a mixture of dread and horror at what she was allowing herself to walk into. Yet, abhor herself as she undoubtedly did, her footsteps did not falter nor did her resolve. The stakes were too high and the rewards at the end of it too great to allow any room for doubt.

She walked into a waiting lift and pressed the button for the top floor without a pause. She kept her chin firm and her teeth set behind steady lips as she took that journey upwards, her clear green eyes fixing themselves on the framed water-colour adorning the back wall of the lift.

It was a painting of the most beautiful villa, set on the side of a hill and surrounded by trees. The walls were white, the roof terra-cotta and the garden a series of flower-strewn terraces sweeping down to a tiny bay where a primitively constructed old wooden jetty protruded into deeper, darker waters and a simple fishing boat stood tied alongside it.

What really caught her interest was the tiny horseshoe-shaped clearing in a cluster of trees to the left of the house. It seemed to be a graveyard. She could just make out the shapes of simple crosses amongst a blaze of colourful flowers.

A strange detail to put in such a pretty picture, she mused frowningly. *Vision* it was simply titled. Whose vision? she wondered. That of the man she was here to see or the artist who had painted it?

'Miss Frazier?'

The slightly accented cool male voice brought her swinging round to discover in surprise that not only had the lift come to a stop without her realising it, but the doors had opened and she was now being spoken to by a tall, dark, olive-skinned stranger. A stranger who was eyeing her so coldly that she had to assume he knew exactly why she was here today.

'Yes,' she confirmed, with a tilt of her chin that defied his right to judge her.

Something flashed in his eyes—surprise at her clear challenge? Or maybe it was more basic than that, she suggested to herself as she watched his dark eyes dip in a very male assessment of her whole body, as if he had some kind of right to check her out like a prime piece of saleable merchandise!

Which is exactly what you are, Mia reminded herself with her usual brutal honesty.

'And you are?' she countered in her crispest, coldest upper-class English, bringing those roving eyes flicking back up to clash with the clear green challenge reflected in her own.

His ears darkened. It was such a boyish response to being caught, blatantly staring, that she almost found it in her to laugh. Only... It suddenly hit her that there was something very familiar about this young man's features.

'I am Leonadis Doumas,' he informed her. 'My brother is this way, if you would follow me...'

Ah, the brother. She smiled a rueful smile. No wonder he looked familiar. The same eyes, the same physique—though without the same dynamic impact as his brother. Perhaps he was more handsome in a purely aesthetic way but, by the way his colour remained heightened as she followed him towards a pair of closed doors, she judged he lacked his brother's cool sophistication.

Leonadis Doumas paused, then knocked lightly on one of the closed doors, before pushing it open, and Mia used that moment to take a deep breath to prepare herself for what was to come next.

It didn't help much, and a fresh attack of nerves almost had her turning to run in the opposite direction before this thing was taken right out of her hands.

But, as she had told Alexander Doumas only yesterday, her father did not deal in uncertainties. He knew she would go ahead with this, just as he had known that Alexander Doumas would go ahead with it, no matter how much it made him despise himself.

Leonadis Doumas was murmuring something in Greek. Mia heard the now-familiar deep tones of his brother in reply before the younger man stepped aside to let her pass him.

She did so reluctantly, half expecting to find herself walking into a room full of grey-suited lawyers. Instead, she found herself facing the only other person present in the room. Alexander was sitting at his desk, with the light from the window catching the raven blackness of his neatly styled hair.

Behind her the door closed. She glanced back to find that Leonadis had gone. Mia's stomach muscles clenched into a tight knot of tension as she turned back to face the man with whom—soon—she was going to have to lie and share the deepest intimacy.

'Very businesslike,' he drawled. 'I believe it's called power dressing. But I feel I should warn you that it's lost on me.'

Startled by the unexpected choice of his first attack, Mia glanced down at her severely tailored suit, with its modest-length skirt and prim white blouse, and only then realised that he had completely misinterpreted why she was dressed like this.

Not that it mattered, she decided as her chin came back up and she levelled her cool green eyes on him. She had dressed like this because she was going on to Suzanna's very strict boarding school directly from here, where strait-laced conservatism was insisted upon from family and pupils alike.

'When you marry me,' he went on, 'I will expect something more…womanly. I find females in masculine attire a real turn-off.'

'*If* I marry you,' Mia corrected, and made herself walk forward until only the width of his desk was separating them. 'Your brother looks like you,' she observed as a mere aside.

For some reason, the remark seemed to annoy him. 'Wondering if your father tapped the wrong brother?' he asked. 'Leon is nine years younger than me, which places him just about in your own age group, I suppose. But he is also very much off-limits, as far as you are concerned,' he added with a snap that made his words into a threat.

'I have no inclination to so much as touch him,' she countered, smiling slightly because she knew then that big brother must have noticed and correctly interpreted the reason his younger brother was looking so warm about the ears. 'Though, you never know,' she couldn't resist adding, 'it may be worth my while to look into whether he would be a better bet than you before I commit myself.'

Again there was the hint of anger. 'Leon is already very much married to a wonderful creature he adores,' he said abruptly. 'Which makes him of absolutely no use to you.'

'Ah, married.' She sighed. 'Shame. Then it looks as if you will have to do.'

With that little ego-deflater, she lowered herself into a chair and waited for his next move.

To her surprise, his mouth twitched, appreciation for her riposte suddenly glinting in his eyes. He was no one's fool. He knew without vanity that he was a better, more attractive, more sensually appealing man than his younger, less dynamic brother.

'A contract my lawyers have drawn up this morning,' he announced, reaching out with a long fingered hand for a document of several pages which he slid across the desk towards her. 'I suggest you read that thoroughly before you sign it.'

'I have every intention of doing so,' she said, picking up the contract. She proceeded to ignore him while she immersed herself in its detail.

It was a comprehensive document, which set out point by point the guidelines by which this so-called marriage of theirs would proceed. In a way, Mia supposed the first part read more like a prenuptial agreement than a business contract, with its declarations on how small an allowance he would be giving her on a monthly basis and what little she could expect from him if the marriage came to an end—which was a pittance, though she wasn't surprised by that.

The man believed she would be a wealthy woman in her own right once all this was over. It suited her to continue to let him go on thinking that way so she didn't care that he was offering her nothing.

It was only on the third page that things began to get nasty. She would live where he wanted her to live, it stipulated. She would sleep where he wanted her to sleep. If she went out at all she would never do so without one of his designated people as a companion.

She would be available at all times for sex on his demand...

Mia felt his eyes on her, following, she was sure, line by line as she read. Her cheeks wanted to redden, but she refused to allow them to, her lips drawing in on themselves because it seemed so distasteful to add such a clause when, after all, they were only marrying because of the sex, which was necessary to make babies.

She would conduct herself at all times in a way which made her actions as his wife above reproach, she grimly read on. She would not remark on his own personal life outside their marriage, and she accepted totally that he intended to maintain a mistress...

The fact that several slick lawyers were privy to all of this, as well as the person who had typed it, made her want to cringe in horror.

In anticipation of her falling pregnant, she would not step off Greek soil without his permission during her pregnancy. The child must be born in Greece and registered as Greek. In the event of the marriage irretrievably breaking down, yes, she would get full custody of their child, she was relieved to read.

Then came his own proviso to that concession, and it made her heart sink. It had to be *his* decision that the marriage must end. If Mia walked out on the marriage of her own volition then she did so knowing she would be forfeiting full custody...

'I can't agree to that,' she protested.

'You are not being given a choice,' he replied, leaning back in his chair yet reading with her word for word of the contract. 'I did warn you that I would not relinquish control of my own son and heir. I have the right to safeguard myself against that contingency, just as you have the right to safeguard yourself against my walking out on you. So it is covered both ways by that particular clause.

'If I decide I cannot bear having you as my wife any longer, then I get rid of you, knowing I will be relinquishing all rights to our child. If you decide the same thing then you, too, will relinquish all rights over him. I think that is fair, don't you?'

Did she? She had a horrible feeling she was being scuppered here, though the logic of his argument gave her no clue as to where. And, in the end, did it matter? she then asked herself. She had no intention of marrying any man ever again after this. If Alexander Doumas wanted to tie himself to this wife for life, let him.

'Is there anything else you want to add to this?' he asked, once she'd read the contract to the end without further comment.

Mia shook her head. Whatever she felt she needed to safeguard for herself would be done privately with her own lawyer in the form of a last will and testament.

Getting to her feet, she picked up her handbag. 'I'll let my father look at this then get back to you,' she informed him coolly.

'No.'

In the act of turning towards the door Mia paused, her neat head twisting to let her eyes clash with his for the first time since this interview had begun. Her heart stopped beating for a moment and her porcelain-like skin chilled at the uncompromising grimness she saw in those dark eyes.

'This is between you and me,' he insisted. 'Whatever is agreed between your father and myself—or even your father and yourself—will be kept completely separate from this contract. But you decide now and sign now or—to use your own words—the deal is off.'

'I would have to be a complete fool if I didn't get this checked out by someone professional before I put my signature to it,' she protested.

'You want a professional here? Give me the name of your lawyer and I will have him here in half an hour,' he said. 'But I think it only fair to warn you first that I refuse to alter one single word on that contract, no matter what advice he offers you. So...' A shrug threw the ball back into her court.

Well, Mia, what are you going to do? she asked herself as she stood, gazing at this man with his intractable expression that so reminded her of her father.

She shivered. He was contemptuous of who she was and what she was, indifferent to what she felt or even *if* she felt. He was ready, she was sure, to make her pay in every way he could, for bringing him down to this.

Oh, yes, she thought grimly. Just like her father. Every bit the same kind of man. Which made her wonder suddenly if that was why Jack Frazier had chosen Alexander Doumas in the first place. Was it because he saw in this man a more than adequate successor to himself as her tormentor?

'Are you at last beginning to wonder if five million pounds is worth the kind of purgatory you are about to embark upon if you marry me?' this particular tormentor prodded silkily.

'No,' she said, dropping both the contract and her handbag back onto the desk. 'I was merely trying to decide whether it was worthwhile calling your bluff,' she explained, 'but, since I have another pressing engagement, I've decided not to bother haggling with you. So...' Her chin came up, her green eyes as cool and as indifferent as they had ever been. 'Where do I sign?'

It took the whole of the long drive into Bedfordshire to pull her utterly ragged senses back into some semblance of calm because from the moment she'd agreed to sign his rotten contract the meeting had sunk to an all-time low in the humiliation stakes.

He hadn't liked her consigning him to second place behind whatever engagement she had, she knew that. It had been exactly why she had said it, hadn't it?

But what had come afterwards had made her wish she'd kept her reckless mouth shut. Punishment was the word that came to mind. He'd punished her by introducing her to the two lawyers he'd called in to witness their signatures as 'the woman who is this desperate to bear my child' as he'd tossed the contract towards them to sign.

It had been cruel and unnecessary but he hadn't cared. The way his hard eyes had mocked the hot colour that swept up her cheeks had shown he'd even enjoyed seeing her so discomfited.

Then had come the final humiliation once the lawyers had been dismissed again.

The kiss.

Her whole body quivered in appalled reaction, her lips still throbbing in memory of the ruthless way he had devoured them. He'd done it so cavalierly, coming around his

desk in what she'd foolishly believed had been an intention
to escort her politely to the door. What he'd actually done
had been to reach out and pull her into his arms then capture her mouth with the same grim precision he had
achieved the day before.

Only this time he had taken that kiss a whole lot further,
Staking his claim, she realised now. Staking his claim on
a piece of property he had just bought, by deepening the
kiss with all the casual expertise of a man who knew exactly how to make a woman's senses catch fire at his will.

And she had caught fire—that was the truly humiliating
part of it. She had just stood there in his arms and had gone
up like a Roman candle! She'd quivered and groaned and
clung to his mouth, as though her very survival had depended on it.

Where had her pride been? Her self-control? Her determination to remain aloof from him, no matter what he did
to her?

What he did to you? her mind screamed jeeringly back
at her. What about what you did to him?

'No…' The word escaped as a wretched groan from anguished lips, and she had to slow the car down because her
vision was suddenly misted. Misted by terrible visions of
her fingers clutching at him—at his nape, and his hair—
holding him to her when she should have been pushing him
away!

He'd muttered something—she could still hear that
driven groan echoing inside her shell-shocked head. Could
still feel the burning pressure of his body against hers, of
buttons parting, of flesh preening to the pleasure of his
touch and the sudden flare of a powerful male arousal, the
crush of his arms as he'd pressed her even closer.

It had been awful. They'd devoured each other like hungry animals, so fevered by desire that when he'd suddenly
let go of her she'd staggered backwards with flushed skin
and dazed eyes, her pulsing mouth parted and gasping for

air as she'd stood there, staring blankly at him as he'd swung away from her.

'Cover yourself,' he'd rasped.

A shudder of self-revulsion shot through her, making her foot slip on the accelerator when she saw in her mind's eye what he must have seen as he'd stood there, glowering at her, with the desk once more between them.

Her jacket, her blouse—even her fine lacy bra—gaping wide to reveal the fullness of her breasts in tight, tingling distension!

'I can't believe you did that,' she whispered, turning her back to him while useless fingers fumbled in their attempts to put her clothing back in order.

'Why not?' he countered flatly. 'It is what you signed up for.'

Humiliation almost suffocated her. 'I hate you,' she choked.

'But I don't think you're going to find the sex a problem, do you?'

Recognising her own taunt from yesterday being flung right back at her, she shuddered again.

'Not surprising, really,' he continued remorselessly, 'when rumour has it that you were a bit of a raver in your teens...'

Her teens? She went very still. The fact that he knew about her wild teenage rebellion was enough to keep her ready tongue locked inside her kiss-numbed mouth.

'Well, let's get one more thing straight before you leave this room,' he continued very grimly. 'You will behave like a lady while you belong to me. There will be no wild parties, no rave-ups. No sleeping around when the mood happens to take you.'

'I'm not like that.' She was constrained to defend herself.

'Now? Who knows?' he said derisively. 'While you are married to me? No chance. I want to know that the child you will eventually carry is my child,' he vowed, 'or you will be wishing you'd never heard the name Doumas! Now, pull yourself together before you walk out of this room,' he concluded dismissively. 'We will marry in three days' time.'

'Three days?' she gasped, spinning round to stare at him. 'But—'

It was as far as she got. 'Three days,' he repeated. 'I see no reason to delay—especially when I know what a receptive little thing you're going to be in my bed,' he added silkily at her white-faced shock. 'The sooner we get this show on the road the sooner I get you pregnant, and you get your five million pounds and I get back what should be mine.'

He meant his island, of course. The stupid bit of Greek rock he was prepared to sell his soul for—or, at the very least, his DNA. The man had no concept of which was really more important. She could have told him, but she didn't.

In fact, she wanted him to go right on believing that his island was worth more to him than his DNA. That way she could finally beat him, which was really all that mattered to her.

The only thing she could do now was think ahead. A long way ahead to a time when—God willing—the awful man would grow tired of her and eventually let her go.

Suzanna was heart-achingly pleased to see her. But the seven-year-old broke down and wept her heart out when Mia told her gently that she was going away for a while.

Pulling her onto her lap, she let the little girl weep herself dry. Heaven knew, there were too few moments when she could give her emotions free rein like this.

'It will only be for a year or two,' she murmured soothingly, 'and I will come and see you as often as I can.'

'But not like you do now,' the child protested, 'because Greece is a long, long way away! And it's going to mean that I will have to spend the school holidays alone with Daddy!'

The alarm that prospect caused the poor child cut deeply into Mia's heart. 'Mrs Leyton will be there for you,' Mia reminded her. 'You like her, don't you?'

'But I can't bear not having you there, too, Mia!' she sobbed. 'He h-hates me! You know he does because he hates you too!'

Mia sighed and hugged the child closer because she knew she couldn't even lie and deny the charge. Jack Frazier did hate them both. He had poured what bit of love he had ever had in him into their brother, Tony. With Tony gone, their father had just got more and more resentful of their very existence.

'Look,' she murmured suddenly out of sheer guilt and desperation, even though her father's warning was ringing shrilly in her ears, 'I promise to call you once a week so we can talk on the telephone.'

'You promise?' the child whispered.

'I promise,' Mia vowed.

She hugged the thin little body tightly to her because it wasn't fair—not to herself, not to Suzanna. May God forgive me, she prayed silently, for deserting her like this.

'I love you, my darling,' she whispered thickly. 'You are and always will be the most important thing in my life.'

She got back to the house after dark, feeling limp and empty.

'Your father's flown off to Geneva,' Mrs Leyton informed her. 'He said to tell you not to expect him back before you leave here. Why are you leaving here?'

The poor old lady looked so shocked that it took the very last dregs of Mia's strength to drag up another set of explanations. 'I'm going to be living in Greece for a year or two,' she said.

'With that Greek fellow that was here the other day?'

'Yes.' Her tired mouth tightened. 'We are—getting married,'

'And your father agrees?' Mrs Layton sounded stunned.

'He arranged it,' Mia said, with a smile that wasn't a smile but more a grimace of irony. Then she added anxiously, 'You'll keep an eye on Suzanna for me, won't you, while I'm away?'

'You should be staying here to do that yourself,' the housekeeper said sternly.

'I can't, Cissy.' At last the tears threatened to fall. 'Not for the next year or so, anyway. Please don't quiz me about it—just promise me you'll watch her and keep my father away from her as much as you can!'

'Don't I always?' the housekeeper snapped, but her old eyes were shrewd. Mia had a suspicion that she knew exactly what was going on. 'That Greek chap has been on the telephone, asking for you, umpteen times today. He didn't sound very pleased that you weren't here to take his calls.'

'Well, that's his hard luck.' Mia dismissed Alexander Doumas and all he represented. 'I'm tired. I'm going to bed.'

'And if he rings again?'

'Tell him to leave a message then go to hell,' she said, walking away up the stairs and into her room where she stripped herself with the intention of having a shower. But it couldn't even wait that long and the next moment she had thrown herself down on her bed and was sobbing brokenly into her pillow, just as Suzanna had sobbed in her arms this afternoon.

CHAPTER THREE

'WHERE the hell have you been for the last three days?'

Mia's insides jumped, her eyes jerking sideways to skitter briefly over the dark-suited figure seated next to her in the car.

Alexander looked grim-faced and tense. She didn't blame him. She felt very much the same way herself, hence her jumping insides, because he had actually spoken to her directly for the first time since that dreadful marriage ceremony had taken place.

'I had things to do,' she replied, her nervous fingers twisting the unfamiliar gold ring that now adorned her finger.

'And I had things I needed to check with you,' he bit back.

'Mrs Leyton answered all your questions,' Mia parried coolly. Hadn't it occurred to him that she was the one who was having to uproot her whole life for this? He'd given her three days to do it in—three damn days!

But that hadn't been the real reason she had refused to accept any of his phone calls. She'd needed these last few days to get a hold on herself, to come to terms with what had erupted between them in his office.

It hadn't worked. She was still horrified by it all, frightened by it all.

'Well, fob me off like that again, and you won't like the consequences,' he muttered.

I already don't like them, she thought heavily, but just shrugged a slender shoulder and kept her gaze fixed firmly on the slowly changing scenery beyond the limousine window.

And it was strange, really, she mused, but here she sat, married to this man. He had kissed her twice, ruthlessly violated her sexual privacy once, had insulted her and shown her his contempt and disgust in so many ways during their two short interviews that it really did not bear thinking about. Yet during all of that, including the brief civil ceremony which had taken place this morning with no family present on either side, not even his own brother, Leon—which had acted as a clear message in itself to Mia—their eyes had barely ever clashed.

Oh, they'd looked at each other, she conceded drily. But it had been a careful dance as to when he looked or she looked, but they had not allowed themselves to look at the same time.

Why? she asked herself. Because neither of them were really prepared to accept that they were actually doing this. It went so against the grain of civilised society that even the Greek in him must be appalled at the depths to which he had allowed himself to sink in the name of desire.

Not sexual desire but the desire for property.

'Why the smile?'

Ah, she thought, his turn to look at me. 'I was wondering if my father was enjoying a glass of champagne somewhere in Geneva,' she lied. 'Celebrating his success in getting us both this far.'

'He isn't in Geneva,' he said, watching impassively as her slender spine straightened. 'He has been staying with his mistress in Knightsbridge since I signed his bloody contract. I presume he wanted to keep out of your way in case you started asking awkward questions about what he actually got me to sign in the end.'

Her chin turned slowly, supported by a neck that was suddenly very tense, her wary eyes flickering over his face without really focusing before she lowered them again. There was something—something snake-like in the way he had imparted all that which made her feel slightly sick inside.

'The two of you can't possibly have agreed anything else to do with me without my say-so,' she declared rather shakily.

'True. We didn't.' He relieved her mind with his confirmation. 'But we did discuss the fact that you have a younger sister...'

Oh, no. She closed her eyes, her heart sinking to her stomach. Her father would not have told this man about Suzanna, surely?

'He wanted me to know what a bad influence you are on the child,' that hateful voice continued, while Mia's mind had shot off in another direction entirely. 'Therefore, while you are with me you are to have no contact with— Suzanna, isn't it? Apparently, you are very jealous of her and can, if allowed to, make her young life a misery...'

So that was how her father was playing it. Her eyes bleak and bitter behind her lowered lids, Mia pressed her lips together and said nothing. No contact with Suzanna would keep her striving to make the grandson her father wanted so badly. No contact with Suzanna was meant as a warning—do your job or forget all about her.

'Is that why he married you off to the highest bidder?' her new husband continued remorselessly. 'To get you right out of your sister's life?'

'You didn't bid for me—you were *bought!*' She hit back at him. 'For the specific purpose of producing my father's precious grandson! So, if the reputation for making sons in your family lets you down,' she finished shakily, 'make sure you don't blame me for the mistake!'

He should have been angry. Heavens, she'd said it all to make him angry! But all he did was huff a lazy laugh of pure male confidence.

'My mother had three sons and my grandmother five. I don't think I need worry on that score. And,' he added as he shifted his lean bulk to glance out of the car window, 'that was not the point I was trying to make. I was simply letting you know that I now know why your father was willing to pay you five million pounds to get you out of his life.'

'Plus a Greek island,' Mia added. 'Please don't forget the island—how much is that worth in cold, hard cash?'

His face hardened at the reminder, the link she was making between them so clear that even he, for all his arrogance, could not deny it was there.

'We have arrived,' he said, bringing an end to the conversation.

Sure enough, the car pulled to a stop and Mia looked out to find they had come to one of the private airfields just outside London. A gleaming white Gulfstream jet sat glinting in the weak winter sunlight, the Doumas logo painted in gold on its side.

Ten minutes after that Mia found herself ensconced in luxurious cream leather—alone.

Her new husband, she discovered, was apparently going to fly them wherever they were going. He disappeared into the cockpit the moment they boarded and she did not set eyes on him again until they landed—in Greece she had to assume because no one had bothered to inform her.

He came striding into the main cabin minus his jacket and silk tie. He looked different somehow, less formal, but all the more intimidating for it.

Male—that was the word that suddenly came to mind. He looked more aggressively male than he had done before. Once again she lowered her eyes before he could glimpse what she was thinking, and bent to pick up her jacket which she, too, had discarded during the flight.

So she didn't see the way his eyes narrowed on the firm thrust of her breasts, outlined by the close fit of her clinging white top. She didn't see those eyes dip lower, over her flat stomach to her slender thighs and then down over pale stockinged legs, before they made the same journey back up her face again.

'Where are we?' she asked, using the cover of fastening her jacket buttons.

'The island of Skiathos,' he told her. 'I have a villa here. It will, of course, be sold when I get back the family island,' he added stiffly.

The family island... Mia shuddered, swallowing on the thick dry lump that formed in her throat at the grim reminder of what this was all about for him.

Then he went on, in a completely different tone of voice, 'That green colour suits you,' he murmured huskily. 'It does something spectacular to your eyes.'

She was so disconcerted by the unexpected compliment that she just stared blankly at the mint green suit with its little fitted jacket and short straight skirt. She hadn't bought it for its colour, but out of respect for the icy winter weather back in London. The suit was made from pure cashmere with matching dyed fake fur collar and cuffs to the jacket.

'Thank you,' she replied, having to fight the rather pathetic urge to blush because he had said something nice to her.

A small silence fell, she wasn't sure why. The two of them stood there, seemingly imprisoned by it, she with her head lowered and he—well, she didn't know what he was doing because she didn't dare look. But the sudden tension between them was almost palpable. Then someone was opening the outer door of the plane and, thankfully, the strange tension was broken.

He left the aircraft first, obviously expecting her to follow. She did so reluctantly, to find another car was waiting for them at the bottom of the short flight of steps—a silver Mercedes.

The sun was shining and the air was much warmer than it had been back in England, but not so hot that she didn't appreciate the warm suit she was wearing.

Alexander was striding round to the driver's side of the car while their luggage was being stowed in the boot. Taking a deep breath, Mia stepped up to the passenger door and then, on a strange kind of compulsion, she paused to glance across the shimmering silver bonnet towards him.

And there it was—the first time that their eyes truly met. Her heart stopped, the breath squeezing painfully in her stilled lungs. He looked grim, those dark eyes frowning back at her with a resentment that utterly belied his earlier compliment.

He hated and despised her for bringing him down to this level. And, what was worse, she didn't even blame him. She hated and despised herself! So why should it hurt?

Yet it did. Of course it hurt. She had feelings, like anyone else! It was her eyes that dropped first, hiding the sudden sharp stab of pain she was experiencing—hiding the deep, dragging sense of self-loathing with which she was having to live.

Heart-weary, she made herself get into the car. He didn't join her immediately. In fact, he remained standing out there for such a long, long time that Mia began to wonder if he had finally come to his senses and changed his mind about all of this. Eventually he appeared, folding his long body into the seat beside her.

He didn't look at her again, and she didn't look at him. The car began to move, and the atmosphere inside it was so thick you could almost suffocate in it. 'It isn't too late to stop this if you want to,' she heard herself whisper, hoping... Hoping for what? she asked herself.

'No,' he replied.

Relief washed through her because that, she realised bleakly, was what she'd been hoping he'd say. No matter how much she hated this she still wanted it—needed it. Needed him.

Her new surroundings were lush and green, with bright splashes of colour from a flush of very early blooming flowers. Give it another few months and the green would be baked brown by the heat of the sun, she mused sadly. The flowers would be mostly gone. It was Mother Nature's way of maintaining a balance—hours of unrelenting sunshine but at the expense of floral colour.

Was she destined to wilt along with the flowers as the months went by? she wondered. She had the feeling that that was exactly what she would do, living a life in an emotion-starved desert with this man.

So, what's new? She mocked her own maudlin fancy. You've been living just like that with your own father. Swapping one heartless despot for another isn't going to be that much of a hardship, is it?

They were travelling along a high, winding road with the sea to the left of them. They passed through tiny hamlets of whitewashed buildings, which would probably be alive with tourists in high season but were at present almost deserted. There was hardly anyone about, in fact. It was a point she dared to remark upon to the man beside her.

'Most people here spend their winters on the mainland,' he explained. 'There is work for them there out of season, and the weather here can be as cold as England sometimes. But in another couple of months the place will come alive again.'

'Is it a big island?' she asked curiously.

He shook his dark head. 'We have driven almost its full length already,' he said. 'The house is situated in the next bay.'

Five minutes later they were driving through the gates of what appeared to be a vast private property hidden from the road by a high wall flanked by tall shrubs and trees. The house itself nestled lower down so the only view she got of it was its red slate rooftop.

It was impossible to tell just how big it was, but as they dropped lower she counted six separate windows on the upper floor and four on the lower, split by a wide white arched double door in the centre of a veranda.

By the time they came to a halt at the veranda steps she had counted at least four men who could only have been security guards by the way they made themselves evident as the car pulled in each one of them in turn, giving an acknowledging flick of his hand before he slunk out of sight again.

'Well, this is it,' Alexander announced, leaning back in his seat as the car engine died into silence. 'Your new home for the duration.'

Mia made no comment—what could she say? Oh, how lovely? How enchanting? I'm sure I will be happy here? She knew for a fact he had no interest in making her happy.

Anyway, she was too busy stifling the fresh set of butterflies that were attacking her system, apprehension for what was in store for her next being their stimulus.

She opened her door and made herself climb out into the late afternoon sunshine. Once again Alexander took his time to do the same, remaining seated inside the car as though it gave him a chance to relax his cold features and let them show what he was really feeling.

Anger, mostly, she guessed, a bitter sense of resentment at her presence in his life, which was going to be her close companion for what he had called the duration.

The white entrance doors began to open. Mia stood, watching, as they swung wide and a short stocky woman stepped out, dressed in uniform grey.

Her expression was utterly impassive as she studied Mia for a few short seconds, then turned her attention away as Alexander Doumas uncoiled himself from the car. Then a smile of such incredible warmth lit the woman's rugged features that it made the comparison between welcome and no welcome with a hard, cruel alacrity.

She said something in Greek, and he replied in the same language as he strode up the steps towards her. They did not embrace, which killed Mia's suspicion that this woman might be his mother. Then they were both turning to gaze in her direction, and all warmth left both of them. Mia's chin came up accordingly, pride insisting she outface the enemy to her last breath.

'Come.' That was all he said, as if he were talking to a pet dog.

Come. Sucking back the wretched desire to tell him to go to hell, she walked around the car and up the steps with her clear green gaze fixed defiantly somewhere between the two of them.

'This is Elena,' she was informed. 'She is my house-keeper here. Anything you require you refer to her. Elena will show you to your room,' he added coolly. 'And get Guido to bring up your luggage. I have some calls to make.'

And he was gone. Without a second look in Mia's direction, he strode into the house and disappeared.

'This way, madam...' Surprising Mia with her nearly accent-free English, the housekeeper turned and led the way into the house.

It was warmer inside, with sunlight seeping in through silk-draped windows onto apricot walls and lovingly polished wooden floors and doors. The furniture was old, undoubtedly antique, but solid, with a well used, well lived with look to it. Not what she would have expected of him somehow.

A highly polished wooden staircase climbed up the wall to the left of her, then swept right around the upper landing.

Elena led the way up and across the polished floor to a door directly opposite the stairs. She threw it open then stood back to allow Mia to move past her.

Her feet were suddenly sinking into a deep-piled oatmeal carpet, and her eyes drifted around soft lemon walls and white woodwork. Oatmeal curtains were caught back from the windows with thick lemon ropes.

'Your bathroom is to your right,' Elena informed her

coolly. 'The master's bedroom is through the door to your left.'

Separate bedrooms, then, Mia was relieved to note. 'Thank you,' she murmured, and forced herself to step further into the room.

Elena did not join her, instead remaining in the open doorway. 'My daughter, Sofia, will come and unpack for you. If you need anything tell her and she will tell me.'

In other words, don't speak to me yourself unless it is absolutely necessary, Mia ruefully assumed from that cold tone.

'Guido, my husband, will bring your luggage shortly,' the housekeeper continued. 'Dinner here is served at nine. Will you require some refreshment before then?'

And doesn't it just stick in your throat to offer it? Mia thought with a sudden blinding white smile that made the other woman's face drop at the sheer unexpectedness of it.

'Yes,' she said lightly. 'I require a large pot of coffee, milk—not cream—to go with it and a plate of sandwiches—salad, I think. Thank you, Elena. Now you may go.'

The woman's face turned beetroot red as she stepped back over the threshold, then pulled the door shut with a barely controlled click. Almost immediately Mia wilted, the stress of maintaining this level of indifference towards everyone taking the strength out of her legs so that she almost sank shakily into the nearest chair.

Right in the very midst of that telling little weakness she sucked in a deep breath, straightening her shoulders and grimly defying it. She had many long months of this to put up with, and if she started turning into a quivering wreck at each new obstacle she wouldn't stay the course.

With that now aching chin held high again, she turned to view the room in general. It was large and light and airy, with two full-length windows standing open to a light breeze beyond. Appropriate furniture stood around the room—a couple of oatmeal upholstered bedside chairs and a small matching sofa scattered with pale lemon cushions. A large dark wood wardrobe stood against the wall opposite the windows, a dressing-table against another, and a tall chest of drawers. Her eyes kept moving, picking out occasional tables and table lamps sitting on lace doilies to protect the polished wood—all very old-fashioned and reminiscent of a different era when tender loving care was poured into furniture like this in the form of beeswax, which she could smell in the air.

And then, of course, there was the bed.

Gritting her teeth, Mia made herself turn and face her major fear. The bed was huge, standing in pride of place between the two open windows, its heavily carved head- and footboards suggesting that the bed was antique. The sheets were white and folded back neatly over a pale lemon bedspread, the headboard piled with snowy white pillows.

Her heart stopped beating, her stomach muscles contracting with dread as she stood there staring at it. She made herself imprint the image of two heads on those snowy white pillows—one dark and contemptuous but grimly determined, the other red-gold and frightened but resolutely defiant.

She shuddered suddenly, realising that contempt and defiance were not going to make good bed partners. Contempt and mute submission would be a far less volatile mixture, she told herself in an attempt at wry mockery.

It didn't work. In fact, there wasn't even the merest hint of the usual mockery that she relied on so much to keep her going.

Oh, hell, she thought heavily, and moved around the bed to go and went to open one of the windows, her lungs pulling in short tugs of clean fresh air in an effort to dispel the ever-present sense of dread—a dread that was drawing nearer with every passing hour.

There was a pretty view outside, she noted in a deliberate

snub to those other grim thoughts. Carefully attended gardens rolled down towards a shallow rock face, but she couldn't see a beach or any obvious way down the cliff to the sea below.

But there was a glass-walled swimming pool glinting off to the left of her, which cheered her up a bit because at least the temperature was mild enough to allow her to take her usual exercise while she was stuck here. Further out, she could see the misted bulk of several other islands not very far away. It made her wish she'd had the foresight to ask where he was bringing her so she could have bought herself a map and acquainted herself with what she was seeing out there.

Then another thought hit her, making a connection that she should have made ages ago. For this was Skiathos, and Skiathos belonged to the Sporades group of islands. The island her father owned was also in the Sporades group. She could actually be looking at her new husband's dream, without actually knowing it.

Suddenly she felt surrounded by reminders of what she was here for. The island. The bed. The isolation in which she was supposed to fulfil her part of the bargain.

Her blood ran cold and she shivered, any pleasure she had experienced because of the beauty of her new surroundings spoiled for ever. She turned away from the window, from the islands, from the bed, and walked straight into the bathroom.

She needed a shower, she decided grimly—needed to soak the tension out of her body with warmth. She had to keep herself together because this was the beginning, not the end, of it.

Guido had arrived with her luggage while she was still in the bathroom and Sofia was there when Mia eventually came back to the bedroom, wrapped in a white terry bathrobe she had found hanging on the bathroom door and with her hair hidden beneath a turban-wrapped towel.

Sofia's glance was very guarded. 'I bring food,' she said in badly broken English, 'and have unpacked for you.'

'Thank you.' No smile was offered so none was returned.

The girl left and Mia moved over to the tray set on a low table beside the sofa. The coffee was too strong and the crusty bread sandwiching the salad too thickly cut for her to have any hope of swallowing it past that lump that was still constricting her throat. Luckily, someone had had the foresight to place a pitcher of iced water on the tray with the coffee so she contented her thirst with that and picked the salad off the bread.

By the time she had finished she felt suddenly and utterly bone-weary. Despite her long shower, the strain of it all was still dragging at her muscles and she could now feel the dull throb of a tension headache coming on.

With a heavy sigh, she at last did what her brain and her body had been pleading with her to do since she'd arrived here. She got up and walked over to that dreaded bed, threw herself face downwards across it and simply switched off.

For the next few blissful hours Mia was aware of nothing, not the day slowly closing in around her or the towel turban slowly uncoiling itself from her head then sliding lazily to the carpet—trailing her hair along with it so the long silken strands spilled over the edge of the bed like a wall of fire lit by the glowing sunset.

When she did eventually come awake she did so abruptly, not sure what had woken her but certain that something had. Her eyes flicked open, her senses coming to full alert and setting her flesh tingling.

She continued to lie there for a few more seconds, listening intently to the silence surrounding her, then something brushed against her cheek and on a strangled gasp she rolled over—and found herself wedged up against a hard male body that was reclining beside her. Alexander's dark head was casually propped up on the heel of one hand.

'I wondered how long your hair was,' he remarked idly. 'Now I know...'

It was then she realised that he was gently fondling a silky skein of her hair. Her scalp was tingling, as well as her cheek, as if he'd teasingly brushed the lock of hair across it.

It must have been his touch that had woken her. 'W-what are you doing here?' she demanded unsteadily.

Stupid question, his mocking eyes said, and he grinned, all white teeth and predatorial amusement.

With a flash of annoyance, meant to disguise the real shaft of alarm that went streaking through her, Mia made to roll away from him again but he stopped her, his arm snaking around her waist to keep her clamped against him.

She met with rock-solid immovable muscle and soft white terry towelling. Her breath caught her eyes dropping to stare at the gap in his bath-robe where tight black curls of rough chest hair lay clustered against warm golden skin.

Her heart stuttered. Her mouth went dry. Something clicked into motion deep inside her—the slowly turning gears of sexual awakening, she realized with dread.

'You sleep like an innocent, do you know that?' he informed her very softly. 'I've been lying here for ages, just watching you, and you barely moved, barely breathed, and your lovely mouth looked so vulnerable it was a strain not to kiss it.'

He did now, though, bending his dark head just enough to brush his lips against her own. Her own head jerked backwards in rejection. 'L-let go of me,' she stammered. 'I n-need—'

'Sex on demand,' he reminded her, speaking right over her protest. 'You agreed to it. Here I am to collect it.'

Oh, God. Her eyes closed, her lips folding in on themselves in an effort to moisten what had gone way beyond being moistened. 'Please,' she whispered with the first hint of weakness she had let herself show him. 'I'm not used to...'

'Performing on demand?' he suggested when her voice trailed off into silence. 'That's not the way I heard it...'

Silence. Mia went perfectly still, a slither of horror sliding down her spine. 'I don't know what you mean,' she said.

'No?' he murmured. 'Then, please, correct me if I am wrong,' he drawled. 'You did have your first full-blown affair at the tender age of sixteen, did you not? With a struggling rock star, I believe. He died several years later of a cocktail of drink and drugs. But not before your wild whoring ways forced your father to place you in a closed institution while they dried you out, made you a half-fit human being then disgorged you back on society in the hope that you had learned your lesson. Did you learn your lesson?'

Mia felt sick, but said nothing. Her father, she was thinking desolately, just couldn't let her do anything with a modicum of dignity. He had to soil it—soil everything—for her.

'Certainly,' that cruel voice went on when she offered no defence, 'you've kept a very low profile for the last seven years. Do you still indulge in drugs?'

She shook her head. Her eyes were closed, and her face so white it looked brittle. It would be no use telling him that she had never—ever—abused her body with illegal drugs because she knew he wouldn't believe her.

'I don't want any child of mine born a drug addict because his mother had no control over herself. What about sex?' he pushed on remorselessly. 'Should I have had you tested before we reached this point? Is there any chance I am likely to put my health at risk if I indulge myself with you?'

Her heart heaved, her aching lungs along with it. 'I have not had a sexual relationship with a man in years,' she told him with as much pride as she could muster.

'You expect me to believe that?'

'It's the truth,' she retorted, her green eyes despising him so much that they actually sought glacial contact with his. 'Believe it or not. I don't care. I don't care if you get a whole army of doctors in here to make sure I am clean enough for you to use. But just do it quickly, will you, so we can get the whole sordid conception over with?'

With that, she managed to break free from him and rolled sideways across the bed. His hand shot out and caught her.

'Oh, no, you don't,' he breathed, and began to pull her to him.

He came to lean right over her, his face tight with anger, his eyes alive with it and his body tense with it. 'Is it true?' he demanded rawly. 'Is everything I've just said the truth?'

The truth? she repeated to herself with skin-blistering mockery. He would like the truth even less than he was liking her father's lies!

'I sold myself for five million pounds,' she spat. 'Does that answer your question?'

It had been a reckless thing to say—foolish, when it was so obvious that he was angry. His dark eyes flashed contemptuously. 'Then start paying your damned dues,' he muttered, and his mouth crushed hers.

It was an insult, an invasion. It promised nothing but punishment for believing she could answer him like that. Yet what actually happened to her then was perhaps more of a punishment than the fierceness of his kiss.

Because she pushed and punched out at him—and then went up like an exploding volcano, her mouth drawing greedily on his like someone with a raging thirst. It was awful—she could feel herself shattering into a million fiery particles but couldn't do a single thing to stop it from happening.

'My God,' he gasped, dragging his mouth free so he could stare down at her. He was shocked. She didn't blame him—she was feeling utterly shattered by it herself!

'You are now contaminated!' she snarled at him in sheer seething reaction.

He just laughed, but it was a rather shocked sound with nothing amused about it. Then he caught her mouth again, sending her spinning back to where she'd gone off to with no apparent effort. It was different now. There was no anger feeding the flames, just a white-hot passion that sang through her blood and sizzled across her skin.

His hands were all over her, his long fingers knotting in her hair, trailing the arching length of her throat, urgently searching for and finding the thrusting tightness of her breast. Then, frustratingly, his hands moving on downwards, finding the knot holding her robe together and impatiently freeing it.

Cool fresh air touched her burning skin and she cried out when it actually hurt. His mouth had left hers and she hadn't even noticed, his body sliding sideways so he could completely unwrap her.

Her eyes were closed, her body trembling with an overload of sensation. He knelt there beside her and watched it all happen while he rid himself of his own robe, his dark face taut and muscles bunched, his own sensual urgency no less controlled than hers was.

When he came back to her, her arms wrapped round him, her fingers clawing into his hair. Their mouths fused hungrily again, and she felt the stinging pleasure of his hair-roughened chest grazing the sensitised tips of her breasts. She felt the power of his arousal pressing against her thighs and instinctively opened them so she could accept him into the cradle of her slender hips.

He groaned something, she didn't know what. She didn't even care. But her eyes snapped open in protest when he denied her his mouth again.

He was glaring hotly down at her. 'Wild,' he muttered. 'I knew you would be wild. No one with this glorious colour of hair and the amount of self-control you exhibit could be anything but wild once you let go.'

'I haven't let go!' she denied, wishing it was the truth! 'I hate you!' she added helplessly

'I hate you too.' He laughed. 'Interesting, isn't it? How two people who can hate each other this much can also feel this naked kind of passion.'

'The passion is all yours,' she said, tight-lipped, then gasped when he suddenly lifted himself away from her to kneel between her parted thighs.

Eyes like black lasers skimmed over her body from firm proud, thrusting breasts to the cluster of tight golden curls protecting her sex.

'Oh…' she choked in appalled embarrassment. No man had ever looked on her quite like this!

But what was a worse humiliation was the way her senses were responding to the way he was looking at her—throbbing and pulsing with an excitement that threatened to completely engulf her.

'I can see you are dying for me to touch you.'

'Please,' she groaned in pained mortification. 'Don't do this to me!'

'You will be wishing me inside you before this hour is through,' he promised darkly.

Then he touched her, sliding a long and silkenly practised finger along the hot moist crevice he had exposed with such a bold disregard to her modesty, and claimed possession by delving deep inside.

It shook her, shook her right through to the very centre of everything she had ever imagined to do with this kind of intimacy. At sixteen she had been too young and too inexperienced to know that she was supposed to have been enjoying this as much as the man who had eventually taken her virginity.

But this—this wild hot surge of stinging pleasure which was taking her over was completely new territory to her. And the fact that it was caused by a man she so utterly despised was enough to send her reeling into shock—the kind of shock that held her helpless as he arched his body over her, capturing her mouth with a hunger that devoured while his fingers began to work a magic on her flesh she had never experienced in her life before.

Oh, help me, she thought on a wave of helpless despair. She couldn't believe this was happening to her, couldn't believe she could lose control like this!

He knew it too, and played with her, like a cat with a mesmerised mouse. An arm slid beneath her shoulders, his body shifting sideways so he was no longer completely covering her, then the real torture began, with slow, light, lazy caresses that told him everything he needed to know about the woman he was exploring.

He touched her face, her nose, her lips, and ran those same fingers down her neck and between the throbbing upthrust of her breasts. He followed the flat line of her ribcage to her tightly muscled stomach, traced the line of her hips, then delved once again into the very core of her, but only fleetingly—too fleetingly—before he was exploring her silken thighs, watching with a dark intensity, which really frightened her, each quiver and jolt of her flesh as he learned what gave her pleasure and what did not.

'Why do you always hide your hair?' he murmured huskily into the dark chasm of sensation that her whirling mind had become. 'I find it very exciting that the same colour nestles here between your thighs. I adore it that your skin is so pale against my own skin, that your breasts are so very sensitive to my slightest touch even though you fight me. And even the fact that you fight me excites me. It makes me wonder what I will feel when you decide to torment me in return...'

'No.' Out of her head with sensation as she was, she heard the silky invitation in his voice and breathlessly refused the offer. 'I won't touch you. You don't need me to.'

The obvious fact that his manhood lay in such daunting erection against her thigh confirmed that fact.

'I will drive you wild,' he warned her, seeming even to enjoy this battle. As if any battle with her was an excitement for him. 'I will make you beg...'

Mia kept her hands clenched in tight fists by her sides as a stubborn answer.

She heard his soft laugh at her stubbornness, then he took one pointed stinging nipple into his mouth and sucked hard at the same time as he slid a finger deep inside her.

Wild, he'd called her. Well, she went wild. It flared up with no constraint. Her hands snaked up and caught at his hair, her fingernails raking into his scalp as she cried out in a wretchedly raw response to what he was doing to her.

He muttered something— it sounded shaken. Then he was repeating the sequence of events so that she reacted in the same way. It was so utterly, mind-blowingly pleasurable that she didn't even feel ashamed of herself, just elated — so exquisitely elated because she had truly believed that she did not have it in her to respond to any man as violently as this.

'You will beg me or caress me,' he warned.

Her eyes flicked open, green fire lasering into burning black. 'I never beg,' she informed him with amazing coolness.

'No?'

With a sudden bright glow in his eyes he slid down the full length of her, landing on his knees beside the bed. 'Beg?' he offered silkily.

'Go to hell, Mr Doumas,' she bit out, using that formal title as an insult.

What he did was bury his mouth between her thighs.

Mia begged. She clutched at him in exquisite agony, and pleaded with him to stop. She wrapped her long legs around him and tried to pull him up and over her. She dug long anxious fingers into his sweat-slicked shoulders. She gasped and writhed and panted and hated him with a vengeance as he held her fast with hands at her hips and drove her to the very edge of sanity.

'Oh—please,' she sobbed, 'please stop now!'

'Say my name,' he muttered against her flesh, his tongue making a snake-like flick at her with the cruel intention of ripping the breath from her body. 'Beg me again and use my name.'

'Alexander,' she whispered helplessly.

'Alex,' he corrected. 'My lovers call me Alex.'

'Alex!' she groaned. 'Alex, please, please…' she murmured deliriously.

'Please—what?' he demanded.

'Please come inside me!' she cried out in aching agony.

It was so humiliating because he laughed as he slid his long, lean, hot body along the full length of her, then entered her with no more warning than that.

'Like this?' he taunted. 'Is this what the five-million-pound wife requires?'

But it was too late for Mia. The cruelty and the insult went sailing right past her because she had shot straight into an orgasm that went on and on and on, and made him go very still in stunned reaction.

He could feel her—actually feel her beating all around him on wave after wave of pulsing ecstasy. It shook him, shook to the very roots his conviction that he'd often experienced what was best in a sexual climax. This woman was experiencing what had to be the best, and not one part of her missed out on the raging feast. Not her fingers where they flexed and clutched at his body, not her breasts as they heaved and arched and quivered, not her mouth as it gasped and groaned and panted.

He caught her mouth. He needed to capture it, needed to join in that wild experience, and at last he began to move inside her, feeling that incredible orgasm go on and on and on while driving him towards his own mind-blowing finish.

When it came he lost touch with himself, with her, with everything. His mind shut down. He felt it happen—felt the flow of blood leave his brain as it surged down to that point of such unbelievable pleasure that it was almost agony to feel it eventually fade away.

Mia thought she might have died a little afterwards. Certainly something deep inside her had been lost for ever. She didn't know what, couldn't begin to try and work out what. But as he lay there, heavy on her, his big body still attacked by the pulsing aftershocks of what they had just created between them, she knew that something vital had gone from her—had been passed, maybe, from her to him, she didn't know.

But it was most definitely gone.

When he eventually moved, sliding sideways onto the mattress to bury his face in the pillow, Mia turned and curled up away from him. She was shocked, shocked by the uninhibited wildness of what had just taken place. Shocked by the power of his passion and her own ability to let go of every ounce of self-control.

And now came the aftermath, she thought bleakly as they continued to lie there, together but separate, intimate but strangers.

Silent, appalled strangers who had been caught in the tangled web of their own sexuality, only to find after it all that they were still very separate entities.

He moved first, sending her muscles into wary tension as he moved to the edge of the bed and sat up with his feet on the floor. She heard him utter a heavy sigh, sensed him raking angry fingers through hair that had been disarrayed by her own restless fingers. She felt the mattress dip as he bent and she knew he was picking up his discarded robe. She felt him begin to cover himself as he pushed himself to his feet.

Tears burned in her eyes as she lay there, facing away from him with her arms and hands clutched protectively across her curved and naked body. She sensed his eyes raking over her, sensed him considering what to say, and waited with baited breath and a hammering heart for the clever insult to hit her eardrums.

But in the end he said nothing, and maybe that was just about the biggest insult he could have paid her as he walked out of her bedroom in total silence.

CHAPTER FOUR

IT TOOK every ounce of determination Mia could muster to step out of that bedroom at precisely nine o'clock that evening, but she had to pause at the top of those highly polished stairs as a bout of cowardly tremors made a sudden last-minute attack.

She was still suffering from shock, she knew. Her body was in shock at the unrestrained way it had behaved this afternoon. Her mind was in shock because it just could not believe it had allowed her to go so out of control with Alex, a man she supposedly felt nothing for. But, more to the point, she was finding it more difficult to come to terms with the knowledge that she had allowed all of it to happen with a man who felt so little for her.

Where had her pride been? Her self-respect?

She didn't know, could not understand what had possessed her during that wild, hot frenzy that had taken place in the bedroom. But she certainly knew where her pride was at this moment. It was floundering around at her feet, along with her lost self-respect.

And the urge to simply turn right around and lock herself in that bedroom rather than have to face *him* again tonight was so powerful at the moment that she almost gave in to it.

Then the sound of a door opening downstairs caught her attention, and she suddenly discovered that her pride was not completely demolished because, with a bracing of her slender shoulders and a defiant lifting of her chin, she found herself walking down the stairs, instead of dashing for cover behind a locked door, because she knew she would rather die than let him see how utterly degraded she felt.

A sound to her left as she reached the hallway set her feet moving in that direction. A door was standing slightly ajar, with golden light shining gently through the gap.

She took a deep breath, ran trembling fingers down her equally trembling thighs then stepped forward, silently pushing the door open just enough to allow her to enter whatever room was on the other side of it.

She saw Alex immediately. Her heart turned over, her throat locking on a fresh lump of tension. He was dressed very formally in a black silk dinner suit, white dress shirt and black bow tie—though what he was wearing barely registered with her at that moment because she was so busy coming to terms with the way she was seeing him now.

Naked.

She shuddered, horrified at herself—appalled by the sudden flare of sexual awareness that went sizzling through her as her eyes looked at him and saw firm golden flesh, covering a beautifully structured framework, instead of the reality of conventional black fabric.

She saw wide satin-smooth shoulders and rock-solid biceps, a hair-roughened chest that was so powerfully muscled it made her own breasts sting in memory of what it had felt like to be crushed against it. She saw a long lean torso with a tight waist, flat hips and strong thighs, supporting a pelvis that housed the full-blooded and dynamic essence of the man.

An essence that made her inner thighs clench, made her go hot all over, made her lungs completely shut down as a whole gamut of sensation went racing right through her. She looked at his mouth and felt it crushing her own mouth, looked at his hands and felt them caressing her skin.

She looked at the man in his entirety and saw a tall dark stranger—now an intimate stranger. But one who had suddenly become so physically real to her that she now realised just how successfully she had been blanking him out before as a flesh and blood person.

Was he aware she had done that? she wondered as she stood there, staring at him in nerve-tightening tension. Did he know that to get herself this far in this dastardly deal they had struck she'd had to pretend he was nothing more than a shadow?

Standing there by a drinks cabinet, seemingly lost in thought as he frowned into what looked like a crystal tumbler lightly splashed with whisky, the only thing she could be sure about concerning him now was that at this moment, while he believed himself alone, he was doing nothing to hide his own sense of loathing at what had erupted between them.

And why not? she asked herself. He despised her as much as she despised him so it followed automatically that he felt the same revulsion for what they'd done to each other.

Shame trickled through her, followed by a wave of pained helplessness. Because this was only the beginning, not the end.

The beginning.

She must have moved, though she hadn't been aware of doing it, because something made his dark head turn. Then he became still, his brooding stare fixing on hers, knowledge making his dark brown irises glint and then burn, which sent a wild flush of hot embarrassment sweeping through her because their new intimacy, she realised, was catching him out, too.

Then the flame changed to contempt, a hard, biting, cruel contempt, before he hooded the expression with long black lashes. Hooded it so he could let his gaze run over her carefully controlled hair and the dramatically plain deep turquoise silk shift dress she was wearing, which skimmed her slender figure without clinging anywhere—deliberately chosen for that reason.

Yet he missed nothing—like herself, she suspected, seeing not the fully dressed woman standing here but the naked one, the wild one, the woman who had surprised him with the power of her own passions. He was seeing her spread out, fully exposed to him and ready.

She felt sick suddenly. Stomach-churningly, head-swimmingly sick.

'Take your hair out of that unflattering knot,' he said in an oddly flattened tone. 'And don't wear it up in my company again.'

It was a shock. The very last thing she had expected him to say, in fact. Her hair? An impulsive hand went to touch the simple knot held in place by a tortoiseshell clasp. Her cheeks warmed and her eyes dropped away from him because she didn't know why he was suddenly attacking her and why he had used that strange tone to do it.

'No,' she said, grimly pulling herself together, the coolly indifferent Mia sliding back into place. 'It's more comfortable for me to wear it like this. It annoys me when it's loose.'

'Then suffer,' he said unsympathetically. 'I hate liars. And that prim hairstyle makes such a damned liar of you. At least when your hair is down...' he took a tense gulp at the drink in his glass '...people are forewarned about what you really are.'

'And what am I?' she asked, the green eyes glinting with challenge—while every fine muscle in her body was held tensely, waiting for him to say the word her father had been throwing at her for so many years now that she couldn't remember when he had not seen her as a whore.

This man would be no different. This man and her father had so much in common it would shock and appal Alexander Doumas to know just how much.

Or maybe he did know, she corrected herself when he didn't say it but took another deep slug from his glass instead.

'Do it,' he commanded as he lowered the glass again. 'Or I will make you do it.'

'Dinner,' a carefully neutral voice announced behind Mia.

She turned abruptly and caught Elena's frosty expression. She knew the other woman had overheard most of their telling little conversation, and looked right through the housekeeper as she strode proudly past her.

But the hand landing on her shoulder brought her to a sudden standstill. How Alex had managed to move across the room so quickly Mia didn't know, but it was certainly his hand, burning its already familiar brand as he detained her.

'Leave us.' He grimly dismissed the housekeeper.

She turned and left as he propelled Mia back into the room then closed the door. A half-moment later and the tortoiseshell clasp that was holding up her hair was springing free, and the silken coil of hair was unfurling over his fingers in a heavy fall of fire that rippled its way to the base of her spine.

The tortoiseshell clasp was discarded and she heard it land with a clunk on a nearby table. Then he turned her round to face him.

'Don't fight me,' he warned her very grimly, 'because you won't like the consequences.'

To prove his point, the hand still lost in her hair tightened, tugging her head backwards until she had no choice but to look at him. His eyes were still hooded, but she could see the anger simmering beneath those heavy eyelids as he began to rearrange her hair to his own satisfaction.

It hurt her inside. For some reason Mia could not work out at all the way he was asserting his control over her like this hurt—when it shouldn't. It was only what she had expected from him from the very beginning after all.

'You don't like who you are, do you?' he murmured suddenly.

'No,' she replied. It was blunt and it was honest.

'It is why you hide your true nature behind prim clothes and stark hairstyles. You are ashamed of what you are.'

'Yes,' she confirmed, again with the same cool bluntness.

'But you could not keep the passion hidden in that bed upstairs, could you? It broke free and virtually consumed you.'

'You weren't so controlled yourself,' she hit back.

'I didn't quite reach the point where I completely stopped breathing,' he countered grimly.

Her cheeks went pale, her lowered eyes squeezing together on a fresh bout of self-revulsion.

'Was it like that with the rock star?' he questioned. 'Did you fall apart as spectacularly for him as you did for me?'

She didn't answer that one—refused to answer. Whatever had gone on in her life *before* this man was none of his business, and she was damned if she was going to feed his ego by telling him she had *never* lost control of herself like that before—ever.

His hand came to her chin, closed around it then tightened, demanding an answer, but her eyes showed him nothing except cold, green defiance. Her mouth, so red and full and still clearly swollen from his kisses, remaining resolutely shut.

'Well, I tell you this much, *yineka mou,*' he murmured very softly. 'You have set your own boundaries with what took place up there. You will not move from this estate without my say-so. You will not be left alone—either in this house of out of it—with another man. You are now, in effect, my personal prisoner.'

'Points you had written into my contract,' she reminded him. 'Did you see me arguing with you about them then?'

'Ah, but I have a... worrying suspicion that you were not so aware of your own passions when you agreed to that contract. Now you do know, and I am going to take no chances with you falling apart like that for any other man— understand me?'

'Yes.' Once more she refused to give him the satisfaction of arguing the point with him because, whatever lessons he thought he had learned about her in that blasted bedroom, she, too, had learned her own lessons about him. This man thrived on argument. His sexual drive fed off it, but he would not be fed by her again.

He knew exactly what she was doing, of course. He was not an idiot. He could read silent messages just as well as she could. But to her surprise, he laughed, a warm, dark, sexily amused sound that curled up her toes inside her shoes as his mouth came down to cover her own.

Their bodies fused, that quickly and that easily, from mouth to breast to hips. They came together as though someone or something had simply thrown a switch to let the whole wretched current of electric pleasure wrap itself around them.

His tongue blended with hers, and her hands jerked up to clutch at his warm, tightly muscled neck where her fingers spread along his jawbone, his cheeks and the smooth line of his chin. She felt his body respond by tensing, felt his hands drag their way downwards until they were clasping her low on the hips, drawing her even closer to the pulsing throb where his manhood was thickening, tightening.

Her own body melted—melted on the inside, melted on the outside, a hot, honeyed meltdown that poured into her bloodstream, filling her breasts and that aching junction between her thighs so she moved wantonly against him. She couldn't stop herself, couldn't put a halt to what was beginning to happen all over again.

She groaned—at least she thought it was her but it might have been him—and her thighs flexed and parted, searching out an even deeper intimacy against the grinding thrust of him. It was terrible. She didn't know herself, couldn't seem to control what was suddenly raging through her system.

When he dragged his mouth free she whimpered and

went in blind search of reconnection while his hands bit like twin vices into the flesh around her hips to keep her pressed tightly against him, though he denied her his mouth. Denied it ruthlessly. So much so that her eyes flickered open, glazed by need and a confusion that went so deep that it took several long agonising seconds for her to realise what he was doing.

Watching her.

Watching her with a bite in his eyes that told her exactly what he thought of her lack of control.

Whore, that expression said. Whore.

She almost fainted on the wave of self-loathing that went sweeping through her.

He despised her for responding like this—as much as he despised her for being here at all.

'Save it,' he said insolently, 'until later. I have a mistress to console before I can come back here and console you.'

It was cruel but, then, he had meant to be. Anger was driving him—anger at himself for wanting her like this, anger at her for making him want her and anger at the whole situation which he could only relieve by venting it on her.

With that final humiliation biting deep into her senses, he let go and stepped back from her. Two seconds after that he was pulling open the door and striding from the room. Not just from the room but from the villa. Standing there, trembling, aching and shamed, she listened to the front door slam in his wake, heard a car start up and drive away with a powerful roar.

And through it all she barely breathed, barely blinked, barely functioned on any level.

Why? Because it had finally sunk in just how much he hated her. It didn't matter that he had already told her so as far back as in her father's study—the point was that she hadn't really taken the full thrust of his words on board.

Words like, 'I will hate and despise you and bed you

with alacrity,' were suddenly taking on their full true meaning. As did his most recent statement, 'I have a mistress to console before I can come back here and console you...'

She would come second. Second to that lucky lady who probably came fairly far down his list of priorities, which made second a very low status indeed.

She was here for one purpose and one purpose only—to conceive his child so he could claim his prize.

'Your dinner, madam...' Sofia appeared from nowhere, her eyes lowered, her expression carefully guarded. 'The dining room is this way,' she prompted quietly.

It took another few moments to pull herself together but Mia managed it, following Sofia into the long narrow grandeur of a formal dining room where only one place setting waited.

He had always meant to leave her alone like this, she realised on a fresh wave of agony.

Then, thankfully, right out of the centre of that very same agony emerged the other Mia—the pragmatic, invulnerable, very mocking Mia. The one who could smile wryly at herself for actually being hurt by Alex's treatment of her.

The one who could sit quite comfortably at a table and eat alone because eating alone was far more preferable to eating with cruel swines like Alexander Doumas—a man like her father.

When the long silent meal was over she left alone, walking out of the dining room with her chin held high as she trod those polished stairs back to the relative sanctuary of her own room where she calmly prepared for bed—and felt the protective casing she had built around herself threaten to crack only once.

That was when she glanced at the bed she had so carefully tidied, before leaving the room earlier. Someone had stripped it, changed the sheets and put on a clean lemon top cover, one which gave not a single hint of what had taken place on that bed earlier—no tell-tale creases, nothing. An act which told tales in itself.

They knew.

She shuddered. The whole damned staff must know what had been going on in this bed earlier.

Did that mean they also knew why it had been going on? By their cold unwelcoming attitude she had to assume that they knew *exactly* why she was here and, worse, that their employer was accepting the situation only under the severest duress.

That brought her swiftly on to the next soul-crushing point—did they therefore know just where he had gone tonight?

The mistress.

The other woman.

Did they know that he had climbed out of her bed only to climb into another bed with his mistress?

Humiliation poured into her blood, searing a path to a temper few knew she possessed. With a flash from her glinting green eyes, she reached down and grabbed hold of that lemon cover, yanking it clear away from the bed and tossing it in a heap on the ground at her feet.

From now on, she vowed, every time she walked into this room she would mess up this rotten bed! If they wanted to bear witness to their employer's bed duty, let them! Let them change this damned bed fifteen times a day and wonder at his incredible stamina!

Keeping two women busy at the same time—the rotten, crass bastard!

Not that she cared! she told herself tightly as she crawled between those pristine white sheets. She couldn't give a damn what the man got up to so long as he was practising safe sex with the other woman. Other than that, she had no interest whatsoever in his sex life!

That was the exact point at which she made her brain switch off because she had a horrible feeling that she might begin to care if she let herself dwell on the subject too much.

Thankfully, sleep came to her rescue with a single lowering of her eyelids. Wearing a nightdress of cream satin and curled on her side with her long hair flowing across the white pillow, she didn't know another thing for hours. Hours and hours of blessed oblivion from the bleak prospect of what her life was going to be like from now on.

A hand grasped her shoulder. 'Wake up,' a deeply masculine voice insisted.

Just as she had managed to push it all away with the single blink of an eye, it was suddenly all back again. 'W-what?' she mumbled in sleepy confusion. 'What do you think you're doing!' she gasped as he rolled her onto her back and pinned her there with his weight. 'No—!'

'Not a word I recognise,' he informed her with a grim kind of sardonicism.

Her lashes flicked upwards, her eyes finding themselves trapped by glinting dark irises that confirmed exactly what his words and actions were stating.

'What's the matter?' she taunted. 'Wasn't she very consolable tonight?'

He frowned, his eyes narrowing for the few moments it took him to grasp her meaning. Then his teeth were suddenly gleaming in the darkness, cruel and incisive like the next few words he lashed her with. 'She was fine,' he muttered, 'but now I want you.'

'You're disgusting,' she said, and tried to wriggle free, but he wasn't about to let her.

'Nevertheless, when I want I take and you deliver,' he said harshly. 'Don't ever say no to me again.'

Then he did take, passionately and ruthlessly, his hungry mouth covering hers, his tongue probing with a dark, knowing intimacy that appalled her even as her own desires leapt like the traitors they were to greet him eagerly.

He still smelled of whisky. His lips were warm with it,

his tongue tasted of it, transferring the evocative taste to her own tongue and filling her lungs with its heady fumes. His hands were trembling slightly as though his urgency was so great he was having difficulty controlling it. His long fingers ran over the smooth slide of satin, skimming her breasts, her ribcage, her abdomen and eliciting sharp little stinging responses that made her gasp, her spine arch, her muscles tighten and her hands move upwards to clutch at his shoulders with the intention of pushing him away.

Only her hands never pushed. They made contact with his hard, warm, naked flesh and clung to him, a wretched groan escaping her smothered mouth as his fingers slid upwards to find her breasts again. In seconds her nipples were erect and tingling, his palms rolling them with an erotic expertise that had them pushing against the confines of her nightdress while his thighs were insinuating themselves between her own.

The throbbing contact of his own powerful erection moving against fine satin was so intensely arousing that her thighs widened even more in an effort to gain greater friction where she most needed it.

His mouth left hers and he laughed. It was a sound far distant from humour but held angry triumph. 'What a hot little thing you are when you let yourself go,' he taunted. 'No wonder you preferred me to that grotesque little man who was knocking sixty. He could not have given you half this much pleasure.'

'Your mind is a sewer,' she shot at him.

'My mind is that low?' he mocked, and grabbed hold of the edge of her nightdress, tugged it up around her hips and entered her. No foreplay, no compunction.

To her utter horror, Mia went wild beneath him. Just like the last time, she was overtaken by an instant orgasm that set her body writhing and her insides throbbing, the tiny muscles inside rippling over him and around him as her head fell back and her throat began to pant out little gasps of riotous intensity while her heart raced out of control.

It shocked him again, held him paralysed for the few stunning moments it took for him to accept just how spectacularly she responded to him. Then his mouth lowered to one tightly stinging nipple. Through the stretched tautness of her nightdress he sucked the pulsing tip deep into his mouth and began to move, thrusting his hips with short blunt stabs that kept her locked in that muscle-clenched storm of hectic climax, the strokes growing longer and deeper and harder as he drove her on and on with no let-up, no chance to make a mad grab at sanity.

She was out of her head and it dismayed her, but she couldn't seem to do a single thing about it. When he withdrew she should really have come tumbling back down to earth with a crash—but she didn't. She stayed up there, lost in that world of electric sensation.

He muttered something, which she couldn't make out. His body slid sideways, the nightgown coming off altogether before his mouth clamped on hers again and his fingers began to discover what his throbbing manhood already knew—what it was like to feel a woman in the throes of a multi-orgasm.

Those tormenting fingers stroked and incited her, his hungry tongue mimicking the action. One of her hands found his nape and clutched at it desperately, holding his mouth down on hers while her other hand went in agitated search of other parts of him.

He was so big, so hard and slick and potent—she wanted him back inside her. She wanted his mouth on her breasts but she wanted him to keep on kissing her mouth like this. In the end and on an impatient sigh her fingers clutched at a handful of his hair to tug his mouth from her so she could present him with her breast instead, and through it all her body was still rocketing through space on its own agenda.

He began to throb against her caressing hand. She felt it

happen and released a sigh of satisfaction that came out closer to a salacious growl. She snaked her body beneath him and guided him into her, two hands clutching at his lean, tight buttocks.

Holding him like that, with his dark head buried between her breasts, she let go of everything, driving him onward with the thrust of her hips. Her cries of anguished pleasure echoed around the darkened bedroom as she felt his own pending climax build, felt the muscles bunch all over him, heard his soft curse as his self-control began to crack wide open, and this time they leapt together, high—so high Mia felt lost and disembodied.

The next morning when she awoke the only sign that Alex had ever been there was his scent on the sheets and on her body—in her mouth and in the soft subtle pulse of her body where he had so effectively stamped his presence.

It was a struggle to make herself get up. She almost stumbled her way into the bathroom, felt hardly any better by the time she came out again, and began to fumble round for something to wear.

It was sunny outside, the heat of the day surprisingly strong for this time of year, she discovered when she pushed open the window in an effort to drag some air into her lungs that did not smell of him.

It didn't work. He was in her system, she knew. Knew the man and his scent were destined to be an innate part of her for ever now.

It was a wretched thought—the kind of thought that made her shiver, as if someone had just walked over her grave, because she knew that no matter how passionately she had affected him last night he would be despising her more for the way she'd responded than he would have done if she'd simply remained cold beneath him.

Oh, face it, Mia, she told herself grimly. You would be despising yourself less if you'd managed to stay aloof—

and that's what is really troubling you. You're disgusted with yourself for being so sexually vulnerable to a man you hold so little respect for.

And, for all you know about him, he probably has the same effect on every woman he takes to his bed.

The great lover, she mocked acidly. The Don Juan of the nineteen-nineties!

Did that mean his mistress was well used to losing her head whenever he deigned to bed her?

Did it matter? she asked herself angrily as a nasty poison called jealousy began to creep through her blood. The point is, you respond like that and it's shameful!

But it didn't alter the fact that she fell apart in his arms like that every night for the next fortnight. During the day she didn't see him. He was never lying beside her when she woke in the morning. She got used to hearing a helicopter arrive and take off again very early—taking him to his offices in Athens, she presumed, though she was never given the opportunity to ask. He came back by the same means, usually just as dusk was beginning to colour the sky.

Where he ate she did not know, but it was never with her. The only contact they ever had was in the hours of darkness when he would slide into bed beside her and drive them both out of their heads with the devastating power of their mutual sensuality. He never spoke unless it was to comment on what they were doing, and he showed no remorse in using her like the brood mare she had sold herself as to him.

When it was over he would lie on his back beside her and she would curl on her side as far away from him as she could get while she waited for the aftershocks to stop shaking her body. Aftershocks she knew he was keenly aware of, and she had a feeling that they were the reason he lingered in that bed with her afterwards—because he saw those tremors as part of his due. They fed his ego—

an ego she knew had been badly damaged by him giving in to this deal in the first place.

Perhaps he even hated himself a little for giving in to it. Certainly, sometimes in the darkness she had glimpsed a look in his eyes that had suggested self-contempt as he'd watched her go wild beneath him and had known—just as she had—that he'd been about to join her.

Whatever he did to her, she did to him. If he did acquire that depth of pleasure with every woman he bedded, then he did not like it happening with her.

But, then, neither did Mia like it. In fact, towards the end of that first fortnight she began hoping—praying—that Mother Nature would be kind to her and make her pregnant. If the potency of their intercourse had anything to do with it, she should be very pregnant. Then at least he would leave her alone.

But it was not to be. The morning she woke with those familiar symptoms that warned her period had arrived she wept.

That day Mia roamed about the big empty house in a sluggish state of deep depression. It didn't help that there was not a friendly face in the place from whom she could gain some light relief from her own sense of grim failure.

Now she had to find a moment to break the unfortunate news to Alex that he had not succeeded in his quest to make her pregnant and, more to the point, that her body was not available to him for the next five days.

But how did she tell anything to a man who only came to her in the dead of night? Leave a note, pinned to the door between his bedroom and hers? she mused bitterly.

The temptation to do just that was so strong that she almost gave in to it. In the end she did the only thing she really could do, and waited up for him to come to her. When eventually she heard the connecting door open she was standing by the window, covered from neck to toe in soft white towelling.

She turned to face him. 'I'm not pregnant,' she announced boldly, and watched him stop dead in his tracks.

He didn't move again for the space of thirty long seconds, his stance so taut that she gained the rather satisfying impression that she had disconcerted him so much that he just did not know what to do next.

It was wonderful, almost worth the disappointment to see him so utterly stumped like this. He was a big man, a man whose body she knew so well by now that she could even read the frustration in his beautiful muscle formation.

'I suggest you use your mistress for the next few days,' she added with icy relish. 'I will, of course, let you know when I am available again.'

Oh, she enjoyed saying that! He treated her like a whore and she was responding as a whore. His dark lashes fluttered, folding down over his eyes then back up again as the full brutal smack of her words hit him full in his arrogant face.

Because he was no fool he recognised that she was not only acknowledging herself as a whore but that he was no better in his treatment of her.

But he got his own back. Heavens, did he get his own back! 'Fine,' he agreed smoothly. 'I will do that.'

The door closed behind him, leaving her standing there where she had faced up to him with her chin high and her stance proud, while the tears trickled unchecked down her pale cheeks.

Why was she crying? She didn't know. What had she expected, after all? For him to show disappointment, concern for her health, a bit of human compassion for her lonely plight?

The man didn't give a damn about her as a living, breathing human being, and went on to prove it by not coming back to the island for the next seven days.

A week to the day later, she was just climbing out of the swimming pool when Sofia came out onto the terrace. 'The master wishes to speak to you on the telephone,' she informed her.

The *master*. Mia mocked the title acidly. The man with everything—*master* of all he surveyed! Except an island he coveted and a child he hadn't managed to conceive.

'Thank you.' She nodded coolly to Sofia, grabbed her beach robe and pulled it over her dripping body as she followed the maid into the house and to a telephone extension in the drawing room.

'A helicopter is on its way to you,' Alex announced. 'It will arrive in about thirty minutes. It has no time to linger so be ready to board as soon as it lands.'

'But—'

That was as far as she got for the line went dead. Frowning slightly and wondering what this new development could mean because she had not been out of the confines of the estate since she'd arrived, she hurried upstairs, showered, dried her hair, then quickly knotted the still slightly damp mass at her nape. She threw on a pale blue cotton sundress, added a white linen jacket and gathered a few things together in a large white linen beach bag because she didn't know if she was going to be away for an hour or two or for a week.

She was waiting when the helicopter touched down on the purpose-built pad situated a little way off from one side of the house. The pilot didn't stop the rotors while he waited for her to duck beneath them and climb on board.

An hour later she was being transported by a chauffeur-driven limousine into the centre of Athens.

The car drew to a stop outside a residential apartment block, the driver getting out to escort her inside. He led her to the lift, smiled politely but briefly as he pressed a button on the lift console then stepped back again, leaving her to travel upwards alone.

Was this where he usually met with his mistress? she wondered, and felt her stomach turn over—felt the usual surge of bitter self-contempt begin to burn at how she let him get away with it.

Was it the mistress's turn to be unavailable?

The doors slid open on a private foyer. Sucking in a deep breath of air, she forced her unwilling limbs to start moving. Chin up as usual and her eyes revealing no hint of what was eating away at her insides, she stepped out of the lift and heard the doors hiss as they closed behind her.

But it was the man propping up a doorframe directly across from her who really held her attention. He was dressed casually in pale chinos and a white polo shirt that clung to the taut contours of his muscle-tight body. His big arms were folded across his wide chest, and one neat ankle crossed over the other. His lean, dark, frighteningly ruthless face was shuttered, his eyes hooded by long lush lashes as he looked her over.

'The hair,' he said.

That was all. Just 'the hair'. As she reached up in mute obedience to loosen the heavy flow of red-gold she saw the intensity with which he watched her fiery tresses tumble around her arms and shoulders.

It was a look she knew well and could feel it touch deep, deep in the very essence of her womanhood.

Desire, unhidden and unwanted.

It was time to begin again.

CHAPTER FIVE

It set the pattern for the next two months. When commuting to and from the island to Athens, Alex came to Mia's bed every night without fail except at weekends when, she presumed, he went to his mistress.

Mia told herself stubbornly that she didn't care, that the five days when he did come to her meant she deserved a brief respite on Saturday and Sunday from his insatiable demands on her.

Anyway, she always rang Suzanna on a Saturday morning and spent long, precious minutes reassuring the poor child that she had not been forgotten.

Those telephones calls hurt as much as they made each passing week bearable. The little girl was lonely. Mia knew what it felt like because she had been there herself during her own loveless childhood. She would usually spend the rest of the weekend sunk in the kind of heavy mood that made Alex's absence a relief.

During the day she had formed her own quiet routine where she swam twenty lengths of the pool before breakfast and the same again late in the afternoon. In between she read a lot, silently grateful that his home possessed such a comprehensive library.

Over the next three weeks Alex had her transported out to him on two occasions when he was away on business—once to Milan and another time to Paris. Each time she found herself being taken to the penthouse suite of one of his own hotels for a night of wild and wanton bedding.

She couldn't call it loving—*wouldn't* call it loving because what they shared was about as far away from that emotion as any two people could get.

At least during those brief trips away from the island they ate together—they talked to each other, even if it was a rather wary and constrained kind of talking. And the sex was different because he would not wait until she was safely lying in the darkness before coming to join her. He would undress her himself, and had her undress him. And sometimes—just sometimes—it would seem as if he almost cared for her a little, the way he would stand there in the middle of a bedroom and caress her with hands that almost seemed to revere the smooth, silken flesh they were touching.

And once during one of these much more intimate beddings that took place away from his private villa—times when he was warmer, kinder, much more attentive towards her, yet still managed to drive her into that mindless state of sensual fervour—he stopped when his body was lost deep inside her, pushed the wild strands of hair away from her face then lay there on top of her, his expression sombre.

'Why do you let me do this to you?' he asked.

Why? The answer almost escaped her kiss-warmed lips but she managed to bite it back. After all, how much mocking mileage would he make out of her admitting that she couldn't help herself?

'I don't know,' she replied honestly enough because she really did not know or understand why this man of all men should be able to move her so dramatically. 'What's your excuse?'

He sighed, something like that old self-contempt, which she had not seen in his face for a week now, clouding his lean, taut features. 'Like you, I don't know,' he answered heavily. For a moment, for a horrible gut-twisting moment, she thought he was going to withdraw from her and leave her in this high state of sexual need, the conscious acknowledgement of what they were doing here enough to cool his ardour.

But, far from withdrawing, what he actually did was bury

himself all the deeper inside her, his mouth trembling slightly as it came down to her own mouth. 'Whatever it is,' he muttered huskily, 'we may as well enjoy because once you are pregnant it will be over.'

It was a statement of intent. A *re-statement* of that intent issued to her, it seemed, so long ago now that she could barely recall the moment in her father's study when he had first made it.

It made their loving all the more urgent that night, made him come back to her time after time after time. The next morning, when she awoke to find him gone from her as usual, she was grateful for his absence, the pride-lowering fact that he never so much as acknowledged her during daylight hours for once a relief because she felt so utterly bereft, though she did not understand why that particular morning should be any different from all the others when she had woken alone like this.

Then the inevitable happened. Three and a half months into this marriage that wasn't really a marriage she missed her period.

Oddly, she said nothing. Oddly, she let him go on making love to her throughout the next four weeks until her second period failed to show itself. Oddly, she felt so terribly depressed by this second missed period that she was glad Alex was in the States again and therefore too far away to send for her for his habitual single night of passion to break up a business trip. Instead, she could use the time to come to terms with her own odd reaction to the one thing this had been all about.

A baby. They had managed to make a baby. A baby that was to make all her most secret dreams come true and would give Alex what he coveted most.

His island, his special piece of rock that lay out there somewhere among that cluster of tiny islands she could see from her bedroom window.

Will it all have been worth it? Mia wondered dully. All

this isolation she had endured, all the nights of loveless passion?

Oh, yes, she told herself flatly, it will have been worth it, and she grimly dismissed the way her heart coiled up tightly then throbbed as if it were hurting for something it had never been given the right to hurt for.

He arrived back at the villa late one afternoon while she was taking her usual exercise in the pool. She watched the helicopter fly over then disappear behind a bank of trees that acted as a wind-break to the pool area. As its rotor blades slowed in the warm still air she grimly returned to her exercise, pounding steadily up and down the pool with a stubborn resolve, refusing point blank to acknowledge any of the fluttering sinking sensations that were crawling around her insides.

She was just pulling herself out of the water when she glanced up to find him standing there.

It was a break from habit, and the irony of that break, coming now, did not escape her. He was still dressed for business in iron-grey trousers and a crisp white shirt, though his jacket was missing and his tie had been tugged loose. He looked tired, she saw. His eyes were hooded as usual as he ran them over her slender figure, encased in white clinging wet Lycra.

Already she was aware of the changes in her body, the extra heaviness in her breasts and their new excruciating sensitivity. She knew her waist was slightly thicker simply because her clothes felt tighter, and she was aware of a swelling around her abdomen that must show under the clinging swimwear.

It was therefore a purely defensive action that made her reach for a towel to cover herself, her eyes dropping away from his with guilt, embarrassment and a multitude of other things that didn't bear thinking about.

One of them was causing disturbance in the deepest parts of her body. It was desire, pure and simple. No matter who he was or what he was—or even why he was—she had grown to need him. She needed what he could do to her to make her lose her grip on the fierce self-control she had spent the best part of her life maintaining for one wretched reason or another.

Alexander Doumas, with his dynamic sensuality, had somehow managed to find a chink in her otherwise impenetrable armour, and in doing so had unwittingly made himself so indispensable to her new need to break free from her own constraints that she did not know how she was going to go on without him now it was, in effect, over.

And the worst thing of all, she acknowledged as she carefully wrapped the towel around her, was that knowing she felt like this about him had to be the most pride-lowering effect of the whole rotten bargain.

'I'm pregnant,' she announced, just like that without any preamble. It came blurting out because it had to be said before he had a chance to say the words she knew were about to come from him. She had seen the look in his eyes and had recognised it. He had been away for longer than a week, and if he had not been able to use the services of his mistress in that time then he had come to search her out like this because he needed her sexually.

If she'd hoped to jolt some kind of response from him by boldly announcing it like that, she failed miserably. Neither by stance nor expression did he hint at anything.

'Are you sure?' he asked quietly.

Her small chin lifted, her green eyes steady as they gazed into his. 'Yes.'

'How far?'

She gave a shrug of one sun-kissed, slender shoulder, and suddenly realised that she was going to have to admit that she'd let him go on taking her while she'd already suspected she could be pregnant. 'I missed my second period last week,' she told him with the usual defiant tilt to her chin. 'I w-wanted to be sure before I told you.'

It was a weak excuse but he made no comment. He just stood there and gazed at her in total silence, his eyes and his expression telling her absolutely nothing.

Yet she sensed in him something—something that kept her very still in the warm sunshine, held in breathless waiting suspense for...

For what? she asked herself confusedly.

Then she knew exactly what because when his answer came it struck so deep that it actually felt as if it might have made her bleed somewhere.

'That's it, then,' he said, and turned and walked away, leaving her standing there feeling cold, cast-down and rejected—feeling empty inside when, physically at least, she wasn't.

An hour later she was standing in her bedroom when she heard the helicopter take off again. With white face, clenched teeth, closed eyes and hands coiled into two tight fists at her sides, she stood there in the middle of the room and listened until the very last whirr of those rotor blades had fluttered into silence.

'That's it, then.' Those cruelly flat words had not stopped lacerating her since he had spoken them. There had been no enquiry as to her health—nothing but those three words that showed his contempt for both herself and their baby. Showed that the man had feelings cast in steel—he wanted the family island and did not care what he was forfeiting to get it.

She had expected nothing more from him but still the words had managed to cut her.

Then, quite without warning, the connecting door to his bedroom swung open. Mia started in surprise, whirling jerkily on her heel to find him standing where he should not have been.

The shock and confusion she experienced was so great that it sent her head spinning and the blood rushing from her brain to her tingling feet. Without really knowing why, since it had never happened to her in her life before, she quietly and silently sank into a faint.

'What the hell happened?' Alex's voice was curt, gruff, grating at her eardrums as she came round again to find herself lying on the bed with him standing over her, his dark face a fascinating mix of anger and concern.

'I thought you'd gone,' she whispered fraiily. 'It w-was a shock when you walked in here.'

'You thought I'd gone?' He sounded so incredulous that she almost laughed. 'I've only just arrived. Why the hell should I want to leave again so quickly?'

'Why the hell should you want to walk into my bedroom during daylight hours?' Mia countered waspishly.

He shifted uncomfortably, his expression becoming closed as he dropped down to seat himself on the edge of her bed. 'I may be ruthless,' he muttered gruffly, 'but I'm not that bloody ruthless.'

It was such a small concession, such a very insignificant gesture on his part, that it really did not deserve the response it actually received yet...

Her arm came up, and of its own volition seemed to hook itself over his shoulder and around his neck as her eyes filled with weak, burning tears. She raised herself up and buried her face in the back of his shoulder—and wept.

Which of them was more shocked was difficult to determine. Mia was shocked at herself because, even in her darkest hours, she had never let herself do anything like this! She'd never cried in front of anyone—hardly ever let herself cry even in private—so she was shocked to find the flood-gates opening as abruptly as they did.

Alex was so shocked that he went rigid. She felt his shoulders grow tense, and his neck. She felt his heart thud against his ribcage as though the shock had jolted it out of its usual steady beat.

Then, with an odd, short, constrained sigh he was twisting around and putting his arms around her, holding her, saying nothing but allowing her to do what she seemed to need to do—to weep in his arms as though her heart were broken.

But, as with all impulsive gestures, this one had to come to an eventual end. When it did, when the sobs changed to snuffles and she became aware of just what she had done and with whom she had done it embarrassment washed over her in a wave. It coloured her damp cheeks and made her shudder in horror. She pulled away from him, scrambled off the bed and made her way to her bathroom, leaving him sitting there with his dark eyes following her.

She didn't look back, didn't want to know what was going on in those eyes. She wanted privacy while she came to terms with what had just taken place in that sunny bedroom.

For the first time in too many years to count Mia had reached out to another human being for comfort. She despised herself for her weakness. She hated him for making her this vulnerable to him. And she hated this whole horrible situation that should never have started, but which now had to continue on its set course.

It was a course which settled her into the next stage of limbo. Surprisingly, Alex did not walk away and forget all about her now his part in the deal they had struck was done. If he was in Athens he came home to the villa every evening. He even began to eat his meals with her, talking, spending the evenings with her. He took her out—picnics to quiet bays in the afternoons, or into Skiathos town during the evenings to enjoy a stroll along the busy L-shaped quayside, now bustling with golden-skinned tourists.

But, true to his word, he never came to her bed again. At night she would lie there, aware that he was lying in his own bed on the other side of that connecting door, and know that he would never cross that threshold again.

Another month drifted by and then another, and a doctor was transported from Athens on a regular basis to check her over. Her weight gain was swift, so much so that she was certain that if she did not keep up her exercise, by swimming twice daily in the pool, she would blow up like a giant balloon.

She didn't see the bloom on her face that seemed to glow with a secret kind of vitality or the way the rich redness of her hair had deepened, having a glossy sheen that shimmered like living fire in the sunlight.

She could not see how voluptuously alluring she looked, with her new maternal shape moulding the front of her body while the rest of her remained incredibly slender in every other way.

In fact, the one and only plus point she could find to all of this was that she loved her baby already. Although she might not like what he was doing to the shape of her body, she did not resent him doing it.

'You grow, my darling,' she whispered softly one morning, as she stood in front of the full-length mirror, ruefully viewing the physical changes while her fingers ran a gentle caress over her swollen abdomen. 'You take whatever you want from your mama to become the strong little man I want you to be.'

And he did take a lot, she had to admit. Took enough to see her safely tucked up in bed before ten each evening and resting several times throughout the day.

Then, on a Wednesday afternoon, two weeks into her fifth month of pregnancy, she was lying on her bed, resting, when she received a telephone call that put the energy back into her with a vengeance. Sofia had answered the call, then came running to get her.

'A Mrs Leyton?' She said the name with difficulty. 'She say it is urgent.'

Mrs Leyton—Cissy, her father's housekeeper—ringing here? Alarm shot through Mia, the kind of alarm that sent her legs to the floor and had her rushing down the stairs to the nearest telephone.

There were only two reasons why her father's house-keeper would be calling here—either something had happened to her father or something had happened to Suzanna.

Pray to God it isn't Suzanna, she begged as she lifted the receiver to her ear with a trembling hand.

It was Suzanna.

Ten minutes after that she was rushing around her bedroom, packing a small case, in a state of high turmoil.

'Listen, Elena,' she snapped at the hovering housekeeper for the very first time since she had arrived here. 'I have to go to England. I don't care how I get there, even if I have to swim! But I do have to go!'

'But the master says you are not to leave the island without him.'

'I don't damn well care what *the master* has said!' she bit back, lifting a flushed face and wild eyes from what she was doing. 'You must have some way you can contact him in case of an emergency! So contact him!' she commanded.

'Contact me for what?' a cool voice enquired from the open doorway to her bedroom.

Mia straightened from what she was doing and spun around to face him. 'Oh, Alex!' she sighed in relief. 'Thank goodness...'

'*Prosehe!*' she heard him shout as sudden dizziness overcame her.

She landed in an ungainly huddle on the bed beside her open suitcase, not unconscious but sickeningly close to it. Beyond the dizziness she could hear him still cursing, and was vaguely aware of him pushing the housekeeper out of the way in his urgency to reach her.

'You stupid, thoughtless female!' he growled at her angrily as he came to stand over her. 'When are you going to learn that you cannot exert yourself like this?'

'I'm all right now,' she whispered, through lips gone strangely numb.

'Oh, you look it,' he mocked grimly, watching the struggle it cost her to sit up again. 'Go any whiter and I won't be able to tell you from the sheet!'

'Just listen!' she cut across him, impatiently ignoring the lingering dizziness, the cloying sense of sickness disturbing her stomach. 'Suzanna, my s-sister, has been taken ill with acute appendicitis. I have to go to England,' she told him. 'She needs me.'

'She needs her father,' Alexander inserted coolly. 'You need to rest and take care of yourself.'

Was that a refusal? Mia glanced up at him and saw that his face was wearing that familiar closed expression. She felt her heart sink when she realised she had a battle on her hands. Elena, she noticed, had disappeared out of the firing line.

'She needs me,' Mia insisted.

Alex walked off towards the bathroom as if she hadn't spoken.

Mia got up, panic beginning to join all the other fears that were flurrying through her. 'Alex...' She met him at the bathroom door, her limbs still shaking and her head still whirling so dizzily that she had to clutch at the doorframe to steady herself. 'Please...' she pleaded with him. 'She's only seven years old! She's in pain and frightened! She needs me there to reassure her! I've always been there for her when she's needed someone!'

'Well, this time it will have to be someone else,' he declared, 'because you are not going. Here...' He offered her the glass of water he had gone into the bathroom to collect.

'I don't want that,' she snapped, and tried to spin away from him, but he stopped her, his free hand closing around her wrist.

'You are amazing, do you know that?' he bit out angrily. 'You walk around this place as if you live on a different planet to the rest of us! You rarely show emotion. You rarely raise your voice or make a move that has not been carefully thought out beforehand! You drift through each day as though you are not really living it. Then some stupid damned phone call comes, and you are suddenly so out of control that you are actually a danger to yourself!'

'What are you talking about?' She frowned at the anger blazing in his eyes.

'You—and the way you live here as if you do not really exist!' he barked. 'You...' his dark face came closer '...almost fainting because you are suddenly doing everything so thoughtlessly that it makes a damned mockery of all that self-control you usually exert over yourself! You!' he said forcefully. 'Almost making the same move just now that sent you toppling on the bed a mere moment ago! And all because of what?' he demanded. 'A sister who has a father to look to her comfort! A sister who can damn well comfort herself because you are not moving off this island!'

'But, you *know* my father!' she cried. 'Do you honestly think he would make time to bother visiting a child he barely remembers exists? She needs me, Alex! Me! And I have to go to her!'

'No.'

It was that blunt—so unequivocal that Mia let out a stunned gasp of appalled disbelief. He ignored it, as he ignored her pale, pained shattered face. He let go of her wrist to walk around her.

'In case you hadn't noticed,' he went on grimly, 'I am back here earlier than usual today because I thought you might enjoy a change of scenery.'

He was back early? Mia blinked at her watch and then blinked back at him, wondering confusedly what the hell that had to do with Suzanna.

'So I have arranged for us to eat a picnic out on a secluded bay I know on the other side of the island,' he continued off-handedly. 'Sofia is preparing the food for us as I speak.'

'I'm not going to sit quietly and eat some damned picnic while Suzanna needs me!' she gasped.

'You will, Mia.' It was so unusual for him to say her name that hearing it now made her blink again and stare at him—made her see exactly why he was using it. He was using it as a don't-push-me-or-I'll-get-nasty warning. 'You will do exactly what I say you can do. Your sister is not your concern.' he said. 'The child you now carry in your womb is your concern. Get your priorities right and forget you even received that phone call for, I promise you, it will be the last one you will receive from this moment on!'

'Oh, I see,' she said, her mouth turning down in a derisive sneer. 'The prisoner has now been placed in solitary confinement—is that it? I am not allowed off this stupid island in case someone guesses the shape of my body may have something to do with you! I am not allowed to speak to anyone outside these grounds in case I stupidly let them know my connection with you! Now I am not to receive phone calls from my own family in case they get the foolish impression that I still have a mind of my own to use now and then!'

'That's it…' he nodded '…in a nutshell. Now, do you want to swim while we are there? If so, pack some swimming gear.'

'I am not going with you!' she shouted at him.

His eyes narrowed, his dark head lifting as if she had just reached out and struck him. 'Don't speak to me like that,' he said, actually sounding shocked.

As an answer to that she walked over to her half-packed suitcase, closed it and hauled it off the bed.

She was a fool to try it, she knew that even as she attempted it. The suitcase was wrenched from her, the hand that came around her swollen body careful of the pressure it applied but demonstrating its intent none the less.

'Now, listen to me,' he said though gritted teeth from behind her. 'You signed a contract whereby I have more rights over you than you have over yourself. You are carrying my child!'

'Your passport to your most coveted dream, you mean,' she tossed at him. 'Other than that, I am nothing to you but the damned loss leader you had to accept if you had any chance of getting your hands on that stupid dream!'

'Loss leader?' he seemed rather stunned at her choice of phrase. 'You see yourself as a loss leader? What the hell do you think I am?'

'A cruel and heartless swine, if you keep me from going to a sick and frightened child who needs me!' she threw at him, and pushed his arm away from her, rather surprised when he let her do it. 'But, unlike you, I can't treat a child's pain and distress as nothing so I'm going—whether you like it or not!'

Reaching out, she snatched up her handbag and began to walk towards the bedroom door. Blow the case, she told herself grimly. She didn't need it. She had money of her own. She could buy fresh clothes when she needed them. She didn't need Alex. She could pay for her own passage off this damned island.

'I will not let you go, you know,' he informed her grimly.

'I am not aware of asking your permission,' she replied, as cold as ice and shaking so badly her legs could barely support her.

'My men will detain you the moment you approach the gates of the villa.'

She was at the top of the landing now, her hand clutching the banister, so she felt reasonably safe in spinning to face him without risking tumbling down those stairs in another silly faint.

He was standing several feet away, but was eyeing her calculatingly, as if he was wondering what she would do if he made another dive for her.

'Are you saying they will physically stop me?' she demanded.

'No,' he conceded, 'but I certainly will. Come away from

the edge of those stairs,' he commanded tersely. 'Your face tells me you are struggling to stay upright.'

'And your face tells me you have no idea whatsoever of what it is like to love someone more than you love yourself.'

'Are you talking about your sister?' he countered.

If anything, she went even paler. 'Yes,' she confirmed. 'Suzanna needs me. I am the only m-mother she has known all her life, and she has a right to expect me to come to her when she's hurting.'

'Go to her without my permission and you break your contract with me.'

Just like that. She stood there and stared at him.

Oh, so clever, she was thinking bitterly. He was calling her bluff. He was reminding her of the one tiny clause she had shown no interest in among all those other clauses he had thrust upon her in that contract—the clause that stated she not leave Greece without his permission while carrying his child or she forfeited custody of the child.

At the time of signing she had seen no reason why she should want to leave Greece until this ordeal was over.

Her heart gave a painful thump, her stomach muscles coiling in sickening understanding. It was time to choose— Suzanna or the baby growing inside her. A baby she loved already and would go on loving far more than this cruel man would ever love it.

Could she do that to her baby—forfeit all control over his little life to this man?

The rest didn't matter. The rest would happen, no matter what she did now. She was putting nothing else at risk but her baby's future.

My God, she thought bleakly, why does fate like to test me like this? Her eyes closed, her throat moving in a constricted swallow. As she hovered there, at the top of those polished stairs, she saw Suzanna's wan little face, looking up at her. Suzanna, with the same solemn green eyes as her own, with the same copper-red hair as her own and with the naturally vibrant personality that went with green eyes and red hair crushed out of her, just as it had been crushed out of Mia.

And, yes, she accepted, with an ache inside that almost sent her doubling up in agony, that she could forfeit this baby for Suzanna. She could do it simply because Suzanna had endured enough misery in her seven short years, whereas at least this baby would be allowed to be himself— that was one distinction she felt she could make between Alex and her father. Both might be despots, both might be ruthless and heartless, but Alex would not punish his son for the sins of the mother.

Mia's eyes fluttered open and looked into those darkly watchful ones. 'I h-have to go,' she whispered. 'I'm sorry.'

With that, she turned and walked down the stairs. Her heart was bleeding and her eyes were blurred by wretched tears because it was like history repeating itself and she didn't think she could bear it.

'Wait.'

She was at the bottom of the stairs before his command hit her eardrums. She stopped, shaking, frozen by the horrible fear that she was going to completely break down and give in to him if he put any more pressure on her.

His soft tread on the stairs as he came down towards her sounded like thunder inside her head. She didn't turn this time. She couldn't bring herself to face him because she knew her own face was showing such a conflagration of emotion that he would probably not understand it.

'Why?' he demanded roughly as he reached her. 'Give me one good reason why this so important to you, why you would throw away all rights to your own unborn child, and I will let you go to your damned sister!'

Her eyes fluttered shut, her heart squeezing in her breast on a pang of agony that only she would ever understand. Give him one good reason, he had demanded.

One good reason.

Well, she had one. 'Suzanna is not my sister,' she informed him unsteadily. 'She is my daughter...'

For the first time in seven years she had let herself say it, and it felt so strange that she shuddered.

'Is that a good enough reason for you?' she said into the bone-crunching silence that echoed around her.

CHAPTER SIX

No ANSWER. Alex didn't say a single word and, after that, neither did she. Mia was trembling too badly to speak, anyway. She didn't know what kept Alex silent, and at that moment she didn't really care.

She was too shocked, dazed by her own admission and paralysed by the burning knowledge that, by saying what she had said, she had just lost Suzanna on a broken promise to another man.

Her father had warned her. It had been part of their bargain, written into that other contract they had signed between them. She was to tell no one of her true relationship to Suzanna before he had his precious grandson.

Now what had she got left? she asked herself starkly. She was standing here, ready to forfeit her claim over her unborn child, and had now, in effect, forfeited her claim over the one she had given birth to seven long years ago!

What did that make her? What kind of mother was she?

The hand was gentle on her wrist when it caught hold of her this time, but it was a mark of how badly she had shaken herself that she didn't even try to pull away from him.

'Come on,' he urged her huskily. 'It will take about an hour to get my plane to the airport here. Come and sit down while I make arrangements...'

He was treating her like someone would a highly volatile substance. She didn't really blame him. She felt very volatile, as though she might just explode with any more provocation.

It was a further mark of how weakened the ugly scene had left her that she allowed herself to lean against him a little as he guided her across the hall and into the sunny sitting room. He saw her seated on one of the pale blue sofas then seemed to hover over her, as though he was preparing to say something.

Mia kept her eyes lowered and bit deep into her trembling bottom lip, waiting tensely for the questions to come.

Yet they didn't come. In the end Alex let out a small sigh and moved away—right out of the room, in fact—leaving her sitting there, still tense, still locked in the appalling fall-out of her own shocking confession.

Later—she wasn't sure how much later—Sofia arrived with a tray of tea-things, which she placed on a table in front of Mia, and then disappeared without a word.

More minutes ticked by. Alex came back and paused when he saw her sitting there just as he had left her. It was he who poured out a cup of tea for her and gently placed the cup and saucer in her hand.

'Drink,' he commanded.

She drank like an automaton. He stood over her, and once again she could sense the questions, rattling around his head. He wasn't a fool. He would already have worked out that if Suzanna was seven years old and Mia twenty-five then Mia had to have been very young when she'd fallen pregnant.

Seventeen years old, in fact. A small grimace touched her bloodless mouth as she lifted the cup to it. Seventeen, and her mother barely cold in her grave after killing herself in a car accident that was her own fault because she had been drinking. Her husband had driven her to look for escape from his mental cruelty in an alcoholic haze—which was still no excuse for leaving Mia alone with a father who hated her and a brother who couldn't care less about her.

So she'd rebelled.

And what a rebellion it had been, she mocked herself now and as bitterly as she had done ever since those wild six months after her seventeenth birthday.

She'd skipped boarding school. Run away. Had got in with a crowd of young groupies who'd followed the current rock group of the time around the country. It had taken the lead singer two months to notice her, a month to take her virginity and a another month to tire of her and throw her out of his life.

So there she had been—seventeen, homeless, penniless and pregnant. By the time Suzanna was born she had hit an all-time low, but it was still a very last resort that had sent her begging to her father.

'Drink some more.'

She glanced up to find that Alex was sitting on the sofa opposite. Her eyes quickly dropped away again, but not before they had taken in the fact that he had changed his clothes somewhere along the line. The business suit he had arrived home in had been replaced by something more casual in a pale linen fabric and a plain white T-shirt.

A sound outside brought her head up again. It was a car, drawing up at the front door. Alex stood up, came over to her and bent to remove her cup. 'Sofia has packed for us,' he murmured flatly. 'All we need to do is go now. OK?'

OK? Why was he asking her if it was OK to leave when he had never bothered to ask her opinion on anything before?

It didn't really matter now, she told herself hollowly as she nodded her head with its neatly styled hair, which should have drawn his anger but was a small detail that seemed to have passed by him unnoticed.

He went to help her rise to her feet again, but she withdrew abruptly from his touch. He was the enemy, she grimly reminded herself. You do not lean weakly on the enemy.

The journey to the airport was carried out in silence. The transfer to his private jet was achieved with the minimum of fuss, and it was only as she sat there, feeling the jet's surge of power as it shot smoothly into the air, that it sank in that Alex was actually sitting beside her.

'You didn't need to come with me.' She found her voice at last, frail and constricted though it was. 'I will come back just as soon as Suzanna is feeling better.'

He didn't answer. His lean, dark face was a closed book as he sat there, gazing directly ahead. Not piloting the plane himself this time, she noted. Not doing anything but sitting here, lost deep within his own grim train of thought.

Tears filled her eyes. She didn't know why. They just did. Then almost directly out of the rubble in which her emotions lay, her chin rose in what had become a familiar habit to those who had been around her during the last few months. Her bloodless mouth straightened and her tear-washed eyes cleared.

'I am not a whore.'

Why she said that was just as big a surprise to her as the tears were that had preceded it.

'You announce yourself in those terms,' Alex quietly replied. 'I have never used the term to you.'

'You don't need to. I can hear it screaming at me every time you look at me.'

From the corner of her eye she saw his grim mouth twist. 'You are your own salesman,' he said. 'Don't blame others for believing what you place in front of them.'

Was that true? she wondered, then sighed because she decided it was most probably very true and that she did present herself as the kind of cool-headed mercenary who would have sold her body for the proverbial pot of gold.

'Well, just in case you're worrying that I might have passed on some dreadful social disease with my whoring ways, I think I had better reassure you that there have only been two men in my life who have used my body—Suzanna's father was one of them, and you the other.'

'If I had been worried about such a prospect I would have insisted on the relevant test to reassure myself. As it is...' his dark head turned to study her whitened profile '...I already knew most of what you have just told me. I had you thoroughly investigated, you see, before I agreed to any of this. The nun's life you have been leading since your wild rebellion eight years ago was easily discovered, which made the way you responded to me all the more intriguing...'

Her cheeks went red, and he lifted a finger to gently stroke that heated skin. 'Only the fact that you have given birth to a child escaped my investigators. Now that,' he added softly, 'was a surprise.'

'And one you are now going to use against me, I suppose.'

'Will I need to?'

It was a challenge. Mia shivered delicately and shifted her cheek so his finger had to drop away. 'I want my baby,' she murmured huskily, 'but I will not keep him at Suzanna's expense.'

'He doesn't warrant the same fierce feelings of love and protection your daughter ignites in you?'

'Yes,' she admitted, one of her hands moving to rest on that firm mound where her new baby lay. 'But Suzanna has paid long enough for the misfortune of having me as her mother. She deserves better and I am prepared to do anything to make sure I am in a position to give it to her.'

'Like sleeping with a man you hold in contempt?' he suggested. 'Like taking any flak he might wish to throw at you, without saying a thing in your own defence? Like allowing yourself to be sent into isolation while he punishes you for his own weaknesses?'

'So you acknowledge you have weaknesses?'

He smiled rather drily. 'I know myself quite well,' he answered flatly. 'I know my weaknesses—and my strengths. I am thirty-six years old, after all,' he added. 'If I have not learned them by now then I truly am in danger of becoming a man like your father. That is how you see me, is it not—as a man no better than your father?'

'You see a chunk of real estate as worth more than life itself so—yes,' she admitted. 'You are no better than him.'

'And you?' he challenged. 'What does that make you?'

Her green eyes flashed—the first sign of life they had shown since she'd walked away from him in that sunny bedroom back at the villa. 'I sold myself to you, not another's life.' She made the distinction. 'And you bought the use of me from my father, not from me. In return he gives you your precious island while he gets what he wants—a male heir to whom he can leave his filthy money. I get Suzanna and this child as payment. So the only thing I have sold to anyone is the use of my own body. You tell me what that makes me.' She threw the challenge right back at him.

His smile was cynical, to say the least. 'You seem to have conveniently forgotten the five million pounds your father is paying you on delivery of his male heir,' he drawled derisively.

Mia's heart-shaped upper lip clamped itself tightly to her much fuller bottom lip and she looked away from him out of the window at the clear blue stretch of sky through which they were flying.

The new silence pulled at the tiny muscles in her throat and around her heart, lining the wall of her tensely held ribcage.

'There is no money,' he bit out suddenly. 'You lied about the five million to throw me off the scent!'

'I have money of my own,' she countered defensively. 'I don't need money from my father.'

'Your mother's money.' He nodded, surprising her with just how deeply his investigators had dug into her life. 'She placed her money in a trust fund for you, which matured on your twenty-fifth birthday. A paltry two hundred thousand pounds,' he added with biting contempt.

Two hundred thousand was a small fortune to most people and more than Mia had ever had access to before. She could easily live off it with a bit of careful planning. She could bring her children up, know they would want for nothing materially.

'You know,' he muttered, 'you *are* a whore in a lot of ways.' With an angry movement he unfastened his seat belt and stood up. 'You sell yourself cheap and you see yourself as cheap!'

With that, he walked away, leaving her sitting there alone while she let the full thrust of his final angry words sink in.

It was getting quite late when they eventually landed, the August evening cool after the evenings Mia had grown used to back in Greece.

'Which hospital?' Alex asked her as they settled in the back of a chauffeur-driven Mercedes.

She told him, and he leaned forward to relay the information to their driver, who was separated from them by a tinted sheet of glass.

It was a small relief that he wasn't making a battle out of going directly to the hospital. She knew she was tired, and knew how that tiredness was showing on her pale, pinched face, along with the worry and strain she was experiencing for Suzanna's sake.

Suzanna. Her daughter. Her stomach flipped over, a frisson of anxiety shaking her system for that poor child she had never been able to claim as her own but who shared, none the less, the kind of bond with herself that really only a mother and child could share.

Mia might have been forced by circumstances to hand over her daughter to her father but he had never managed to break that bond, though he had tried—many times. 'She's my daughter now,' he had announced with grim satisfaction the day the adoption papers were signed. 'Ever be tempted to tell her who you really are and it will be the last time you will ever see her.'

Mia shivered as she sat there beside a silent Alex, remembering the choices she had been offered the day she went home to her father, frightened, desperate, destitute and carrying her new-born baby girl in her arms, to beg from the last man on earth she wanted to go crawling to.

'I won't have any gossip about my promiscuous daughter and her bastard child,' he'd warned her brutally. 'If you want my support, let me adopt her, though, God knows, I don't need another damned female hanging around me. You can be a sister to her,' he had decided, 'but as far as anyone is concerned she is my child, not yours, and don't you let yourself forget that.'

So she'd placed her own life on hold and had stayed living with her father so she could be close to her daughter. It was she who had brought Suzanna up since she was a baby, she who had seen to her needs throughout her young years, and she who had visited the child every weekend since her father had placed Suzanna in that dreadful boarding school. 'To toughen her up,' he'd announced heartlessly. 'The way you mollycoddle her, she will never learn to take care of herself if I don't split you up.'

But really he had sent Suzanna away to school because he knew how it would hurt the two of them to be separated like that. And because it placed Mia under yet more obligation to him. 'You can have her to yourself during the vacations,' he'd promised. 'So long as you remain living here with me, that is.'

Then Tony had been killed, and his whole attitude to both Mia and Suzanna had taken on a radical change. In Tony he had seen the continuance of himself. He hadn't needed to look any further for a male heir to his fortune. That was when Mia had become a tool for him to use for a different purpose—and Suzanna was the bait he had used to make Mia agree to everything he'd demanded.

'You get me a grandson and I'll let you have full custody of Suzanna. I'll choose the man. I'll discover the weak link that'll make him marry you. All you have to do is go to bed with him—not a problem for a whore like you.'

Not a problem. In the dimness of that luxury car she grimaced. Well, it hadn't been a problem in the end, had it? In fact, going to bed with Alex had turned out to be a pleasure! Which probably meant her father knew her better than she knew herself. Did he know she was already pregnant? Had Alex told him? She certainly hadn't. She'd had no contact whatsoever with her father since she'd got married. But Alex would have been eager to announce their success to Jack Frazier, she was sure.

In four more months or so her father would get the boy to whom he wanted to leave all his money, Alex would get his island and Mia would get custody of Suzanna.

All pacts with the devil, with this small baby growing inside her the unwitting champion for the three of them.

'Does she know you are her mother?'

The question made her jump, coming out of the blue as it did.

'No,' she replied. 'I am not allowed to tell her until this child is safely delivered.' Then her breasts heaved as she sucked in a tense breath of air and let it out again before she added huskily, 'I was not allowed to tell you either. If my father finds out that you know, he will say I have broken the contract I have with him and keep Suzanna, just for the hell of hurting me.'

The hospital came into view, its brightly lit windows announcing that time here had no real meaning. Work here went on twenty-fours a day.

Alex came with her, travelling through the corridors with a tight-lipped silence that kept his presence remote from Mia, who had become barely aware of him as her anxiety grew the closer they got to the ward to which they had been directed.

They came upon a nursing station first, with a pretty young nurse standing behind it who glanced up then smiled the warmest smile Mia had been offered in months. 'You must be Suzanna's sister,' she declared immediately. 'You look so much like her.'

'How is she?' Mia asked worriedly.

'Fine.' The nurse came around the station to touch her gently on the hand. 'The operation went off without a hitch. The appendix hadn't burst so she should have no complications. She's already out of Recovery and back on the ward here, though we do have her settled in a room off the main ward so we can keep a special eye on her.'

'Can I see her?' Mia's eyes were already darting off in the direction the nurse's hand had indicated.

'Of course. She's asleep,' the nurse warned as she moved off, with them following, 'but you can take a quick peek at her to reassure yourself. She has been asking for you constantly...'

The room was nothing more than a tiny annexe, with brightly painted pictures, done with childish hands, pinned all over the white-painted walls. But it was the little bed in the middle of the room that held Mia's attention. Her eyes darkened, her face losing what bit of colour it possessed as one trembling hand went up to cover the sudden quiver of her mouth while she stared at her daughter lying so pale and still.

Without taking her eyes off that sleeping face, Mia walked over to the bed, then gently stroked the child's pale cheek before she bent and replaced the hand with a kiss.

'She looks so vulnerable,' she whispered, worry-darkened eyes running over that little face with its shock of bright hair tied back to keep it tidy.

'She'll be sore for a few days,' the nurse said quietly, 'but she shouldn't feel too much discomfort. Her worst worry was that you wouldn't manage to come.'

Mia winced. Somewhere beyond the periphery of her own vision someone else winced also.

'Apparently, you were not in the country when she became ill.'

'I got here as soon as I could,' Mia said huskily. 'Has my father been in to see her?'

'No.' The nurse's tone cooled perceptibly. 'Only the lady who came in the ambulance with her. A Mrs Leyton—your father's housekeeper, I believe? She stayed until Suzanna was safely back up here again before she left.'

'Thank you,' Mia murmured. 'I'll sit here with her for a little while, if you don't mind.'

'Of course not,' the nurse said. 'There is a chair just behind you,' she added, and with a curious glance at the man who was standing in the far corner of the room, but who had contributed nothing to the conversation, she left them alone.

Mia didn't even notice. Her whole attention was fixed on Suzanna as one of her hands searched blindly behind her to find the chair so she could sit down on it.

Then she reached for and gently closed her fingers around Suzanna's small fingers, lifting them to her cheek and keeping them there. 'I'm here now, darling,' she murmured softly.

The child didn't move. She was still too heavily sedated to be aware of anything that was going on around her. But that didn't stop Mia talking gently to her, murmuring the kind of reassuring phrases a mother seemed to find instinctively.

Maybe the child did hear within the fluffy clouds of her own subconscious because something seemed to alter about her. Her slender limbs lost a tension that hadn't been apparent until it had eased away and her pale, rather thin face seemed to gain some colour.

As silently as he had observed everything, Alex observed the change in the child also, and just as silently he walked

out of the little room and left them to it, sensitive enough—
no matter how Mia believed the opposite about him—to
know he was intruding on something private.

He came back an hour later and, after pausing in the
doorway to frown at the look of exhaustion straining Mia's
features, he stepped forward and touched her shoulder. He
waited for and received the expected start that confirmed
to him that she had forgotten his presence.

'It's time to go,' he said quietly. 'We will return tomorrow, but you need to rest now if you don't want to end up
too tired to be of any use to her.'

A protest leapt to her lips—then hovered for a moment
before it was left unsaid. He was right, she conceded. She
was so utterly weary she could barely function. So, without
a word, she stood up, bent to the child's cheek then straightened, and without so much as a glance at him she turned
and walked out of the room.

As soon as she was settled in the car again her head went
back against the leather headrest and her tired eyes closed.

'You are very alike,' Alex remarked quietly. 'Does she
have your colour eyes, too?'

'Mmm.' Mia didn't want to talk—didn't even want to
think very much. Relief was, at this moment, playing the
biggest role in making her feel so exhausted. She had travelled from Greece to the hospital in a state of high nervous
tension, not knowing what she was going to find when she
got there. Now she had reassured herself that Suzanna was
going to be all right it seemed to make everything else
deflate inside her.

'Has no one ever made the natural connection between
the two of you?' Alex persisted. 'It seems impossible to
me not to consider a stronger bond than sisterhood when
the likeness is so strikingly obvious.'

'My brother had the same colouring,' she explained.
'People suspected Suzanna was my brother's child but not
mine because I was so young when I had her.'

'I thought you told me your father did not believe you were his daughter.' He frowned. 'But if you and your brother have the same colouring, surely he has to accept the blood connection somewhere?'

'We have the same mother,' she said. 'Exactly who it was that fathered us was a different thing entirely.'

'And a son was easier for your father to accept as his own than a mere daughter,' he concluded grimly, 'because it suited him to accept a son where, because of his bigotry, he didn't need to accept the daughter.'

'Now you're catching on,' Mia said very drily. 'If you want the full truth of it, I don't think my father is capable of fathering children,' she announced quite detachedly. 'More to the point, I think he knows it, which is why he set you and me up for this kind of deal when he could, at his age and with his money, have quite easily got himself another wife and produced a dozen more sons of his own. What's more,' she added, 'I think my mother was unfaithful to him from the day she married him.'

It was another confession that managed to shock her simply because she was actually telling it to Alex of all men.

'She came from a very socially acceptable family that had lost most of its money to inheritance tax. My father wanted to be accepted by that society so he bought himself into it, by marrying my mother. He wanted very socially acceptable sons to carry on his name for him, but when she didn't produce them he began to get nasty, calling her all those unpleasant names people can call women who don't have children easily. So she went out and got herself a lover. Conceived a child—though she was never absolutely sure whether either of her children belonged to her husband or her lover because she continued to sleep with both of them right up until the moment she managed to kill herself.'

'And the lover?'

'He died of cancer a couple of years ago,' Mia said, then

added reluctantly. 'He was Karl Dansing, the electronics magnate.'

There was a stifled gasp of shock from the man beside her. 'Are you trying to tell me,' he murmured gruffly, 'that you could be Karl Dansing's daughter?'

'Does that impress you?' Mia drawled. 'Well, don't go off the deep end about it,' she said mockingly before he could say anything further. 'As father figures go, neither impress me much. Karl Dansing must have known that Tony and I could have been his children but he never once owned up to it while he was alive, and didn't even give us a mention in his will.'

'But—.'

'Look—' She sighed wearily. 'Can we stop the inquisition, please? I'm too tired to deal with it and just too indifferent to want to talk about it! If you want to know anything else, put your investigators to work,' she suggested grimly. 'I'm sure they will come up with something juicy for you if you pay them well enough!'

With that, she closed her eyes firmly again, aware that she sounded embittered by her own sordid history. After all, who wanted to claim as parents the kind of people she had just described? She certainly didn't. Even spoiled, selfish, supremely avaricious Tony hadn't. 'I'll make do with what I've got,' he'd said to her once when Karl Dansing's name had come up. 'He may be worth a hell of a lot more than Jack but he has four other kids to share his money, whereas I'll be getting the whole lot from Jack one day.'

Only he hadn't got anything in the end, had he? Because Tony had died very much the same way their mother had died—in a car accident, while driving too fast with a skinful of booze and heaven alone knew what else.

She still missed him. Oddly and surprisingly, considering his selfish view of life. But they had shared a kind of affection for each other. And Tony had been good to Suzanna. In his own way she suspected he had even loved the child, which was enough for Mia to forgive him his other faults.

Suzanna...

Her mind drifted back to that poor, defenceless child she had left sleeping in her hospital bed. All at once depression swept over her. What was she going to do? she wondered fretfully. How was she going to bring herself to leave Suzanna again when Alex decided it was time to go back to Greece?

A more urgent question was how long he was going to let her stay here. A couple of days? A week? Maybe two, if she was lucky?

Whatever, it was not going to be long enough. Just seeing the little girl lying there had told Mia that Suzanna needed her to be closer to her!

It was the long vacation from school at the moment, which meant Suzanna would have to go back to her father's house when she was eventually discharged from hospital. The child couldn't cope with Jack Frazier on her own. She never had been able to. He only had to look at her to petrify her.

Cissy had told her during that hurried phone call today that her father had accused Suzanna of fabricating the pain in her side. He'd called it attention-seeking, and had told her that if she expected to get Mia back by playing on his sympathy then she was in for a disappointment because Mia was never coming back so she may as well get used to it.

Oh, God. How could one human being be so cruel to another? What had made Jack Frazier the cold hearted monster he was?

Her hand came up to rub at her eyes, where the ache behind them was beginning to drag at what was left of her severely depleted stamina.

Beside her, Alex moved. She went still, her nerve-ends beginning to sing beneath the surface of her skin because she had a horrible feeling he was going to reach out and touch her. If he did touch her, she was going to fall apart completely.

Then the car stopped and, bringing her hand away from her wary eyes, she found that his attention was fixed outside the car and not on her at all.

Which was a levelling experience, she discovered as she watched him open his door and climb out, impatiently waving the chauffeur away so he could come around the car and open Mia's door himself.

'You are almost dead on your feet,' he muttered, watching her sway slightly as she joined him on the pavement.

'I just need a good night's sleep,' she replied.

'What you need,' he grunted, as he helped her up the steps of a very exclusive white-painted town-house she presumed must be his home when he was in London, 'is to be yourself occasionally, and not all these other personalities you conjure up, depending on who it is you are having to deal with!'

'Oh, very cryptic,' she mocked.

'Not cryptic—tragic,' he corrected grimly. 'A good psychoanalyst could make a life study out of you,' he muttered, stabbing an angry finger at the front doorbell. 'Today alone I have met the vixen, the ruthless negotiator, the loving mother and the cynic,' he said, with tight-lipped sarcasm. 'As the old saying goes, would the real woman please stand and reveal herself?'

'Not for you she won't,' she tossed back frostily.

'Oh, I've already met her,' he insisted tightly. 'In her bed, in the darkness. And she is quite the most fascinating one of all, I assure you.'

'You're mistaken,' Mia replied. 'That was the whore you met there— Why are you ringing this bell, instead of using a key to get in the house?' she asked frowningly.

'Because—obviously—the house does not belong to me,' he replied sardonically.

The front door swung open, and she was suddenly faced with exactly whose house this was.

Oh, hell! she thought wearily. What now? Why this? What was it supposed to mean?

It was Alex's younger brother, Leon.

CHAPTER SEVEN

'AH,' LEON smiled politely enough. 'So you are here at last. We were beginning to give up on you.'

But Mia could see by the way his eyes barely touched her that he was no happier to see her standing on his doorstep than she was to be here. He obviously still resented her intrusion into Alex's life, and was not going to bother to hide it.

'Come on in,' he said.

Her shoulders drooped wearily, the long, long day spent enduring all the other stresses leaving her with nothing with which to fight this next ordeal.

An arm came warmly about her shoulders, and for once she huddled gratefully into it, going into retreat because it was the only thing she could do as Alex propelled her into a warmly lit hallway then paused to murmur something to his brother in his own language.

She didn't know what he'd said—didn't want to know—but she sensed the hint of a warning beneath the casual tone and the arm around her shoulders tightened briefly, as if to offer support.

With what she suspected was a forced lightness, Alex enquired rather drily, 'Where's the wicked witch?'

'I heard that,' a sharp female voice responded.

What now? Mia wondered, raising very wary eyes to see the most exquisite vision of blonde loveliness, dressed in tight faded jeans and a skinny white top, appear at the top of the stairway in front of her.

Very tall and incredibly slender, she had the bluest pair of eyes Mia had ever encountered but what was most disconcerting was that those eyes were smiling at her warmly—genuinely warmly.

'Hi,' she said pleasantly. Then, before Mia could answer, she went on, 'Oh, good grief, but you look dreadful! What's the matter with you, Alex?' She frowned at him. 'Trailing a pregnant woman all over the world, as if she's some piece of baggage! How is your sister?' she asked Mia, without waiting for Alex to answer either. 'Is she very poorly? Mia, isn't it?' She smiled that warm smile again. 'I'm Carol,' she announced. 'The lucky one because I got the nicer brother. You drew the short straw, I'm afraid, when you got Alex.'

'Mia is exhausted,' Alex interrupted rather irritably. 'She doesn't need all your crazy chatter right now. She needs her bed.'

'Oh, sorry,' Carol said, sounding rather disconcerted by his curt tone. 'This way, Mia. Gosh, you look done in. Will you let me help you? You can lean on me, if you want to. I don't mind.'

'I can manage, thank you,' Mia answered quietly.

'Yes. Right.' Carol nodded, and after a short pause, when she glanced from one brother to the other, she turned and began to lead the way up the stairs while Mia followed, having to draw on the very last dregs of her stamina.

She was shown into a prettily decorated bedroom, with blue walls and apricot furnishings. There was a connecting bathroom, where Carol took it upon herself to run Mia a bath while all Mia could do was lower herself onto the side of the bed and wilt.

By the time Carol came back into the bedroom Mia knew all about Leon, the great love of Carol's life. How they met, where they met and where he had proposed to her. She now knew that they had been married for two years but were not going to start a family yet because Leon had insisted that his children were born in Greece and they couldn't go and live in Greece until the new hotel they had just bought and were refurbishing here in London was finished up and running.

'The bath's ready,' Carol announced. 'All you have to do is get undressed and sink into it. I'll be back in half an hour to make sure you're all right...'

Silence. At last a blessed, beautiful silence fell upon the room at her exit. Mia remained where she was for a few precious minutes and simply let that silence flow all around her, then made herself get up and trail her weary body into the bathroom.

By the time she had hauled herself in and out of the bath again she was so utterly worn out that she had to sit down on the bathroom stool to recover. Hell, she thought as her head began to swim, a quick shower would have been more sensible in your condition. You really should have known that!

'How are you doing in there?'

Carol was back already, Mia noted wryly.

'One moment,' she called back, hurriedly donning the short white silk slip-style nightdress Carol had thoughtfully hung behind the bathroom door for her. She ran a quick brush through her hair and, on a deep fortifying breath, let herself out of the bathroom.

'Wow!' the other woman gasped. 'Look at all that hair! You're gorgeous, aren't you? No wonder Alex has been walking around looking as though he doesn't know what's hit him! I hope my figure looks as good as yours does with a bump stuck on the front of it. Here, get into bed. You'll be more comfortable there...'

Without a word, Mia did as she was told. A tray landed across her lap. Her pillows were fluffed up.

'Now...' Standing back to view her ministrations, Carol frowned and then smiled when she realised she was frowning, as though she was trying very hard to make Mia feel wanted. 'I'm going to leave you—Alex's orders.' She grimaced. 'He's frightened I'll say something I shouldn't—

like I think its disgraceful the way he's been treating you, no matter what the circumstances. See?' She grinned. 'I've said it anyway!'

Not that she seemed to care!

At last she disappeared. Mia wilted again, and in the next second her mind switched off. As if it had taken more than enough for one day and was refusing to accept any more, it dropped her into a slumber from which she didn't even stir when the bedroom door opened again an hour later.

Alex stood on the threshold, staring at the way she had fallen asleep, half sitting up and with the untouched tray still lying across her lap.

With stealth he closed the door, then moved across the carpet to stand over her. She looked exhausted, even in sleep, the signs of stress evident in her washed-out face. Without disturbing her, he removed the tray and set it aside. Then, after another brief grim study of her, he turned and walked into the bathroom.

Ten minutes later he was back, showered, shaved and wrapped in a thin black cotton bathrobe. Silently he moved around the room, switching off several lamps Carol had left burning. Then, with the darkness enfolding him, he came back to the bed, removed the bathrobe and slid his unashamedly naked body into the bed beside her.

Still she did not so much as move a muscle. He lay there on his side and watched her for ages before—on a grimace that said he didn't much fancy what he was about to do next—he leaned over her so he could slide an arm beneath her shoulders and lift her just enough to remove one of the pillows from behind her.

As he settled her back again in what he hoped was a more comfortable position her eyes flickered open, green homing directly onto guarded brown.

Mia blinked slowly, her sleep-sluggish mind taking its time to remember that it had been long months since she had woken to find him leaning over her in the darkness like this.

As she did remember, her eyes widened warily.

'It's OK,' Alex said softly. 'I was not about to seduce you while you were sleeping. I was simply trying to make you more comfortable.'

'What are you doing here?' she whispered, still staring owlishly into those rich, dark, slightly rueful eyes of his.

'Carol's idea,' he said. 'She naturally assumes we share a bed, and I was not up to one of her question-and-answer sessions, by informing her that we did not.'

Grimacing, he moved away from her, going to lie on his back and stare at the ceiling while Mia took a few moments to take in this totally unexpected new situation.

He intended to share her bed, she seemed to find it necessary to tell herself. They had been married for almost seven long months, and *never* shared the same bed as a married couple normally did.

Now this. It felt weird, like lying next to a stranger.

'Do you mind?' he asked quietly.

'Its a big enough bed.' She shrugged. 'I suppose we will manage.'

Silence fell, the kind of tight, stinging, uncomfortable silence that caught at the breath and increased the tension in the darkness of the room.

'Why did you bring me here to your brother's house?' Mia asked when she could stand it no longer.

'It is the *family* house,' he said. 'Leon and Carol are in residence right now because Leon is based here at the moment. They expect me to stay with them when I am in London. It would have been...awkward if I had taken you to a hotel.'

'I won't do or say anything that could embarrass you,' she assured him huskily.

His dark head turned. Mia felt his eyes on her. 'You have a very low opinion of me, don't you?' he said.

Mia's head turned so that their eyes clashed again. 'It's mutual,' she countered.

He didn't answer, those lush, long, coal-black lashes flickering slightly as he continued to lie there studying her in the darkness—a darkness they had always been more comfortable in. A darkness where most of their most intimate moments had taken place—their mutual passion, their ability to drown in each other.

Drown, as Mia could feel herself beginning to drown right now—drown in those deep, dark, sensually knowing eyes that could probe right inside her and touch places only this man had touched, ignite senses only this man could ignite.

'Go to sleep,' he ordered softly.

Sleep. Yes, she agreed, dragging her eyes away from his. Don't look at him, she told herself sternly as she turned her head on the pillow. Don't even think about him, lying here next to you.

And don't, for goodness' sake, remember what it feels like to have him make love to you!

The stern lecture made no difference because she did imagine him making love to her. She could feel his hands caress her body, feel his mouth move sensually on hers, could feel her breathing growing shallow as her heart picked up pace and that place between her thighs begin to pulse with a message so erotic that she had to lie very still with her muscles tightly clenched in an effort to subdue the feeling.

What made it all worse was that it was all happening under his steady gaze. She could sense him watching her, knew he was witnessing the increase in her breathing and the way her eyes couldn't close because she was holding herself so tense beside him. A tension that was fizzing in the air around them. Sexual tension.

'Go to sleep,' he repeated in a soft, silken voice that

utterly rejected every message her stupid body was sending him.

Dismayed, she threw herself onto her side and away from him, so agonised by her own weaknesses that it actually hurt like a physical pain.

It took her ages to relax and ages to drift back into a restless slumber—only to come blisteringly awake again the moment she felt him move beside her.

With her heart beginning to pound in her aching chest, she listened to him release a heavy sigh then carefully slide out of the bed. There was a rustling sound as he pulled a robe over his body. Even in the darkness, with her back towards him, she could feel his grimness and knew—just knew—that the grimness was there because he hated this situation so much.

Hated having to lie here beside her in this bed when he was probably wishing himself a million miles away.

With his mistress, most probably.

He threw himself down in one of the easy chairs by the curtained window. She heard him sigh again, then—nothing. Nothing for long minutes while she held herself still, listening until she could stand to listen no longer and turned over in the bed to gaze at the dark bulk by the window.

He was asleep, stretched out in the chair with his dark head thrown back and his face a mask of grim perseverance.

Tears began to burn at the back of her eyes. Weak tears. Wretched tears. Foolishly hurt tears! She fell asleep like that, with the tears still clinging to her lashes.

When she awoke next morning she was alone as usual. The knowledge that Alex had found it impossible to spend a whole night in the same bed with her lay like a lead weight across her chest.

Then she remembered Suzanna and got up, showered quickly and dressed herself in a pair of comfortable stretch white leggings and a pale blue overshirt, before taking a deep breath and letting herself out of that bedroom to go in search of the others.

She was just coming down the stairs when Alex walked out of one of the rooms off the hallway. He saw her and paused to watch her descent through those impenetrable brown eyes of his.

'You still look tired,' he observed huskily.

Still stinging from last night's humiliating rejection, she dropped her eyes from his and concentrated fiercely on the stairs in front of her. 'It's worry, not tiredness,' she contended. 'I would like to ring the hospital,' she went on coolly. 'Is there a telephone I could use?'

'Of course.'

Stepping back to the room he had just walked out of, he opened the door and gestured her through it. She found herself standing in a study that was very male in style—a lot of polished wood, walls lined with books and the more modern state-of-the-art communications hardware.

There was a desk by the window, with a telephone sitting on it. Mia thanked him quietly and walked over to pick up the receiver.

Her thanks had been a polite way of dismissing him but, to her annoyance, he didn't leave her to her privacy but came to lean on the desk beside her so he could watch her face while she spoke to the hospital.

Suzanna had spent a comfortable night, she was assured. She also knew that Mia had been in to see her late last night, and the fact that she was actually here in London had cheered the child up remarkably. 'She keeps on asking when you are coming in again,' the nurse told her.

'Later this morning,' Mia replied. 'Tell her I will be with her just as soon as I can be.'

'OK?' Alex asked quietly as she lowered the receiver.

Mia nodded, her lips pressed together to stop them from trembling, but it still hurt to think of that little girl spending the whole of yesterday sick and in pain and probably very frightened of what was happening to her.

'Then what is the matter?' he asked. 'You look almost— hunted.'

'I'm fine,' she lied. 'I n-need to ring my father next, that's all.'

'Ah,' he said, as if that explained everything. 'Would you prefer me to make that particular call for you?' he offered.

Instantly her chin lifted and her eyes met his with their usual defiance to give him his answer. He smiled wryly. 'You trust me about as much as you trust him, don't you?'

Mia didn't answer—didn't need to. He knew exactly how little she trusted him.

The housekeeper answered her call. The moment she heard Mia's voice she went off on a harried burst of speech that showed just how anxious she had been about Suzanna.

Mia listened with her eyes lowered and her fingers clenched. Her knuckles were white around the receiver as she strove to contain the black anger that was building inside her.

For three days Suzanna had been complaining of pain— and for three long, wretched days her father had cruelly dismissed the child's distress as a ploy to bring her precious Mia back.

Her eyes began to flash and her heart to pump on an adrenaline rush. Beside her, Alex shifted his position a little, catching her attention and bringing those green eyes flashing upwards to pierce him with enough burning venom to make his own blink.

'No—no, Cissy,' she murmured smoothly, in reply to whatever the housekeeper had said to her. 'I'm right here in London. I visited Suzanna last night, and I'm going back to the hospital this morning so you don't have to worry about her now.'

Another volley of words hit her burning eardrums and

Mia had difficulty containing what was screaming to be released inside her.

Alex brought a hand up to grab her chin, then tugged it around in his direction. His eyes were black, boring into hers with stunned fascination. 'My God,' he breathed. 'You're cracking up! The ice is beginning to melt at last!'

'Is my father there?' she asked the housekeeper in a voice as cool and calm as a mill pond on a winter's day, while her eyes spat murder into those probing black ones. 'Can I speak to him, please?'

Cissy told her that her father had meetings all day and that he had left the house very early, without even bothering to ask after Suzanna. Why? Because the child held no great importance in the real plan of things! She was simply a very small pawn he used to make Mia jump to his bidding.

Another loss leader.

It was cruel, it was sick and it was downright criminal. By the time Mia replaced the telephone she was shaking like a leaf and ready to hit out at the nearest person.

Alex.

Angrily she turned away from him, her slender arms wrapping around her own body in an effort to contain what was desperately clamouring to burst free.

'Mia—'

'Say one more word,' she bit out, 'and I am likely to spoil your handsome features!'

There was a choked gasp from behind her. 'What did she say to you?' he demanded roughly.

'Nothing you would find unacceptable,' she retorted. Then, because she knew she needed to calm down because she could feel the usual dizziness surging up to pay her back for allowing herself to get this agitated, she took a jerky step towards the door. 'I need to—'

'No!' The hand that closed around her wrist stopped her from going anywhere. 'I want to know what she said to make you so angry,' Alex insisted grimly.

Mia rounded on him like a virago. Her teeth bared and her eyes spitting green fire, she hit out at him with her free fist. It missed its target because he ducked out of its way—which in turn sent her off balance so she stumbled and would have fallen if he hadn't caught her to him.

'What the hell was that for?'

'Three days!' she choked out. 'She was ill for three whole days before my father condescended to let Cissy bring in a doctor!'

'And you think I could be that callous?' He looked white suddenly—white with anger. 'I am *not* your damned father!' he railed at her furiously.

No, she thought, you are just the man who is breaking my heart in two! 'Oh, God,' she said brokenly when she realised just what she was telling herself. 'Let go of me,' she whispered, feeling the all too ready tears beginning to build inside.

Maybe he sensed them threatening—certainly he could feel the way her body was trembling as he was holding her so close—because, on a driven sigh, he let go of her. 'You should not let yourself get upset like this,' he muttered. 'In your present condition it cannot be good for you.'

Ah, her present condition. Mia allowed herself a tight smile. 'I'm fine,' she said grimly, pulling herself together. 'It's my sister's health that worries me, not my own.'

'Your *daughter*,' he corrected.

'Sister,' she repeated. 'She will not be my daughter again until I have safely delivered this child I am carrying now.'

Alex came with her to the hospital that morning, though Mia wished he could have shown a bit of sensitivity and let her have this first very painful meeting with Suzanna alone.

As it was, the child took one look at her as she walked in the room and dissolved into a flood of tears. Mia just gathered her gently into her arms and held her there, struggling hard not to weep herself.

'Daddy said you wouldn't come,' the child sobbed as she clung to her. 'He said you didn't want me any more because I'm a nuisance.'

'That's not true, darling,' Mia murmured reassuringly. 'You will never be a nuisance to me and I will always come if you need me. Always. Didn't I promise you that the last time I saw you?'

'But he said you'd gone away to start your own family!' the child sobbed out accusingly. 'S-so I'd better get used to you not being around! But I missed you, Mia!'

It was a cry from the heart that cut so deep even Alex, a silent witness to this tragic overload of emotion, could not stay silent any longer.

'Hello,' he said, stopping Suzanna's tears as if he'd thrown a switch.

Her face came out of Mia's shoulder so she could look towards that deep, smooth, very male voice, first in surprise because she hadn't noticed him come in with her precious Mia and then with all the natural wariness of a child towards any total stranger.

A very tall, very dark, very handsome stranger, who was smiling the kind of smile that made Mia's heart flip because she recognised it as the same smile he had once used on her—before her father's bargain had effectively killed it.

'My name is Alex,' he introduced himself. 'Mia is my wife.'

Wife. Her heart flipped a second time. He had formally acknowledged her as his wife for the first time ever, and the word seemed to echo strangely inside her head.

Like a lie that wasn't quite a lie but still sounded like one nonetheless.

'And you are Suzanna...' With each gently spoken word he came closer, holding Suzanna's attention like a hovering hawk mesmerising a wary rabbit. He came down on his haunches beside the bed where Mia was holding the child against her. 'I am very pleased to meet you.'

He offered Suzanna his hand in greeting. Her tear-spiked lashes flickered to the hand, then uncertainly back to his face again—before finally looking to Mia in search of some hint as to how she should respond.

Don't ask me, Mia thought drily. I still haven't worked that one out and I've been living with him for months. She smiled reassuringly. 'It's OK. You can like him. He's nice.'

'Thank you,' Alex murmured in a dry undertone that said he'd caught the mocking intonation behind the remark.

By then Suzanna was cautiously placing her little hand in his, and Alex's full attention was back on the child.

It was a revelation, simply because Mia had never known he had it in him, but within minutes Suzanna had forgotten her tears, forgotten her woes. In fact, she seemed to have forgotten everything as, with amazing intuition, Alex breached the little girl's natural shyness with men in general by encouraging her to describe—in lurid detail—every stage of her emergency dash to the hospital in an ambulance and the ensuing course of events that had led to her waking up here in this bed with stitches in her tummy.

'They're horrid,' she confided. 'They hurt when I move.'

'Then try not to move too much,' advised the man, whose simple logic seemed to appeal to the child.

'Thank you,' Mia murmured gratefully an hour or so later, when Suzanna had drifted into a contented sleep.

'For diverting her mind from the horrors your father has fed into her?' He got up from the bed where somehow he had managed to swap places with Mia so she had ended up seated more comfortably on the bedside chair. 'That does not require thanks,' he stated grimly. 'It requires defending.'

He was right. It did. Mia didn't even take offence at the comment. 'He is not a nice man.' She sighed. 'He likes to control people. You, me, Suzanna—anyone he can gain power over.'

'Which does not justify her being treated to that kind of mental torture,' Alex countered harshly.

Mia went pale, but she nodded in agreement. 'Maybe now you can understand why I had to marry you. I had to do what was necessary so I can remove her from his influence.'

'An influence she should never have been exposed to in the first place!'

They had been talking in low voices by necessity in such close proximity to the sleeping Suzanna, but those words cut so deep into Mia's bones that she could not sit still and take them on the chin as she really knew she should do.

She got to her feet and walked right out of the room on legs that were shaking so badly they could barely support her.

When Alex eventually came looking for her he found her standing in the corridor, staring out of one of the windows that overlooked the hospital car park.

'I'm sorry,' he said heavily as he came up behind her. 'I did not mean to sound so critical of you. It was your father I was condemning.'

She didn't believe him. 'You think I am the lowest of the low for handing my child over to him,' she murmured unsteadily. 'And don't think that I don't know it!'

'That is your own guilty conscience talking,' he said with a sigh. 'I only wish you could have told me from the beginning why you had been forced to agree to this marriage!'

'What was I supposed to say?' she said cynically. 'Oh, by the way, I'm doing this because I had another child but I gave her away and this is the only way I can get her back again?' Her eyes flashed, her cheeks blooming with anger. 'That would really have made you respect me, wouldn't it?'

'And you want my respect?' he asked huskily.

Her heart hurt with the truthful answer to that question. 'I just want to get through these next few months without falling apart,' she answered shakily.

Silence greeted that, a grim kind of silence that held them both very still in that hospital corridor. Alex stood behind her, a dominating force as he stared over her shoulder at the car park beyond.

Mia felt like crying. Why, she didn't know—except maybe it had something to do with the need pounding away inside her breast that wanted her just to turn around and throw herself against the big, hard chest behind her.

'Do you have copies of the adoption documents?' Alex asked suddenly.

She steadied her lips and nodded. 'Yes,' she whispered.

'Where are they?'

Mia frowned at the question and turned to face him. 'I keep them with my other papers in my vanity case back at the villa in Skiathos,' she told him. 'Why?'

'Because I would like to see them, if you have no objection.'

No objection? Of course she had objections as a sudden fear drained her face of its colour. 'You want to use them against me, don't you?' she accused him shakily. 'You think that if I gave my child away once then a court of law would not give me custody of a second child! You—'

'You,' he cut in angrily, 'have a nasty, suspicious, insulting mind!' He was so very right!

'And that makes you feel very superior to me, doesn't it?' she flashed back hotly. 'Well, let me tell you something, Alex. I won't ever think you superior to me while you go on believing that a lump of rock somewhere in the Aegean is more important to you than your own DNA!'

CHAPTER EIGHT

ALEX rocked back on his heels as if Mia had struck him. He looked frighteningly angry and Mia couldn't breathe— she didn't dare to in case she released whatever it was she could see threatening to explode inside him. Her heart began to hammer, the world beyond his stone-like stance blurring at the edges. Then he moved, and so did she, sucking air into her starved lungs on a tension-packed gasp.

What she'd thought he'd been about to do to her she had no idea, but when he turned on his heel and strode away she stared after him with horror that verged on remorse.

Because it hit her—really hit her as she watched him go—that she had just inadvertently struck at the very heart of him, though she did not know how or with what!

When she was ready to leave Suzanna, after eating her tea with the little girl, it was Carol who appeared in the doorway to the little room.

'Oh, you have to be Mia's sister because you are like two peas from the same pod!' she declared, making Mia jump nervously and scan the empty space around Carol in the flesh-tingling fear that Alex would be there.

He wasn't. For the next ten minutes Carol talked Suzanna into a blank daze as she produced, during her mindless chatter, little presents from the capacious black canvas bag she'd had slung over her shoulder when she arrived.

A pocket computer game. 'From Alex,' she explained to Suzanna. 'He thought it may help to fill the time in when Mia has to rest. She's making a baby—did you know she's making a baby?'

Suzanna gave a nod about the baby, whispered a thank-you for the computer game and stared at the beautiful Carol with something close to star-struck idolisation as the other woman chatted on as if they'd known each other all their lives.

'Now, I've been ordered by Uncle Alex to take Mia home and make her rest,' Carol informed her latest conquest, 'so she can be fresh as a daisy when she comes back here tomorrow.'

'Will you come, too?'

Mia felt the wall around her heart crack, oozing a warm, sticky liquid called heartache for this child of hers who was so hungry for this kind of warm affection.

'I'll be coming to collect Mia after I've finished work.' Carol nodded.

When Mia bent down to receive her goodnight kiss the little girl clung to her neck. 'You will come back again, won't you?' she whispered anxiously.

'Tomorrow morning,' Mia promised.

'What did you say to put Alex in such a bad mood?' Carol asked the moment they were inside her car. 'He's been stomping around the hotel like a demolition man all afternoon.'

'You work there, too?' Mia asked in surprise.

'You think I'm a real blonde bimbo, don't you?' She grinned. 'I'm not, you know. I am an interior designer. I work on all the Doumas projects.'

She changed gear with a flourish and changed lanes with the deftness of someone who was used to taking on London rush-hour traffic.

'It's called keeping it in the family,' she explained. 'Leon is the construction expert, Alex the one who makes every new project pay. We are in a rush to get this one in London completed so we can start on the island project once you've had this baby. Only the island will be a private renovation,' she explained, oblivious or just completely indifferent to the way Mia had stiffened up at the fact Carol knew exactly why Alex had married her.

'The house has been left to decay while your father has been in possession. The land around it has turned back to scrubland that only goats find idyllic. Once it was a beautiful place...' she sighed wistfully '...and we intend to return it to its former glory. Now you know that I know exactly what goes on between you and Alex, will you tell me what you said to upset him?'

'None of your damned business,' Mia said abruptly, feeling angry, bitter and utterly, cruelly betrayed. And, worse than all that, feeling as if every rotten word she had thrown at Alex earlier had just been well and truly justified!

'Since you seem to know *all* my business,' she added angrily, 'do you think I could have a bedroom of my own, please? Knowing it all must surely mean that you also know that Alex never sleeps in my bed! So let's make life easier for him and give him his very own bed in his very own room so he doesn't have to spend the night stretched out in the chair in my room!'

'Oh my...' Carol drawled after a long taut silence. 'I think I've put my big mouth in it again! Did he really sleep in the chair?' She had the cheek to giggle. 'That'll teach him not to play mind games with his next of kin!'

'I don't know what you're talking about,' Mia said crossly.

'I know,' Carol laughed. 'That's what makes it all so amusing!' The car pulled to a stop outside the white townhouse. 'Are you sure you want a separate bedroom?' she goaded teasingly. 'He's supposed to be a dynamic lover— so rumour has it. Won't you miss him slipping between your sheets to have his evil way with you?'

Too angry to care any more, Mia retaliated spontaneously. 'You have it all wrong,' she snapped, grappling for the car door lock. 'He will still slip between my sheets when the mood takes him. He just does not approve of spending the whole damned night with a whore, that's all!'

As an exit line it was perfect, except she had nowhere to exit to. She hurled herself out of the car, certainly, but she had to stand by the closed front door and wait until Carol opened it with her key before she could make her real exit.

'I'm sorry,' Carol murmured as she stepped up beside her, and for once the other girl sound genuinely subdued. 'Believe it or not, I wasn't trying to offend you,'

No? Mia thought. Well, you could have fooled me!

'I was, in actual fact, teasing you at Alex's expense,' she admitted ruefully. 'He was the one who insisted that you share a bedroom, you see...'

Which meant—what? Mia wondered. That he was attempting to save face in front of his family? Well, if that was the case, he should have kept his mouth shut about the rest of their arrangements, shouldn't he?

'Do you have a key for this door or do we stand here until someone arrives who does?'

'I have a key.' Carol sighed, and fitted it into the lock, then pushed open the door. 'Mia—'

But Mia was already stalking towards the stairs and so furious she was barely managing to contain it.

'He's going to kill me if I have to confess what I've said to you!' Carol cried pleadingly after her.

'Good,' Mia said between gritted teeth. 'Do me a favour and kill each other—it will solve all my problems for me if you do!'

'This isn't a joke!' the other girl shouted.

Then Mia did explode, turning round at the base of the stairs to glare back down the hallway. 'You're right it's no joke!' she cried. 'I am seriously having his baby! And he seriously impregnated me to get it! So don't you dare make a mockery out of— Oh,' she groaned as the hall began to swim around dizzily.

The next thing she knew she was huddled on the floor, with Carol leaning over her, her lovely face chalk-white with shock. 'My God,' Carol gasped. 'What happened?'

'It's all right,' Leaning against Carol's shoulder, Mia closed her eyes and waited for the world to stop spinning. 'It happens sometimes,' she breathed. 'Nothing to worry about. I'll be fine in a moment or two.'

'But you fainted!' Carol gasped. 'That can't be normal, can it?'

'It is for me,' Mia said, a trifle ruefully. 'If you could help me get to my feet, I think I would be better lying down in bed now.'

'Of course.' Eager to help, but feeling guilty for bringing on the faint, Carol helped Mia to her feet. Together they mounted the stairs.

In the bedroom Mia dropped weakly onto the bed and lay there with her eyes closed while Carol hovered anxiously, uncertain what to do next.

'Can I get you a drink or something?' she offered in the end.

'Mmm.' Mia nodded carefully. 'That would be nice. Just a glass of water, please.'

Two minutes later Carol was back with the water and Mia was able to sit up and drink it, without feeling dizzy. 'Mia...' Carol began cautiously. 'Please don't let Alex know what I said before,' she begged. 'He's always going on about my big mouth. If he finds out I've been baiting you with it my life isn't going to be worth living around here...'

Thinking about it now the anger had subsided, along with the dizziness, Mia supposed the other woman was right. What was the use in causing yet more friction in a situation that was already too full of it?

'If you don't tell him that I fainted just now,' she bargained. 'He knows it happens,' she quickly assured Carol at her immediate protest. 'But he'll stop me from visiting

Suzanna if he hears about it, and at the moment the little girl needs me.'

'OK,' Carol agreed, but she sounded reluctant, to say the least. 'I'll say nothing about you fainting if you'll not chuck him out of this room so he knows my mouth's been working overtime again. Deal?'

'Deal,' Mia agreed, then lay back again as the front door slammed and the sound of two male voices drifted up the stairs.

'I'll go and head him off,' Carol said, shifting quickly to the door. 'If he sees you looking this washed-out he'll know something's wrong with you.'

Then she was gone. Mia could hear their voices through the half-open door. 'Where's Mia?' Alex was demanding. 'Why is your bag lying on the floor with its contents tipped all over the place?'

'Mia is tired and has gone to bed,' Mia heard Carol answer. 'She said to tell you not to disturb her when you came up. And my bag is on the floor like that because I was so desperate for the loo when I got home that I just dropped it and ran. Any more questions?'

It was a challenge, and one issued with her usual flippancy that belied any hint of deceit. The voice changed and became the brother's, whose tones were warmer as he greeted his wife the way loving husbands did.

After that, all went quiet as the three of them disappeared into the kitchen and Mia dragged herself up, got herself undressed and into her nightdress then fell between the sheets.

She slept very heavily and woke the next morning feeling thick-headed and lethargic. By the imprint on the pillow beside her, Alex had shared her bed last night, though whether he'd stayed there all night or had spent half of it stretched out in the chair she didn't know or care.

She was still angry with him for discussing their private business with the rest of his family. It made her feel exposed, more the outsider than ever, even though, on the face of it, he had allowed her closer to his family here in London than he had done while they were living in Greece.

When she went downstairs she found Carol alone in the kitchen. The men had apparently already left for work, and it was Carol who drove her to the hospital. Mia spent the morning entertaining Suzanna, who was allowed out of bed today and was walking around although she found it sore to do so.

They had just finished lunch, and Suzanna was resting on her bed while Mia read a story to her, when Alex walked in. He sent Mia a fleeting glance and then directed his attention at Suzanna.

'You look much brighter today.' He smiled.

The child smiled, too, her face lighting up like a puppy starved of affection who saw the chance of some coming its way in the shape of this man.

'I've drawn you a picture,' she told Alex shyly, and asked Mia to pass her a new sketch pad Carol had given her yesterday. 'It's to say thank you for my computer game...'

Inside were three pictures, although there was another one, which Mia had already been given for herself, of a church with a bride and bridegroom standing outside it and a child standing beside them, her hand tucked in the groom's. It said such a lot about the child's secret wishes that Mia had had to fight the urge to weep when Suzanna had handed the picture to her. Now she had it safely tucked away in the carrier bag in which she had brought Suzanna's gift—the set of story books they had just started reading. One of the set, *The Lion, the Witch and the Wardrobe*, was Suzanna's favourite story.

Now the child was solemnly handing Alex his picture. It showed blue skies and a large sun, beaming down on a man, a woman, a little girl and a baby around a swimming pool with a pretty house in the background.

More secret wishes unwittingly portrayed for the discerning to read. Mia had told Suzanna all about Alex's villa on Skiathos, and she had drawn herself there with them because that was where she most wanted to be.

No, thought Mia, Alex was not a fool. The way his eyes were hooded as he studied the picture meant he was reading all the right messages.

'I have one for the other lady, too,' Suzanna told Alex shyly.

'Carol,' Mia said.

'Carol,' Suzanna obediently repeated. 'She brought me these felt tips and the sketch pad,' she explained to Alex. 'She wanted me to draw my operation so I have—do you think she'll like it?'

This picture was gory in the extreme. When Alex finally managed to drag his attention away from his own offering to look at Carol's picture, he couldn't help the rueful smile that touched his mouth. 'I should think she will love it.' he murmured very drily. 'Thank you for my picture.'

From being ready for a nap, Suzanna was suddenly so animated Mia felt something painful clutch at her heart as she watched the little girl hunt in the clutter on her bed to unearth her computer game, which she handed to Alex.

'Would you like to have a go?' she offered eagerly, switching it on for him. 'You press this button here, then—'

It was like watching a light go out. One moment all three of them seemed to be basking in the brilliance of Suzanna's excitement and in the next, darkness fell in the form of a metaphorical big black shadow. The child had glanced up, that was all—just glanced up distractedly—and, wham, she was a different person.

Mia was sitting on the side of the bed, with Alex seated in the chair on the other side. She looked up, too, and rose jerkily. Alex glanced up, saw who was standing in the doorway and frowned as his eyes flicked to the other two then back to the door again.

Jack Frazier was standing there, transfixed. His eyes were locked on Mia's body, greed glinting in their cold grey depths as he absorbed the obvious evidence of her pregnancy.

'So it is done,' he said with unmasked satisfaction. 'Why didn't you tell me?' The accusing words were flashed at Mia. 'When is it due?' He laughed, and turned to Alex, who was rising slowly to his feet. 'I can't damn well believe it! Well done, man. Well done!'

Not seeing or completely ignoring Alex's grim expression, Jack Frazier walked forward to grab his hand and began to pump it up and down.

'When do we close the deal, then?' he asked eagerly.

On the other side of the bed Mia was reaching for Suzanna's hand as the child's hand searched for hers. Neither smiled. Neither spoke. As far as Jack Frazier was concerned, they might as well not have been there for all they mattered. Mia only mattered as a vessel required to make him his so-called grandson and Suzanna didn't matter at all.

'We will let you know at the appropriate time,' Alex said coldly. 'As it is, Suzanna's health is the main concern in this room.'

As a pointed reminder of his duty, Jack took the hint and at last condescended to notice Suzanna. 'Got your Mia back, then?' he taunted drily. 'The lengths children will go to get their own way.'

'She didn't stage-manage appendicitis,' Mia said tightly, as the poor child lowered her head so she didn't have to look into those coldly indifferent eyes.

'No?' He sounded dubious. 'Well, never mind about that. I want to know about my grandson. Were you going to bother to tell me at all, or was I supposed to wait until the damned thing was over and done with before I found out anything?'

She didn't answer—she refused to. She had nothing whatsoever to say to him that he didn't already know.

'Like that, is it?' He grimaced. 'Well, at least you carried through. I did wonder with this long silence whether you'd chickened out at the last hurdle. But...' he glanced at Suzanna's lowered head again '...we all have our price, don't we, Mia? And your price almost became a non-runner. I wonder what you would have done then?'

It was such a cruel thing to suggest that Mia actually swayed in horror. Luckily, the child didn't understand what he was talking about—but Alex did. In one step he had hold of Jack Frazier's arm.

'Let's go for a walk,' he suggested grimly. 'We have a few things to say to each other, I think...'

He had them both out of the door before Mia could react. The dire threat in his words filled her with such a dark sense of impending horror that her legs went from beneath her. She slumped down beside Suzanna and pulled the little girl close to her breast.

He couldn't mean what she feared he'd meant, she told herself desperately. Alex wouldn't break a confidence and tell her father that he knew about Suzanna, would he?

Oh, please, she prayed as she held the little girl even closer. Please don't let him say anything stupid!

'Daddy hates me,' Suzanna whispered painfully.

'No, he doesn't, darling,' Mia said soothingly. 'He just doesn't know how to love anyone, that's all.'

It was the truth. Her father was incapable of loving anyone. The man was a single-minded egotist who measured his own strength in his ability to close his heart to others. He had done it with her mother, with his children and with all his competitors when he'd squeezed them dry without conscience. He saw himself as omnipotent, his only regret in life being the loss of his son to carry on his name even if he hadn't been his blood heir. To Jack Frazier that hadn't mattered so long as Tony bore his name.

Now he had to accept second best in a child who would bear the name of its father and not its grandfather, but it was written into the contract he had drawn up with Alex that the child Mia carried would be given the second name of Frazier. For Jack Frazier, that was going to be good enough for him to bequeath his millions.

He made her sick. The whole filthy situation made her sick! The sooner it was over the sooner she could begin to wash her life clean again.

Alex didn't come back. Mia spent the rest of the afternoon worrying about what he'd said to her father. By the time Carol arrived, with Leon in tow, she felt so tired and wretched she was more than ready to leave.

But Suzanna was still feeling the effects of Jack Frazier's visit, and at least Carol's bright chatter helped to lift the child's mood again. Leon was quiet but, then, he always was. He glanced often at Mia who had removed herself to the window and stood there, gazing out with a bleakness that isolated her from the rest of those present.

While Carol was sitting on the bed, drawing a bold picture in Suzanna's sketch book, Leon came over to stand beside Mia.

'Are you all right?' he asked quietly.

It surprised her enough to glance at him. 'Tired, that's all.' She tried a smile and almost made it happen before she was turning to stare out of the window again.

'Alex was coming back to get you himself, but something came up only he could deal with. He asked me to ask you if you would mind waiting until he gets in tonight before you retire because he has something important he wishes to discuss with you.'

Something to do with her father? Mia wondered fretfully, and gave a nod of acquiescence.

'Thank you.' Politely Leon moved away from her again. He didn't like her, Mia knew. He resented the pressure her father had used on his brother. He resented her presence in his brother's life.

Back at the house, Mia found enough energy from somewhere to help Carol prepare dinner, then sat and ate with them in the dining room, though she felt like an intruder. But it was either eat with them or go to her room and eat alone, which would have been rude in the extreme. By the time they had cleared away after the meal, and Alex still hadn't put in an appearance, Mia couldn't take the tension any longer and excused herself with an apology.

'I just can't keep awake any longer,' she explained. 'I'm so sorry.'

She had just climbed wearily into bed when the bedroom door opened. *Alex looks less than his usually immaculate self* was the first anxious thought to hit her. He needed a shave and his clothes looked decidedly the worse for wear. His hair was rumpled, as if he had been raking impatient fingers through it.

'I'm sorry I'm so late,' he said, when he saw she was awake, 'but this could not wait until the morning.'

He closed the door and continued to stand there for a few moments, his tired face brooding as he studied the pensive way she was sitting in bed, banked by snowy white pillows, waiting for him to say what he had to say.

Then he sighed—heavily. 'Look, do you mind if I take a quick shower before we talk?' he asked tiredly.

'N-no, of course not,' she replied, but she would have preferred him just to get on and say what he had to because she didn't like the grim mood he was in, and she needed to know what he had discussed with her father. But he had already walked off into the bathroom, leaving her sitting there trapped in an electric state of tension.

True to his word, though, he was back in minutes. He had showered and shaved and looked marginally less weary, though no less grim, wrapped in a blue towelling bathrobe that left too much naked golden flesh on show for her comfort because her imagination was suddenly conjuring up images that set her over-sensitive breasts tingling and made that place between her thighs begin to throb.

Her knees came up, her arms loosely wrapping around them in an instinctive act of defensive protection for those susceptible parts of her body. But her eyes never left him as he came over to the bed and sat down on it beside her, the tension seeming to sing loud in the quietness of the softly lit bedroom.

'What's wrong, Alex?' Mia asked anxiously, unable to hold the question back any longer.

His dark eyes flicked up and clashed with hers, then he smiled a rather rueful smile at her that did nothing for her equilibrium. 'Nothing,' he assured her, then went silent, those deceptively languid eyes of his studying her worried face for a few moments before he eventually went on, 'Nothing that you need worry about, anyway...'

He did a strange thing then. He reached up to touch her hair, gently combing it away from her cheek and one creamy shoulder. The electricity in the air sharpened, sprinkling that well-remembered static all around her. Her heart began to race, those two over-active parts of her body sending her another jolt that reminded her just how irresistible she found this man.

'I have to return to Greece,' he announced, making her blink and forcing her to come back from wherever she had flown off to—bringing reality tumbling back into perspective. 'I expect to be gone for about three weeks.'

His hand dropped away. She wanted to shiver, as if she'd just been shut out in the cold, and hated herself for being this vulnerable to him.

'I accept that you cannot leave Suzanna yet,' he continued while she struggled with her foolish emotions, 'so I have arranged with Carol and Leon for you to stay here for now.'

At least he wasn't making her return to Greece with him,

Mia noted with relief, although remaining under this roof with his brother so clearly resenting her presence didn't exactly fill her with joy. Still, she'd lived with worse, she told herself bracingly. And she could spend most of her time with Suzanna—keep herself as scarce around here as possible.

'The other problem is Suzanna,' he went on, as if his own train of thought was following the same lines as her own. 'She is due to be discharged from hospital in a couple of days.'

'I'll go with her to my father's house,' Mia offered instantly. 'It seems the best thing all round. I won't be putting anyone here out.'

Alex was already shaking his head. 'No,' he said. 'I will not have you exposed to your father in your condition so I have done a deal with him.'

Mia stiffened instantly. 'You didn't tell him you knew the truth about her, did you?' she asked tensely.

'Of course not!' he snapped. 'What do you take me for— a monster? You think I was blind to the way that child shrivelled up in his presence—the way you did the same thing yourself? You think I enjoy watching any child react to an adult like that?'

Mia lowered her lashes and said nothing—after all, it wasn't that long ago that he'd enjoyed seeing her cringe from him.

The air grew thick, laden with anger, then he sighed heavily. 'You cannot bring yourself to trust me even a small amount, can you?' he muttered. 'So, what do you suspect I am about to say to you now? That I have sold you into purdah for the duration of your pregnancy?'

'Why not?' she shot back. 'I was in purdah before we came to London. Why not put me back there again?'

'I have offered to take Suzanna off your father's hands for the next three weeks until she returns to her school,' he cut in tightly. 'Your father has agreed, so long as you both reside at this house and Suzanna is not taken out of the country!'

'He's agreed to that?' Mia couldn't believe it.

'He almost bit my damned hand off!' Alex rasped in disgust. 'Apparently, his housekeeper is about to take her annual vacation, which meant him having to hunt around for someone who could temporarily take charge of the child. So you being here fitted in very well with his own situation!'

'Oh,' she said, disconcerted by the amount of thought he had put into all of this. 'Thank you,' she mumbled belatedly.

'That is not all,' he continued, all that softness she had glimpsed in him a moment ago well and truly gone. 'I have my own provisos to add to your father's. The main one is that you promise me you will come back to Greece the day you take Suzanna back to school. The reason I demand this is because I will not be able to get back to London to collect you myself so I am going to have to take your word for it that you will come back to me.'

'I'll come back,' she promised, frowning because she had never so much as considered doing anything else. They had made a deal, one where she had agreed to give birth to his son on Greek soil. 'I will drive Suzanna back to school, then catch the next scheduled flight to—'

'My plane will be waiting for you at an airfield close to Suzanna's school,' he interrupted. 'And you will not drive yourself anywhere while you are here,' he went on grimly. 'One of my own drivers will be left at your disposal for the rest of your stay here.'

'But I have a car!' she protested. 'It's sitting, doing nothing, at my father's house! It would be nice to drive myself again while I'm here in London!'

'Not while you keep fainting,' he said.

'I do not keep fainting!' She hotly denied that.

'But those dizzy spells affect you too readily for you to

be safe behind the wheel of a car. I saw the way you barely managed to hold yourself upright in front of your father at lunchtime,' he added tightly when she opened her mouth to protest yet again. 'So you agree to my terms or I take you back to Greece with me now. The choice is yours.'

He was, after all, only protecting his investment! 'Yes, oh, master,' she said sarcastically.

He had been about to stand up when she'd said that, but now he stilled and Mia felt a frisson of warning shoot down her spine as he turned those dark eyes on her—she recognised the look, recognised it only too well.

'You know...' he said, super-light, super-soft, 'you are in real danger of baiting me once too often, *agape mou*. And, despite the delicacy of your condition or the fragility of that protective shell you like to hide behind, I am going to retaliate,' he warned her. 'And you're not going to like it because I know your secret.'

'I d-don't know what you're talking about,' she said warily.

'No?' he said quizzically—and his dark face was suddenly very close to her face. Her eyelashes began to quiver, and her fingers clutched nervously at the sheet. 'Well, let us see, shall we?' he suggested silkily, and his mouth covered her trembling one.

It was like being tossed into a burning furnace—she caught fire that quickly. Her mind caught fire, as well as her body, and she wasn't even aware of how spectacularly she had done it until he was having to use force to prise her clinging fingers from his nape before he could separate his mouth from her greedily clinging one.

'Now that...' he drawled, touching a punctuating fingertip to the pulsing fullness of her lips, 'is your secret. You may prefer to hate me, but you cannot damned well resist me!'

His words made her want to hit out at him, but he caught

the hand before it landed its blow and arrogantly pressed his warm lips to her palm.

That was the point where her sense of humiliation plumbed new depths because the moment she felt his tongue make a salacious lick of her palm she was lost again. Her eyes closed and her breathing ruptured as that lick sent its sensual message down her arm and through her body, arrowing directly at the very core of her.

'I can delay my departure for an hour or two, if you want me to...' he offered.

That stung a different part of her entirely. Her eyes opened, angry fire burning alongside the passion. 'Only an hour or two?' she said scathingly. 'Well, that just about puts your attitude to sex in a nutshell, doesn't it? One quick fix then you're off again before the sheets get warm!'

He should have been angry- she'd said it all to make him so angry that he would walk out! But he completely disconcerted her by arrogantly taking up the challenge.

'You want more than that? A whole night of wild passion, maybe?'

'You aren't capable of spending a whole night in the same bed as me!' she said scornfully.

His eyes darkened. Mia felt real alarm take a stinging dive down the length of her spine. 'That lousy opinion you have of me really does need amending,' he said curtly. Suddenly he was standing up, determined fingers already working on the knot to his robe.

'W-what are you doing?' she choked. 'No, Alex...' she protested huskily, not even trying to pretend that she didn't know exactly why he was stripping himself.

It didn't stop him. Her heart began to race, her tongue cleaving itself to the roof of her dry mouth as she watched in a paralysed mix of greedy fascination and mind-numbing horror that magnificent naked frame of his appear in front of her.

The air left her lungs on a short, sharp gasp at the unashamed power of his pulsing arousal. Her eyes moved upwards to clash with the fierce flame in his as he bent to lift the edge of the sheet.

At last she found the motivation to attempt an escape, slithering like a snake to the other side of the bed. His arm caught her before she could get away. It drew her back across the smooth white linen, then turned her so she was facing him.

'I'm pregnant,' she reminded him shakily, as if that should be enough to stop him.

It wasn't. His arm slid beneath her shoulders then angled downwards across her spine so his hand could arch her slender hips towards him. The firm roundness of her stomach was pressed into the concaved wall of his taut stomach. He sighed a little unsteadily, his darkened eyes closing as if this first physical contact he was having with their unborn child was moving him deeply.

Enthralled by his totally unexpected reaction, Mia released a soft gasp. He heard it—felt the warm rush of air brush across his face—and opened eyes which had gone pitch black and seemed to want to draw her deep inside them.

Which is exactly what he did do. He didn't speak—he didn't need to. That expression had said it all for him. It was need. It was desire. It was hunger too long-standing for him to fight it any longer.

The last conscious thought she had before he completely took her over was that he'd been right. She can't resist him, not when he looked at her like that, anyway.

Her eyes began to close, her soft mouth parting as it went in blind search of his. They fused from mouth to breast to hip. It was that easy to give in to it in the end.

For the next few hours they became lost in each other, the world outside with all its complications shut right out.

'Why?' Mia asked a long time later when they were lying

in a heated tangle of sensually exhausted limbs. 'When you rejected me the first night we came here.'

'I promised you I would not touch you again once you were pregnant,' he replied.

'You made that promise to yourself, Alex,' Mia corrected him quietly. 'I never asked you for it.'

He was silent for a moment, then gave a small sigh. 'Well, it is now a broken promise,' he announced, 'and one I have no intention of reinstating.'

Then he kissed her again, slowly, languidly, drawing her back down into that deep, dark well of pleasure from where she eventually drifted into a sated sleep, her arms still holding him and his still wrapped around her. It felt wonderful—so different from anything they had shared before that it was like a statement of future intent.

Yet when she awoke the next morning he was gone—as usual.

Which meant—what? she wondered grimly. A return to the status quo, with the sex thrown back in to spice it all up a bit?

CHAPTER NINE

SUZANNA was discharged from hospital three days later, and the time that followed went by much too quickly. Time that turned out to be a lot pleasanter than Mia had expected it to be, mainly because Leon's manner towards her had softened remarkably—though forced to do so, she suspected, by a child who was so very eager to please that even Leon Doumas didn't seem to have the heart to be anything but pleasant around Suzanna.

And that meant he had to include Mia.

Everywhere the little girl went, her fluffy rabbit, her pens and paper and her computer game went with her. Every night she insisted Mia read a story from her set of books. When in their company, her wistful green eyes followed Leon and Carol around like a love-starved puppy, eagerly waiting to be noticed. When not in their company she talked about them constantly, starry-eyed and happy, so pathetically grateful to the couple for allowing her to come and stay with them that sometimes it brought tears to Mia's eyes to witness it.

With the resilience of childhood she recovered quickly from her operation, and with the vulnerability of childhood she worried constantly about the moment when she would have to go back to school because she knew that was also the time when Mia would be going back to Greece.

'You might forget all about me when you have the new baby to love,' she confided one evening as she lay in the bed Carol had allocated her in the room next to Mia's.

'New babies don't steal love from one person for themselves, darling,' Mia said gently. 'They only ask that you let them share it. Do you think you can do that? Share all the love I have for you with this new baby?'

'Will Alex let me come and visit sometimes, do you think?' she asked anxiously. 'Will he mind if I share you with the new baby?'

'Of course not,' Mia said. 'Who was it who convinced Daddy to let you come and stay here until you go back to school?'

'Carol said Alex likes children,' the child said, with that painfully familiar wistful expression. 'She said Alex likes me because I look so much like you.'

Well, that was a very kind thing to say, Mia acknowledged, and made a mental note to thank Carol when she next saw her.

Carol just shrugged her thanks aside. 'It was only the truth,' she said. 'Alex does like children and he's got himself so tied up in knots over you that he's bound to like Suzanna simply because she looks like you.'

Tied up in what kind of knots? she wondered. Sexual knots? 'You don't know what you're talking about,' she replied dismissively.

'No?' To her annoyance, Carol started grinning. 'Did Alex ever tell you about his mistress?' she asked. When Mia instantly stiffened up Carol nodded, 'I thought he would. I know how his mind works, you see, and he would have told you about her just to score points off you. But I bet he hasn't told you that within a week of marrying you he had sent her packing.

'No,' Carol continued drily at Mia's start of surprise, 'I didn't think he would. Too bad for his ego to admit that, having had you, he couldn't bring himself to touch another woman. But that's our dear Alex for you,' she went on. 'Committed. Totally committed to whatever he turns his attention to.'

'Like an island he wants to repossess,' Mia said derisively, refusing to believe a word Carol was saying because believing would make her start seeing Alex through different eyes, which in turn could make her weak.

And she couldn't afford to be weak where Alex was concerned. She was already vulnerable enough.

'Certainly, recovering the family island has been the goal that has driven him for the past ten years,' Carol agreed. 'But marry some strange woman and produce a child with her in the quest for that goal?' She shook her blonde head. 'Now that was going too far, even for Alex. Or so I thought,' she added sagely, 'until I met you. Then I began to wonder if half the trap wasn't of his own making.'

'It wasn't,' Mia said coolly. 'My father is a master tactician.' And then some, she added bitterly to herself.

'Your father knew why Alex wanted the island back so badly,' Carol acknowledged. 'A solemn promise to his dying father—you can't really get a bigger incentive than that for a Greek. But I still say—'

'His father?' Mia cut in sharply. 'Alex promised his dying father?'

'Didn't you know?' Carol looked surprised. 'Come on,' she said suddenly, taking hold of Mia's hand as she did so. 'It will be easier to show you,' she explained, pulling Mia into the hall and then into a room Carol used as a working studio. 'See,' she declared, bringing Mia to a halt in front of a large framed painting.

It was titled *Vision* and Mia's heart stilled as she recognised it as the original of the print she had seen in the lift at the Doumas office building.

'Their father had this painted when he knew he was going to have to sell the island,' Carol explained. 'Until then it had been in the family for ever. See the little graveyard.' She pointed it out. 'Every Doumas, except their father, is buried there, including their mother and their older brother. They were killed in a flying accident when Alex was a teenager and Leon a small child. The accident devastated their father. He adored his wife and worshipped his eldest son.

'With them gone, he felt he had nothing left to live for, hence the sudden drop in the Doumas fortunes. His own health suffered until he eventually died prematurely—but not before he had extracted a promise from Alex that he would get the island back and have his remains transferred there. Do you understand now?' she demanded finally.

'Understand?' Mia repeated. Oh, yes, she acknowledged heavily, she understood. Alex's island in the Aegean was not just a piece of rock for which he was willing to sell his soul. It was home. It was where his heart lay, right there with his mother and his brother and where his father needed to lay his own heart.

She finally did understand that the grip her own father had on Alex was easily as tight as the grip he had on herself. Blackmail—emotional blackmail. A far more powerful vice than mere financial blackmail.

Her hand came up to cover her mouth. 'I'm going to be sick,' she choked, and had to run to the nearest cloakroom.

It was ironic, really, that Alex should choose to call her that same evening. 'Are you all right?' he demanded the moment she announced herself on the phone. 'Carol said you were sick earlier.'

'Something I ate. I'm fine now,' she said dismissively, hoping Carol hadn't told him exactly why she had been sick.

And what had made her sick? Her own words coming back to haunt her. Cruel words, dreadful words, where she'd condemned him for selling himself for physical gain while she'd self-righteously seen herself as selling herself for love.

'You must not overdo it now that Suzanna is out of hospital,' he commanded rather curtly.

'I won't,' she said. 'She's quite an easy child to entertain.'

'I noticed,' he muttered. 'Too damned easy to please. Have you seen your father?'

Mia frowned at his sharpened tone. 'No,' she replied.

'Good,' Alex grunted. 'Let us hope it stays that way.'

'Is that why you're calling?' she asked. It was so unusual for him to bother. 'Because you're concerned about my father showing up here? He won't, you know,' she assured him. 'Having reassured himself that all is going to plan, he won't waste thinking time on me again until the baby is due.'

'Does that bother you?'

Bother me? Again she frowned at the strangely sharp question. 'No,' she said firmly. Her father's lack of interest in her as a person had stopped hurting her a long time ago.

'Good,' he said again. 'I have two reasons for calling you,' he went on, suddenly becoming all brisk and businesslike. 'You are due your monthly check-up with the doctor this week. Since it is not logical to transport you to Athens for a simple doctor's appointment, I have therefore arranged an appointment at a clinic in London for you.'

He went on to give her names, addresses, dates and times which she had to hurriedly write down.

'And the other reason I called,' he continued, 'is because I have just discovered that I have your passport here in Athens with me. I must have stashed it in my briefcase without thinking about it, when we travelled to London, and there it has stayed until I unearthed it this morning. I also happened to notice that it still bears your maiden name, which makes it invalid.'

'Oh,' she said. She hadn't given a single thought to either her passport or the fact that it was no longer valid. 'I suppose that means I will have to apply for a new one.'

'I am already arranging it,' he announced. 'Leon is seeing to the paperwork so we can get it rushed through before you leave for Greece. You will need to put your signature to the forms Leon is preparing and supply a new photograph. Can you see to that first thing in the morning?'

'Of course,' she said, 'but I could just as easily have seen to the rest as well. I'm pregnant, not an invalid, you know!'

'I never meant to imply you were.' He sighed. 'But I presumed you would prefer to devote your time in England to Suzanna,' he said, in a tone meant to remind her exactly where her priorities lay.

Which it did—irksomely. 'Is that it?' she said, sounding childishly uncivil even to her own ears.

She heard him mutter something that sounded very much like a profanity. 'Why do you have to turn every conversation into a battle?' he said wearily.

'Why do you have to be so damned arrogant?' she shot back, for want of something to toss at him.

'Because I'm trying to save you a lot of unnecessary hassle.'

'I don't like my life being organised for me!' she snapped.

'I am trying to help you, damn it!' he exploded. 'When are you going to stop being so damned bitter and realise that I am your ally, not your enemy!'

When you stop tying my emotions in so many knots that I just can't tell what you are any more! she thought wretchedly, and slammed down the phone before she actually yelled the words at him!

Then she stood, shaken to the very roots by her own anger, because she didn't know what she was angry about!

Yes, you do, a little voice inside her head told her. You want him to show you a little care and consideration, but when he does you get so frightened it isn't real that you simply go off the deep end!

Leon produced the relevant forms for her to sign the next evening—several of them, which made her frown.

'Copies in case I mess up,' he explained dismissively.

She shrugged and signed where he told her to sign, and handed over the requested photographs—four surprisingly good snaps, taken in a passport booth in the local high street. Carol had gone with her and so had Suzanna, and between them they had turned the excursion into a game.

Mia now had in her possession several photos of Suzanna pulling silly faces into the camera, and even a couple of Carol, doing the same thing.

She kept her appointment at the exclusive London clinic Alex had arranged for her. They gave her the full works, blood pressure, blood tests, physical examination and an ultrasound scan. No problems anywhere, she was relieved to hear. The dizzy spells were a sign of low blood sugar levels, easily remedied by keeping light snacks handy. Other than that, she was assured, they were nothing to worry about. She left the clinic feeling very relieved to have a clean bill of health—and a black and white photograph of her darling baby curled up inside her womb.

'Did it hurt?' Carol asked suspiciously as she studied the picture.

'What, the scan?' Mia asked. 'No,' she said. 'It just feels a bit strange, that's all—and they did prod and poke the poor thing a bit until they could get him to lie in a good position.'

Carol handed back the photograph, but there was an odd look in her eyes that Mia couldn't interpret—a look that bothered her for days afterwards, though she didn't know why.

Another week went by, and Alex didn't call again—not that she expected him to after the last row they'd had. But it hurt in some ways that he hadn't even bothered to call to see how her visit to the clinic had gone—though she would rather die that let him know that.

Then other, far more immediate concerns began to take precedence, not least the way Suzanna grew quieter and more withdrawn as their three weeks raced towards their imminent conclusion.

Carol found Mia one evening, weeping over Suzanna's school trunk which Mrs Leyton had had sent over to the house that day.

'Oh, Mia.' Carol sighed, and knelt to put her arms around her. 'Don't do this to yourself,' she murmured painfully.

'I can't bear to leave her,' Mia confided wretchedly. 'I don't know how I'm going to do it! She hates that school!' she sobbed. 'She hates being away from me! It's going to break her poor little heart and it's going to break mine, too!'

'Oh, dear God,' Carol groaned thickly. 'I can't cope with this. Mia, listen to me!' she pleaded. 'You—'

'Carol...'

It was the flatness in Leon's tone that stopped Carol from saying whatever she'd been about to say.

'Don't meddle,' he warned.

'But, Leon!' Carol cried. 'If Alex knew how—'

'I said, don't meddle,' he repeated.

He was standing in the open doorway to Mia's bedroom, and he sounded so formidable that when Mia glanced at him through tear-washed eyes she thought she could see Alex standing there. Alex, grim with resolve.

She shivered. They had a bargain, she and Alex, she reminded herself staunchly. A bargain that was too important to both of them for her to stumble at one of the very last hurdles.

'It's all right,' she said, pulling herself together so that by the time she had pulled herself to her feet all that cool dignity she had used to bring her this far was firmly back in place. 'I'm all right now.' She smiled a brittle smile at the tearful Carol as she also straightened. 'But thank you for caring.'

'We all care, Mia,' Carol murmured anxiously. 'Though I can well understand why you wouldn't believe that.'

The next day Suzanna's trunk left for the school by spe-

cial carrier. The morning after that, pale but composed—
they'd both been through this many times before, after all—
Mia and Suzanna came down the stairs together, the child
dressed in her dour black and grey school uniform and Mia
in a sober grey long-jacketed suit, prim high-collared white
blouse and with her hair neatly contained in a rather aus-
tere, if elegant, French pleat.

She expected to find Alex's chauffeur waiting for them,
but she had not expected to see both Leon and Carol standing there also.

'We're coming with you,' Carol explained. 'Alex's orders.'

Alex's orders. She almost smiled at the phrase, only she
couldn't smile.

The journey to Bedfordshire was utterly harrowing.
Suzanna sat between Mia and Carol in the back of the car
while Leon took the front seat next to the driver.

One of the little girl's hands was locked in Mia's and,
clicking into a sort of autopilot, Mia talked softly to the
child as they swept out of London onto the motorway and
kept on talking as the car ate up the miles far too quickly.

As they left the motorway Suzanna began to recognise
her surroundings and grew tense, her hand clinging all the
tighter to Mia's. A couple of miles away from the school
entrance the tears began to threaten. Carol muttered something very constricted, then reached out jerkily to grab at
Suzanna's other hand.

'Hey,' she said, with very forced lightness, 'this is an
adventure for me. I've never been this way before!'

'I hate it,' Suzanna whispered.

'But look!' Carol urged. 'There's a private airfield over
there! I can see a beautiful white plane sitting on the tarmac.'

Airfield.

Mia shivered. It ran through her like a dousing from an
ice-cold shower.

'You know,' Carol was saying brightly, 'Alex has a plane just like that one! Do you think he may have come to—?'

'What's going on?' Mia interrupted sharply as the car suddenly took a *sharp* right turn. She leaned forward, staring out of the car window. 'Why have we turned here?' she demanded.

To her confusion, Carol chuckled. 'A magical mystery tour,' she chanted excitedly.

The car stopped. Mia stared and her heart began to pound heavily in her chest for in front of them, just as Carol had indicated, stood a gleaming white Gulfstream jet, with its engines running.

'No,' she breathed, 'No!' she gasped more strongly as a horrified suspicion of what was actually happening here began to take a firm hold on her. 'Carol, this is—!'

But Carol was already clambering out of the car—and taking Suzanna with her!

'Leon!' Mia entreated jerkily.

'Trust us,' he said, then climbed out of the car—and that was when panic suddenly erupted.

'You can't do this!' she protested, scrambling out of the car in time to see Carol and Suzanna disappear onto the jet. 'No!' she shouted after them. 'Oh, God!' Leon's arm came round her shoulders. 'Leon, for the love of God, you don't understand!'

'Believe me,' he said soothingly, 'I do understand. It's OK...' He began urging her towards the plane. 'Alex has fixed everything. You have no need to worry. Trust him, Mia. He has your best interests at heart...'

Best interests at heart? Her blood pressure began to rise in a swirling red mist that almost completely engulfed her. She stumbled up the steps, dangerously out of control and near collapse. With her eyes she frantically searched out and found Suzanna—then saw the man who was squatting next to the child, talking to her.

'Alex,' she gasped in confusion.

His dark head came up, his eyes giving her a look of such grim determination that any small threads of pretence she might have been clinging to that this was not what she feared it was snapped at that moment.

As if in rehearsed confirmation, Suzanna's voice reached out towards her, shrill with rising excitement. 'I'm coming to Greece to live with you, Mia! I don't have to go back to that horrid school!'

'No,' she breathed in pulse-drumming horror. 'Alex, you just can't do this!'

'Go and sit next to Carol and fasten yourself in, Suzanna,' Alex urged the ecstatic child.

He straightened, lean and lithe and dauntingly real in a casually loose taupe linen jacket, black trousers and a black T-shirt that did nothing to disguise the tight contours of his body as he began striding towards her. Even in the midst of all this trauma Mia found herself in a tense state of suspended animation, her senses remembering the man's sensual might and not the might of his ruthless intellect.

'Be calm,' he was murmuring soothingly. 'There is no need to panic...'

No need to panic. The words rattled frantically around her. No need to panic? Of course there was a need to panic! This was wrong! This was crazy! It was going to ruin everything!

Behind her she heard the muffled thud of the plane's outer door sealing into its housing and the jet engines give a threatening roar. Her whole body quivered in violent reaction, the clammy heat of horror suddenly racing through her blood, and on a whimpering groan of pained accusation aimed at those compelling dark eyes that were coming ever closer she pitched dizzyingly forward into total oblivion.

She came round to find herself stretched out across two soft leather chairs, with a pillow tucked beneath her head and Alex squatting beside her, his fingers impatiently dealing with the tiny pearl buttons that held her blouse collar fastened at her throat.

He looked pale, grim-faced and extremely angry. 'I swear to God, with everything I have in me,' he railed at her the moment he saw her eyes flutter open, 'that you will spend the rest of this pregnancy locked away in a bloody stress-free environment!'

The blouse button sprang free. He sat back on his heels, his eyes flashing with rage when he saw her catch in a greedy breath of air.

'And the power dressing gets its walking orders as well!'

Still too dizzy to fight back, Mia lifted an arm to her face so she could cover her aching eyes with decidedly icy fingers. Almost instantly, the hand snapped away from her eyes again. They were already in the air! She could hear the aircraft's engines as nothing more than a faint purr as they flew them ever further away from England!

Shakily she pushed herself into a weak-limbed sitting position, her green eyes flicking urgently around the plush cream interior of the cabin.

They were alone. 'Where's Suzanna?' she demanded jerkily.

'In the galley with Carol, having the time of her life,' Alex said sardonically. 'We told her you were sleeping. She didn't see you swoon into my arms so she believed us.'

Is that what I did? Swooned right into the arms of the enemy?

So, what's new? she grimly mocked herself. You've been swooning into those arms from the very beginning! Knowing he was the enemy has never made any difference.

'Is anything else too tight on you?' Alex asked. His hands were already pushing the grey jacket down her arms.

'Will you stop doing that?' she snapped, trying to slap his hands away.

But the jacket came off, and his grim face did not unclench from the tension locking it as he angrily tossed the jacket away. Then he seemed to make a concerted effort to get a hold on his temper. A deep sigh ripped from him, his big shoulders flexed...

'I'm sorry about the cloak and dagger stuff,' he said heavily. 'I did not intend to frighten you so badly with it. I was afraid that if I had told you what I was going to do you would have panicked and warned your father.'

Which she would have done—Mia freely acknowledged that. 'But why, Alex?' she cried. 'Why are you doing this when you must know it will be Suzanna and me my father is going to punish for this bit of senseless defiance!'

'No defiance,' he said, shifting his long, lean frame into the chair directly opposite her own, where he leaned forward, placed his forearms on his spread knees and then, with the grimly controlled expression of a man who was about to drop a bombshell on the heads of the innocent, he announced impassively, 'I am calling the deal off.'

Mia just sat there, her blank, staring eyes telling him that she had not taken in what he was saying. He remained silent, waiting, watchful, noting the way her lips parted to aid the very frail thread of her breathing and the way her pale skin went even paler, the green of her eyes beginning to darken as the full import of his words finally began to sink in.

Her reaction, when it came, was not what he was expecting. 'Our deal?' she whispered tragically.

'No.' He frowned and shook his head. 'That is a completely separate issue, which I am not prepared to deal with right now. I am talking about my deal with your father. I am calling it off and, because I know that my decision is going to have a direct effect on you, I am placing both you and Suzanna under my protection. Which is why we are flying to Greece.'

'Protection?' she repeated. He was placing them under his protection when the very act of how he was doing it was effectively removing the only form of protection they had! 'How can you say that?' she cried. 'Legally, Suzanna is still his daughter! Legally, he can take her back whenever he wants to!'

'You *wanted* to leave her behind?' he challenged. 'You *wanted* to dump her at that school and walk away?'

No. 'But that's not the point,' she said with a sigh. 'My father—'

'Can do what the hell he likes,' Alex cut in grimly, throwing himself back in his seat in an act of indifference. 'But he will have to do it through legal channels because it is the only way he will get to see either of you again!'

Mia gasped, her mind burning up in horror at his cavalier attitude. 'But, Alex—this is abduction!' She pleaded with him to see the full import of what he was doing. 'You could be arrested for it! You could go to prison!'

'Try having a little faith,' he said.

Faith in what? she wondered deliriously. In him? In what he was doing? 'Suzanna doesn't even have a passport!' she told him shrilly.

His expression didn't alter by so much as a flicker as he reached into his jacket pocket and came out with something he tossed casually onto her lap.

Two passports. Two new British passports. Her stomach began to quiver, her icy fingers trembling as she made herself open both of them. She stared down at the two similar faces, which were staring right back at her.

One was an adult, the other a miniature version of that adult.

'H-how did you get this?' she whispered, picking up Suzanna's very own passport.

'With careful planning,' he replied drily.

'But…' Her eyes flickered downwards again, looking at the photograph of her daughter which was a match to the several sets she had tucked away in her bag.

Carol.

The full duplicity of what had been going on around her

for the last weeks finally hit her. 'You've all been very busy, it seems,' she managed to say at last.

'I am, by nature, very thorough,' Alex casually attested.

'Even to the point of getting my father's written permission for this?' she mocked,

'You authorised it.'

'What?' She stared at him blankly—only her eyes didn't remain blank because they were suddenly seeing that blur of forms Leon had got her to sign. 'Copies,' he'd called them, 'in case I mess up.'

'We will *all* end up in prison!' she said wretchedly.

To her absolute fury, he started to grin at her! Mia wanted to hit him! He never smiled at her—*never!* Yet he chose to do it now, in this dire situation.

'Oh, stop fretting,' he told her, leaning forward to take the two passports back and replace them in his jacket pocket before she had a chance to stop him. 'No one is going to question your connection with Suzanna when she looks so much like you!'

'It's still wrong, Alex!' she flashed back at him. 'And why go to all of this trouble, anyway?' she cried. 'It would all have been sorted out above board in a couple of months!'

To her utter confusion, his face closed up. 'I am not prepared to deal with that question at this present moment,' he said abruptly, and got up, his whole demeanour so grimly inflexible that she panicked.

'But, Alex!' she choked, jumping up to grab hold of his sleeve as he went to walk away from her. 'I need you to deal with it right now!'

'No,' he said, shook his arm free from her grasp then grimly walked away.

The rest of the long flight was achieved in an atmosphere of severely suppressed tension—suppressed because Suzanna was so clearly delighted with the whole wretched business that it would have been cruel to spoil it for her.

But it wasn't easy, and Mia retreated behind a cloak of cool repudiation where no one could reach her, except Suzanna.

They landed in Skiathos in the full heat of mid-afternoon, and Mia broke out in a cold sweat which didn't leave her until they were safely off the airport confines and driving away.

At every turn she had been expecting to see a group of officials bearing down on them to detain them—by order of her father.

But—no. She found herself safely ensconced in the passenger seat of the silver Mercedes, with Alex behind the wheel and Leon and Carol crushed into the back seat, with an excited Suzanna sitting between them.

The child chatted and bounced and asked question after question that, thankfully, the others answered because Mia couldn't lift her mood to fit the little girl's.

She felt shut off, bricked in behind a wall of anger, stress and a terrible sense of betrayal. She had begun to let herself like these people—to trust them even, which was no mean feat for someone who had learned a long time ago that trusting anyone was a terrible weakness.

Suzanna trusted them—Mia's eyes began to water. Suzanna was opening up like a blossoming flower to the warmth of their affection!

The car turned in through familiar gates and swept down the driveway to pull to a halt outside the front veranda.

Car doors opened, and they all climbed out. The sun was hot, the sea was blue and the white-painted walls of the house stood framed by the dense greens of the hillside behind.

'Is this going to be my new home?' Suzanna trilled in breathless wonder. 'Is it truly—is it?'

Mia spun to face Alex across the gleaming bonnet of the Mercedes. 'If you hurt her with this, I will never forgive you!' she said thickly, then turned to run into the house.

CHAPTER TEN

ALEX caught Mia in the hall, one hand curling around her slender wrist while the other clamped itself to her waist.

'Let go of me!' she protested.

His grip only tightened as he guided her—almost frog-marched her—up the stairs and into her bedroom. The door shut with the aid of his foot. Then he was tugging her round until she was facing him, his arms anchoring her there while she glared through a mist of bright, angry tears into his set face.

'I am *not* going to let anyone hurt Suzanna!' he blasted at her furiously. 'I am *not* doing this to hurt you!'

'Then why are you doing it?' she spat right back at him.

'I told you!' he rasped. 'I am pulling out of my deal with your father!'

'But *why?*' she repeated. 'Why, Alex, why?'

He let out a string of rasping profanities, frustration and anger blazing out of his eyes. 'Because of this!' he muttered, and caught her mouth with a kiss that knocked her senseless.

When he eventually let her up again for air she could barely stand up straight.

'I want you, I want our child and I want Suzanna *more* than I want my island!' he growled fiercely. 'Does that answer your question?'

Answer it? It virtually consumed it! He wanted her, really wanted her that badly?

Her face went white, her eyelashes flickering as she started to tremble. Her deeply inbred sense of caution stopped her from believing what he was actually trying to tell her. What his eyes were telling her as they blazed pas-

170

sionately down at her. What her own senses were pleading with her to believe!

'Don't faint on me!' she heard him mutter, and suddenly she was being lifted into his arms. 'Why is it,' he rasped as he strode towards the bed, 'that you either pass out or take my head off whenever I try to hold a meaningful conversation with you!'

He sat her down on the edge of the bed.

'You are driving me out of my mind!' he growled, coming down on his haunches in front of her. 'I cannot get close to you unless I use sex as a damned weapon!' he ranted. 'I cannot talk to you without feeling as if I am walking through a minefield of mistrust! And if I actually do manage to get through to you, you do this!'

'I'm not doing anything,' she whispered.

'You are trembling all over!' He harshly discarded her assurance.

'That's because you're shouting.'

'I'm not— Damn,' he grunted, as he caught himself shouting out a denial.

He sighed, lowered his head to run impatient fingers through his silky black hair, then sprang abruptly to his feet and moved right away from her over to one of the windows. He stood there with his hands thrust into his trouser pockets while he stared grimly outside, as if he needed time to recover his unexpected loss of composure.

'I want you to understand,' he muttered suddenly, 'that I have done what I have done because I needed to be sure that you and Suzanna were safe before I made a move on your father.'

'But why bother going to all this trouble at all?' she asked, still none the wiser as to why this had all been necessary. 'In a couple of months we could have had everything! You—your island, me—Suzanna, and my father his precious grandson!'

'No.' He refuted her words.

'Yes!' she insisted, coming to her feet on shaky legs that did not want to support her. 'Deciding to renege on your side of the deal now is not going to change the fact that I am pregnant with your son, Alex—which is all my father ever wanted anyway!'

'No, you're not.'

Mia blinked. 'I'm not what?' she demanded, her bewildered eyes fixing on the bunched muscles of his back.

The big shoulders flexed, his expression when he slowly turned to face her so sombre that she was arming herself for a really bad shock even before she knew she was doing it.

'You are not carrying my son.' He spelled it out more clearly.

'I beg your pardon?' Mia choked, then released a shaky laugh. 'What do you think this is, Alex?' she said mockingly, indicating her swollen abdomen. 'A mirage?'

'It's my daughter,' he replied.

'What?'

'Sit down again!' he barked at her when the colour drained out of her face, his long legs bringing him back to her side so he could push her back on the bed. 'My God,' he breathed harshly, 'I never would have thought such a strong-willed and fiery woman could be this physically frail!'

'I'm not frail,' she said in a broken whisper. 'I'm just shocked that you could say such a thing!'

'It is the truth.' He sighed. 'The scan you had last week shows no male genitalia—'

'But...' She was frowning in utter bemusement. 'Your family only makes male babies!'

'Not this time, it seems.' He grimaced.

'No.' She shook her head. 'I d-don't believe you. You weren't even there to see the scan!'

'Your doctor faxed a photocopy to me.'

He did? She blinked up at him, surprised to learn that

Alex had taken that much interest in her pregnancy. Then she remembered that she had her own copy of that scan, and she was as sure as she could be that it had not given any indication *what* sex their baby was!

She began glancing around her urgently, looking for her bag so she could check for herself what Alex was claiming.

He beat her to it, by gently placing his own small black and white print into her shaking fingers. After that she didn't move— not a muscle or even an eyelash. This photocopy of her scan was different from her own copy. Her baby had moved—and was showing clearly that Alex was telling the truth.

'Oh, heavens,' she gasped. 'How did that happen?'

It was a stupid question in anyone's books, and he said sardonically, 'By the usual methods, I should imagine.' The comment was probably well deserved—except Mia was in no fit state to appreciate it.

It was all suddenly becoming so wretchedly clear to her. What he'd gambled and what he'd lost. What he'd ended up being saddled with when he hadn't wanted any of it in the first place!

'Oh, Alex,' she breathed. 'I'm so very sorry!'

'Why should you apologise?' he drawled. 'We both know who takes responsibility for the sex of any child.'

'But your precious island!' She was barely listening to him.

Suddenly he was squatting in front of her again. 'Do I look like a man in need of sympathy?' he demanded. 'Look at me, Mia,' he insisted, when she kept her burning eyes lowered to that damning picture, then made her look at him by placing a gentle hand under her chin and lifting it.

His eyes weren't smiling exactly, but they were not miserable either. And his mouth was relaxed—a bit rueful maybe, and incredibly—

She sucked in a sharp gulp of air, shocked as to where

her mind had suddenly shot off to—and at such a calami-
tous moment like this!

'I have to confess to being rather pleased to be the first
Doumas to father a daughter in over a hundred years,' he
admitted sheepishly. 'I am also pleased,' he added more
soberly, 'that this unexpected development has saved me
from having to find another way of getting your father out
of all our lives.'

'He's not out of mine and Suzanna's yet,' Mia shakily
reminded him.

'But he will be,' Alex pledged.

'He's going to come after her, you know.'

'I want him to.' He nodded gravely, then raised his hands
to her trembling shoulders. 'Trust me,' he urged. 'Suzanna
is safe here. He cannot touch her. I know this absolutely,'
he declared. 'and by the time he arrives here I will be in a
situation to make *him* know it also!'

Mia wished she could be so sure about that. She knew
her father, knew how he responded to insubordination of
any kind. She shuddered.

Outside, a sound drifted up from the garden. It was the
laughter of a happy child.

A sob broke from her, and the hands on her shoulders
tightened. 'I make you this solemn pledge,' Alex vowed
fiercely. 'No one—will ever—take that laughter away from
her again!'

Tears slid into Mia's eyes. Alex watched them come,
watched her soft mouth begin to quiver, and something
painful seemed to rip free inside him. He shuddered. 'You
are so damned vulnerable sometimes it makes my heart
ache just to look at you!'

So was he, she realised with a shock that stopped her
heart beating altogether. Alex was painfully vulnerable to
her vulnerability!

'Oh!' she choked—why, she didn't even know—but in
the next moment her arms were sliding up and around his

neck, and just as she had done once before without any warning, she buried her face in his throat and clung to him as if her very life depended on it.

How they got from there to kissing feverishly she didn't know either. Or how they ended up in a heated tangle of naked limbs on the bed. But she knew by the time she took him into her body that something very radical had changed in their relationship because there were no barriers, no resenting the way he made her lose control of herself.

'I adore you,' he murmured against her clinging mouth. 'You crept into my heart, without my even knowing how you did it. Now I cannot seem to take a breath without being made aware that you are there, right inside me.'

'I know,' she whispered in soft understanding because he had done the very same thing to her. 'I love you so much that it actually hurts me to think about it.'

He reacted like a man who had been shot in the chest. He stopped moving, stopped breathing. 'Say that again,' he commanded hoarsely.

His eyes were black, his skin pale, his beautiful bone structure taut under stress. Mia lifted gentle fingers to cover those taut cheeks and held those black eyes with her own earnest green ones. 'I love you,' she repeated.

He caught the words in his mouth, stole them, tasted them and made her repeat them over and over again until the whole thing carried them off into one of those wildly hot passionate interludes that had always managed to completely overpower them even when they'd thought they hated each other.

'This is it,' Alex murmured lazily when they were lying, limp-limbed and sated, in each other's arms. 'I will never let you go now.'

'Do you see me trying to get away?' She smiled.

'No.' He frowned. 'But—' A knock sounded at the closed bedroom door.

'Alex!' his brother's voice called out. 'Frazier is on the phone! You had better get down here!'

'Well?' Mia asked anxiously. She was hovering in the doorway of Alex's study where he stood, leaning against the desk behind him, his dark face lost in brooding thought.

He was dressed in the same clothes she had taken off him earlier, whereas she had delayed long enough to drag on a lightweight dress of cool blue cotton, before hurrying downstairs.

He glanced up and smiled, but it was a brief smile. 'He is on his way,' he told her. 'In flight as we speak.'

Mia shivered. 'W-when will he get here?'

'Tomorrow at the earliest.' he replied, then grimaced. 'The airport here does not accept incoming traffic after dark so he has no choice but to stop over in Thessalonika...'

'W-what if he brings the police with him?'

'He is not going to do that.' He sounded so absolutely certain about it that she was almost reassured.

Except that she knew her father. 'Alex...'

'No,' he cut in, and began to walk towards her, his lean face grimly set. 'You are not to worry about this,' he commanded. 'I know what I am doing.'

In other words, he was asking her to trust him.

But it was no longer Alex she didn't trust—it was her father. 'I'm going to find Suzanna,' she murmured, turning away.

He let her go—which only increased her anxiety. It took real effort to lift her mood to meet Suzanna's bubbling effervescence as they explored together this wonderful paradise Suzanna was now calling home.

'You've got to believe in him,' Carol said quietly when she caught Mia in a moment's white-faced introspection while Suzanna was enjoying her bath, before going to bed in the room she had picked out for herself. 'Alex is amazingly efficient when he sets his mind on something.'

'He lost his island.' Mia smiled bleakly at that.

'Ah, but that was because it came down to a straight choice between his old dream and his new one,' Carol explained. 'The new dream won, hand over fist. If it hadn't he wouldn't have given the island up, I can assure you,' she said. 'He has astonishing patience, you see. He would simply have kept you barefoot and pregnant until you produced the son he needed to stake his claim on the island.'

Suzanna interrupted them at that moment, dancing out of the bathroom wrapped in a towel and looking so blissfully happy that Mia firmly thrust her worries away so she could pretend that everything was as wonderful as the child seemed to think it was.

The call that Jack Frazier was on his way from Skiathos airport came very early the next morning while they were all sitting around the breakfast table, trying to look perfectly relaxed.

But, really, the waiting had got to everyone by then. No one ate, except Suzanna. No one spoke much, except Suzanna. In fact, it was all so very fraught that when Alex took the call on his mobile it was almost a relief to know the waiting would soon be over.

'Right,' he said briskly. 'This is it.' He sounded so invigorated that Mia suddenly wanted to hit him! 'Carol, you were going to show Mia and Suzanna your upstairs studio, I believe,' he prompted very smoothly.

'Oh! Yes!' Like a puppet pulled by its master's string, Carol jumped to her feet and turned towards Suzanna. 'Come on, poppet,' she said over-brightly. 'This is going to be fun! Wait until you see the size of the piece of paper we are going to paint a picture on!'

Eager to fall in with any plans, Suzanna scrambled down from her chair and was at Carol's side in a second.

'Mia?' the other woman prompted.

'I'll be there in a minute,' she said, turning anxiously

towards Alex as the other two walked away. 'Tell me what you are going to do!' she pleaded.

'Later,' he promised. 'For now I want you out of sight until your father has been and gone.'

'But—!'

It was as far as she got. 'No!' he exploded, turning angrily on her. 'I will not have you exposed in any way to that man!' he swore. 'So do as you are told, Mia, or, so help me, I will make you do it!'

Her chin came up, her green eyes coming alight with a defiance that showed the old Mia, whom he had spent the whole previous night loving into oblivion, had come rising up out of the ashes of all that time and effort. 'Back to purdah again, I take it!' she said cuttingly.

'He's at the gates.' Leon's voice came shiveringly flat-toned from just behind her.

'Damn and blast it, woman!' Alex rasped out frustrat-edly, and in the next moment Mia found herself cradled high in his arms and he was striding up the stairs with a face apparently carved from granite.

He dumped her on a chair in her bedroom. 'Stay!' he commanded. Then he strode angrily back out of the room, slamming the door shut behind him.

She stayed. She stayed exactly where she was as she listened to the sound of a car coming down the driveway, listened to it stop outside the house, heard a door slam— shuddered and closed her eyes on a wave of nausea when she heard her father's voice bark something very angry. She heard Leon's dark-toned level reply, heard footsteps sound-ing on the veranda floor...

Then nothing. The whole villa seemed to settle into an ominous silence. She tolerated it for a while, just sat there and let that silence wash over her for several long wretched, muscle-locking minutes.

But that was the limit of her endurance, and the next

moment she was up, stiff-limbed and shaking, walking out of the bedroom and to the head of the polished stairway.

As she moved downwards she could see the study door standing half-open, and hear the rasp of her father's voice as he blasted words at Alex.

As if drawn by something way beyond instinct, she walked silently towards that half-open doorway.

'I don't know what you think you're damned well playing at!' She heard her father's angry voice as she approached. 'But you won't get away with it!'

'Get away with what?' was Alex's bland reply.

'You know what I'm talking about!' Jack Frazier grated.

Mia saw him then, and went perfectly still. He was standing with his back to her, every inch of him pulsing with a blistering fury as he faced Alex across the width of the desk. Alex was seated, looking supremely at ease in the way he was lazing back in his chair, his dark eyes cool, his lean face arrogantly impassive.

But what really struck at the very heart of her was to see Leon, standing at his brother's shoulder.

Her breath stilled, her eyes widening as she instantly realised just what she was looking at. It was like being shot back to another scene like this— in another study, in another country altogether. Only here the roles had been reversed. This time it was her father who was pulsing with anger and frustration and Alex who was looking utterly unmoved by it all.

Leon's sole purpose was to stand silent witness, whereas in London it had been Mia who had played that role.

A deliberate set-up? she wondered, and suspected that it most probably was. Jack Frazier had humiliated Alex that day when he had made him surrender his pride in front of Mia. Now it was her father's turn to know just what that felt like.

She shivered, not sure that she liked to see Alex displaying this depth of ruthlessness.

'All I know,' she heard Alex reply, 'is that you have been standing here, throwing out a lot of threats and insults, but I am still no wiser as to exactly what it is you are actually angry about.'

'Don't play bloody games with me,' her father grated. 'You've reneged on our deal, you cheating bastard! And you've stolen my youngest daughter! I want her back right now—or I'll have you arrested for abduction!'

'The telephone sits right there. By all means,' Alex said invitingly, 'call the police if you feel this passionate about it. But I think I should warn you,' he added silkily, 'that the police will demand proof of your claim before they will act. You have brought that proof with you, I must presume?'

Silence. It suddenly consumed the very atmosphere. Mia's spine began to tingle, her breath lying suspended in her chest while her eyes fixed themselves on her father's back as she waited for him to produce the proof that she of all people knew he had.

Yet...he didn't do anything! He just stood there, unmoving, in that steadily thickening silence.

It was Alex who broke it. 'You have a problem with that?' he questioned smoothly.

'We don't need to get the police involved in this if you are sensible!' her father said irritably.

'Sensible,' Alex thoughtfully repeated. 'Yes,' he said agreeably, 'I think I can be *sensible* about this. You show *me* your proof of claim, and I will hand Suzanna over to you with no more argument.'

Mia felt the blood freeze in her veins, an excruciating sense of pained betrayal whitening her face as she took a jerky step forward. Then her pained eyes suddenly clashed head-on with a pair of burning black ones as Alex finally saw her there, and she went perfectly still.

No! those eyes seemed to be telling her. Wait! Trust me! Trust him. Her hand reached out to clutch at the polished doorframe. Trust him! her mind was screaming at her. If you don't, you will lose him! He will never forgive you!

Trust him. She swallowed thickly over the lump of fear that had formed in her throat and remained where she was.

'I keep that kind of stuff with my lawyers,' her father snapped out impatiently, 'not on my person!'

Mia lost Alex's attention as he fixed it back on Jack Frazier. 'I possess all the usual communication equipment,' he pointed out. 'Call up your lawyers, tell them to fax the relevant information here and all this unpleasantness could be over in minutes.'

He even rose to lift the telephone receiver off its hook and held it out to her father! His body was relaxed, his face utterly impassive, and he did not so much as flicker another glance in Mia's direction as a new silence began to stretch endlessly, along with Mia's nerve-ends as she stood there, clutching the wooden doorframe with fingers that had turned to ice.

Then she jumped, startled as Alex suddenly slammed the telephone back on its rest. 'No,' he said through gritted teeth. 'You cannot do it, can you, because there was no official adoption!'

His hand shot out, picking up something from the desk and then slapping it back down again in front of Jack Frazier.

'You conned Mia into believing she was signing away all rights to her baby,' he bit out, 'when in reality what she did sign was not worth the damned paper it was written on!'

Her father was staring down at whatever it was that Alex had slapped down in front of him. Mia's eyelashes fluttered as she, too, looked down at the desk where she could just see a corner of a sickeningly familiar document.

It was her own copy of what her father had made her sign seven years ago. It had to be. Alex must have gone through her private papers, without her knowing it.

'She did sign it, though!' Jack Frazier suddenly hit back jeeringly. 'In fact, she was only too bloody eager to hand over her bastard child to me!'

'Oh,' Mia gasped, having to push an icy fist up against her mouth to stop the sound from escaping.

He wasn't even bothering to deny it!

'Or be out on the streets, as you so charitably put it at the time!' Alex tagged on scathingly. 'You played on her youth, her naïvety, her desperation and her inability to tell a legal document from absolute garbage!' he went on. 'And you did it all with a cold-blooded heartless cruelty that must make her very happy that you are *not* her real father!'

'What's that supposed to mean?' Jack Frazier jerked out.

'This is what it means...' Another piece of paper landed on the desk. 'Your blood group,' he said curtly, then slapped another piece of paper on top of it. 'Karl Dansing's blood group.' Another piece of paper arrived the same way. 'And finally—thankfully—my wife's blood group!' Alex said with grim satisfaction. 'Note the odd one out?' he prompted bitingly.

'Any questions?' he then asked. 'No, I thought not, because you knew this already, didn't you? Which is why you have been punishing her all these bloody years. Well...' He leaned forward, his dark face a map of blistering contempt for the other man. 'It is now over,' he said. 'And you are no longer welcome here.'

'But what's the matter with you, man?' Jack Frazier blustered in angry frustration. Something had gone wrong with all his careful planning and he still had not worked out exactly what that something was. 'If I am prepared to accept Mia as my daughter, then the damned island is yours when she gives birth to my grandson!'

'But Mia is not carrying your grandson,' Alex coolly contradicted. 'She is carrying my daughter.'

'What? You mean she couldn't even get that right?'

Dark eyes suddenly began to look very dangerous.

'Watch what you say here,' Alex warned. 'This is my home—and my wife—you are maligning.'

'A wife you didn't damned well want in the first place!' Jack Frazier said scornfully. 'But if you've decided to keep her, there will be other children no doubt—sons!' he added covetously. 'All you have to do is give me back Suzanna, and Mia will be as compliant as a pussy cat, I promise you. Another year and you could still have your island!'

'You can keep the island,' Alex countered coldly. 'I have no wish to set foot on it again. In fact,' he added, 'you have nothing I want that I have not already taken away from you. Which makes you defunct as far as any of my family are concerned. So, as you once put it so eloquently to me— the door, Mr Frazier, is over there.'

'But—!'

'Get him out of here,' Alex grated at his brother, his face drawn into taut lines of utter disgust.

Leon moved, and so did Mia, jolting out of the stasis that had been holding her to move shakily back to the stairs. She had no wish to come face to face with Jack Frazier. She had no wish to set eyes on him ever again.

She was standing by the bedroom window when Alex came looking for her.

'I hope you are pleased with yourself,' he said in a clipped voice.

'Not really.' She turned to send him a wryly apologetic smile. He still looked angry, his beautiful olive skin paler than it should have been. 'I almost blew that for you,' she admitted. 'I'm sorry.'

'Why did you come down there when I specifically asked you not to?'

'I don't know.' She shrugged. 'It was a—compulsion. I couldn't see any way that you could make him give up Suzanna, without giving him what he wanted, you see.'

'And in return for your lack of trust in me you learned

a whole lot more about yourself than you actually wanted to know!'

That made her eyes flash. 'I learned that you had the bare-faced cheek to go through my private papers!' she hit back indignantly.

'Ah...' At least he had the grace to grimace guiltily at that one. The anger died out of him, his warm hands sliding around her body to draw her close. 'I was desperately in love with a woman who refused to trust me as far as she could throw me,' he murmured in his own defence. 'Men that desperate do desperate things. Forgive me?' he pleaded, bending his dark head so he could nuzzle her ear.

Mia wasn't ready to forgive anyone anything. Her head moved back, away from that diverting mouth. 'When did you go through my private papers?' she demanded to know.

He sighed, his smile at her stubbornness rueful. 'I came straight here after leaving you in London,' he told her. 'Initially, I wanted to see if there was any way we could reverse the adoption,' he explained, 'but the moment I read that damned thing I knew it was not legal!' His angry sigh brushed her face.

'But I needed to get that confirmed with my own lawyers before I dared take action. And you had signed it, *agape mou*,' he added gently. 'My lawyers were afraid that if I faced your father with what I had discovered while you were still in London, he could have used the fact you had signed away your right to Suzanna to make the child a ward of the British courts while we fought over her.'

'And thereby gain himself a different way of blackmailing us into doing what he wanted us to do.' Mia nodded understandingly.

'It was safer for me to get you both here to Greece before I faced him with what I knew.'

'So you kidnapped us.'

'Yes.' He sighed. 'I'm sorry if I frightened you.'

Frightened her? He'd put her through a hell of uncertainty over the last twenty-four hours! 'You are as under-hand and cunning as my father,' she said accusingly. 'Do you know that?'

'I love you madly,' he murmured coaxingly. 'I would not hurt a hair on your beautiful head.'

In answer to that blatant bit of seduction, Mia turned her back on him again—though she made no attempt to move out of those strong arms still holding her.

And Alex was not going to stop the verbal seduction. 'I adore you,' he whispered softly against her ear. 'I *ache* for you night and day I am so badly bitten.'

'Which is why you keep a mistress, I suppose.'

As a mood-killer it worked like a dream. His dark head lifted. 'Ah,' he said ruefully once more. 'The mistress. You are after your pound of flesh again, I think.'

I want more than a pound of your flesh, Alexander Doumas, Mia thought covetously. I want it all! 'I apologise,' she said with deceptive contrition. 'I forgot for the moment that I am contracted not to mention the mistress.'

He laughed, not fooled at all by her tone, and the arms holding her tightened their grip. 'There is no mistress,' he informed her drily. 'And there never *was* a mistress.' His mouth was tasting her ear again. 'I have not looked at an-other woman since the first night I saw you across a crowded room and was instantly smitten—as I suspect you already know!'

Mia smiled a smile of feline satisfaction. 'Carol did im-ply something of the kind,' she confessed, and arched her neck to give him greater access to the ear lobe he was tasting. 'I just wanted to hear you say it.'

'I'm going to rip that crazy contract up...' he promised.

'Good,' she said approvingly.

'And make you sign another one that will tie you to me for life,' he added.

'What makes you think I will sign it?' she challenged.

His mouth moved to her throat, his tongue arrowing directly for a particular pulse point he knew all about. 'I have my ways,' he murmured against that exact spot—and laughed softly as she drew in a sharp, shaken gasp of air. Her body was already beginning to throb in his arms with pleasure when a sound outside caught her attention.

Glancing downwards, she saw Suzanna appear, with Carol and Leon in tow. They were dressed for swimming, with towels draped around their necks. Hand in hand, they walked off towards the swimming pool area.

'She has them wrapped around her little finger,' Mia drily remarked.

'I know the feeling,' Alex murmured. 'Her mama has me tied up the same way.'

Mia smiled and said nothing, her gaze following the trio until they disappeared out of sight, then she lifted her gaze to the larger view of this, her new home. Out beyond the gardens the sea was shimmering lazily, and beyond it stood the misted green-grey string of smaller islands.

'Which is your island?' she asked.

He didn't answer for a long moment, seemingly much more interested in tasting her. Then his dark head came up. 'The one you can see directly in front of us,' he said, 'with the two crescent-shaped patches of golden beach...'

Is that why he had bought this villa, she wondered, because it looked out on his true home?

'Your vision,' she sighed. 'I'm so sorry you lost it.'

'I'm not,' he replied, with no hint of regret. 'Visions can change. Mine has changed. All I want is right here with me, in my arms.'

'Still,' Mia said sadly, 'it seems so very unfair that you have to break a promise to your father because my so-called father is such a dreadful man.'

'I have you,' he said. 'I have my child, growing inside you.' His hands splayed across her abdomen in a gesture of warm possession. 'And I have a miniature version of you in Suzanna, who worships the very ground I walk upon because I rescued her from your father. I am very content, believe me.'

'Well, your contentment is going to fly right out of this window if you move your hands much lower,' she informed him quite pragmatically—then tilted her head, her green eyes twinkling wickedly up at him.

And he laughed, a deep, dark, very masculine sound that had her turning in his arms to face him. That was all it took. Their bodies fused…so did their mouths…and they were lost in each other.

Special Offers

Every month we put together collections and longer reads written by your favourite authors.

Here are some of next month's highlights— and don't miss our fabulous discount online!

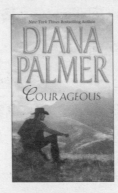

On sale 5th April   On sale 15th March   On sale 5th April

Save 20%
on all Special Releases

Find out more at
www.millsandboon.co.uk/specialreleases

Visit us Online

0413/ST/MB410

Mills & Boon® Online

Discover more romance at
www.millsandboon.co.uk

🌹 **FREE** online reads

🌹 **Books** up to one
month before shops

🌹 **Browse our books**
before you buy

...and much more!

For exclusive competitions and instant updates:

 Like us on **facebook.com/romancehq**

 Follow us on **twitter.com/millsandboonuk**

 Join us on **community.millsandboon.co.uk**

Visit us Online   Sign up for our FREE eNewsletter at
www.millsandboon.co.uk

WEB/M&B/RTL4

The World of Mills & Boon®

There's a Mills & Boon® series that's perfect for you. We publish ten series and, with new titles every month, you never have to wait long for your favourite to come along.

Blaze®

Scorching hot, sexy reads
4 new stories every month

By Request

Relive the romance with the best of the best
9 new stories every month

Cherish™

Romance to melt the heart every time
12 new stories every month

Desire™

Passionate and dramatic love stories
8 new stories every month

Visit us Online

Try something new with our Book Club offer
www.millsandboon.co.uk/freebookoffer

M&B/WORLD2

*What will you treat
yourself to next?*

*Ignite your imagination,
step into the past...*
6 new stories every month

INTRIGUE...

Breathtaking romantic suspense
Up to 8 new stories every month

*Captivating medical drama –
with heart*
6 new stories every month

MODERN™

*International affairs,
seduction & passion guaranteed*
9 new stories every month

n o c t u r n e™

*Deliciously wicked
paranormal romance*
Up to 4 new stories every month

⊃IVΛ™

*Live life to the full –
give in to temptation*
3 new stories every month available
exclusively via our Book Club

You can also buy Mills & Boon eBooks at
www.millsandboon.co.uk

*Visit us
Online*

M&B/WORLD2